Audrey Corr is in her fifties and works as a buyer of props for films. She lives in County Mayo, Ireland.

Also by Audrey Corr

Dead Organised

The Outing

Audrey Corr

POCKET BOOKS
TOWNHOUSE

First published in Great Britain by Pocket/TownHouse, 2003
An imprint of Simon & Schuster UK Ltd,
and TownHouse Ltd, Dublin

Simon & Schuster UK is a Viacom Company

1 3 5 7 9 10 8 6 4 2

Simon & Schuster UK Ltd
Africa House
64–78 Kingsway
London WC2B 6AH

Simon & Schuster Australia
Sydney

TownHouse Ltd
Trinity House
Charleston Road
Ranelagh
Dublin 6
Ireland

A CIP catalogue record for this book is available
from the British Library

ISBN 1 903650 35 6

Typeset by SX Composing DTP, Rayleigh, Essex
Printed and bound in Great Britain by
Bookmarque Ltd, Croydon, Surrey

For Denis

Chapter One

Maureen Carmody did not hold with outings. She said as much to Deborah as she squeezed her lemon into her gin and tonic and stirred it vigorously with her plastic spoon. 'A recipe for trouble, Deborah, that's what it is. A Molotov.'

'I don't know how you stick it, Maureen, I really don't. I think you are marvellous. Anyone who does what you do . . .'

'Well I have been trained, Deborah. It is not a job anyone off the street could do as I have continually pointed out to the board of management. But do you think they listen to the likes of me? Me, a mere SRN.'

'I thought you hadn't finished your training.'

'A technicality, Deborah. Merely a technicality. What is a piece of paper compared to a lifetime of experience?'

'You are right of course, Maureen,' Deborah agreed quickly, 'it is only a piece of paper.'

'But you'd know all about life experiences, Deborah, wouldn't you? In and out of your little day job. No responsibilities. Only number one to think of.'

'I didn't mean any offence, Maureen. I only meant . . . I know how responsible your job is.'

'I sometimes wonder about you, Deborah.'

'I sometimes wonder about me, too,' Deborah sighed under her breath. 'What am I doing here?'

Maureen Carmody and Deborah Murphy met up in the cocktail lounge of the Russell Hotel every Friday. It was one of those arrangements that seem to just happen. Although they had known each other on and off for years and hadn't been particularly close when they bumped into each other at the same singles evening, Deborah had been so relieved to see someone she knew that she threw her arms around Maureen and greeted her like a long lost friend. They fled the do together, agreeing it was awful and not their sort of thing, and that standing around with your name on a badge seemed to suggest to all and sundry that you were in some way a social failure.

They arranged to meet for drinks. In the beginning it was casual, then it became a regular habit and, all too soon for Deborah, it had become sacrosanct. They sat in the same seats, had the same drinks, and the conversation ran the same way, week after week. Maureen dominated the conversation, pausing now and then to let Deborah get a word in before she took off again.

Maureen liked the atmosphere of the cocktail bar, not that they ever ran to cocktails. 'Showy,' she would say, if Deborah suggested they have one. 'What would people think?' She felt it was a proper sort of career woman's place to be seen in. Maureen liked her tipple but she wouldn't dream of going into an ordinary bar. She had the most irritating notions about what she considered proper and Deborah asked herself, for the umpteenth time, why she continued with the charade. Deborah's problem was that all her friends were married, or in relationships, and she had had her fill of evenings with couples. The ones in love, the ones in the middle of a private war, and the ones rushing to phone babysitters while telling her how lucky she was to be free. Better to sit in the Russell Hotel with Maureen, where there was at least the possibility of meeting someone new, than to spend yet another evening alone, in front of the telly. In fairness, Deborah had to admit, Maureen wasn't too bad until she got on to the subject of her job, or her vocation as she liked to put it.

Maureen worked as nursing supervisor in the Cross and Passion Nursing Home where she dealt with the day to day problems of caring for the elderly. There, although not fully qualified – if any of the residents got seriously ill they were transferred to a special medical unit – Maureen could safely aspire to the title of Matron. A small, self-contained flat went with the job which meant her salary was her own. No rent, gas, or electricity bills to worry about. The only expense was her telephone which, she confided to Deborah, she seldom used. If she wanted to have long chats, or phone her people in Tipperary, she crept down to reception at night and used the main line. Deborah thought it was a terrific advantage having a free flat but one mention of that to Maureen and she got on her high horse and there was no stopping her. Deborah prayed that this was not going to be one of those evenings. The best option was to let Maureen get all her job moans off her chest and then hopefully they could get on to another topic.

'What about the outing tomorrow, Maureen? You were telling me about the outing. Are you going?'

'I have been trained, Deborah, contrary to your theory, and I know from experience that these outings only serve to unsettle my patients. Why, only yesterday Mr Flood got so excited about the trip he took his penis out twice and nothing but a cold bath could calm him down.'

'Oh, Maureen.' Deborah felt a shiver at the thought of calming the penis of an excited octogenarian.

'It's been going on all week. Ever since that notice went up. Do these do-gooders ever stop to think of the trouble they cause?'

'All the same, Maureen, it is nice that the old folk have something to look forward to.'

'Nice. That's rich, Deborah, coming from you, considering you don't know the first thing about it.'

'I only meant . . .'

'Do you mop up the spills? Do you have to issue extra incontinence pads? Do you?'

'You know I don't.'

'Then keep your nices for things that are nice. Why is it there's always someone to put in their tuppence-ha' penny worth when they don't know what they are talking about.'

'I'm sorry, Maureen. You are right. I only thought . . .'

'The subject is closed, Deborah. This is my night off and I don't intend spending it talking shop. I am washing my hands of this whole business. The do-gooders can cope with the consequences. I told the board that I am having nothing to do with it. That Iris Fox person, the dreadful woman organizing the thing, can go to hell for all I care. Now, it's my round. We will have another drink and then you can tell me all the news from your life-experiencing little world of commerce.'

Deborah shrank back in her chair. She hated it when Maureen decided it was her turn to tell of her week's events. She racked her brains to come up with something, anything, that Maureen might find entertaining, but nothing ever happened in her job, certainly nothing that could compare with Maureen's trials and tribulations. Deborah did the wages and costings for a firm of aluminium manufacturers in a sprawling industrial estate. Her daily routine – into the car, drive to the office, time sheets, tax certs, overtime and wet time – could hardly be described as life experience. The only highlight was the odd Friday when she delivered the wages to sites, too far out for the men to collect their cheques, and could dally on the way back, stop somewhere for coffee or do a bit of shopping. The boss never said anything. He knew they couldn't replace her. It wasn't that she herself was indispensable but no social-seeking young one would be seen dead in the place. There were no pubs, no shops, no cafés to browse in at lunchtime, just the canteen with forty or so married glaziers, aluminium fitters, and a Mrs Thompson who did the books. The funny thing about it was that Deborah hated aluminium windows and for the life of her couldn't imagine how she had ended up there. She knew she was in a rut but felt incapable of doing anything about it. Every so often she resolved to give her notice, get out of the place, do something with her life. She scoured the employment notices in the evening papers but the thoughts of getting a CV together and going for interviews left her exhausted. You couldn't say that to Maureen. Maureen thought she had a cushy number. 'You and your desk job,' she always said. 'Honestly, Deborah, you're on the pig's back. I don't know what you have to moan about.'

Iris Fox and her friend Helen Keogh sat in the corner of The Gleeson Lounge and counted the takings from the pub quiz.

'Twenty tables at four pounds a table, that's eighty pounds. Would you check that Helen, while I make up the raffle money? You know I think with this lot and the stash from the car-boot sale we will have reached our target.'

'Don't remind me about that raffle, Iris. I didn't know where to look when that man from table three came up for his prize. A fiver's worth of tickets and he wins an oven glove. I thought you were going to make up parcels, not raffle each item individually.'

'No one was forced to buy a ticket, Helen.'

'But an oven glove, Iris.'

'That's the luck of the draw. I don't know why you are harping on about gloves when there were loads of other great prizes. Look at the amount of bottles of booze the pub donated. Not to mention the chocolates from next door and the super evening out for two. You seem to be forgetting the whole point of the exercise. We are trying to make money for the old folks. What does it matter who won what?'

Weeks of organizing and fund-raising had been put in by Iris and Helen for the OAP outing. Iris had been determined that none of her old folk would have to put their hands in their pockets for anything other than the little extras they might want to buy for themselves. She had planned everything down to the last detail. The bus, one of the new 123 City Swifts, from Drimnagh to Marino, plus a full tank of diesel, had been donated by the Dublin Bus Company, so a day's wages for the driver would be the first outlay. Lunch, at five pounds a head, had been booked at the mystery destination. Breast of chicken and chips, or mash, with mushy peas, followed by apple tart and cream and tea or coffee. There would be comfort stops each way. Tea and biscuits was the fare for the comfort stops. You couldn't have a coachload of pensioners plus driver and stewards using the toilets and not order anything. It would be a tight squeeze to get it all paid within the budget, plus keep a little slush fund for emergencies, but both ladies felt they could cover it, and Iris, though she swore she wouldn't use it, would bring her Visa card along as an added precaution.

'Hey, Iris. There's eighty-seven quid here. Someone paid too much. Can we treat ourselves to a drink?'

'Go on then. I suppose we do deserve one. Only the one mind you, tomorrow is going to be a tough day.'

'Is there any chance you could manage without me, Iris? I don't mind the fund-raising but I'm not much good with –'

'Forget it. I can't manage without you. Anyway, I know you, Helen. Once we get under way you'll really enjoy it.'

Twenty-four-year-old Stevie Mahon left the bus depot on Friday evening with his new blazer under his arm. Tomorrow would be his big chance. He had passed his basic training with flying colours and the supervisor, Mr Maloney, had told him he could look forward to a permanent job with the bus company. There had been twenty-five trainees on the course but only nine had passed and these nine could now, legally, remove the L-plates and, as soon as the current go-slow was over, drive the new one-man City Swifts from terminus to terminus. Out of that nine Stevie had been selected to drive for a mystery tour the following day. Mr Maloney briefed him about the trip and told him it would be an invaluable experience in dealing with the public. He couldn't believe his luck – if there hadn't been a go-slow one of the older drivers would have been on the trip, but now, because he hadn't officially started as a bus driver, he wasn't breaking union rules.

A brand new official blazer. A brand new state-of-the-art City Swift. This was the start of a whole new career. His mother was so proud of him she wept.

Chapter Two

The day for the outing had arrived. Iris showered and dressed with care. She wanted her outfit to suggest smart but casual, efficient yet comfortable, so, after much deliberating, she decided on her black skirt, the white T-shirt with the little rose on the pocket, and her black fleece. The new black tracksuit bottoms would go in her bag. That way she could mix and match and be prepared for all contingencies – you could never tell what way things would go, weather-wise. Black and white. You could go anywhere in black and white. Sneakers or her good ankle boots? Sneakers. Definitely sneakers. Her ankle boots would look funny without tights and, with her little problem, there was no way she was wearing tights. She swept her hair up into a ponytail, fixed it in place with an elastic band, and slipped two extra elastic bands on her wrist, just in case. Finally she hung her dad's whistle round her neck. A whistle could be very handy when rounding up the elderly. She stood in front of the mirror, did a few knee bends, and gave herself a smile of satisfaction.

Iris booked a taxi for seven-thirty a.m. The plan was to collect Helen, meet the driver in plenty of time to run through the schedule with him, and decorate the bus. She laid out the banner for the front of the bus, the streamers and the balloons, copies of the itinerary, the names and phone numbers of the premises they would be stopping at and, most important, her seating plan. Iris prided herself on her organizational ability. 'You should have been in the army, Iris,' her dad had said more than once. 'You have great organizational skills.' Poor Dad. That was before he lost his mind and thought she really was in the army. Before they put him in the home. She would never forget his last words to her. 'Look after your old soldiers, sergeant. It could be you one day.'

It was the memory of her dad that prompted Iris to do all she could for the old folk. She had done her best to look after him but it became impossible. He needed constant care and attention. When it came to the point that she was taking so much time off work she was in danger of losing her job, the social worker arranged for him to go into a home. 'He was happier in the Complex.' How often had she said that to herself? Although it had taken his entire pension and half of her salary to keep him comfortable, she got neither help nor sympathy from her siblings. When he died, and it was discovered she had been left the family home, they were convinced she had forced his hand. Iris had spent the next few years making it up to them. Dishing out what money she could, baby-sitting their children, and generally keeping an open house for all of them, it wasn't as if they were short.

They all had their own homes, ran cars, had foreign holidays. Things she could never afford for herself. Nothing she did was enough. On one particular morning she woke up and told herself, 'Iris, enough is enough.' She could never satisfy them. There were plenty of people out there in more need than they were. She threw herself into all sorts of activities and found it extraordinarily liberating. Christmas parties, charity functions, and weekend volunteer in the Simon Community shop. This was the second summer outing Iris had organized and she was confident it would go well. She felt with that one under her belt she knew all the pitfalls.

Iris packed everything, ticking each item off as she put it in a box. She left the banner till last. She was worried that it might be still a tiny bit sticky. She was tempted not to bring it at all but that same banner had taken her the best part of a week to make. She had tried everything. Paper, cardboard, felt, nothing looked right until she had the brainwave of cutting some old sheets into three-feet lengths, sewing them together and painting the sign in emulsion. When the paint finally seemed dry – it had hung out on the washing line for days – there was a little puckering but Iris was sure no one would notice once it was strung out along the bus.

There was stony silence in the cab as Iris and Helen travelled to the assembly point. Helen groaned, opened the window all the way down and stuck her head out.

'How could you, Helen?'

'How could I what?'

'Turn up with a hangover. Today of all days.'

'I haven't got a hangover. I couldn't sleep, that's all. I'll be fine in a minute.'

'I knew it. I can always tell. Quite apart from the fact that your eyes have disappeared and your breath smells like a brewery.'

'Knock it off, Iris.'

'Just the one, we said. What did you do?'

'I went home. I went to bed.'

'And?'

'Christ, Iris. What is this? An inquisition? I went home, I went to bed and the phone rang . . .'

'Go on.'

'. . . It was the people upstairs, they were having people in. They had invited me but with that bloody pub quiz I'd forgotten all about it. I didn't want them to think I was being stand-offish so I went up for a while.'

'You couldn't tell them that it was too late? That you had an important engagement today and had to be in the pink for it.'

'There was no point. The music was so loud I wouldn't have been able to sleep anyway.'

'I suppose it went on until all hours.'

'It wasn't that late, Iris, because, well actually, a bit of a row broke out. Ruth – you've met Ruth, Iris, don't you remember? Well, Ruth got upset so she came down to my place and nothing would do Tess but to follow her and, anyway, they'd had too much drink to drive home so they ended up crashing in my spare room. They had been to an outing.'

'I see. So their outing is more important than ours? Is that what you are trying to imply?'

'It wasn't that sort of an outing. It was a coming out.'

'A what?'

'Oh rev up, Iris. Tess got upset because she came out and Ruth decided at the last minute she didn't want to. That was what the party was for.'

'What?'

'It's understandable really. It's a big step . . .' Helen's voice trailed off.

'Nothing about your friends is understandable. Why you? Are you some sort of lesbian counsellor all of a sudden? I give up, Helen. Here we are, taking a bus full of old folk out, trying to give them a day to remember, and you turn up—'

'Knock it off, Iris. You are too hard on them. As a matter of fact they both said if we needed extra hands we have only to—'

'No way, Helen. I need that like a hole in the head. You told them we were going on an outing. Did you say what sort of an outing?'

'Well I did say it was for old folk.'

'And they still wanted to come?'

'They thought it was very brave . . . of the old folks . . . I think, or maybe of us. I can't bloody well remember. What does it matter anyway?'

'It matters, Helen. It matters if your lesbian friends think my old folk are coming out and not going out. Did you say it was a going out?'

'I just said it was an outing, Iris. An Outing.'

'Well that's it then, isn't it. We are up the Swanee

without a paddle. How could you do this to me?'

'I didn't do anything to you, Iris. You are doing it to yourself.'

'Don't mention anything about outing to our bus driver when we get to the park.'

'But, Iris . . .'

'Shut up, Helen.'

Helen tried to laugh but only succeeded in hurting her head.

Fairview Park, the Marino end, was the assembly point for the Annual OAP Mystery outing. As the taxi turned the corner from the Strand Road, Iris and Helen could see the bus parked on the hard shoulder and the driver standing on the footpath, looking up and down, and checking his watch. Stevie, in his navy blazer, grey trousers, gleaming black shoes, and dark glasses, had been there for almost an hour. Assuming that the tour would be for foreigners – Americans or Germans or the like – he had invested in a pair of shades intending to give a debonair, man-of-the-world impression. First impressions are very important, his super had told him, especially on a tour. He wore his shades diffidently.

'Oh my God, Iris. Our driver is blind.'

'Don't be ridiculous, Helen. For Christ's sake get your act together. Over there driver, pull up beside that bus.'

Iris paid the cab driver while Helen, struggling with the enormity of getting through the day, still drunk from the night before, got all the paraphernalia for the bus out of the taxi. Iris strode up and introduced herself to Stevie.

'I'm Iris. Iris Fox, and this is Helen Keogh, my right-arm man. Helen, meet Stephen.'

'My mates call me Stevie.'

'I think we will keep to Stephen on this little trip. My OAPs would have more confidence in a Stephen, don't you think?'

'Your whats?'

'My OAPs. My outing-goers.'

'What are OAPs?'

'I can see you are quite a card, Stephen. My pensioners. Don't tell me that nice Mr Maloney didn't explain the nature of our little trip?'

Stevie looked with amazement as the nature of the little trip was being unfurled by Helen. WELCOME ONE AND ALL TO THE ANNAL OAP OUTING.

'Jesus, Iris,' Helen said, 'you've surpassed yourself this time with the banner.'

'Thank you, Helen. Not bad, even though I say it myself.'

'There is just one thing.'

'What one thing?'

'You left out the U.'

'What do you mean I left out the U?'

'Annual, Iris. Annual has a U.'

'Trust you to nit-pick, Helen. It's only a tiny mistake. We can make a little pleat when we hang it up and no one will notice.'

'Are all those frills meant to be there?'

'Frills? What frills? Just get on with it, Helen. Stephen, if you come on board with me we can go through the details while Helen is decorating the bus.'

'Mr Maloney didn't mention anything about decorations,' Stephen said. 'He told me to wind on to SPECIAL, that's all. I don't think he would like decorations.'

'Nonsense. You can't have an outing without decorations. Helen. Where are my kitchen steps?'

'Steps? What steps?'

'I put my kitchen steps in the boot of the taxi because otherwise we would not be able to reach high enough to hang our bunting. You've left them in the boot, haven't you? What have I done to deserve this? There is nothing else for it. You will have to go somewhere and borrow a ladder. Stephen. On the bus please. Let's get this show on the road. Our old folk will be here any minute and we won't be ready for them. Stephen.' Iris's voice rose an octave and Stephen, who had been standing dumbstruck by the side of the bus, jumped on board. 'Most of our pensioners will be embarking here and the rest we will pick up in the Cross and Passion Nursing Home in Drumcondra. It's going to be a great day for them. Did you bring some tapes? I asked your Mr Maloney for some tapes so we could have a singalong. The senior citizens love a singalong. I'm not half bad on the old vocals, though I say it myself. In fact my dad, God be good to him, thought I should be on the stage.' Iris looked out of the bus window. 'Helen. Will you stop gawping and go and get a ladder? We all have to pull together if this day is going to work. I want that banner up before our guests arrive.' Iris gave Stephen a little conspiratorial look. 'You'll have to forgive her, Stephen. She's a little under the weather. Trouble in the family.'

Helen zigzagged across the road through the heavy morning traffic to a tobacconist's opposite the park and explained the situation to the shopkeeper.

'I've no steps, love, only a ten-foot ladder, but you are welcome to that. It's great what you girls are doing for the old folk —' Helen muttered an obscenity under her breath but happily wasn't overheard. '— You will have to get it over yourself. I can't leave the shop.'

'Christ.' Helen grabbed the ladder and staggered out of the shop. As she reached the middle of the road the ladder, caught in the traffic cross wind, pitched this way and that.

'Helen,' Iris screamed above the din. 'What are you playing at? Do hurry up.'

'I'm going to kill her. Let me by, damn you, let me through. Stevie, help.' The ladder swung dangerously as she made a lunge through the cars.

'Lunatic!' A man whose car bonnet had been knocked roared after her. 'Get off the road.'

'Jesus Christ, Iris. I could have been killed.'

'Oh stop being so dramatic, Helen. We have no time to waste. Stephen, would you give her a hand with the banner or she will be at it all day. And she still has all the balloons to blow up.'

Chapter Three

'Welcome. Welcome aboard everyone.' Iris ticked names on her clipboard. 'You'll find your names on the back of the seats . . . come along ladies, my word, you all look gorgeous. Mind the step there, Lillie. We don't want you putting that hip out again now do we? I'll take your bag, Olive. My goodness it's heavy. You didn't need to bring all that food with you, Olive, it is all organized you know . . . Now, Reggie, which one of these ladies do you want to sit beside . . . It's a mystery tour, Violet. You're not supposed to know where you are going . . . Move them along, Helen. Further down the back of the bus. It will make it easier for the Cross and Passioners when we get there . . . Whatever you don't need on the bus the driver will put in the boot for you . . . Did I hear a clink? Con. Don't you remember what we said after last year? No drink on the bus. You better leave that with me . . . I know it's yours, Con. No, Con, I am not keeping it for myself. It's for safety's sake. Come back, Con. Of course you can keep it with you if you really want to . . . How are we doing down the back, Helen? Could you count heads? . . . I think we are finally ready for the off . . . What are you doing up here, Helen? You can't sit up here. You must station yourself at the back. Avante, Stephen. Stephen?'

Stevie was looking in his rear-view mirror. The pensioners, sitting rigid in their seats, all seemed to have their eyes fixed on the back of his head. As he gripped the wheel he felt a trickle of sweat run down the back of his neck. He checked his side mirrors, indicated, and began to pull out into the traffic. Once he was in the flow he began to relax. Iris, perched on the little pull-out seat at the front of the bus, faced her charges and held the specially installed microphone to her mouth.

'WELCOME TO THE MYSTERY TOUR EVERYONE.' As Iris's voice boomed round the bus, Stevie slammed on the brakes and the pensioners leaped out of their seats with fright. Helen clasped her head in pain as cardigans, raincoats, sandwiches, knitting, large-print Mills and Boons, plastic over-shoes and fruit spilled out of bags and ran all over the bus. Mai Byrne fell on to the lap of Con Pierce while Lillie Fogerty, who had clutched her chest when Stevie hit the brakes, wrenched a button off her good lilac blouse.

'Whoops. So sorry. Have to adjust the volume.' Iris fiddled with the microphone unaware of the chaos in front of her. Stevie steadied himself as Helen, crawling round the bus on all fours, helped to retrieve the spilled articles, and a bit of calm was restored.

'I have the knack of it now.' Iris beamed. 'Settle down everyone. Get ready to enjoy yourselves.'

'Iris. Iris.'

'What is it, Cissy? You really musn't shout on the bus. It will only distract the driver.'

'It's Willie. Over there on the path. We can't go without Willie. He's been looking forward to the trip for ages.'

'He was on the bus,' Iris said. 'I saw him.'

'He hopped off to get something in the shop.'

Iris glared down the bus at Helen. 'I did ask you to count heads, Helen. How could you let this happen? We will have to go back for him, Stephen. We can't leave him behind.'

The traffic was too heavy for Stevie to reverse. He had to drive on until he could turn right at Buckingham Street, right again at Summerhill and head down Ballybough to get back to Fairview. A huge cheer went up as the pensioners approached the park again.

'Sit down, Mr Ryan. Where are you going?' Helen ran down the bus after Mr Ryan and took his hand. 'We're not home, Mr Ryan. We haven't started yet.' She steered him back to his seat. 'We are going back for Willie. *Willie*,' she roared into his good ear. Reg Ryan checked his fly.

'There he is. There's Willie.' Cissy opened the window and stuck her head out. 'Yoo-hoo, Willie. It's the posse. We're coming to get you.'

Willie was standing outside the park clutching his bus pass. He was trying to figure out where the bus had gone. He looked up startled when he heard his name, but he was looking in the wrong direction, and nearly got himself killed by stepping out on the road. Stevie pulled the bus up and stopped just behind him.

'You don't need your bus pass, Willie,' Iris said, helping him on to the bus. 'Put it away in case you lose it.'

Bus pass. Bus pass. The word spread through the bus and all hands went fumbling in handbags and pockets for the magic little cards.

Iris picked up the microphone. 'For the last time, everyone, this is a mystery tour. Don't ask where you are going. Don't eat your sandwiches or you won't be able to eat your lunch, and put away your bus passes.'

'The last mystery for me was me wedding night.' Cissy Nolan cackled down the bus through the static of Iris's microphone. 'What a disappointment. Them statues have a lot to answer for.'

'What were you expecting, Cissy?'

'Not what I got.'

'What's that smell?'

'It's me hard-boiled eggs.'

'Thank God for that.'

'I couldn't eat the dinner last year. I wasn't taking any chances.'

'I brought haslet. It's Deveney's.'

'Has anyone got any chicken? I'll swop you.'

Iris sat on her little seat in despair. She might as well have been talking to herself. 'Attention. Attention, everyone. When we have picked up all the ladies and gentlemen from the Cross and Passion, and we are all aboard, I will explain a little about our trip.'

'Abroad. Abroad? I didn't know we were going abroad.'

'For God's sake, Lillie,' Cissy said. 'When you've one foot in the grave and the other one is limping in after it what does it matter where you are going?'

'I heard the free travel is only circumcised in England. Did you hear that?' Olive turned to the people behind her.

'You could say that, Olive,' Helen said. 'but I think the word you want is subsidized.'

'Driver. Driver. Stop the bus. I think I left the gas on. I'll have to phone my daughter.'

Stevie Mahon changed down a gear. 'Some bloody mystery tour,' he muttered to himself. 'We haven't even got out of Fairview.'

'It's all right, Stephen. Don't stop the bus. Settle down, everyone. Don't worry, Reggie. We can phone your daughter from our first comfort stop.'

'Olive, isn't that your Frankie? There. Over there, going into the bookies.'

'I'll kill him. I'll be dug out of him. He told me he wasn't well, that's why he didn't come on the trip. Just wait till I get home, Frankie Doyle, I'll bookie you.'

'He can't hear you.'

'Do you know,' Dessie Rourke said morosely to his neighbour, 'you can't piss in this town but the whole world knows.'

'I heard that, Dessie Rourke,' Mai shouted down at him.

Chapter Four

Maureen Carmody tapped her keys impatiently on the front desk. 'Typical. Just typical. Forty minutes late already.' She looked through the glass window behind the desk into the Cross and Passion day room. 'Trouble,' Maureen sniffed. 'There's bound to be trouble.' She had done her best to dissuade the board from sanctioning the trip but that young Doctor Kennedy had brushed aside her misgivings.

'Nonsense, Sister Carmody. Do them the world of good, a trip like that. Recharge their batteries, liven them up a bit, meeting other senior citizens. In fact it's a great chance to try out a little idea of mine. To have open house here once a week. Invite pensioners from outside to join us for social evenings. It would be good for those living alone, and the ones living with their families, give them a bit of a break. What do you think?'

'What an idea, Doctor Kennedy,' said Maureen. 'Over my dead body, is what I think,' she hissed under her breath. She knew better than to put up any argument on the spot. She had seen doctors come and go. Let him plan away. When he had been here a while he would soon change his tune.

Inside the day room, the residents of the Cross and Passion sat in hushed silence. The day room, with its highly polished parquet floor, its stiff chairs, the rows of Zimmer frames, with Cross and Passion emblazoned on the steel frames, the spray of artificial flowers on the piano and the life-sized statue of the Virgin Mary, had the effect of reducing both residents and visitors to a churchlike reverential hush. Three of the ladies, Mrs Scott, Miss Bourke and Mrs Joan Clancy sat on a couch in front of the blank television. Miss Poole clacked away on her needles, knitting yet another jumper for her nephew. Mr Carr and Mr Flood played draughts, Mr O'Connor played patience and Mr Connolly and Mrs Walsh sat side by side in knee rugs, staring straight ahead. Mr Eoin O'Neill, in his usual chair by the bay window overlooking the drive, watched for the long-awaited visit from his son.

'I won't be joining you on the trip.' Mr O'Neill spoke softly to Mr Mooney who was wandering aimlessly up and down the day room. 'I feel sure my son will arrive today.'

Maureen bustled in. She loved the sound of her swishing apron, the squeak-squeak of her rubber-soled shoes on the parquet floor. It had been suggested that there would be no objection to her wearing a more casual uniform, but she wouldn't hear of it. Maureen looked around the room, reassuring herself that everything was as it should be. Neat, orderly, harmonious.

'Do sit down, Mr Mooney. You will tire yourself out. Are we all here? I see Mr Perrin is not with us. I thought he put his name down for this shebang.'

Mr Perrin was a thorn in Maureen's side. He had come to the Cross and Passion to convalesce but had stayed longer than expected. He didn't fit in to Maureen's category of residents. He was too independent. He still had his flat in the city and would take himself off now and then. Disappear. 'Sorting out his affairs,' he would say to Maureen. He had a mobile phone, for goodness sake. Maureen knew he didn't belong there but he paid the exorbitant monthly bill without a murmur and the trustees were only too willing to have his cash.

'Mr Perrin. Mr Perrin.'

Maureen marched upstairs to his room and knocked on the door. That was another thorn. He refused to allow anyone into his room without permission. 'Such nonsense in an establishment like this,' Maureen told the other members of staff. 'What does he think this is, a hotel?'

'Is the coach here yet, Maureen?'

As Mr Perrin opened the door, Maureen swept in. Maureen indeed. All the other residents called her Sister Carmody, but not Mr Perrin. It was Maureen this and Maureen that. She wished he would leave but she didn't dare offend him. She forced a bright smile.

'It's on its way, Mr Perrin. It would be more convenient if you were downstairs with the other residents.'

'Why, Maureen?'

'Well, obviously . . .'

'I will come down when I hear the coach. Thank you, Maureen.' Mr Perrin showed her to the door.

'Will you look at this place,' Lillie said. The bus had finally swung into the long drive leading up to the Cross and Passion Nursing Home. 'It's like a bleeding palace.'

'Now, Lillie,' Iris said. 'Let's be civil.'

Iris hadn't exactly hit it off with Maureen Carmody and she wanted to get in and out of the Cross and Passion as quickly as possible. She weaved her way down the back of the bus to Helen who was slumped on the back seat.

'I'll hop in and get the rest of them, Helen. You stay on the bus. If Hatchet-face sees the state of you she won't let them go.'

Helen who had no intention of moving lifted her bleary head. 'Ask her if she has any ether, or better still, get me a flask of oxygen.'

'Very funny, Helen.'

'Sorry, Iris. Just give me another hour and I will be as right as rain. I promise.'

'You'd better be.'

Stevie stopped the bus in front of the main entrance and turned off the engine. There was no sign of life except for one elderly man sitting at the window. As Stevie gave a friendly toot on the horn, Iris charged back up the bus.

'Stephen, don't.'

'Just being friendly, Iris.' Stevie was hurt.

'This isn't the sort of place you toot in, Stephen. We have to mind our Ps and Qs here.'

Iris ran up the steps, giving a big friendly wave in to the residents who had gathered nervously at the bay window. The door was opened by Maureen who stared incredulously at the decorated bus.

'Goodness gracious, Miss Fox. I mean to say. This isn't exactly what I would have expected for my residents.'

'Great isn't it.' Iris followed Maureen's eyes and smiled. 'To be honest I never thought we would get it together. Fair dues to Helen. She made a great job of it. Is everybody ready? I hope you didn't make sandwiches. Sorry we are a bit late. We had to go back for Willie. Hello. Hello, everyone. I'm Iris.' The residents were trickling out of the day room into the hall and out of the front door. 'We won't delay introducing ourselves — we can get to know each other on the bus . . .'

Underneath the banner, which ran across the front of the bus, and the bunting Helen had draped from window to window, the Fairview OAPs stared in silence as the Cross and Passion residents streeled down the steps.

'. . . Mind how you go, folks. Oops a daisy. Stephen, could you assist here please.'

Stevie opened the little door to his seat and took each trembling hand as the newcomers clambered in.

Maureen watched in silence as her charges got on the bus. 'A Molotov,' she told herself.

When George Perrin walked out past her and with a dapper lift of his homburg said, 'You're not joining us, Maureen?' she pursed her lips and dusted an imaginary speck off her uniform. 'I'm sure you are missing a good day out. Don't worry, young man, I'm quite able-bodied.' Stevie had stretched out to assist him on to the bus. He ignored the seat Iris was indicating and went down the back of the bus where he sat beside Helen.

'Hello,' he introduced himself. 'I'm George Perrin.'

'Hi. I'm Helen. I'm not at my best.'

Iris gave Maureen a copy of the itinerary and an approximate time for their return, then she hopped on the bus with a big wave. 'At last,' she said. 'We are finally off. On we go, Stephen.' Iris giggled into her microphone. 'And don't spare the horses.'

Chapter Five

'Who told you that?'

'No, it's true. When you see cows sitting down in a field it's a sign of rain.'

'Would you get off. The sun is splitting the trees.'

'Well don't say I didn't warn you.'

Iris's seating plan was now obsolete. All the ladies were sitting together at the front of the bus and the gents had congregated towards the back. Iris had no one to blame but herself as she had inadvertently caused this new arrangement. There hadn't been a word out of anyone as the bus pulled out of the nursing home and headed through town. The Cross and Passioners sat, cowed and muted, as Iris ticked them off on her clipboard. The Fairview contingent were subdued, and for the first time since they had met up that morning there was no chat out of any of them. Iris had tried hard to get everyone going.

'Let's give a big hello to our new guests. I'm sure we will all get on famously. Hello. Hello, everyone.' There was no response from any of the passengers. 'Is this thing working?' Iris shook the mike. 'Testing. Testing. One, two three, four. Testing.'

'What's she doing?' Lillie asked.

'She's testing,' Cissy said. 'You've seen it on the telly.'

'Hello, Hello,' Iris repeated, cupping her ear to encourage response. 'Perhaps we should mix everyone up. Stephen –' she poked her head into his cab '– could you stop the bus while we swop seats. No, maybe not, it would delay us even further, although it would make things more friendly. I'll make a little announcement about our trip that should help to break the ice. Attention everybody. I am sure you are all dying to hear about the plan. I won't give you the final mystery destination but I will tell you we will be making two stops before lunch. Two beauty spots which I promise won't disappoint you. The first renowned for its botanical prowess –' Iris paused for effect '– and the other . . . dearie me, I was hoping for a lively guessing game from all of you before I went on. The other, a certain watering hole which, I have no doubt, you will all have seen on picture postcards. Does anyone have a clue?'

The pensioners, unmoved, continued to stare at her.

'I know what we'll do. What about a singsong to get us in the mood? Who knows "The Fields of Athenry"? Dum dum, de dum dum dum, la la, la la la la. Come on now, I know you know it, it's lovely in the Fields of Athenry.' Iris sat on her little seat singing into the microphone. 'Don't tell me you are shy.

Helen. I don't hear you, Helen. Let's take it from the top. And a one and a two. Dum dum, de dum dum dum.'

'Sorry, Iris. I wasn't ready.'

'Are you ready now, Helen?' Iris's voice was getting dangerous.

'I don't really know that one.'

'Nonsense. Everyone knows "The Fields of Athenry".'

'Couldn't you leave it until a bit later? At least till we get out of town. I'm sure no one is ready to sing just yet. Especially me.' Helen's voice dropped to a whisper.

'Would you like me to stop the bus, Helen, so you can . . . Oops.' Iris slipped sideways off her perch and landed with a thump as Stevie, slowing and then accelerating on command, temporarily lost gear control and the bus hiccuped twice and stopped.

'It's all right everyone.' Iris spoke through the microphone from the floor. 'No harm done.' Stevie, recovering from the shock of a full view of Iris's white knickers tried to mouth an apology. 'You'll have to be more careful, Stephen. We have precious cargo on board.'

Nothing could have worked better than Iris's little slip to break the ice. Falls. The terror of the pensioners' lives. Falls, slips, hips, knees, each of the ladies had a story to tell. Eyesight, hearing, itching, twitching, veins.

'Move over there, Reggie, till I talk to this lady . . .'

'Shift yourself, Dessie. I'm sure I met Mrs Bourke at the Post Office.'

They changed seats. They sighed. They sympathized. They laughed and went one better. They showed each other scars.

'Do you see this one? I got that just crossing the road.'

'. . . And I told that Doctor Bejani, I said I wasn't having the knife . . .'

They knew each other's stories. They had all been there. The good sons. The good-for-nothing ones. The daughters who had married animals. The daughters-in-law who couldn't cook, never darned. Photographs came out from handbags and were shared.

'You nearly put me eye out, Cissy,' Willie complained, 'with your blooming handbag.'

'Go down the back of the bus then and talk gee gees with the rest of them.'

The gents, never at ease with personal stories, huddled together.

Stevie hit the Motorway and the bus cruised along at a steady fifty. Appreciative gasps were heard from the passengers as the housing estates were left behind and fields and rolling hills came into view. When the first cows were spotted a great cheer went up and Lillie started a cow count. As the bus climbed slightly, and a glimpse of Dublin Bay appeared on their left, they ooh'd and ah'd and reminded themselves how beautiful County Wicklow was and how, only a stone's throw from the city, you had all this at your feet. Even Helen, who was sufficiently impressed to stop thinking about her sore head, joined in their enthusiasm.

*

'Seventeen, eighteen.'

'You can't count them, Lillie. They're not cows.'

'What are they then?'

'If you stop being so vain and put your glasses on you would see that they are ostriches.'

'Give over.'

'I swear to God.'

'Ostriches? In Ireland?'

'I read about it in the *Indo*. Some geezer started an ostrich farm as a way of protecting cows, like.'

'I read it as well,' Mai Byrne said. 'They're for vegetarians.'

'Goodness me, no,' Mr O'Connor, from the Cross and Passion group spoke up. 'They are an invaluable source of protein. I believe the ostrich is a great delicacy in the Far East.'

'Far or near, Mister, you won't catch me eating ostrich.'

Stevie slowed the bus and the pensioners all gazed out of the window into the field.

'Look at them, they've no place to play. I think it's cruel. How could anyone eat them?'

'It's no more cruel than eating cow or hen. Not to mention little lambs.'

'Can we stop, Iris? Can we get out and see the ostriches?'

'I'm afraid not. We're on a tight schedule. Maybe on the way back.'

'I thought you were having me on,' Lillie said, 'but they do look a bit like outsize turkeys don't they.'

'I'd like to see you trying to pluck one, Lillie, or get one of them into the oven at Christmas time. You'd have to make the stuffing in the bath.'

'Helen, could you come up to the front please.'

Helen threw an eye to George Perrin. 'The royal command. What does her majesty want now? If it's another song I am going to throw myself off the bus.'

'If it's another song, Helen, I will be right behind you.'

'A quiet little confab, Helen.'

'You are talking into the mike, Iris.'

Iris put the mike down and whispered in Helen's ear. 'I have decided we should bypass Ashford, Helen. We don't want to be late getting to Arklow for the lunch.'

'But the place is booked, Iris, and anyway there is no bypass for Ashford. We have to go through the village. They're bound to see us.'

'They won't even notice us.'

'You've got to be joking, Iris. Look at us. We're like a mobile pageant. Even the tractors are hooting as we go by.'

'There are hundreds of tour buses on the road. Don't make difficulties where there are none.'

'Not with banners and bunting and a coachload of old ones roaring out the window every time we pass a sheep or a cow.'

'It can't be helped.'

Cissy called out. 'We're coming to a village, Iris. Are we going to stop?'

'Not today, Cissy.'

'When can we get off, Iris? My veins are swelling with the motion.'

'Yeah, Iris. We want to get off.'

'It won't be long now.' Iris picked up her microphone. 'Ladies and gentlemen, we shall be making our first stop at the Vale of Avoca where, as I am sure you all know, Mr Moore wrote some of his famous melodies . . .'

'That's who it was who said that about the cows.'

'Thomas Moore?'

'No. Old Moore, in his almanack.'

'His what?'

'They serve Armagnac in Freeny's.' Reg Ryan leaned across the aisle. 'I have the odd one at Christmas.'

'She said almanack, Mr Ryan,' Helen kindly explained to Reg on her way back down the bus. '*Almanack*.'

Reg checked his raincoat.

'Bang goes our first chance to get off this bloody bus,' Helen said to George Perrin when she got back to her seat.

'What did she mean, not today? Are you planning more trips?'

'Mr Perrin, don't even think about it.'

'George. Call me George.'

'We were supposed to have twenty minutes here. I don't know what she's at.'

'. . . we could sing one of Mr Moore's songs . . .'

'Oh Christ. Not again,' Helen whispered.

'. . . I will lead you in with a bar. "Oh there's

nought in the wild world a valley so sweet as the vale in whose bosom the bright waters meet." After the count of three. One two three. "Oh there's nought . . ."'

Thin warbling voices took up the refrain while Iris kept time with her hand. Miss Bourke started to weep. 'I'm so sorry. That song always makes me cry. It reminds me of my husband. He was killed in the war you know.'

'Was he posted overseas?'

'Oh no, dear. He was a milkman. He was injured on his rounds.'

'Oh the poor man.'

Poor Stevie, whose nerves were raw, couldn't contain himself. He started to laugh.

'Stephen,' Iris said. 'It's very sad, you shouldn't laugh.'

'Injured on his rounds,' Stevie chortled. 'That's a good one. Ha ha ha . . .'

'Pull yourself together, Stephen. A little decorum please.'

'. . . ha ha ha . . .' Stevie couldn't stop '. . . ha ha ha ha ha.' His laughter was infectious and within minutes the entire bus, with the exception of poor Miss Bourke who was weeping copiously into her hanky, was in hysterics.

Ashford, a pretty little village, prided itself as the gateway to Wicklow. Among its attractions it boasted the Mount Usher gardens and Hunters Hotel, famous for its afternoon teas. The café, in the middle of the village, was a haven for all types of travellers, businessmen commuting to Dublin, day trippers, and bus tours. No one passing through could miss it – PATRICK SCULLY – GOOD FOOD AT A FAIR PRICE was painted in bright red over the entrance. Mr Scully had one of his assistants on the lookout for the pensioners' bus. He had promised Iris he would do something special so he and his staff had set up trestle tables, chairs and stripy umbrellas on the grass out the back. The young girl stationed herself on the pavement.

'There's something coming, Mr Scully. It looks as if it might be them.'

'Right everyone,' Mr Scully called out, 'all hands on deck.'

The staff bustled about putting the finishing touches to the tables.

'Look, Iris. There's someone waving at us.'

'Cissy. Put your hand down. Do not attempt to wave back.'

'This must be where we are stopping.'

'Hooray. At last.'

'Settle down. Settle down everyone. We are not stopping here. Stephen, I want you to get through this village as quickly as possible. I will create a diversion on the bus to occupy our guests.'

Mr Scully's assistant had stepped out into the middle of the road and was waving and gesturing to guide the bus towards the café car park.

'Quickly, Stephen, turn off the road. Turn off the road.'

'Where?' Stephen shouted.

'Over there, quick, before they recognize us.

There's a little turn to the right, just beside that bridge.'

'It's too narrow, Iris. The bus won't fit.'

'Of course it will fit, Stephen. Do as I say.'

Stephen had no time to indicate. He swerved across the road and took the sharp right turn Iris had indicated. Sparks flew as the bus skidded and screeched on the bend.

'Hold on, everyone,' Helen called out from the back. 'Hold on tight. Oh my God. Iris. Are you all right?'

Iris had vanished. She had been thrown sideways off her seat and was jammed in the well at the bottom of the steps.

'Holy Mother of the Divine and gentle Jesus,' Mai Byrne blessed herself, 'It's the end.'

'Help. Help.'

The bus scorched along out of control, the passengers pitched and tossed, as the rear of the bus swung from side to side, banging off the stone walls on each side of the boreen.

'Hard on the throttle, young man.' Mr Flood, who hadn't said a word during the entire journey, suddenly found his voice and shouted from his seat. 'Keep her head up!'

Mrs Scott and Miss Bourke were wrestled to the floor. Miss Poole found herself embracing Mrs Joan Clancy, whom she was never very fond of. Mr O'Neill called for his son, while Dessie Rourke, never one to miss a chance, roared above the din, 'Marry me, Lillie, before it's too late.'

Stevie fought hard and finally managed to stop,

helped in no small way by the flattening of a large road sign announcing: WELCOME TO ASHFORD, THE GARDEN OF IRELAND.

Chapter Six

The phone at the reception desk in the Cross and Passion Nursing Home rang several times before Ann Roberts stopped her doodling to answer it. She was bored out of her drawers. She hated this Saturday job her mother made her do. 'If you want pocket money, Ann, you have to earn it.' Ann would much rather work in a shop or a restaurant but her mother had got her this job. 'It's very worthwhile, Ann, and you will be making money.' Ann's duties were to man the phone, do the elevenses and accompany the residents in the garden on fine days. This was a fine day but there were no residents. All but the bedridden had gone off on a trip. She could have had the day off but the dragon had made her stay at the desk. She shifted her chewing gum to the side of her mouth.

'Hello, Cross and Passion . . . Who do you want? . . . That'll be Sister Carmody. She's in charge. Hold on and I'll see if I can find her for you, sir.' Ann put the receiver down and wandered off in search of Sister Carmody. She found her in the staffroom.

'What are you doing here, Ann? Why aren't you at your desk?'

'There's a guy on the phone . . .'

'What do you mean, a guy? Did you not get a name? Really, Ann, you will have to take your receptionist duties more seriously.'

'I don't know what guy. Some guy from Ashword or Ashford or somewhere.'

'Ashford. Did you say Ashford?'

'Yeah, Ashford, that's it. He's holding on.'

'You left him holding on?'

'What was I supposed to do?'

'You stupid, stupid girl.'

'You can't talk to me like that. I'll tell my mother.'

Maureen charged out of the staffroom and down the corridor to the phone. 'Hello, hello. Sister Maureen Carmody here. I'm so sorry . . . What? What time were they expected? . . . And it's now . . . Yes yes I do know the time . . . No, sir, certainly not. I can assure you it may be inconvenient for you, sir, but the disappearance of a coachload of senior citizens is far more important than your trestle of coffee and digestive biscuits . . . I am not taking *any* tone. Good day, sir.'

Ann Roberts and the rest of the Cross and Passion day staff edged into the hall as Doctor Kennedy, who had come down to find out what all the commotion was about, approached the desk.

'I hope you're happy now, Doctor Kennedy. We have lost our residents.'

'Oh my God, Maureen. Was there a crash?'

'Lost, Doctor Kennedy. Lost.'

'Maureen, get a grip on yourself. What has happened?'

'Our senior citizens are lost. They never turned up in Ashford.'

'Pull yourself together, Maureen. You are getting hysterical over nothing. They haven't gone to Outer Mongolia.'

A titter was heard from the little group at the end of the corridor.

'How can you be so flippant, Doctor Kennedy? My citizens are out there, lost, and all you can do is make jokes.'

'Now, Maureen, take it easy. I am sure there is nothing to worry about. It's probably something as simple as a puncture; we're bound to hear from them sooner or later. I must get back to my office, I have a patient waiting. Why don't you get Ann here to make you a nice strong cup of tea? You'll feel better in no time.'

Maureen waited until Doctor Kennedy had closed his office door then she picked up the phone. 'Deborah. It's Maureen. I can't explain too much over the phone but we have a crisis on our hands and I need your help. You must come round immediately . . . yes, immediately. Pick me up at the front door. I will explain everything when I see you.' Maureen hung up the phone. 'Ann. I want you to phone every garda station between here and Ashford. Get the number of the bus from the depot in Dublin and give it to the guards. Photocopy this.' She handed Ann the itinerary. 'It is a list of their intended schedule. Check every stop the bus was to make. I shall follow the route by car and will telephone you at intervals with an update of our progress. Pass me that mission box. I am going to need all the change I can get. Oh, to have a mobile phone in times of need. Stay by your post, Ann. I am relying on you.'

'Wow.' Ann stopped chewing her gum. 'Wow.'

Deborah was halfway up the drive of the Cross and Passion when she saw Maureen pacing up and down at the front steps. For a moment she was tempted to turn and drive away but Maureen spotted the car and came rushing up to the window.

'I don't want to seem ungrateful, Deborah, but you did take your time.'

'It's Saturday, Maureen. I was in bed where I had hoped to stay as long as possible. What is the big emergency?' Deborah opened the car door to get out. 'I thought the place must be on fire.'

'Stay in the car. There is no time to lose.'

'What on earth is going on, Maureen?'

'Reverse. Reverse and turn, Deborah, while I tell my staff we are off.'

'Off where?'

Deborah got no reply. Maureen had run up the steps and was shouting into the hall. 'Man your post, girl. What did I tell you? My friend has arrived and we are off to find our residents.'

'Wow,' Ann replied. 'Double wow.'

'Thank goodness I had the foresight to insist on a copy of their itinerary.'

'Whose itinerary? Maureen if you don't tell me what's going on . . .'

'The outing, Deborah. The outing that you thought would be so nice for my residents. They are missing. They have not turned up where they should. Drive, Deborah, drive.' Maureen delved into her pieces of paper. 'They were supposed to stop in Ashford for coffee, then Avoca for the meeting of the waters, and then on to Arklow. They are booked in for lunch at two-fifteen.' Maureen looked up. 'Why are we still stationary, Deborah?'

'I am not gifted with ESP, Maureen. Where do you want me to drive to?'

'East, Deborah, east. Where are your maps?'

'I don't have any maps.'

'We will have to stop and get some. That's typical, isn't it. A car driver with no maps.'

'We don't need maps to get to Arklow. It is only thirty-five miles from Dublin.'

'On the main road, Deborah. But my residents are lost. Stuck on the side of a road. Broken down, I shouldn't wonder, with only that incompetent do-gooder in charge of them. I can't bear to think of it.'

'I'll have to get petrol. You can buy a map at the garage.'

Deborah drove to the nearest petrol station. As she filled the tank Maureen dashed into the shop. 'A map of Wicklow, please.'

'We don't have Wicklow specifically. There should be one on the shelf over there of the East Coast.'

'I don't want the East Coast. I want an Ordnance Survey map of Wicklow.'

'Then you better go to the Phoenix Park, Mrs. That's the only place you're going to get an Ordnance.

We do have a *Walking in the Wicklow Hills* that might do you. Just as good, in my opinion.'

'I'll take it. How much?'

'For you, Mrs, seven pounds, sixty.'

'Seven pounds, sixty? I could get a whole atlas for that.'

'That's the price, Mrs. Take it or leave it.'

'Daylight robbery,' Maureen said, counting out the money.

'I don't set the prices, Mrs. You needn't take it out on me.' Maureen swept out of the shop. 'Bloody woman. I hope she gets lost.'

'Get us out of town, Deborah. I'll navigate after that.'

'Did you get the map?'

'Not the one I wanted but it will do.' Maureen picked up the itinerary and began to read it aloud. 'Depart Fairview, eight-forty-five. Collect local pensioners and proceed to C and P.'

'C and P?'

'Cross and Passion. For goodness sake, Deborah, stay alert.'

'Oops, sorry.'

'Ashford, ten-twenty a.m., coffee break, twenty minutes. Avoca, midday – coffee break and leg-stretch – thirty minutes. Arklow, two o'clock, lunch plus one hour free time. Depart Arklow, three-thirty p.m. Roundwood – via Wicklow gap – four-thirty tea break – twenty minutes. Drumcondra – six-thirty. Deposit Cross and Passion pensioners. Fairview, seven p.m. Deposit remaining pensioners and dismiss coach.'

'That sounds fairly well organized to me, Maureen.'

'Organized? There is nothing organized about it, Deborah. Look at it. Coffee break twenty minutes, it would take twenty minutes to get my residents off the bus. No wonder they are lost when the organizer has no practical experience. We will head for the N11 motorway, Deborah, and follow their route from there. Someone must have seen them.'

'This is a wild goose chase, Maureen. They're probably sitting in some cosy café having tea and sticky buns.'

'I have extremely sharp instincts, Deborah, and those instincts are telling me that all is not well.'

Chapter Seven

Ann got out the Cross and Passion telephone book, looked up the Dublin bus company and, following Sister Carmody's instructions to the letter, phoned them, got the bus number, and wrote it down carefully on the top of the itinerary. So far so good. Police stations next. She flicked through the book. There were pages and pages of police stations. Now what was she going to do? It wasn't fair. How was she supposed to know which ones were en route to Ashford and which ones weren't? Sister Carmody never said. She could ring 999. No, she'd better not, her mother would kill her if she rang 999. Ann went back to the first page. Dublin Metropolitan Region Headquarters. Headquarters. She could ring them and then they could get on to the others. They could put out an APB. She didn't know what an APB was but they always said that on the telly.

'Is that the police? I was told to ring you on account of the residents who Sister Carmody says are not where they are supposed to be. I want to put out an APB.'

'Who is this?'

'I'm Ann Roberts.'

'Where are you calling from, Ann?'

'The Cross and Passion. I work here.'

'All right, Ann. Tell me from the beginning.'

'My mother made me do this job and when I came in this morning all the residents were gone out on a trip and now they are missing.'

'Missing?'

'Yeah.'

'How missing are they, Ann? You said they were on a trip?'

'Oh, very missing. Sister Carmody is mad. She and her friend are gone to look for them and she told me to ring you with the bus number.'

'The bus number?'

'Yeah. And it's ZXY 276.'

'I'm at a bit of a loss here, Ann.'

'How could you be lost when I rang you at the station?'

'How old are you, Ann?'

'I'm fifteen.'

'And what did your sister say to you exactly?'

'She said, "ring the depot and get the bus number and then ring you", and that's what I did.'

'Let me get this straight. You work at the Cross and Passion Nursing Home. The residents are gone on a bus and your sister says they are missing.'

'No, no. You've got it all wrong. She's not my sister, she's Sister Carmody. She's in charge. Listen.' Ann took a deep breath. 'All the old ones went on a trip and they are missing and Sister Carmody and her friend are gone looking for them and she wants me to ring all the police stations between here and Ashford and I'm to stay on the phone and give her messages when you find them.'

'Are you sure, Ann, this isn't some kind of prank?'

'Oh no, mister. Honest. Cross my heart. I have all the names and all and where they were going only they didn't get there and . . .'

'How many old people are we talking about, Ann?'

'Hold on till I get the list. There's Mrs Scott, Joan Clancy, Miss Poole, Mr Carr, Mr Flood, Mr O'Connor, Mrs Walsh, Eoin O'Neill, Mr Mooney, and George Perrin on our list and then there's another list that says . . .'

'George Perrin. Did you say George Perrin?'

'Yep, but he's not as old as the others so you probably don't have to worry about him, and the other list says . . .'

'Ann. This is very important. I need to know exactly where they have gone and who they are gone with.'

'I don't know who they went with and I don't know where they are gone. I only know they are not where they are supposed to be because Sister Carmody gave me the list and I already gave you the bus number.'

'Stay exactly where you are, Ann. I'll send a squad car round immediately. Don't let that list out of your sight, and Ann, don't worry, we'll find them, if we have to chase them all the way to Waterford.'

'Wow.' Ann sat behind her desk. 'A squad car.' This was great. Like being in a whodunnit. She had never dreamed she'd have a chance to be involved in a real police chase. Wait till she told her mates. They wouldn't believe it. Chase co-ordinator. Ann lifted the phone and dialled a number. 'Mags. Is that you? Wait till I tell you. You're never going to believe it . . .'

Sergeant Kelly hesitated before going into the Superintendent's office. This was bad news, in fact it couldn't be worse. If George Perrin was missing, the George Perrin who had been placed in the Cross and Passion Nursing Home, it could blow their whole case apart. It would have to happen when the Chief and all of his crack team were off for the weekend and the Sergeant was left with rookies, rookies and the Chief's new assistant, Detective Desmond Meyers who, as far as Sergeant Kelly was concerned, didn't know his arse from his elbow. The rookies were keen, he had to give them that, but between the lot of them, they hadn't clocked up enough experience to catch a paint-spraying delinquent, let alone handle a case like this. As for Meyers, the less said the better. He was a buffoon, somebody's relation, who had been brought in from outside to gain hands-on experience.

Operation Steamroller had been a difficult and intricate case. It had taken months of hard work to set up, endless man hours of liaison with Customs and Excise, the Fraud Squad and the Motor Department. Due to the total dedication of the team, they had finally been able to put the case to bed. The main villain, Lefty Morgan, was temporarily behind bars and the team's star witness, Alex Smith – alias George Perrin – had been placed in a safe house until the trial. But without Smith they had no case. Morgan would walk. Any clever lawyer could get him off and Morgan had the money to pay for the best.

In the interest of security only the Chief Superintendent and his team knew the whereabouts and true identity of George Perrin. Round-the-clock surveillance had been discussed but the Chief had felt it might attract undue attention. The gang would know that a twenty-four-hour watch on an old people's home could only mean there was something there to protect. George had been instructed to keep his head down, maintain a low profile, and only make contact with the incident room every other Thursday. He had been supplied with a police-issue mobile phone for this purpose. Sergeant Kelly braced himself and went in to the Super's office to brief Meyers.

'Gentlemen.' Sergeant Kelly addressed the rookies. 'As you may or may not be aware, we have a serious problem on our hands. I will now hand you over to acting Chief Desmond Meyers who will explain the situation to you.'

'Now men.' Chief Meyers looked around the incident room. 'I don't have to tell you how important this case is. You've all heard about Operation Steamroller . . .' The rookies looked at one another not wanting to admit to the Chief that they hadn't the faintest notion what he was talking about. '. . . Don't bother to deny it, I know how things get round the station. What you do not know is that our star witness is missing, AWOL. I have received a call from the safe house and I have reason to believe that what was supposed to look like an innocent pensioners' outing, may, in fact, be a cleverly contrived plot to snuff our witness out. Let me fill in the details for you. Alex Smith was placed in the Cross and Passion Nursing Home, under the assumed name of George Perrin, for his own protection and safety. No one, save the team, knew of this plan. I can only surmise that either George unwittingly drew attention to himself or the gang have someone on the inside. What is it, Jones?'

'I was wondering, Chief. What is this Alex alias George Perrin a witness to? It would help if we knew what we were tackling.'

'I'm glad to hear that the station grapevine hasn't got that far, Jones, but I'm not at liberty to divulge that information at present. All you need to know is that George Perrin is missing and he must be found. Gather round the flip chart, men. Jones, pull the blinds.' Chief Meyers picked up a baton and lifted the chart cover. 'I don't have to tell you men that anything you hear in this room is strictly confidential. Here –' the Chief pointed to a large house drawn out on the flip chart '– is the Cross and Passion House. As you can see, it has extensive grounds. There are two exits, here and here.' He banged the chart in two places to emphasize the exits. 'Both of these exits are covered by security cameras which, unfortunately, only operate at night. The main exit, here, leads out on to Drumcondra Road. From there it's only a short walk to O'Connell Street, so any obvious suspects could be assured of an easy getaway. They could lose themselves in the crowd or jump on a bus. The other exit leads on to the canal. We can rule that one out. Even the most stupid of criminals is unlikely to have a barge tethered on the canal. Our informant tells us that at least ten of the residents left on a coach for an outing. Needless to say they have not arrived at their destination. We are dealing with some very clever adversaries. Who would suspect a coach full of old people to be anything other than a harmless trip?'

'Do we know the coach, Chief?'

'As I speak a squad car is heading for the Cross and Passion. I believe our informant has been able not only to get the coach number, but to obtain a list of all the passengers. I firmly believe that this is an inside job. Our man on the beat has been instructed to find out the names of all the staff past and present. Sergeant Kelly will let us know immediately if any of those names are familiar to us.'

'What do you want us to do, Chief?'

'I want four cars. Two in each car. As soon as we have the information each team will be given their assignment. The intended destination, as far as we know, is Ashford. That might be a good place to start from. Someone there must know something about it. The coach driver would have to have been given instructions before he started out.'

'Do you think he's in on it as well, Chief?'

'I'm not ruling anyone out for now, Jones.' The Chief closed the flip chart. 'Now gentlemen, you all know the drill, you will have covered this in basic training. Keep off the air as much as possible. Use code names only and, if you suspect your calls are being picked up, use public telephones. Communicate directly with Desk Sergeant Kelly. What is it, Jones?'

'Do we get to pick our own code names, Chief?'

'We'll keep this simple. Operation Steamroller, car one, or car two, as the case may be, will be enough. Sergeant Kelly will take it from there. Keep out of sight. If any of you spot the coach don't attempt to apprehend it. Call in, follow it, and wait for reinforcements. Any questions?'

'Chief. Do you think we should wear disguise?'

Sergeant Kelly, who had been standing quietly at the back of the incident room during the briefing, winced visibly.

'Disguise won't be necessary. Neat and tidy, men. The last thing the public expect is plain clothes being neat and tidy. Remember, men, I am relying on you. And men, be careful out there.'

Four blue unmarked Escorts screeched out of police headquarters heading east. Once out of sight they pulled over and had a quick confab. 'Neat and tidy,' the Chief had said, and they weren't about to let him down. They all agreed that before they went on this important assignment they should go home and change.

Chapter Eight

Shaken, but unharmed, the passengers of the 123 City Swift gathered themselves together. All, that is, except the driver. Poor Stevie couldn't move. His hands were glued to the wheel and he was staring straight ahead of him. Helen rushed up to the front of the bus.

'Stevie, Stevie. Are you okay?' Stevie was so overcome he couldn't reply. 'You're not hurt, are you?'

A large tear dropped into Stevie's lap as he shook his head slowly from side to side.

'Iris.' Helen looked down into the well of the bus where Iris was splayed against the door. 'Are *you* all right?'

'Yes. Yes. I'm fine. Help me up. What about everybody else?' Iris asked as Helen grabbed her arm and tried to haul her up.

'Don't worry. They're some tough old birds. It didn't take a feather out of any of them.'

'Stephen. We can't go on like this. This is our second mishap.'

'Leave him alone, Iris. He's very upset.'

'You call this a mishap, Iris?' Cissy Nolan said. 'It's the second time we have been hurled to the floor. That young fellah is trying to kill us.'

'Off the bus please,' announced Iris. 'Everyone off the bus. Leave your belongings and step off the bus as you are.'

'Jesus, it's just like *Aeroplane*. Did you see it? They all get off and the plane bursts into flames and after walking hundreds of miles they start eating each other.'

'Give over, Lillie.'

'Was it *Aeroplane* or was it Desert something?'

'Eejit. *Desert Song* was the one where Lawrence of Arabia fell off his horse.'

'I don't want to interrupt, my dear, but I don't think horses are natural to the desert.'

'Nice to hear you speak, Miss Poole.' Con took Miss Poole's arm and helped her off the bus. 'I thought the cat had got your tongue. You haven't said a word since we left town.'

'I didn't mean to . . . oh dear . . . have I said something?'

The pensioners were off the bus and George Perrin and Iris stood behind Stevie.

'It's all right, Stephen lad, you did a great job. No one is hurt.'

'What are we going to do now, Mr Perrin? I don't know what to do.'

'Take a deep breath, Stephen. That's it. Let yourself

relax.' Mr Perrin prised Stevie's hands off the wheel. 'Do you want to get off for a minute?'

'He can't do that, Mr Perrin,' Iris said. 'We have a schedule to keep. We must get going.'

'I'm OK, Mr Perrin.'

'Are you sure you are up to it?'

'I'll be fine.'

'Take your time. When you are ready we'll try to get her started.'

'What do I do?'

'Turn on the ignition, put her in reverse and back up slowly. We need to get that sign out from underneath before we do anything else. That's it, Stevie. Easy now. Keep your foot on the accelerator and just ease her back.'

Stevie turned on the engine and a cloud of black smoke billowed out from the undercarriage, followed by a terrible grinding noise.

'It's wrecked. It's completely banjaxed.'

'Language, Stephen,' Iris reprimanded him, 'language. My senior citizens . . .'

'It's all your fault, Iris. You made me take that turn. I knew we'd never make it.'

'Now now. We won't get anywhere by squabbling,' Mr Perrin said. 'We need to get that sign up and get the bus out of the ditch before anyone reports us to the police.'

'The police,' Stevie howled.

'It's going to be OK, Stephen.'

'Push,' Iris urged, hanging out the door of the 123,

'push, everyone, put your backs into it.' The elderly pensioners, shoulders to the bus, tried to inch it off the sign.

'You could get off and give us a hand, Iris,' Helen said. 'We are all exhausted.'

'My weight doesn't make the slightest difference, Helen. It's all to do with aeronautics. You'd be a lot better off conserving your energy for the task in hand than wasting valuable strength on useless remarks. One more big push and then we can take a breather. On the count of three. Ready, everybody. One, two, three. Push.'

Stevie rammed the bus into reverse and it shifted enough for Mr Perrin to drag the sign out from underneath. 'Well done, everyone. Well done.'

The pensioners sank to the ground around the bus.

'My doctor told me I'd have to have physio,' Lillie said, 'but after this trip, I reckon I won't need it.'

'Now. When you've all had a little rest and got your breath back, I need volunteers to hoist the sign.'

'Christ. I swear, in another life, she was in charge of a Gulag.'

'Gentlemen? I need all able-bodied men to the sign as soon as possible.'

'Iris,' Helen said, 'enough is enough. Someone will have a heart attack.'

'I'm not enjoying this either, Helen, but it must be done.'

Reg Ryan, Mr Flood and Mr O'Neill held the buckled sign in position as the ladies collected stones and deposited them round the base. The pile got bigger and bigger as the wall beside the bus was dismantled.

'That's it, ladies. Keep them coming. We need a lot more in case it blows over in the wind.'

'They'll have pilgrimages to this,' Reg said. 'The moving sign of Ashford.'

'Iris,' Lillie called into the bus.

'What is it, Lillie?'

'Can we have our sandwiches?'

'Not now, Lillie.'

'You might as well let them, Iris,' George Perrin said. 'It could take some time to assess the damage to the bus.'

'Helen, could you come on the bus and collect up all the edibles?'

'You're on the bloody bus, Iris, why don't you pass them out?'

'Really, Helen. Can't you see I am busy with the technical side of things here?'

'She's not going to go, Mr Perrin,' Stevie said in despair. 'What am I going to do?'

'Don't panic, Stephen. We'll get her going all right.'

The pensioners grouped round the bus as Helen passed out the bags of food.

'I think they would be safer in the field, Helen,' George Perrin said. 'Guide them into the field.'

'You can't expect my senior citizens to climb into a field, Mr Perrin. They could hurt themselves climbing over walls.'

'They won't have to climb, Iris.'

Iris looked out of the bus window at a large gap in the wall. 'Oh my God, Helen. What have you done? Don't you know stone walls are part of our Celtic culture? They are our national heritage. How could you let this happen?'

'Into the field, everyone. We'll have our picnic in the field. Don't break your necks over our national heritage or Iris will get upset.' Helen steered and guided her charges one by one through the gap, over the ruts and boggy ditch and into the field. 'Keep to the right, everyone. It's not so wet on the right.'

'Operation Steamroller to base. Operation Steamroller to base. Come in, base.'

'Base here. Kelly speaking.'

'Roger, Foxtrot, Alpha, Brava, Charlie. Are you receiving? Over.'

'Of course I'm receiving. Cut the crap and get on with it.'

'Hi, Sarge. It's me, Jones.'

'Don't use your name, Jones. When you call in use your car code.'

'We are proceeding east on the N11, Sarge. No sign of suspects yet. Over.'

Sergeant Kelly sighed deeply. 'Rookies, nothing but rookies.' He pinned a red marker to the large Dublin and Wicklow District map on the wall in front of him and spoke into the phone again. 'Car two. Come in, car two. Are you receiving? Where the bloody hell are you, car two? Give me your position.'

'Jones here, Sarge.'

'Jones. I thought you were car one.'

'I was, Sarge. But O'Hara passed me out on the motorway so now I'm car two.'

'Are you telling me you are all together? The whole lot of you are travelling in convoy?'

'Sarge?'

'You are supposed to be undercover, Jones. The public are supposed to be unaware of your presence.'

'Sorry, Sarge.'

'Get yourselves sorted out. And fast.'

'Yes, Sarge.'

Jones waved down the other cars and they pulled up, one behind the other, at the roundabout.

'Lads,' Jones called out to them. 'The Sarge was on. He says we have to keep ourselves out of sight.'

'Do you think we should split up?'

'Yes. You may be right. We'll split up and rendezvous in Ashford. Oh, and he's a bit confused about our car codes. We'll be number one . . .'

'I thought we were number one?'

'. . . No. We're number one. You can be number two and you lot can be three and four. Everybody got that?' The other men nodded.

'Where will we meet?'

'I know Ashford. There's a café in the middle of the village. We can meet up there.'

'Won't it look funny if we're all there together?'

'It's always full on Saturdays. No one will notice us. Not the way we are dressed. Two of us will stay on the motorway, the other two take the back roads, and remember lads, no mention of either

Alex Smith or George Perrin. OK then, off we go. See you there.'

'Adios amigos.'

'Hasta la vista, muchachos.'

The Ford Escorts drove off.

Chapter Nine

Chalkey Deveroux and his girlfriend, Janice, were out for a spin on Chalkey's bike. This was a new departure for Chalkey. He wasn't one for country trips. Two miles out of the city was enough to make him feel queasy. Chalkey's Saturday afternoons were always spent in The Hideout, in Rathmines, shooting pool and having a few beers with his mates. The Hideout was where you made your contacts, where you heard what was going down, where if the boss wanted you he knew where to find you. It was his spiritual home. Janice had been on his case, whingeing and nagging, all morning, 'I don't care where we go, Chalkey. Just one afternoon in the country. One afternoon away from your mates. Is that too much to ask?' until in the end he gave in. He knew a few bikers who hung out in the Hell Fire Club. He could look them up. The club wasn't too far out. It would get Janice off his back and give him a chance to meet up with the lads.

They had stopped for a smoke at the roundabout on the N11, arguing about which turn-off to take, when the four blue Escorts pulled up near them.

'Jesus Christ, Chalkey, they look like police cars. What have you done this time?'

'Nothing, doll. I swear it. Nothing at all.'

'You must have done something.'

'They'd never send four cars out just for me.'

'I don't like the look of this, Chalkey.'

'You're right, doll. There's something funny going on.'

'Chalkey. What are you doing? Chalkey.' Chalkey was edging towards the cars.

'Act nonchalantly, Janice.'

'What's that supposed to be when it's at home?'

'Pick some bleeding flowers or something.'

Janice looked at the bank of weeds beside the hard shoulder and sighed.

'Boss. It's Chalkey here. I'm ringing you on the mobile. I thought you might want to know there's something funny going on.'

'Spill it, Chalkey.'

'Me and the mot were out for a spin on the bike. I wanted to go to the Hell Fire Club but she wouldn't hear of it. "Riff-raff," she says. I said, "Hold on, doll. You can't call my mates riff-raff. No one calls my mates riff-raff and lives." "In your dreams," she says . . .'

'Chalkey.'

'Yes, Boss?'

'You won't have dreams, wet or otherwise, if you don't get on with it.'

'We're stopped, arguing like, at the start of the motorway and guess what? . . . eh, sorry boss . . . eight non-uniforms stop in front of us and start shouting up and down at each other. Now you know me and the fuzz, Boss, I'd normally run a mile but eight of them together. It had to be something big. So, here's what I do. I inch the bike closer, to get an earful like, then I listen and then I get out the phone and I call you.'

'Chalkey. Get to the bleeding point.'

'They were talking about Alex Smith and a George Perrin.'

'What? Tell me exactly what you heard.'

'They said, "No mention of Alex Smith or George Perrin . . ." '

'Bingo. Go on, Chalkey.'

'. . . and that they were going to Ashford. That's all I heard, Boss. But I thought you'd want to know seeing as how Alex Smith is going to testify against you.'

'For once in your dumb, stupid life, Chalkey, you've done good. Get yourself to Ashford. Find out what's going on. I'll round up some of the boys.'

'I don't think the mot wants to go to Ashford, Boss.'

'Dump her. No. On second thoughts she'll be good cover. Chalkey. Did they make you?'

'Naw, Boss. They couldn't have. I had me helmet on.'

'Jump on, doll. You win. We're not going to the Hell Fire Club.'

'Where are we going then?'

'Some bleedin' place called Ashford.'

'Do you have to always talk like some gangster, Chalkey?'

'I am a gangster.'

'But you're giving that all up for me, right, Chalkey?'

'Sure, doll. Sure.' Chalkey was watching the police cars over Janice's head.

'We're going to get married, and join the Credit Union, and you are going to get a proper job like you promised, right Chalkey? That's what you said, isn't it?'

'That's what I said.' The cars were pulling out. Two turned off, up a side road, to the right and the other two went straight on. Chalkey revved the bike. 'Get on, doll.'

Janice got on the back of the bike and gave him a tight cuddle. 'I love you, Chalkey,' she sighed into his leather jacket.

Chalkey took off at a steady pace. Normally he would have bombed down the motorway but he didn't want to draw attention to himself. Nice and easy. Just keep the cars in sight. A spin with the mot. Nothing more innocent. He put one hand behind him and gave Janice a squeeze. He was all right there. He'd get his leg over again tonight. Maybe even earlier if they found a spot. Not only that but the boss was pretty pleased with him. Janice felt a little thrill as he touched her. It was going to be wonderful. She'd have a white wedding and all her friends would be there. Her mother was wrong about Chalkey. She said he was a bad lot. Said he'd never change. But she would change him. She bent her head forward and let her helmet rest against his back.

Chapter Ten

Maureen sat on the edge of her seat fretting and fussing as they inched their way through the busy Saturday morning shopping traffic and out towards the motorway.

'Every red light, Deborah. We have hit every red light in the city. You'd think it was on purpose. Why they can't synchronize the traffic? It can't be that difficult. It would make you sick thinking about all those people getting tax payers' money to organize the streets. Money for old rope. That's what they get. Chaos and gridlock. That's all you see. Everywhere you look it's chaos and gridlock.'

'Shut up, Maureen.'

'Look at that.' A car towing a caravan crossed lanes in front of them. 'Honk, Deborah. Honk your horn. Bloody tourists. Those things shouldn't be allowed on the roads. Pass him out, why don't you? Can't you go any faster?'

'This is a thirty-mile zone, Maureen. I am not risking getting a ticket.'

'At last.' Maureen had spotted the blue MOTORWAY AHEAD sign. 'Thank goodness for that. Now Deborah. Step on it. Foot to the ground. Faster, faster. Keep on the outside lane. My God, Deborah. If the only thing you are going to pass out is a home on wheels we might as well forget it.'

'There is no point working yourself up into a lather, Maureen. This car doesn't go any faster.' Deborah was fighting to control her temper. One more word out of Maureen and she was ready to go home.

'Why you have such a banger of a car, Deborah, is beyond me.'

'It suits me. I like bangers.'

'You never stretch yourself, do you? Always second-hand this and second-hand that. Why don't you get a loan and buy yourself a new car?'

'Because, Maureen,' Deborah hissed under her breath, 'I don't have a free flat and free electricity and all the perks that you have.'

'Pardon, Deborah? I didn't hear you. What was that?'

'Nothing. Nothing at all.'

'Isn't it lovely out here. Do you know, if I wasn't so worried about my residents, I could enjoy this little spin. We should do this more often. Does the soul good, little jaunts in the country.'

'You could have fooled me.'

When they finally reached the village of Kilmacanogue, Maureen consulted her map, and directed Deborah off the main road.

'Thank God for that, Maureen. I didn't fancy being

bumper to bumper all the way to Ashford.'

'Look at the hedgerows and those meadows, Deborah. We must be mad to live in the city. If it wasn't for my job, and all my responsibilities, I would move tomorrow.'

'There's plenty of retirement homes in the country, Maureen. You could easily get a job in one of them.'

'Continuity, Deborah. Where would my residents be without continuity? I couldn't just up and leave them. They'd be lost.'

'They are lost and come to think of it, so are we. This doesn't look right.'

'What was that? Don't be offended if I tell you, Deborah, but you do have an annoying little habit of talking under your breath. What was I saying? Oh yes, hedgerows. What was it Yeats said about the hedgerows?'

'Maureen. Would you stop waxing on about your hedgerows and concentrate a moment. Are you sure this is the right road? It looks very off the beaten track to me. We haven't seen another car for ages.'

'Don't be irritating, Deborah, of course I'm sure. Trust me I know what I'm doing. This is a short cut that will take hours off our journey. I've been following the map and the route is clearly marked. The N11 to Kilmacanogue, the R765 to junction 200, then we keep climbing, 300, 400, until we reach 1123. I expect we will see a signpost telling us where we are at that point.'

The car drove higher and higher and the fields, to the right-hand side of the road, sloped away until there was a sheer drop.

'I don't like this, Maureen. I don't like this one little bit. What's that noise?'

'What noise? I don't hear any noise.'

'I definitely heard a funny noise.'

'Really, Deborah. This is too much.'

'This isn't a cable car, Maureen, it wasn't intended for mountaineering. Jesus, listen to that, we'll have to stop. The engine is overheating.' Deborah pulled over to the side of the road and got out. She looked around. Pine forest now stretched below them for miles and the road ahead was almost vertical. 'We'll never make it. We'll have to go back.'

'Nonsense, Deborah. We're almost there. Once we reach the crest of the hill it's downhill all the way. You can freewheel to the bottom.'

'I'm going to walk to the top. Say what you want, Maureen, but if I can't see a proper road I am turning back.'

Deborah walked up the hill with Maureen lagging behind her. She was furious with herself. How had she allowed Maureen to talk her into this? Why had she not just refused? No wasn't such a difficult word to say. No, no, no. It was her own fault. She knew that. She had no one else to blame for her lack of backbone. Here she was on the side of a mountain with a woman in full nurse's uniform walking behind her. If it wasn't so pathetic it would be hilarious.

As soon as she reached the top of the hill Deborah's annoyance and irritation fell away. The view was breathtaking. It was so beautiful. She felt she was standing on the top of the world. 'Maureen. Maureen, come and look at this.' When she turned around and saw Maureen struggling to reach the top she couldn't help smiling. Maureen, puffing and panting up the hill, was being twirled in the wind. Her nurse's apron was flying out in front of her and she was having difficulty holding on to her cap.

'Look, Maureen. Over there. That is definitely Glendalough. I can see St Kevin's rock and the lake.'

'I told you it was a short cut, Deborah. According to the map we need to get to the other side of that lake.'

'I don't think you can.'

'There is a definite road marked on the map which goes over those hills, alongside the lake, and then drops down near Rathnew. From there it's a straight run to Ashford.'

'You're the boss.'

'Look down there. See, I can make out a bridge. You can take a left turn and follow the road.'

'Oui, mon capitaine.'

'Sarcasm doesn't become you, Deborah. You shouldn't feel bad. We can't all be gifted with a talent for leadership.'

The ladies returned to the car. Deborah started the engine and they crawled slowly to the top.

'Hold on to your hat, Maureen. Here we go.'

They both laughed as the car took up speed and their ears began to pop.

'Oh no.' Deborah cried.

'What is it now, Deborah?'

'Look ahead, for God's sake. We are running out of road. It's a dead end.'

*

The tractor towed Deborah's car out of the deeply rutted forest trail.

'It's awfully good of you to rescue us like this,' Deborah said. 'You must think we are very stupid to have got stuck like that.'

'You're lucky I was about. I am not often about this way on Saturdays. Where were you thinking you were driving to?'

'The authorities will hear of this,' Maureen said. 'To sell maps that lure strangers into this, this . . .'

'My friend,' Deborah tried to explain to the farmer, 'got rather mixed up . . .'

'That's typical of you, Deborah, blame me when I followed this map to the letter.'

'Give it to me.'

'No.'

'Give me the map.' Deborah snatched the map out her hands. 'She mistook this line here for a road. I am sure you could point us in the right direction.'

'You'll not be travelling on in that vehicle. Her back axle's broke.'

'Oh no. I don't believe it. It can't be.'

'We have got to get to Ashford,' Maureen said. 'It is imperative that we get to Ashford.'

'You'll not get to Ashford on this road unless you walk her. I can take you as far as the motorway. You can thumb it from there.'

'What about my car?'

'There's a good mechanic below. Ask in Scully's. They'll direct you.'

'You see,' Maureen spoke to the farmer, 'we are looking for a coachload of pensioners. We must find them.'

'They'll not be in Ashford.'

'How do you know that?'

'They were in Ashford but they're not there now.'

'Why didn't you tell us before?'

'You didn't ask.'

'Then we must go on to Avoca. That's their next stop.'

'To hell with Avoca, Maureen. I'm taking the lift into Ashford. You can do what you like.'

The farmer got into the tractor and started up the engine. 'I can't fit you in the cab. I've the dog in here. Step up there in the front bucket.'

'Maureen. Come on.'

'I can't get into that contraption. I have my position to think of.'

'Maureen.' Deborah roared at her.

'This,' Maureen said, 'is the most humiliating experience of my life.'

Maureen and Deborah clambered into the tractor bucket and held on for dear life as the farmer raised it off the ground.

'To think I would ever end up in a tractor bucket,' Maureen wailed.

'You and your damn map. Walking, Maureen, did you not look at the front cover?' Deborah clenched her teeth as the tractor rattled along, 'Walking the bloody Wicklow Hills.'

'Walking, driving, what difference does it make?'

'Junction 200. Jesus. 200 was the bloody altitude.' Deborah imitated Maureen's voice. 'Two hundred, three hundred, and when we reach a thousand we are in the clouds.'

'There is no need to go on about it, Deborah. Anyone can make a mistake.'

Deborah couldn't reply. The tractor hit a bump and the ladies were bounced up and down in their bucket.

'Stop. Stop.' Maureen saw the main road up ahead and tried to signal up to the cab. 'Why doesn't he stop, Deborah? I don't want anyone to see us. Stop. You can let us off here.'

'He can't hear you, Maureen.'

'We will have to jump for it then. I am not being seen on a main thoroughfare in this thing.'

'Don't be mad, Maureen. We'll be killed.'

'We'll have to try and get his attention then. Yoo-hoo, sir.' Maureen waved up again. She jumped up and down in the bucket and the farmer's vision was temporarily blocked as her chest was almost level with the cab window.

When the farmer finally stopped the tractor and lowered the bucket, Maureen and Deborah tumbled out on to the side of the road. They got to their feet wiping traces of hay, muck, and other unrecognizable debris from their clothes and, through the noise of the tractor, tried to mouth their thanks.

'We will never get a lift looking like this, Maureen.'

'Nonsense, Deborah. The public have an enormous respect for the nursing profession. One look at me and they are bound to stop. Look. There's something coming already. Stick your hand out. Wave.'

Two blue Ford Escorts sped past, slowed, and then backed up a bit and, just as the ladies were about to run forward to accept a lift, the cars took off again.

'Cads,' Maureen screeched after them. 'Hitch teasers.'

'Stop, Maureen. For God's sake stop.'

'Did you see what they did?'

'They are police cars, idiot. Do you want to get us arrested as well as everything else?'

'Squad cars. Don't you realize, Deborah? They are probably looking for us. Stop, stop,' Maureen hollered after the receding Escorts. 'You are looking for us.' Maureen stepped out into the middle of the motorway waving both arms above her head. 'Do something, Deborah. Do something.'

'Maureen. Look out.'

Maureen was nearly swept off her feet as Chalkey and Janice zoomed by on the motorbike. Deborah covered her eyes. She was sure the bike was going to plough straight through her. Chalkey swerved to the wrong side of the road to avoid her and then straightened up again.

'Lunatic.' He shook his leather-gloved fist at Maureen who, paralysed with shock, was standing stock-still in the middle of the road.

'Are you all right, Maureen?' Deborah led her back to the side of the road. 'Maureen, speak to me. Are you all right?'

'Deborah. If anyone, ever, speaks to me about the peace and tranquillity of the countryside I will not be responsible for my actions. Bucket farmers, police who do not even know who they are looking for, Hells Angels on wheels . . .'

'It wasn't the biker's fault, Maureen.'

'He should never have been there in the first place. His kind shouldn't be allowed out.'

'Maureen, you better calm down. You are not making sense.'

'Sense? You are looking for sense when I have lost my charges, will probably need a hysterectomy after that bucket experience, and was nearly run over by an alien in leather? You make sense of it if you can.'

'There's a lorry coming, Maureen. They're usually good at giving lifts. Stay here while I try.'

'Dear Lord,' Maureen prayed, 'I know you are only trying to test me but I am now on the brink. Deliver me back to the city with my residents intact and I will never beseech you for anything again.'

'Maureen. Come on. This gentleman is going through Ashford. He's going to give us a lift. Come on, get in.'

Maureen tried to get her leg up on the first step of the big truck but couldn't reach it.

'Hold on there, Mrs, and I'll give you a bunt.' The driver got out from his side of the lorry and came round to Maureen. 'Up we go.' He put his hands under her bottom and gave her a shove.

'Is there to be no end to this humiliation, Lord?' Maureen sprang upwards as his hands made contact.

As they drove towards Ashford, Deborah chatted with the driver while Maureen tried to avert her eyes from the area over the truck window. 'Disgusting,' she sniffed to herself. 'What real women could be shaped like that?' Rows of half-naked pinups adorned the truck. Women, blondes mostly, with large breasts, not to mention the other parts of their anatomy on view for all the world to see. Some of them, she noted, had even shaved off their pubic hair. She folded her arms tight across her chest and, without realizing it, crossed her legs as well. How Deborah could keep a normal conversation going when faced with all that decadence was beyond her.

'It was very good of you to stop,' Deborah was saying.

'I always pick up hitchers. Helps to pass the time. When you are on the road all day you need something to help you focus.'

'We can see only too well the sort of focus you have in mind, bucko,' Maureen said to herself.

'What has you two ladies out on the road? If I'm not being too personal, you don't resemble your average backpacker.' The lorry driver laughed.

'My car broke down further back. Well actually, we took a wrong turn and got stuck in a forest, that's how it happened.'

'Deborah!' Maureen leaned forward and spoke to the driver across Deborah, trying to force a smile. 'I'm sure this gentleman doesn't want the nitty-gritty details of our trip.'

'I am just trying to explain, Maureen, how we came to be on the side of the road. And in such a state. We had to get towed out by a tractor,' Deborah continued. 'I'm afraid my car might have had it.'

'Easy enough done. I've been in many a ditch myself.'

'I'm sure you have.' Maureen gritted her teeth. 'Lorry drivers. Deborah is far too naïve. Next thing you know he'll have his camera out and Deborah and I will end up as focuses on his wall.'

'Do you always travel with your own nurse?' The driver looked across to Maureen. 'Or are you on your way to a fancy dress?'

'Oh no,' Deborah said. 'I know this must appear very strange to you, but there is an explanation. She is looking for some of her patients. They went on a day trip, an outing, and haven't got to where they were supposed to be. We set out to look for them. This isn't making any sense at all, is it?'

'Not a lot but don't worry about it. My name is Bill, by the way, Bill Thomas.'

'Deborah. Deborah Murphy, and my friend's name is Maureen Carmody. She likes to be called Sister Carmody when she's on duty.'

'Is she on duty now?'

'In a manner of speaking.'

'Nice to meet you, Deborah. Nice to meet you, Sister Carmody,' the driver shouted over. 'I've known a few nurses in my time. Great girls, all of them.'

Maureen threw her eyes to heaven and immediately wished she hadn't. Her glance fell on one of the pictures. It was a photograph of a member of the nursing profession, bent over a patient, in a most awkward position. There was a caption on the bottom of the photograph in large letters, SISTER DIVINE. The only thing Sister Divine was wearing was her nurse's cap and her stethoscope.

'Great photograph, isn't it.' The driver had seen Maureen looking at it. 'I bet you'd look good in a stethoscope.' He winked at Deborah to show he was joking. 'We're almost there, ladies. Allow me to escort you into Scully's. I often stop there en route. They won't half be surprised if I appear with a lady on each arm.'

'We'd be delighted,' Deborah said. 'The least we can do is buy you a coffee.'

The driver pulled in to the car park.

'Hold on there and I'll help you down.' He got out and walked around the back of the truck but before he could reach the passenger side Maureen had opened the door and thrown herself to the ground.

'Look. There's a garage over there. Would you mind if we talk to a mechanic about my car before we go in for coffee?'

'A good idea, Deborah. We must get back on the road as soon as possible.'

'After you, ladies,' Bill said.

Assistant Chief Superintendent Meyers paced the floor of the incident room. There had been no word from the squad since they called in their position which, at that stage, was on the outskirts of the city at the N11 roundabout. Sergeant Kelly was trying to reach them but without success. 'So much at stake,' Chief Meyers kept repeating to himself, 'the reputation of the whole department on the line.' He buzzed through to Sergeant Kelly.

'Any news yet, Kelly, from our flying squad?'

'Nothing yet, Chief.'

'Keep on it.'

'Yes, Sir. I will inform you the minute I hear from them.'

Meyers double-checked his watch. He would give it another twenty minutes. If there was no news within the next twenty minutes he would have no option but to join the search for Alex Smith himself. He would start with that nursing home. Someone there must know something.

It had been some time since Meyers had been out on a case. In his own district, in County Louth, he ran all operations from his office and had clocked up a considerable reputation for his tough, no-nonsense approach. Law-breakers there, from sheep stealers to poteen makers, knew what they were up against. They all quailed under his rule. How was it going to look in his report if, on his first outing as acting Chief, he had lost not only a main witness, but four cars and a bunch of rookies.

'Kelly.' Chief Meyers rang down to the front desk.

'Yes, Chief?'

'Get a car round to the front. I'm going out.'

Chapter Eleven

Helen was sorting out the bags of sandwiches when she heard the cry.

'Help, help.' Mrs Scott's feet were stuck fast in the ditch.

'To the right, I told you. Jesus. Con, Reggie, help me with Mrs Scott. The rest of you wait where you are.'

'I'm not going in there,' Con said.

'We can't leave her stuck. Don't move, Mrs Scott.'

'I can't move dear.'

'Right. Con, Reggie, you take her arms while I try and unstick her legs.' Helen lifted Mrs Scott's feet one after the other until they had manoeuvred her out of the ditch. 'You will be all right now, Mrs Scott. Try and dry off your feet. Holy shite. Miss Poole, Miss Bourke, come back.' Miss Poole and Miss Bourke were halfway across the field. 'I told you to stay where you were. Iris. Get off that bloody bus and help me.'

'I don't know what it is about you, Helen.' Iris poked her head out of one of the windows of the bus.

'You can't even organize a few elderlies into a field.'

'I'm not a bloody shepherd, Iris.'

Iris stomped off the bus and pulled her whistle out from under her shirt. She blew it several times. 'To the whistle, please. Everyone to the whistle. You mustn't wander off dears, it causes no end of trouble. If we could all stay together until our little crisis is over. Helen will share out the supplies. I must lend support to our heroic driver and we will be off again before we know it. Helen, take the whistle.'

'I don't think much of the garden of Ireland,' Cissy said between bites of egg sandwiches. 'There's not a flower in sight.'

'Oh but there is.' Miss Poole interrupted her. 'There is a wealth of flora here.'

'All I can see is thistles and nettles. I hope I don't need a pee. You wouldn't know where to squat.'

'If you look closely you will see that that is a *Carlina Vulgaris*.'

'A what?'

'And look. Over there is a *Centaurea Scabiosa*.'

'She must be a Protestant,' Lillie whispered. 'You can always tell when they start that sort of thing.'

'Shush, Lillie. She'll hear you. And what's a cent whatsit, Miss Poole?' Cissy asked loudly to stop Lillie saying more.

'A *Centaurea Scabiosa*, or Greater Knapweed as it's commonly called, looks like a thistle but the leaves are very different. They have no prickles. There is a legend that Chiron the Centaur, who is reputed to have had a great knowledge of herbs, used it for some of his cures.'

'Imagine that now,' Cissy said, 'Chiron the Centaur.'

'Oh yes. And Culpepper mentions the Greater Knapweed as a cure for sore throats, nose-bleeding and all sorts of other ailments.' As Miss Poole's voice trailed off the pensioners stared at the weed.

'*Scabiosa*.' Con said. 'You can sort of see nose-bleeds and scabs all the same. Pick a scab and your nose bleeds, right?'

'And what's the other one, Miss Poole. The vulgarian one?'

'The *Carlina Vulgaris*? Deary me. That bold, stiff and prickly plant . . .'

'You'd want to listen to this, Dessie Rourke.' Cissy cackled.

'. . . except in dry weather, of course, when the flower-head spreads out to dry in the sun. Named *Carlina Vulgaris* because of a tradition that the root of the thistle of the same family was shown to Charlemagne by an angel as a remedy for a plague which was prevalent in his army . . .'

'Jesus.'

'I told you she was a Protestant.'

'. . . So you see,' Miss Poole tearfully addressed the group, 'I only went over to the field because I thought I saw a rare *Anacamptis Pyramidalis*. I didn't mean to cause any trouble . . .'

'You didn't cause any trouble, Miss Poole,' Helen said.

'. . . Sister Carmody doesn't like any trouble.'

'If Miss Poole wants to see her ana-thing she is going to see it.' Cissy got up. 'Come on. Anything is better than sitting here on the damp grass getting ourselves a chill.'

'My Betty's young one is always getting nose-bleeds,' Lillie said.

The pensioners and Helen trailed across the field with Miss Poole leading the way. '*Rotundifolis, Serpyllifolia* . . .' she sang out.

'Eh, Miss Poole. Can you give us the English version?'

'. . . Oh dear me, I am sorry, of course. Red Deadnettle, Heartsease, Meadow Buttercup . . .'

'I know that one.'

'Eejit. So does everyone else.'

The group reached the far side of the field where they were out of sight.

Stevie, Mr Perrin and Iris were off the bus peering into the engine.

'What do you think, Mr Perrin?'

'Well, we could soldier on, Iris, so long as we take it very easy, or Stevie and I could go back to Ashford and find a mechanic.'

'No. We can't go back, Mr Perrin. We must go on.'

'Where is our next stop?'

'Avoca, the meeting of the waters, and then on to Arklow. Our lunch is booked for Arklow.'

'I don't know if we would even make it to Avoca on this road, Iris,' Stevie said.

'Nonsense, Stephen. I am sure once we back the bus up and get out of this hedge we will have no trouble. It's more scenic anyway. I couldn't have planned it better. Just think. Before highways and dual carriageways were built our ancestors came over these roads.'

'Yeah, Iris. In donkeys and carts. Not a Drimnagh to Marino City Swift.' Stevie looked at the narrow road ahead and shook his head. The road twisted upward, towards corkscrew bends; it didn't look possible to get the bus up there. As he looked, two blue Ford Escorts appeared and disappeared round the bends. 'Get down everyone, get down,' Stevie called. 'It's the police. The police are coming.'

'What. Where? I don't see any police.'

'It's the police, I'm telling you. Coming down that road. Someone put them on to us.'

'Don't be ridiculous, Stephen. What would police cars be doing on a little side road like this?'

'I don't know and I'm not waiting to find out. Hide everyone quick.'

'Really, Stephen. You are overwrought. If they are the police it's a blessing in disguise. They can help us out of our little predicament. Tell him, Mr Perrin. Mr Perrin?' George Perrin had joined Stevie who was lying flat on the ground beside the hedge.

'Get down, Iris,' Mr Perrin said. 'You don't want our day destroyed by endless questions, do you?'

'But . . .'

'Down, Iris.'

'I am not lying down on that dirty verge no matter who it is.'

'Well stretch yourself over us and you won't touch the ground.'

Iris lay across the backs of Stevie and Mr Perrin. Her face was inches from the earth on one side, and her legs stretched out and up behind her in an effort to keep her feet out of the mud.

'Not a sound, Iris,' Mr Perrin said. 'They might just go past without seeing us.'

Cars three and four came round the bend at breakneck speed. They didn't want to be late for their rendezvous in Ashford. When they spotted the bus, half in and half out of the hedge, car three braked so sharply that car four nearly went up its bumper.

'This is car three speaking. Come in, car four.'

'Car four here, lads.'

'There's a bus ahead stopped by a hedge.'

'We see it, car three. Can't be ours. It's not a coach. It's a City Swift. One of the new ones. Probably test-driving it out here away from the traffic.'

'Should we check it out?'

'Negative, car three. It will waste too much time. The Chief wouldn't be too pleased if we wasted time on a domestic. We must remember our main objective. To recover the witness and get him safely back to town.'

'I don't see the driver.'

'Probably taking a leak.'

'What the hell is going on out there?' Desk Sergeant Kelly butted in over the airwaves.

'Who said that? Car three, was that you?'

'Negative, car four.'

'I repeat. What the hell is going on? Where is the leak? Inform headquarters immediately if you suspect . . .' Sergeant Kelly's voice squeaked unintelligibly through the system.

'Did you hear that?' Car four drove up alongside car three, wound the window down and spoke across to car three.

'Couldn't make it out.'

'We seem to be in a black spot, lads. We better keep off the air.'

'Roger, car four.'

'You don't have to say roger, Nigel, when we are talking to each other face to face.'

'Wilsomedytelmewhaisgoingon?' The rattle came through from the Sergeant again.

'I think we should turn the radios off for a while. There's too much interference here among these trees.'

'Good idea. We'll race you to Ashford, lads.'

'Did you hear that?' Iris said. 'What on earth were they talking about?'

'Beats me,' Stevie said, 'but if they are going to Ashford, I'm not.'

Mr Perrin didn't say anything. He knew what the police were talking about. Someone must have twigged that he had left the Cross and Passion. A spot check. The Superintendent did that occasionally. It would have to be today of all days. Well they could search. He wasn't going to give himself up. He was relaxing for the first time since that whole business had started. At least it was the police looking for him and not the gang. He would phone in and reassure them as soon as he got a moment alone.

'Iris.'

'Yes, Stephen?'

'Do you think you could get off us now? Your knee is digging into the back of my neck.'

'Coo-ee, everyone. We are in business. Stephen and Mr Perrin have got our bus back on the road. Where is everyone?' Iris looked into the field where she expected to see the pensioners. 'Helen. Helen, where are you?' Iris cupped her hand and shouted as loud as she could. 'Stephen. Press your horn. Keep pressing until we get some response. This is the last time I trust Helen to do anything.'

'It's all right, Iris. There they are. They're coming.'

'What have they done?'

The pensioners, their arms full of all sorts of greenery, branches, weeds, ferns, and flowers, were making their way back to the bus.

'You can't do that,' Iris called out. 'Put them back.'

'Look what we've got, Iris.'

'You can't rip up the flora like that.'

'They're cures, Iris. We've got cures for everything under the sun. Miss Poole told us what they are all going to do for us, didn't you, Miss Poole. We're going to save a fortune in the chemist's.'

'I didn't mean them to pluck roots and all, Miss Fox, it's all my fault really it is.'

'Well it can't be helped now. No one is to bring that stuff on to the bus. It's alive with creepy crawlies. Put it all in the luggage booth. Stephen, open the luggage thingy and let them put it all in there.'

Iris stood guard as, one by one, the pensioners deposited their spoils in the space under the bus.

'Et tu, Helen,' Iris said sadly, as Helen placed her little posy of lavender with the rest.

'Cut it out, Iris.'

'Do you know, Miss Poole,' Dessie Rourke said as they all took their places on the bus, 'you are a walking wonder. No, I mean it. You should be up there in the botanicals. I should know. I have a natural bent for horticulture myself.'

'Naturally bent, Dessie,' Lillie said, 'I'll give you that. But not over shrubs and flowers.'

'She loves me.' Dessie winked at Miss Poole.

'I have an allotment,' Willie said softly. 'Down by the canal. I love that allotment.'

'You are very lucky to be in such a place with such beautiful grounds,' Helen said to the Cross and Passioners. 'Do you have a bit of the garden you can tend yourselves?'

'Oh no, dear,' Mrs Scott said, 'Sister Carmody is very strict when it comes to the grounds.'

'That Sister Carmody sounds like a bit of a tartar.'

'You don't understand. It's for our own good. She is only thinking of us, isn't she?' Mrs Scott turned to her companions. Murmurs of agreement were heard from the other residents. 'She always says that our welfare is her welfare.'

'You'd wonder,' Cissy said. 'See Mai here. Mai was in a nursing home. Sold her house and all. Her son had to take her out. Hardly uttered a word since they took her in. We couldn't get a word out of you, could we, Mai. She took everything in though. You took everything in though, didn't you, Mai.'

'Her son took her out,' Eoin O'Neill echoed.

'I don't go much now,' Willie continued. 'Not since Bartley passed on.'

'Who is Bartley?"

'He had the patch next to mine. It's a bit empty going down without Bartley. He'd a wonderful way with Brussels sprouts.'

A little cloud of gloom descended over the pensioners.

'Don't worry, Willie,' Iris said in an effort to brighten things up. 'For all we know Bartley is up there giving God a nice plate of Yorkshire pud and Brussels sprouts for his lunch.'

'Do you think so, Iris?'

'I wouldn't put it past him.'

'Talking about lunch, Iris,' Helen said, 'is there any danger that we might be heading in that direction?'

'Of course we are heading in that direction. We are on our way to our first comfort stop. We shall have a quick respite there and then head directly to our lunch rendezvous.'

'We'll be lucky to get there in time for dinner at this rate,' Helen said to George Perrin, who had returned to his seat at the back.

'Think of it not as the arrival, Helen, but as the journey.'

'Eh, Miss Poole, I wonder, could I have a word?' Iris sat down beside Miss Poole without waiting for a reply. 'Miss Poole, I have a little problem you might be able to help me with.' Iris leaned over and whispered into her ear.

'Cystitis, my dear. Isn't that the bride's —'

'Shush, please, Miss Poole. I don't want the whole bus hearing.' She whispered in Miss Poole's ear again.

'Chafing,' Miss Poole replied in a very loud whisper. 'How very uncomfortable for you, dear. I'm sure I can recommend something. Just give me a moment.'

'Thank you, Miss Poole. I felt sure you could help. There's no rush. We can talk with a bit more privacy when we get off the bus.' Iris made her way back to her own seat.

'What's the matter with Iris?' Cissy asked down the bus. 'Has she got an ailment?'

'She has an itchy twat,' Dessie Rourke said grinning from ear to ear.

Stevie crawled along in second gear. He wanted to be prepared for any surprises. He felt if he stayed in second he could stop the instant an obstacle appeared. As the road got a bit wider he began to get his confidence back. This was more like it. The bus was purring along nicely so he ventured into third gear. Ask yourself, Stevie, he thought, what else could go wrong? When they got to the lunch spot he would slip away to a garage and have the undercarriage checked out. Mr Perrin didn't think there was too much damage. He'd even offered to help out with any costs. A very nice man, that Mr Perrin, very decent. You don't meet many like him nowadays.

Chapter Twelve

Car one and car two pulled up outside Ashford for a consultation.

'Remember our basic training, lads,' Jones said. 'We've got to suss out the area thoroughly before going in. Here's the plan. We do a quick reconnoitre, just in case the bus got here after all, before we hit the café. You men take the left-hand side of the street and we'll take the right. Keep your eyes peeled but don't attract undue attention. You all know what we are looking for.'

The cars moved on slowly and, to the astonishment of the few locals in the two grocery shops, the one hardware shop and the butcher's, they cruised up one side of the village and down the other.

'All quiet on the right. There's no sign of a Dublin coach.'

'Roger, car one. Ditto on the left.'

'On to the café then.'

The Escorts parked directly outside the front door of Scully's and the four rookie special branch men got out and sauntered into the café. As they approached the self-service counter the restaurant went quiet and the customers who had been watching them through the window all turned in their direction.

'What can I get you?' the waitress asked.

There was a huddled conversation among the rookies. '. . . But we can't sit here with nothing in front of us.'

'Right. Grab a table and I'll order. Get one against the wall. That way we can watch everything. Tea, Miss, and four rasher sandwiches, please.'

'Take a seat. I'll pop them over to you.'

'Thank you, Miss.'

'We can't see anything facing the wall.' The rookies sat at a table for four which left two of them with their backs to the rest of the customers.

'Bring your chairs around this side then.'

They moved seats. When the waitress came over with the tray, the four men were sitting, squashed in a row, at one side of the small table.

'Here you go, gentlemen. Are you sure you can manage like that?'

'Quite sure, thank you.'

'Funny. I thought you people didn't eat rashers.'

'You people?'

'Jehovahs. I thought you didn't like blood or animal fats.'

'We are not Jehovahs. We are . . .'

'Shush. That's all right, Miss. We have an exemption. It's a special day.'

'But . . . ouch.' The driver of car two received a sharp kick under the table. 'What did you do that for?'

'Jehovahs. That's a great cover. We don't want them to know who we really are, do we? Now eat your sandwich and make it look good, like it's something special.' The rookies tucked in.

'Yum, very nice.' They beamed across at the waitress smacking and licking their lips.

'All right, lads. No need to overdo it.'

Chalkey and Janice, leathered and helmeted, entered the café arm in arm. The waitress pointed to a sign over the door. 'All helmets must be removed.'

'I'm not taking me helmet off,' Chalkey said.

'Don't be stupid, Chalkey,' Janice said. 'How can you drink your coffee if you don't take off your helmet? You're drawing attention to yourself. Will you take the bleeding thing off? He's just shy, Miss,' she said to the waitress. 'He'll take it off when he sits down.'

'I can bring you your coffee outside if he wants to keep it on.'

'Chalkey. Take off the bloody helmet. No fiancé of mine is going to make a show of me in a public place.'

Chalkey slithered to a corner, sat down, and took off the helmet. He couldn't explain the situation to Janice, that he was supposed to be incognito, and not get recognized. After a few minutes he sneaked a look at the other table. He needn't have worried. The rookies weren't paying any attention to him. They were sitting in a row, eating sandwiches, and laughing and joking among themselves. Maybe he was wrong. They didn't look as if they were on a mission. Maybe it was a special-branch outing. He hoped not. What would he say to the boss?

'There you go, Chalkey. I got you a nice éclair. Have to keep your strength up, eh Chalkey?' Janice gave him a dig in the ribs. 'Cream is supposed to be very good for men if you know what I mean.' She winked up to the waitress who had been in on the joke. 'Do you see those fellahs there? The ones in a row? The girl said they were Jehovah's Witnesses and they're allowed to have rashers just for this one day. Funny isn't it.'

'Jesus.' Chalkey spluttered into his cup.

Cars three and four drove into the car park of Scully's and sat for a moment sizing up the situation.

'Should we go in?'

'The others are in there.'

'It might look odd if we're all in there together. We'll sit outside, that way we can keep our eye on the street. Nigel, you go in and order coffee for all of us. Let the others know we are here but don't arouse any suspicion. Make contact and when you get a chance signal one of them to go to the toilet where we can meet up and talk unobserved.'

'Why me? Why is it always me who gets the coffee?'

'You're the newest recruit, that's why.'

'It's the same in the office. Nigel do this and Nigel do that.'

'Don't you realize that this is our big break? Look, Nigel, you always get it in the office, right? You said so yourself. If the others saw any of the rest of us getting the coffee they would be surprised, wouldn't they. They might break their cover. With you getting the coffee everything is normal. We won't be taking them unawares. You do see that Nigel, don't you.'

'I suppose so. When you put it like that. But this is the last time.'

Patrick Scully popped his head out of the kitchen and was somewhat mollified to see the café begin to fill up. He was still annoyed by the non-appearance of the coach from Dublin, especially since it had been booked so far in advance. In future, if he was going to go to that much trouble, he would insist on a deposit. Still, at least one group of customers had taken advantage of his trestle tables and had gone out to the garden. He retreated back to his kitchen and missed Maureen and Deborah's entrance.

When they got into the café, Maureen excused herself and headed straight for the ladies' toilet to try and tidy herself up. She was furious with Deborah. What had possessed her to invite that Bill Thomas person for coffee? A short lift down the street hardly required eternal gratitude. Leaving aside the pornography, Maureen had no time for men who had two Christian names in place of a proper, decent, surname. It was made up, of course, to avoid detection. He was obviously the sort of man who latched on to unescorted women. A highway de Sade. Deborah was so naïve she couldn't see it. An image, too horrible for Maureen to contemplate, crept through her mind. Deborah, wearing little else except a smile, pinned up over that man's wheel. Maureen shuddered and splashed a little water on her face to dispel the distraction. She must think only of her residents. As soon as he had had his coffee, Mr Bill Thomas would get his walking papers.

They needed a car. But from where? The first thing to do was phone Ann, back in the nursing home, and see what news she had of the police search. It might be possible to link up with a squad car. Maureen checked the mirror, readjusted her nurse's cap, and fluffed her apron. She wasn't too happy, but it was the best she could do with her appearance, under the circumstances. She got out her bag of mission change, went in search of a telephone, and dialled the number of the Cross and Passion.

'Cross and Passion Nursing Home.' Garda Cullen, who had been stationed in the Cross and Passion, picked up the phone before Ann could get to it.

'Hello. Hello. Who is this? What are you doing on my telephone?'

'Your telephone?'

'Put me on to Ann immediately, or Doctor Kennedy.'

'Who is this speaking?'

'This, as you put it, is Sister Maureen Carmody and I demand to know what is going on.'

'Hold the line.' Garda Cullen cupped the phone and spoke to Detective Superintendent Meyers who was waiting in the hall. 'Chief. It's the nurse, Carmody. The one who went after the coach.'

'Give me that.'

Chief Meyers took the receiver. 'We have to be careful,' he whispered to Garda Cullen, 'she may be in on the plot. Sister Carmody, this is acting Chief Detective Meyers here . . .'

'But, Chief,' Garda Cullen interrupted, 'she's the one who got young Ann here to phone us.'

'A clever ruse to put us off the scent, Cullen. They knew we would find out sooner or later. By pretending concern, calling us themselves, they could be protecting their inside source.' Garda Cullen looked at the Chief in admiration. That's how you get to be chief, he thought to himself. One step ahead all the time.

'Go ahead, madam.'

'Thank goodness. A Chief Superintendent. What news have you, Chief? Have you found my residents?'

'I was hoping, Sister Carmody, that you would have news for me. Where are you calling from?' The Chief nodded to Garda Cullen. 'Take this down.'

'Ashford. Deborah, that's my friend with the car, and I are in Ashford. We were waylaid on our way here. Ambushed, so to speak, or I would have phoned sooner.'

'Ashford. Ambushed. Waylaid.' The Chief repeated the words for Garda Cullen's benefit.

'Oh yes, Chief. A terrible incident that involved a tractor and a lorry. I can't go into it just now.' Maureen lowered her voice. 'But I shall be reporting that lorry driver for obscenity as soon as I return to the city. Deborah is still with the lorry driver and I have a feeling it will be difficult to get rid of him.'

'Say no more, Sister Carmody. I'm reading between the lines. Waylaid, ambushed and subjected to obscenity.' Garda Cullen wrote furiously. 'Friend still in the clutches of lorry driver. Sister Carmody. I have eight plain-clothes men in the field, tracking down your coach, as we speak. The driver we can apprehend before he meets up with the rest of his gang.'

'Gang? Oh my goodness, are there more of them? Are you talking about a ring?'

'I'm afraid so, Sister.'

'Thank you, Chief. It's such a relief to me knowing that you are taking this attitude. Morals are very important to me. People seem to think they can get away with murder.'

'Murder!' The Chief's expression went dark. 'It won't come to that, Sister Carmody. I give you my word.' The Chief hung up the phone.

'Now, Chief Superintendent, about my residents. Hello. Hello . . .'

'I may be wrong about the nurse,' the Chief confided to Garda Cullen. 'She said that she and her friend were held hostage and threatened with obscenity and the word murder was mentioned. I'm not so sure, it could be a red herring, a plan to throw us off the scent, but on the other hand, we must keep all options open, that's the secret of good policing.'

'What do we do, Chief?'

'Wait and watch, Garda Cullen. Wait and watch.'

'I'm not waiting,' Ann Roberts suddenly spoke up. 'Sister Carmody told me to stay by the phone but you won't even let me answer it so there is nothing for me to wait for.' Ann had been standing beside Garda Cullen all through the phone call. She had been so quiet the Chief hadn't noticed her. He couldn't let her go now. He couldn't risk her talking when she got outside.

'I'm afraid that's not possible, Ann. You are a material witness. You will have to stay here.'

'Witness to what? I didn't see anything. I'm going to phone my mother, she'll come and get me, she's not afraid of anyone.'

'. . . Chief Superintendent.' Maureen was still trying to get a response. 'Have you had any news at all about my residents?'

Chalkey Deveroux watched Maureen go to the phone. He felt there was something odd about her he couldn't put his finger on. He mooched over, pretending to look at a motor rally poster hanging near the phone, and strained to listen to her conversation, but it was no use, he couldn't hear anything. He had a call of his own to make and he was dreading it. 'Jehovahs', Janice had said. What if she was right? What would he say to the boss? He could have sworn he heard them say Alex Smith. Maybe there was more than one Alex Smith. Christ. Why had he phoned the boss at all? Why hadn't he just kept out of it?

'I'm going to the Gents, doll,' he said to Janice. 'don't go talking to any fellas while I'm gone.'

'What do you take me for, Chalkey?' Janice said indignantly, thrilled skinny that her Chalkey was so jealous.

'Maureen. Over here.' Deborah called Maureen over to where she and Bill Thomas were sitting. 'We got a window seat specially for you, Maureen, in case you spotted your bus.'

'They're not here, Deborah. The farmer told us that already.'

'It must be a worry for you, Maureen,' Bill said, 'losing a party of old folks. If there is anything I can do . . . maybe drop you off somewhere else?'

'Thank you, but we can manage ourselves.' Maureen had no intention of getting back into that lorry. Especially now that the Chief had more or less implied that he might be part of some gang. She would have to find a way to let Deborah know without arousing his suspicions.

'We need transport, Maureen. You heard the mechanic say there was no way he could do anything about my car until Monday. Bill has offered to take us . . .'

'That won't be necessary, Deborah. I have been speaking to the Gardaí.' Maureen stared directly at Bill when she spoke. 'A Chief Superintendent Meyers, who has despatched a team to help us with our search.'

'If you are sure, Maureen.'

'I am sure.'

'Are they going to pick us up?' Deborah asked.

'Deborah. Let's bring our coffee out to the garden, shall we? I'm sure Mr Thomas doesn't want to be detained any longer.'

'Oh I don't mind at all, Maureen. In fact a breath of fresh air will do me good before the rest of my trip.'

'Where are you headed, Bill?'

'Rosslare, Deborah. Then the ferry to France. I drop my cargo off in France and return on Monday.'

'Sounds wonderful. I'd love a trip abroad.'

*

Chalkey went into one of the toilet booths. He was about to make his call when, one by one, the rookies gathered at the urinals.

'Did you see anything?'

'Like what? Does anyone know what we are looking for?'

'Anything or anyone who looks suspicious.'

'Do you think we should call in?'

'And say what? Do you want us to look like fools?'

'But Chief Meyers said to keep in touch.'

'OK. I'll ring Sergeant Kelly. Give him our position and get some feedback. Filter back to your places, men, and remember, unobtrusive.'

As soon as the coast was clear, Chalkey left the booth. He was right all along. Janice and her bleeding Jehovahs. He reckoned he'd hold off phoning the boss until he had gathered more information. This would be worth at least a ton to him, maybe more, not to mention the kudos he would have built up with the big boys.

Jones sat in the Ford Escort outside Scully's and spoke to headquarters. 'Jones to, oops, sorry, Sarge. Car one to base. Come in base, over.'

'Car one. Where the bloody hell are you? I've been trying to reach you for the last bloody hour.'

'We were maintaining radio silence as ordered, Sarge.'

'You stupid bleeding . . .'

'Sorry, Sarge.'

'What is your position?'

'We have rendezvoused in Ashford. No sign yet of the missing coach.'

'Of course there is no sign of the coach, you idiot. They're not in Ashford. We only know about this ruse because they never got to Ashford. Have you spoken to the café owner?'

'Not yet, Sarge.'

'Well speak to him. Speak to the rest of the staff and while you're at that keep a sharp eye on all the customers. Find out who made the booking. Does the owner know the bus driver? Oh, and speaking of drivers, keep an eye out for a lorry picking up women along the road.'

'Pardon, Sarge?'

'Apprehend any lorry you see picking up women. There's been an incident. The Chief suspects there could be a connection between our gang and a certain lorry.'

'What sort of a lorry, Sarge?'

'I don't know what sort of a lorry. Stop any lorry travelling suspiciously and get particulars. Oh, and a tractor as well.'

'A tractor, Sarge?'

'Yes. A coach and a lorry and a tractor. Is that too much for you to handle?'

'No, Sarge. We're on to it. Leave it to us.'

Jones, of car one, stepped back into the café and, mindful of Sergeant Kelly's instructions, hovered round the tables trying to listen in on the conversations. He paused at Maureen and Deborah's table, on the pretext of looking for someone out the window, as Bill was talking about his destination: 'Rossslare, ferry to France. Cargo.'

'You can have this table if you like,' Deborah said. 'we're moving out to the garden.'

'It's OK, thanks. I'm just looking for somebody.'

'We're all looking for somebody.' Deborah smiled at Jones. 'It seems to be the day for it.'

Jones moved on to where his fellow rookies were still at their coffee. 'The garden,' he hissed. 'Take your coffee out to the garden so we can't be overheard. I've been on to Sergeant Kelly and he's given me more information. We may have extra vehicles to look out for.' He slithered past them and out the back door.

'I've finished mine. I can't take an empty cup out to the garden.'

'Get another one then. Get more for all of us.'

'I forked out for the last lot.'

'Stop making such a fuss. Do you want to draw attention to us? Keep the receipt and you can put in for them when we make up our expenses.'

They stood up, tucked their chairs neatly under the table and followed Jones outside.

Chalkey was on his guard. He had been watching the nurse, trying to make a connection between her and the police, when he saw the plain-clothes pause at her table, move on, hiss something at another table, and then go out the back. So his hunch was right after all. They were all in cahoots. Now the nurse and her lot were getting up. Shite. Which ones was he supposed to watch? Cool it, Chalkey. It's OK. They're all going out the back.

'Chalkey, love. I could do with another cuppa. Chalkey. Another cuppa please. Chalkey I hope this is not a sample of the sort of attention I'll get after we're married.'

'Sorry, doll. My mind was miles away. What do you want?'

'The same again please.'

'Right. I have to go to the Gents. I'll get it for you on the way back.'

'You've just been to the Gents.'

'Yeah. But I couldn't do nothing.'

'What do you mean, you couldn't do nothing. What sort of bleeding English is that?'

'The booth was occupied.'

'Were you going for a number two?'

'What do you mean, number two?'

'Chalkey, you know what I mean.'

'Look, doll. I just need a piss.'

'Then why do you need a booth? Are you taking something in there? If you are taking something, Chalkey Deveroux . . .'

Chalkey had left the table.

The rookies, sitting together under the umbrellas, were listening while Jones repeated Sergeant Kelly's instructions.

'I don't get it. A lorry and a tractor as well as a coach?'

'Here's what Sergeant Kelly thinks. There's a woman involved. They were hijacked by a lorry somewhere along the road. Don't ask me where the tractor comes in because I don't know yet. Anyway, that's what the Sarge thinks, but I think this is a subterfuge to keep us from following the vehicle that our witness is in.'

'Maybe they did a swap. Swapped the woman for our man.'

'But what's it got to do with her? She's not a witness. It doesn't make sense.'

'Exactly. And because it doesn't make sense is precisely why they think we will fall for it. We chase the woman and what happens? It divides us up. Sends half of our party off on a wild goose chase. Well we are too smart to fall for that little trap. Waste time on lorries and tractors, no siree.'

'But I thought you said Sergeant Kelly wanted a tractor and a lorry stopped.'

'That's because he fell for it. Don't you get it?' Jones looked at his bemused colleagues. 'Between ourselves, lads. I think the Sarge has gone off the boil. Look at it this way. He's still a sergeant isn't he? No promotion for years. I mean, a tractor? Think about it. Would any criminal risk their man in a tractor? I say we stick with our main target, the coach.'

'OK but where do we go from here?'

'Let's review the facts as we know them. Fact one. We know that Alex Smith, alias George Perrin, left the Cross and Passion Nursing Home with a party of pensioners on a coach. Fact two.'

'We don't have a fact two.'

'Yes we do. Fact two. Alex, alias George, is a very important witness and must be found. Fact three. The coach definitely headed out of town in this direction.'

'So what do we do?'

'We keep searching. We will continue on out the N11 until we find them. Two cars on the high road and two on the coast road . . .'

'And we'll get to Scotland before ye,' Nigel sang out spontaneously.

'Stop kidding about, Nigel. Until we spot them. Then we swoop on the coach. If we do this right, men . . . think of it . . . we bring in a major witness and our future in the force is secure. We might even get medals. And just to be on the safe side, we won't burn our boats. We'll pick up a lorry driver to please Sergeant Kelly.'

Chalkey was frustrated. He could hear the voices from outside but he couldn't make out what they were saying. 'Damn. I've got to do something.' He lifted the toilet seat, stood on the rim, and tried to force open the small frosted window. 'Gotcha.' Chalkey stretched up and strained his head towards the garden in time to catch Nigel's, 'We'll get to Scotland before ye,' 'What the? . . . They're bleeding singing.' He listened again. 'Then we swoop on a coach. Land the major witness and pick up a lorry on the N11.' Before he had a chance to interpret this his foot slipped off the rim and landed in the bowl.

'Fuck.'

Janice had slipped into the Ladies. She was humming to herself. She had finished her business, washed her hands, and was fixing her hair when she heard Chalkey's shout through the partition wall.

'Chalkey!' She ran from the Ladies and into the

Gents. 'Chalkey. What's the matter?' Chalkey was standing in the middle of the floor shaking water from his left leg. 'Oh, my poor Chalkey. Did you miss? Don't worry. I understand.'

'You don't understand fucking anything,' Chalkey shouted.

'What was that?'

The rookies looked around. There was nothing to see. Apart from themselves only one other table in the garden was being used and its occupants were chatting, innocently, among themselves.

'Kitchen, I expect. The chef probably scalded himself.'

'We can't be too careful, men. The gang could have spies anywhere.'

'How would they know where we are?'

'They don't. But we must be on our guard anyway. Our big advantage is the element of surprise.'

'If no one knows where we are, and we don't know where they are, how are we going to surprise anyone?'

'Don't be so negative, Nigel. I have a plan which, though I say it myself, I think is foolproof. Car one, that is myself and driver, will interview the owner, the staff, and the customers here in the café. Car two. You will station yourselves out on the street. If anyone tries to slip out of the café to avoid interrogation you will be on hand to intercept them. Cars three and four will proceed by different routes to the next village where we shall have our next rendezvous. Any questions?'

'That's a roger for car two, Jones.'

'And car four.'

'Car three. Do you have a problem?'

'Eh, no. Not really.'

'What do you mean, not really?'

'I'd like to do the interviewing. I haven't had much chance to interview.'

'Don't worry, Nigel. You'll get plenty of chances to do interviews when we apprehend the gang.'

'I hope so.'

'Right. As soon as we've finished here I will contact Sergeant Kelly and inform him of our movements. You men go on ahead but remember what the Chief said. If you see anything suspicious don't attempt confrontation. Phone in immediately. Good luck, men.' The rookies got up to go to their cars. Jones and his partner went back into the café.

Chalkey followed Janice from the toilets as she stormed back to their table to retrieve her jacket and her helmet.

'I'm going home. If you think you can treat me like this, Chalkey Deveroux, you have another think coming.'

'Look, doll. I didn't mean it.'

'Don't "doll" me. I was only trying to help. You'd think it was my fault you wet yourself, the way you roared at me.'

A low murmur could be heard among the customers as they turned to Chalkey and saw the pool of water which had trickled down his leg, over his shoe, and out on to the floor.

'My mother was right about you. She said you were no good.'

'That's right, bring your bleeding mother into this.'

'You can't talk about my mother like that.'

'Oh can't I? And who's going to stop me?'

Janice covered her face with her hands and burst into tears.

'You shouldn't talk about her mother like that, young man.' The woman from the next table spoke up. 'Look how you've upset her.'

'She brought her mother into it first.' The accusation came from a gentleman at table number five.

'Only as a reference point.'

'That's women all over,' said the man from table five. 'Throw in something and then when the answer doesn't suit, burst into tears.'

'No one asked you for your opinion, sir.'

'That, madam, is not an opinion — it is a fact.'

'I see Ashford has its fair share of misogynists,' a well-dressed lady from the back of the café threw in.

'I resent that, madam.' The gentleman stood up in protest.

'So do I.' His companion jumped up and stood at his side.

Chalkey and Janice were forgotten as the argument spread throughout the café while the waitress, not knowing how to handle the situation, ran to the back for Mr Scully.

'You better get out here quick, Mr Scully.'

Mr Scully, who was being interviewed by the detectives, rushed from his kitchen followed by Jones and his partner. 'What the hell . . .' The place had erupted. All his customers were shouting and arguing with each other across the café.

'Let's get out of here, Janice.' Chalkey took Janice's

arm and steered her towards a side door. They slipped out just as Jones, taking his badge out of his pocket, shouted above the noise.

'Police. Sit down everyone. In your places or your names will go on record.'

Chalkey inched out, dragging Janice behind him. He knew one of the Escorts was parked out the front. He had to get past it without being spotted. He needn't have worried. When he peeked around the front, the rookies from car two were out of their car peering through the café windows.

'Come on, Janice, make a run for it. We don't want to be stuck here answering stupid questions all day.'

'Police, Chalkey? And I thought they were Jehovahs. It goes to show, doesn't it, Chalkey, there's just as much crime in the country as in the city if they have plain clothes at the ready in every café.'

'You said it, doll.' Chalkey wheeled his bike through the car park. He didn't want the engine noise to attract undue attention. As he passed car one he could hear the car radio.

'Headquarters to car one. Come in car one. I repeat . . .'

Chalkey had to think fast. 'Janice. Would you nip over to that garage and get some fags while I start the bike?'

'And what's wrong with your own legs, Chalkey Deveroux?'

Chalkey tried a sheepish look and pointed to his trouser leg. The trick worked.

'I'm sorry, Chalkey love. Of course I will. Back in a tick.'

Chalkey raced over to the Escort and picked up the radio mike. 'Car one here.'

'You took your time, car one. We have a position for the bus. Proceed to Avoca. We have confirmation that the passengers stopped there for refreshments and will continue on to Arklow. Do not apprehend. I repeat, do not apprehend. Follow, observe and, if there is any deviation from this route, phone in. Over. Jones, have you got that?' Sergeant Kelly got no response. Chalkey had put down the mike. 'Jones?'

'Now this is what I call bliss,' Deborah said. 'Sitting out in a garden like this. The sun shining, nature at its best. What more could anyone want?'

'My residents, Deborah, or have you got so carried away –' Maureen threw a look at Bill '– that you have forgotten all about them? I am going back to the phone. Chief Meyers must have some information by this time.'

'Residents?' Bill asked as soon as Maureen was out of earshot. 'I thought she was looking for some missing pensioners?'

Deborah brought Bill up to date with the details of the outing. 'And I'm quite sure, Bill, when we do come across the pensioners they'll be having a great time and wondering what all the fuss was about.'

'It does seem a bit far fetched, the whole thing. On the other hand –' Bill spoke softly '– if it hadn't happened, I wouldn't have met you.'

Deborah flushed slightly and passed off his remark as if she hadn't heard it.

'Your Maureen is a bit highly strung.'

'Highly strung! That's a nice way of putting it, Bill.'

'Deborah. Deborah.' Maureen came running back out from the café. 'I don't know what's going on in there. It seems an enormous fight has broken out among the customers. We must get away from here as quickly as possible.'

'Well, Maureen, Bill did offer to drive us on to your next point of call.'

'Very well. But only as far as the next village. I must get to a telephone box as soon as possible.'

'I have a CB radio in the cab, Maureen. You are welcome to use it.'

'You know you could be a bit gracious about this, Maureen,' Deborah whispered as they walked back to the truck. 'I think Bill is being more than obliging.'

'If you only knew what I know, Deborah.'

'Don't start, Maureen.'

'Well, don't say I didn't warn you.'

'About what?'

'Shush. He'll hear us.'

Chapter Thirteen

The bus reached Avoca with only one further delay. A donkey had strayed from a field and was standing, stock-still, in the middle of the road. Stevie beeped his horn a few times but the animal refused to budge. As Stevie got out, waving his arms about and making shooing noises at the donkey, nothing Iris could say or do could prevent the pensioners getting off after him and taking snaps of each other beside it.

'Isn't he gorgeous,' Lillie said. 'Wouldn't you love to bring him home?'

'I can see it, Lillie, you and your little donkey and cart going down to the shops for the messages.'

'You know what I mean, Cissy. There's something about donkeys you have to love. Even Jesus Christ loved donkeys. He rode one in Jerusuleum.'

'He was a bit big for that if you ask me. When you see the holy pictures with him on the donkey's back . . . it wouldn't happen today. If it was today you'd have the anti-blood sports people after you, not to mention the warrior people.'

'What warrior people?' Dessie Rourke asked.

'The fellas in rugs up the trees trying to save them, like.'

'What has that got to do with donkeys?'

'It's the same thing.'

'The female mind is a wonder to behold.'

'No one asked you to behold anything, Dessie Rourke. Don't be butting into other people's conversations and trying to change them.'

'God forbid that I would try to change anything you say, Cissy. No man would have the neck to do that.'

'Just you remember that, Dessie Rourke. And remember the last man who tried is dead.'

'Did your God ride donkeys, Miss Poole?'

'I beg your pardon?'

'Did your God ride around on a donkey like ours? Ours went to Jericho and Bethlehem and all over the place on a donkey.'

'Lillie!' Cissy was shocked.

'What? I only want to know.'

'It's the same God for Protestants as well as Catholics.'

'It can't be if ours went round on a donkey and theirs didn't.'

'They just don't believe in Our Lady. Everything else is the same.'

'Not believe in Our Lady? How can they not believe in Our Lady? Sure if it wasn't for her there would be no Jesus.'

'Would you shut up, Lillie. Do you want to hurt Miss Poole's feelings or are you trying to stir up a controversy?'

'I was only asking.'

'You pick the strangest things to ask, Lillie Fogerty. Don't pay her any mind, Miss Poole. She never knows what she is talking about.'

'Oh I don't mind, Cissy. When I was a girl I used to love nothing better than a good old theological debate.'

'No more than myself, I'm sure, Miss Poole,' Dessie put in. 'No more than myself.'

'Get up on his back, Stevie, get up till we get a shot of you.'

'No way.'

'Ah go on, Stevie. It'd make a great shot. Come on, girls, get him.'

The Fairview ladies charged at Stevie. They grabbed him by the arms and legs and lifted him off the ground.

'Help,' Stevie shouted. 'Put me down. You'll ruin me blazer.'

'Get him up, girls. Here, you men, help us get him on.'

Stevie, afraid to resist in case he hurt the pensioners, was half-dragged, half-carried over to the donkey and hauled across the donkey's back.

'That's the boy, Stevie, now throw your leg over and get up on him properly.'

Stevie tried to straighten up but the donkey started to buck and all he could do was cling on as the donkey tried to shake him off.

'Mind he doesn't kick you. Watch out for his back legs.'

'Has anyone got a carrot?'

'Get me off this,' Stevie shouted. 'He's going to throw me. Hold him someone.'

'Quick, get a shot before he falls off.'

'Hold on, Stevie. Hold on till I aim the camera.'

'He's a great sport, isn't he?'

Stevie slid to the ground as the donkey gave a final shake before wandering off up the road unperturbed by the commotion.

'Did you get a shot?'

'I couldn't. I was laughing too much.'

'Very funny,' Stevie said, as he picked himself up and dusted off his blazer.

'You're not hurt are you, lad?'

'Look. Neddy's taking off,' Lillie said. They all laughed as the donkey broke into a trot, took a sharp left into a field, and disappeared behind a hedge.

'He can't get away from you lot quick enough,' Dessie said.

'Goodbye, donkey. Goodbye.'

'He can't hear you, Lillie.'

'It would be wonderful to have a pet donkey,' Miss Poole said.

'There must be a few acres out the front alone at the Cross and Passion. You could have the donkey and Willie's allotment in there and not even notice it.'

'Wouldn't it be so wonderful,' Miss Poole said. 'Perhaps we could get up a petition and approach the board.'

'What about your Nurse Hatchet? The one we saw at the hall door. I bet she'd have something to say about allotments and animals on the front lawn.'

Helen and Iris had watched the photograph session

from the bus. 'Do you know, Helen. This makes it all worthwhile. Seeing our elderlies having such a good time.'

'Here we are, everyone. The Meeting of the Waters. Isn't it lovely? You can see now where Mr Moore got his inspiration from. Take your time now getting out. We have half an hour here for refreshments and bathroom visits.'

The staff at the Waters Inn made a great fuss of the pensioners, especially when they heard about their near miss accident with the bus. The more sympathy they got the more the story was embroidered. Iris had to call a halt when she found Reg Ryan attempting to display an old war wound to one of the waitresses, intimating that the piece of shrapnel, buried high up in his thigh, had been disturbed by the impact of the bus and the hedge. The weather was perfect for sitting outside and everyone was delighted to be off the bus and able to stretch their legs. After their coffee and biscuits, the pensioners made their way down to a little viewing platform at the water's edge where the ladies encouraged the gentlemen to remove their shoes and socks and have a paddle. Iris heard the shrieks and went to investigate.

'Gentlemen, gentlemen. No more paddling please. I don't want anyone catching cold.'

'You try it, Iris. Go on.'

'Very funny.' Iris laughed. 'You all want to see me fall in, don't you?'

'Go on, Iris, be a sport.'

'Oh all right then.' She took off her socks and

sneakers and stuck her toes in the water. '*Ooh*, it's freezing, it's ice cold. Helen,' she called up the bank, 'come on down, Helen. You'll love it.'

Helen had no intention of dipping her feet in the stream. She sat up, waved encouragingly, and then lay back on the grass where she was soaking up the sun.

'Iris. Iris.' Miss Poole called down to where Iris was standing. 'You know, Iris, river water is very good for your little complaint.'

'I can't hear you, Miss Poole. You'll have to speak up.'

'River water is very good for your little complaint,' Miss Poole shouted as loudly as she could.

Iris stopped splashing about playfully and stood stock-still in the water as everyone turned to look at her.

'Whoosh a little on to the chafed area, dear. It will do wonders for your problem.'

'What's that, Miss Poole? I can't hear you.' Iris resumed her splashing, hoping to drown out Miss Poole's voice.

'Douse your twat, Iris,' Dessie Rourke said. 'That's what she is saying to you. Douse your twat.'

'Dessie Rourke. Have you no shame? Leave the girl alone. He shouldn't be let out. Randy old coot.'

'It's a pity we have to leave, Iris,' Helen said as she and Iris gathered up their bits and pieces and put them on the bus. 'It's so relaxing. Could we not have our lunch here and then call it a day? I'm sure the staff would have no problem sorting us out and it would make up for all the wasted time.'

'We can't, Helen. We don't have enough money. I paid a big deposit to the hotel in Arklow and we can't afford to lose that. It is a pity but it can't be helped.' Iris began to collect the charges. 'All aboard, everyone. All aboard the mystery express.' She blew her whistle a few times to summon everyone and, while the Fairview contingent dawdled along, the Cross and Passioners hurried as best they could back to the bus. 'Take it easy, everyone. Mrs Scott, you'll hurt yourself rushing like that. Mr O'Neill, there is no need to break your neck, the whistle was only a gentle reminder. Ladies, gentlemen, please, take your time.'

'We didn't want to be late, Iris. The staff in the nursing home get very cross if one is late.'

'Well no one is cross here, Mr O'Neill. We are out to enjoy ourselves, aren't we?'

'This is the best time I have had in ages,' Joan Clancy said. 'It's a real adventure.'

The other residents joined in. 'Such fun.'

'Singsongs.'

'Paddling.'

'And sandwiches in a field. What would Sister Carmody say if she could see us now?'

'God,' Helen thought to herself. 'Listen to them. It would make you wonder about some of those nursing homes.'

'Where is Mr Perrin?' Iris addressed the group at large. 'Has anyone seen Mr Perrin? Stephen, have you seen him?'

'He went into the bar a little while ago, Iris,' Stephen said ruefully. Stevie would have loved to join him but he didn't dare. He was in enough trouble as it was. Until he got the undercarriage of the bus sorted he wasn't taking any chances. 'I haven't seen him since.'

'Right. Everyone get on the bus. I will find Mr Perrin.' Iris marched herself to the bar.

George Perrin had bought himself a large brandy. He had intended making that phone call to headquarters but he knew what the consequences would be. The Superintendent would send someone hotfoot to pick him up and that would be the end of it. It would frighten the old dears to see a police car taking him away and, apart from that, he would have blown his cover with the Cross and Passion. God knows where they would put him next. It was better to leave it altogether. They'd be back in town before any damage was done. If the Chief made a fuss he would say that it was a spur of the moment decision and there wasn't time to call. What was wrong with taking a few hours off, anyway? He was finishing off his brandy when Iris appeared at his elbow.

'Mr Perrin. While I realize you are not technically a pensioner, I must ask you, for the sake of all our guests, to refrain from sneaking off for alcohol. It's unfair to the others and setting a very bad example. If some of our Fairview contingent knew you were in here they would not hesitate to join you and there would be no getting them out. We had an incident last year, which I won't go into, that threatened to spoil our entire day and I shall not risk having it repeated.'

'So sorry, Iris. I'm coming now. I didn't mean to upset you.' Mr Perrin meekly followed Iris out of the bar.

'Mum's the word as regards drink, Mr Perrin.'

'Scout's honour, Iris.'

'What have you got in your handbag, Mrs Scott?'

'Pebbles. Pebbles from the river, Iris.' Mrs Scott had had trouble getting up the steps and on to the bus. Her bag banged and clattered off the sides as she got on board and made her way to her seat.

'Let me take it for you. It looks far too heavy to sit on your lap. It might stop your circulation. I'll put it up the front for you.' Iris leaned over and tried to take the bag.

'You can't have it.'

'Don't be silly, Mrs Scott. Give it to me.'

As Iris wrestled the bag from Mrs Scott, tea spoons, knives, a salt and pepper set, and a milk jug fell to the floor.

'It's only a few souvenirs, Iris. A little memento of our trip.'

'I hope no one else has any little mementos.' The pensioners looked at each other sheepishly. 'Come on. Own up. You won't be in trouble if you own up. I want to be sure no one has anything dangerous on their person.' Iris walked up and down the bus examining the contents of bags, pockets, and anywhere else spoils could be hidden. When she finished she sat down beside Helen and Mr Perrin with a final tally.

'I don't believe it, Helen. Fifteen spoons, twelve

knives, nine forks. God knows how many salt and pepper sets, and twenty-four cloth napkins. Mrs Walsh has a full set, cup and saucer, milk jug and sugar bowl. What am I going to do? They're like locusts descending on the crops.'

'Don't worry, Iris. I'm sure the hotel is insured against this sort of thing.'

'That's not the point, Mr Perrin.'

'What is the point, Iris?' Helen asked. 'You're not going to go upsetting everyone over a few measly bits of cutlery and a milk jug I hope.'

'No of course not. It's just . . .'

'If you are that worried, Iris, I will send them a cheque to cover the amount.'

'That's awfully good of you, Mr Perrin. You've put my mind at rest.'

'Now for God's sake, Iris, forget about it. Look at them.' Helen gestured down the bus where the pensioners, some in tears, sat subdued and silent.

'My goodness. What's this? We can't have this on our magical mystery tour. Mrs Scott, it doesn't matter about your mementos. And as for you, Mrs Walsh, you do know I expect to be invited round for tea? Now, who can guess where our next destination is? We've been through Ashford, left Avoca, and we are on our way to? If I tell you it also begins with an A, would that help? What about Ark . . .?'

'It's the zoo?' Willie burst out.

'No, Willie. It's not the zoo. It's Ark . . . l . . . ow. And it's only a skip and a jump from here. We are all going to sit down to a slap-up meal, then there's an hour of free time, so anyone who wants to do a little

a problem and it comes to a showdown with the cops, kill him.'

'What about the others, Lefty? Do we torch the bus?'

'No. It will draw too much heat . . .'

'Too much heat. That's a good one, Lefty.'

'. . . Knock it off, Muller, let's keep the funnies out of this. There's an old airfield in Tinahealy. Bring them there, take the keys, and get the hell out as quickly as you can. I want the guys driving the buses picked up by the back-up cars. I don't want anyone left on the scene. That's it. Any questions?'

'No, Boss. That's clear.'

'Right. It's one-fifty-five. Get back to your cells and wait for the bell. When your visitors arrive give them my instructions.'

'OK, Boss.'

'I want results.'

'Sure thing, Boss.'

'Remember. If we get Smith the whole case against me folds. As it stands they can only charge me with possession. We're talking months, weeks even, instead of years. My lawyer is talking bail: with Smith out of the picture I could be out by this time tomorrow.'

Acting Superintendent Detective Meyers paced up and down the reception area of the Cross and Passion. He was worried. There had been no fresh news from Sergeant Kelly's men and the longer this went on the more time Lefty Morgan's gang had of discovering the whereabouts of George Perrin. He had questioned the remaining Cross and Passion residents but got nothing there. Most of them were either too old, or too feeble, to understand what he was talking about, let alone give him any information. The staff were unhelpful. He had interviewed them individually, careful not to reveal the true identity of George Perrin, and drawn a blank. They seemed to regard the whole thing as amusing and implied that anyone who took Sister Maureen Carmody's word about an abducted bus was seriously in need of medical attention themselves.

'I must protest, Chief Inspector,' Doctor Kennedy said when he was being questioned. 'This whole business is preposterous. I don't know what Sister Carmody told you but you are blowing this up out of all proportion. An outing for a few pensioners, that's all it is. You are going to feel pretty foolish when they return, safe and sound, after a good day out.' Meyers knew he could eliminate the staff. His years of experience in County Louth told him that they knew nothing. He turned his attention to Ann Roberts, the only part-timer and therefore in his estimation the most likely suspect, making her repeat her conversation with the nurse so often that Garda Cullen had to restrain him.

'Let's go over this one more time.'

'I've told you everything, over and over,' Ann said. 'I don't know anything else.'

'If you are keeping something from me, Ann, you know where you'll end up. Twenty years behind bars.'

'I'm a kid. I can't get twenty years.'

'You start off in a home for delinquents. Then,

when you're sixteen, you get transferred to the women's prison. Do you know what they do to people like you in the women's prison?'

'I want my mother.'

'I bet you do, Ann. But if you are holding back on me, the next time you see your mother will be through mesh. Cuff her, Cullen.'

'Chief,' Garda Cullen interrupted as Ann started screaming. 'I think you better take it easy, Chief. The Chief was joking, Ann. He's a terrible man for the jokes, aren't you, Chief? Why don't you go and make us a nice cup of tea . . .'

Ann fled down the corridor towards the kitchen.

'Sorry, Chief. I thought I better . . .'

Chief Meyers sat down abruptly and took a few deep breaths. 'We won't mention this line of questioning, Cullen.'

'I heard nothing, Chief.'

The Cross and Passion phone rang and Garda Cullen picked it up. 'It's Sergeant Kelly, sir,' he said, handing the phone to Chief Meyers.

'Meyers here.'

'Chief. I've had word from the prison. There's something going on. Lefty called a meeting with his boys. I think they know about Perrin.'

'What's the news from your men?'

'Nothing new so far, Chief,' Sergeant Kelly said. 'I have informed them of the stops the bus intends to make so I expect they have headed straight there.'

'Expect, Sergeant Kelly? Expect? Why the hell don't you know?'

'They're keeping radio silence, sir.'

'I'm coming in, Kelly. I will co-ordinate operations from headquarters.'

'Righto, Chief.'

'And Kelly, I want all our informers contacted. Pull in every source you can think of. I want the word on the street.'

'That's not going to be easy, Chief, you do know it's Saturday.'

'Do we have a tap on Morgan's phone?'

'All the phones in the Scrubs are monitored, Chief. Morgan is definitely not using the prison phone boxes, but he does have a mobile.'

'A bloody mobile?'

'You know the governor at the Scrubs, sir. If a prisoner requests a mobile phone on humanitarian grounds, he's entitled to one.'

'Get on to them. I want that mobile confiscated.'

'Chief. Do you want the Arklow station contacted?'

'Put them on alert.'

'What's our story? Do we fill them in about Smith or . . .?'

'Suspected drugs drop. That's what we tell them. Cullen.' The Chief turned to Garda Cullen. 'I am returning to the station. You stay here. Keep us informed of any changes.'

Ann crept up the corridor with the tea.

'It's all right, Ann,' the garda said to her, 'there's no need to be frightened. The Chief Inspector is gone back to the station.'

The residents of Ashford watched as car three and car four sped through the village followed closely by

Chalkey and Janice on the motorbike. They hardly had time to turn their heads when a truck with a nurse and a patient sitting up beside the driver, pulled out of Scully's car park and headed in the same direction. As they turned their attention to Scully's, a gentleman in a dark suit, carrying an umbrella and a walking stick, emerged from the café to talk to two other gentlemen who were pressed up against the glass.

'What on earth do you think is going on?' one of them asked. 'Should we notify the guards?'

'Best leave it, they're from the city. You never know what city people are up to.'

The rookies, realizing they had gathered a crowd around them, called across the road. 'Move along now, folks. The show is over. There is nothing to see here.'

The crowd shuffled up the street a little bit and then mooched back trying to see more.

'What's going on, officer?'

'Nothing, madam. Just a routine check.'

'A routine check for what? What are you looking for?'

'We are assisting the health inspectors.'

'Is there something wrong?'

'No madam. Nothing at all. Now please, move along.'

'What's with the walking stick, Jones?' the rookies asked.

'I had to confiscate it, and the umbrella. They were being used as weapons in the affray.'

'So what do we do now?'

'We'll have to hold these people in the café. We

can't afford to let them out and disclose our cover. Get inside and keep your eyes on them. Don't let anyone use the telephone. I'll contact Sergeant Kelly and let him know the situation.'

Mr Scully had managed to restore calm. 'Please, please, sit down everyone. These gentlemen just want to ask you a few questions. If we all co-operate they will be on their way. In the meantime, refills of tea and coffee are on the house.'

'Questions? What sort of questions?'

'Who are these men?'

'These gentlemen are policemen,' Mr Scully explained, 'and they are seeking information about a bus which was supposed to stop here but didn't.'

'Stay where you are,' Jones called out to a Miss Cotter of Ivy Cottage as she attempted to get up and leave. 'Don't anybody move.'

'Are they making a movie?' enquired Miss Cotter, who was a little hard of hearing. 'Are we extras? When can I have my umbrella back?'

'Car one to Sergeant Kelly. Come in, Sergeant Kelly.'

'Kelly here, come in, Jones. Chief. It's Jones.'

'We have a situation here, sir, that's a little bit tricky.'

'What? What's tricky?' Chief Meyers shouted over the intercom. 'Have you a definite lead, Jones?'

'There is a problem, sir. We were forced to blow our cover and are detaining several people . . .'

'He must mean some of Morgan's gang,' Chief Meyers said to Kelly. 'Good work, Jones. What is your position?'

'Like I said, sir, Scully's café in Ashford. We, car one and car two, are detaining several persons here.'

'Are they armed, Jones?'

'No, sir. Not in the firearms sense. They do have objects which could be classed as semi-dangerous.'

'What the hell is he talking about, Kelly?'

'I'm just not exactly sure, Chief.'

'Hold on to them, Jones. Help is on its way. Kelly, get on to it, stat.'

'How many persons are we talking about, Jones?'

'I cannot give you the . . .' Jones's voice descended into a crackle.

'I've lost him, Kelly. Something's gone wrong with the system.'

'. . . exact numbers, Chief. They may decide to co-operate and not give the game away in which case there would be no problem . . .'

'Jones. Are you reading us? Come in, Jones.'

'. . . I must advise you, sir, these people are not directly involved in our present case. A fracas which developed in the café resulted in myself and my partner blowing our cover . . .'

'Can't you do something, Kelly? I'm losing half his report.'

'. . . Naturally, sir we are aware that speed is of the essence; we don't want to waste valuable time here when our main objective is elsewhere. Could you send reinforcements to relieve us? Then we, that is car two and ourselves, could proceed with the pursuit . . .'

'Jones. Are you reading us?'

'Cars three and four have gone on ahead, sir . . .'

'I've got them. Kelly. I've got them back.'

'. . . and we have arranged to meet them at the next point of call. As soon as we are released from our present situation we shall follow post haste. Over.'

'Damn. He's gone. What do you make of it, Kelly?'

'I'm not sure, Chief. It doesn't sound . . .'

'Well the way I read it is this. Jones has somehow managed to corner a few of Morgan's gang and he's holding them in Ashford while the rest of the team have gone ahead to monitor the bus. That's a good sign. It means Morgan is still sniffing around. He doesn't have the goods on the bus. Here's what we'll do. Get on to the local station. Get some of their men over to the café and free up Jones and his team. Stick to the drugs story. Acting on information received about a drop in Scully's café etc., etc. You know what to say Kelly. Jones knows about the stop in Avoca and the lunch in Arklow?'

'Yes, Chief. I relayed the message to him as soon as we had confirmation.'

'Good. That's where they are headed then. Smart fellow, that Jones. I didn't think he had it in him.'

'Neither did I, Chief. Neither did I.'

'Do you know,' Maureen said to Deborah and Bill, 'the more I travel through the countryside the more convinced I am that the city is the only place left with any sanity?'

'What do you think that to-do in the café was all about?'

'I have no idea, Deborah, but I intend to add it to my list of reasons for not venturing into the country ever again. How far are we from Avoca, Bill?'

'About ten miles or so.'

'Can't we go any faster? I want to get there before my group have moved on.'

'I'm afraid not, Maureen. There is a speed limit for trucks. It wouldn't do to get stopped.'

'How do I use your CB?' Maureen had started fiddling with the CB radio trying to figure it out. 'There's nothing to dial with.'

'Press the red button on the side.'

'Like this?' Maureen pushed the button.

'That's it. Now when you get air space and someone comes on the line you give your handle and . . .'

'Your what?'

'Your handle, your call sign.'

'Nothing's happening. I'm pressing as hard as I can but nothing is happening.'

'Give it a minute then press again.'

Maureen pressed the button several times, staring intently at the radio.

'Stomping Mary to California Billyjoe.' Deborah and Maureen jumped as the voice came through loud and clear from the speaker on the dashboard. 'Hi there Billyjoe, what can I do for you?'

'Press, Maureen, press.'

'Hello. This is Sister Maureen Carmody here. I would like to be connected to the Cross and Passion Nursing Home.'

'You can't be transferred, Maureen. Give him a message and he will pass it on.'

'Don't be ridiculous. I cannot give an important message to a Stomping Mary.'

'Hi, Stomp, it's Billyjoe. We need your help. We're

trying to locate a bus touring in the area. A Dublin bus with a party of pensioners on board.'

'Gee Billyjoe. That's a tough one. There's a lot of tour buses on the road.'

'Tell him this one is decorated,' Deborah said. 'The bus is covered with banners and bunting. You couldn't miss it.'

'Heard that, Billyjoe. I'll pass the word. Someone's bound to see it.'

'Thanks Stomp. Oh, and Stomp, ask the office to contact me, I need them to make some calls.'

'No worries. Keep in touch and keep rolling.' The radio went dead.

'You mean that's it?' Maureen said. 'Well correct me if I am wrong but I don't see how that's going to help anything.'

'Wait and see, Maureen. Stomp will contact every trucker on the road. If anyone can find your people the truckers can and when the office call you can give them your numbers.'

'Well done, Bill,' Deborah said. 'That's a great idea. Don't you see Maureen? There must be hundreds of trucks on the road. They're the very people to ask.'

'I suppose there may be a small amount of merit in it but I still need to get to a proper phone box. I must speak directly with my staff and Chief Meyers.'

'We take the next right and that will bring us to Avoca.'

'I hope it's not taking you too far out of your way.'

'For ladies in distress, nothing is too far.'

Cars three and four had continued out on the N11

until they came to a fork in the road where they were meant to split up. A slight argument as to which car was to take the coast road and which the more difficult upper road was resolved by the toss of a coin.

'It doesn't matter anyway,' Nigel said, having lost out on his choice by getting tails. 'We can swap on the way back.'

'Should we pretend to know each other when we get to Avoca?'

'Better not. If we need to communicate we can use the same strategy as before.'

'Which is?'

'Meet in the Gents.'

'Oh, we'll take the high road and you'll take the low road.' Nigel burst into song as his Escort took the right fork and headed for Woodenbridge. 'And we'll get to Scotland . . .'

'Shut up, Nigel.'

Chapter Fifteen

'Arklow, everyone, Arklow.' Iris called out. 'We have arrived at last. Helen, can you prepare our passengers? Make sure they leave all their personal belongings on the bus. We don't want things getting lost.'

Iris directed Stevie through the main street to Cassidy's Hotel while Helen tried to rouse the pensioners, the majority of whom were by now fast asleep.

'Drive right up to the main entrance and let us off there, Stephen. I don't want our charges having to walk all the way from the car park. Move your bus and then join us for lunch when you are ready.'

'If it's all right with you, Iris, I want to go to a garage and get the bus checked out.'

'Of course it's all right, Stephen. I'll arrange for your lunch to be kept for you.' Iris hopped off the bus and went on ahead into the lobby to alert the manager of their arrival.

'Wake up, Cissy, Lillie. Wake up everyone. We're

here. We're in Arklow. Miss Poole, Mrs Bourke, Reggie.' Helen went from row to row gently shaking each one of the sleeping pensioners.

'Are we home yet?' Reg Ryan opened his eyes and looked around.

'No, Reg. We're in Arklow. We're going in for our lunch.'

'Do you know, Lillie, I'm that stiff and sore from all the travelling I don't know if I'll be able to get off the bus,' Cissy said.

'I know what you mean, Cissy. I can't move me legs. What's that thing you get when your arms are limp and your legs feeling like leaded lights?'

'Old age, Lillie.'

'Come on, ladies. You can't give up now. You'll be grand when you've got a bit of food into you. Give me your arm, Mr O'Neill. That's it. Ups-a-daisy, that's the way. Miss Clancy, do you need a hand?'

One by one the pensioners staggered off the bus and dazed and bedraggled, made their way into the dining room.

'Welcome. Welcome, everyone. Welcome to your mystery destination. Deary me.' Iris looked at the exhausted pensioners. 'We really must cheer up, this is the highlight of our day.' She bustled about setting out place names and pulling out chairs. 'Isn't this exciting? Now, look for your names, everyone. I've put a name on each plate. It will save a lot of confusion if we all know where we were sitting. Mr O'Connor, you're here. You're over there, Cissy, beside Miss Poole. This side, Mr Flood, stay this side. No Con, we mustn't move names, go round the other side of the table. Oh my goodness, Helen, I nearly forgot. I left the paper hats on the bus. Can you run out and get them before Stephen leaves?'

'It's not Christmas, Iris.'

'I know it's not Christmas, Helen, but there's nothing like paper hats to create a party atmosphere. Quick as you can please, the staff are ready to serve.'

'Does she ever let up?' Lillie whispered as she took her seat.

'I don't think she can help it,' Cissy said. 'Some people are like that.'

'This place is like a morgue. How come there's no one else here?'

The huge dining room was empty save for the pensioners. Tables had been pushed together for the lunch booking, leaving a large gap in the centre of the floor.

'We are a little late. I imagine the other lunchers have gone sightseeing. Look,' said Iris pointing to the gap, 'they've left us room for dancing.' She skipped over to the middle of the room, did a few twirls and ended with a flourish. 'What do you think of that? Not bad for a soldier's daughter.'

'I think she's lost it.'

'Humour her or we'll never get our dinner.'

'Very nice, Iris. You've missed your vocation.'

'Do you think so? You know, I've always wanted to go on the stage. My Dad always told me I had a flair, he said I was a natural.'

'Well he wasn't lying, Iris.'

'Why thank you, Cissy, how nice of you to say so. Oh good, here comes Helen with our hats. Give them out, Helen, as quickly as you can. Hats on everyone, that's it. Isn't this fun? Helen, we haven't got *our* hat on. We can't get started until everyone has their hat on.'

'I feel ridiculous,' Helen said as she put the gaudy paper hat on her head. 'I hate these things.'

'We're not going to be a spoilsport, are we, Helen? We won't let her, will we folks?' Iris grinned round the table at the pensioners as they sat facing the empty plates, each with a paper hat on their head. 'Could everyone look this way and smile?' Iris rummaged in her bag and got out her camera. 'I think this would be the perfect time to take the outing photo. Smile everyone, say . . . someone is missing.' Iris looked at the vacant chair beside Mrs Walsh. 'Mr Perrin. I should have known. This is most annoying. Helen, would you? No . . . I'll get him myself. I have a fair idea where he is.' Iris got to her feet and headed for the door marked BAR, but before she reached it George Perrin entered the dining room followed by two waitresses carrying trays of steaming drinks.

'I thought hot ports all round might be a good idea, Iris. I hope you don't mind.'

'Hot port,' Dessie said. 'Nice one, Mr Perrin. Never mind if she minds, pass one along here.'

'Of course I don't mind, Mr Perrin. My goodness, you must think I'm a terrible spoilsport. I would have done it myself if our budget had run to it.'

'Three cheers for Mr Perrin. Hip hip.'

'Hooray!' the pensioners shouted together.

'I'm very partial to a hot port.'

'They say it's very good for the blood.'

'I heard it was good for the bowels.'

'It helps the circulation. If you take a glass of stout and a small port everyday you'll never want for iron.'

'Is that so?'

The pensioners, revived by the hot drinks, began to cheer up.

'A few more of these, Iris, and I'd skirt the floor with you myself,' Dessie said.

'Get out of it Dessie Rourke. The only thing you can skirt is a bar stool on your way to the gents.'

'Little do you know, woman. I took the ballroom championship title for two years running in Butlins Holiday Camp.'

'Yeah,' Cissy said. 'And they're still running after you to give it back.'

'Ladies, gentlemen, best behaviour please. The staff are about to serve.'

'I took the liberty of asking them to hold it a little longer, Iris,' Mr Perrin said. 'I thought one more round of ports would be in order.'

'Really, Mr Perrin,' Iris tried to suppress a snort of disapproval. 'I sincerely hope we don't have consequences.'

The meal was finally served. The waitresses rushed in and out of the swing doors bearing platters of chicken, followed by bowls of chips and mashed potatoes, peas, and jugs of gravy which were placed in strategic spots up and down the table.

'Tuck in everyone. Don't let it get cold. Oh. Perhaps we should say grace?'

'After all we've been through,' Cissy whispered, 'we'd be better off with the five sorrowful mysteries.'

'I don't think we should, Iris.' Lillie jerked her paper hat in Miss Poole's direction. 'Some of us aren't of the faith.'

'Give over, Lillie. Even cannibals say grace.'

'Do they, Cissy? I never knew that. Do you know, you learn something new every day?'

There was no fear of the meal getting cold. The pensioners tucked in with a vengeance and got through the main course, the dessert, and the after-meal cup of tea in no time and all eyes turned to Iris expectantly.

'Can we go home now, Iris?' Con asked.

'Dear me, no. We have our hour of free time when everyone gets to do their own thing. There's loads to see in Arklow.' Iris took a sheaf of leaflets from her bag and handed them to the pensioners. 'They have some very historic buildings here, and there's the pottery factory if you want to bring back presents, and a heritage centre. I have marked out all the places of interest. My goodness, you'll be begging me for more time once you get going. I suggest you go in small groups, then you won't have to queue for things. Helen and I will station ourselves in the lounge while you go and enjoy yourselves.'

'Do we have to go, Iris?'

'Yes you do. I've spent a lot of time working on those leaflets. You know I wouldn't insist if I didn't know how much fun you will have. Look at your pages everyone. The main attractions are circled in red and those blue lines are the streets leading back here to the hotel so there is no need to worry about getting lost. Synchronize your watches. We meet back here in one hour.'

'We never go out, Iris,' Miss Poole said. 'We're not used to going anywhere on our own.'

'You won't be on your own, Miss Poole. The ladies and gents from Fairview can team up with members from the Cross and Passion. That way you will all have a jolly time and get to know each other better. Now off you go.'

The pensioners reluctantly got to their feet and, led by Dessie Rourke, made for the exit. They stood on the street outside the hotel, still wearing their party hats and clutching their leaflets, unable to decide which way to go when Dessie made the decision for all of them.

'I don't know about you lot but there is no way I'm going tramping up and down this town looking at bloody pottery.'

'What'll we do, Dessie? We can't go back in, she'll see us.'

'There's where I'm going,' Dessie pointed to a bar across the street. 'I'm having a pint and a game of darts. Any takers?'

'You can count me in.'

'And me.' The gentlemen of the group followed Dessie across the road.

'If they're going in to that bar,' Cissy said, 'so am I. I'm too tired to go sightseeing.'

'I'm right behind you, Cissy. What do you say, ladies? Will we all go in?'

'Oh yes please, Lillie,' Miss Poole said. 'I think I

speak for all the ladies from the Cross and Passion when I say we don't want to sightsee either.'

'That's settled then.'

'Do you know, I used to be rather a whizz at darts in my younger days?' Miss Poole said. 'I played on the ladies' team at college.'

'Don't tell Dessie Rourke that,' Cissy said. 'We'll get a few bob out of him before our hour is up. Ladies versus men. A challenge.'

The ladies linked arms and crossed the street to The Lancers.

'Do you think it was safe to let them go, Iris?' Helen and Iris were relaxing over a drink in the hotel lounge. 'What if some of them get lost?'

'They'll be fine, Helen. All the sights are on the one street. They have only to follow the map I gave them and they arrive back here. Anyway, Stephen is not back yet with the bus. If they had stayed here you know what would have happened. The Fairview contingent would be in the bar like a shot, and drink more than they are capable of handling.'

'Did Mr Perrin go with them?'

'I do not know and I do not care. I have had quite enough of Mr Perrin for the moment. He practically took over the lunch.'

'Oh come on, Iris. He was only trying to get things going.'

'He could have consulted me first before ordering drinks like that.' Before Helen could reply a voice came over the intercom.

'Telephone call for Miss Fox. Telephone call for

Miss Fox. Could Miss Fox come to reception please?'

'That's you, Iris.'

'Me? How could it be for me? How could anyone know I was here?'

'You better go and find out.'

'Who was it?' Helen asked when Iris returned.

'The receptionist from Avoca. She was wondering if we were coming back. She said our bus had pulled up, followed by an ambulance, and she was phoning to make sure everything was all right.'

'She was obviously mistaken.'

'That's what I told her.'

'Why would Stevie go back to Avoca? Nothing was left behind. And an ambulance?'

'That's what she said.'

Lefty Morgan's gang had driven directly to Avoca. When they approached the Meeting of the Waters, the replica bus and the ambulance pulled over while the back-up cars drove on slowly and waited up the road out of sight. The drivers got out and walked around the building, sizing up the area, and planning where the best place was to make their grab. Chalkey was leaning against his bike, having a smoke, and taking in the view, when he spotted the gang. He quickly glanced around, making sure no one was watching, and then strolled across the grass. When he got within earshot he hissed out of the corner of his mouth: 'They've moved on to Arklow, boys. The cops haven't arrived here yet but I imagine they're on their way, so you better skedaddle.'

'Gotcha, Chalkey.'

'Where in Arklow, Chalkey? Did you find out where?'

'It's a one-horse town. There can't be that many places a gang of auld ones can hide out.'

'Don't worry, we'll find them.'

'What do you want me to do?' asked Chalkey.

'Follow us to Arklow. You flush them out, pass the word to us and we nab them. When you spot them, start a row with your bird and let it spill out on to the street. A bit of commotion will draw attention away from us.'

The bus and the ambulance drove off.

'Who's that lot, Chalkey?' Janice asked. 'How come you know them?' Janice had been enjoying herself throwing stones in the water and striking little poses she thought would impress Chalkey when she spotted him talking to some men in the car park. She climbed up the bank, annoyed that she hadn't had his full attention.

'What lot, doll?'

'I'm not stupid, Chalkey. I saw you talking to them. What is it about you, Chalkey? You always seem to have more time for other people than you have for me.'

'We're moving on, doll.'

'But I don't want to move on, we only just got here. Come on, Chalkey, the water's lovely. Come on and have a paddle with me.'

'We're going on to Arklow.'

'Why?'

'That's a good one. You're always whingeing that

we don't go anywhere. Now I'm taking you round and you're complaining.'

'I'm not complaining, Chalkey love. I just thought it would be nice to stay here a little while longer.'

'You stay then if you want to.'

'Don't be stupid, Chalkey. Of course I'll come with you. Who were the men you were talking to? I hope they're not the reason we're going.'

'They're just fellas, doll, just fellas I know from town.'

'You're amazing, Chalkey. You can't go anywhere without knowing someone.'

'Yeah, well it's a small world isn't it. Get on the bike, we don't want to be late.'

'Late for what?' Janice's voice was drowned out by the sound of the motorbike.

The receptionist in the Meeting of the Waters, Annette Connell, had satisfied herself that there were no problems with the group of pensioners who had stopped earlier for coffee. The organizer had mentioned where they were having lunch and she had called and spoken to her. 'Talk about coincidence,' Annette said to the staff, 'two City Swifts in the one day.' She had only hung up the phone when a lorry stopped outside and a nurse in full uniform came dashing into reception.

'I'm Sister Maureen Carmody. I want to enquire about a bus full of pensioners who were to stop here for coffee. Have they been here?'

'They were here but they went on to Arklow. Is there a problem? I've just been speaking to the tour organizer and she said everything was fine. I got worried when I saw the bus and the ambulance . . .'

'Ambulance? Did you say ambulance?'

'. . . but she assured me that all was well. Are you all right?' Maureen had taken a step backwards and clutched at her chest.

'I must use your phone. My worst fears have been realized.'

'You can use that one on the desk. I hope it's nothing serious. Those lovely old people. The trouble is, at their age, you never know when the blow will strike.'

Maureen ran around the reception desk, picked up the phone and dialled the number of the Cross and Passion. 'Bill Thomas,' she said aloud. 'He mustn't be allowed to go on. Take this.' She handed the phone to Annette. 'When you get an answer it will be Ann Roberts. Tell her to get Doctor Kennedy immediately.'

'But . . .' Annette was left holding the telephone.

Maureen ran from the reception desk back out to where the lorry was parked and shouted up to Bill and Deborah. 'There is a crisis. An ambulance has been called. Keep your engine running, we may have to make a dash for the hospital.' She ran back in to Annette, who had just got through to the Cross and Passion and was being handed over to Garda Cullen.

'Miss,' Maureen continued, gasping from her spurt, 'tell me exactly what the situation is? Where did the ambulance go? What hospital does it serve?'

'I don't know, madam.'

'Hello, hello.' Garda Cullen's voice could be heard squeaking on the line. 'Speak up, please. Hello.'

'How can you not know? Don't you take the slightest interest in the state of your customers?'

'There is no need to shout, madam. I can hear you perfectly well.'

Maureen took a deep breath and repeated her question as calmly and as deliberately as she could. 'What hospital does that ambulance serve? Where did it take your customers?'

'Is there anybody there?' Garda Cullen was saying. 'Who do you want to speak to?'

'They weren't my customers. I have definite confirmation that my customers took their own bus to Arklow.'

'Are you sure?'

'I am absolutely sure. My customers went to Arklow. The second bus and the ambulance pulled up briefly and then drove off again. They never came in.'

Maureen stared in front of her digesting this information and then made for the door.

'What do you want me to do with this call?' Annette held the phone out.

'Hang up. Don't say anything, just hang up.'

'Damn.' Garda Cullen had asked for a trace but the caller had hung up before it could be implemented. 'You're sure the caller didn't say who she was, Ann?'

'I told you. She only asked for Doctor Kennedy. You're not going to tell that inspector are you? He'll blame me again. I know he will.'

'We'll keep this to ourselves, Ann.'

*

'To Arklow,' Maureen leaped up into the lorry with new-found agility. 'My people have gone to Arklow.'

'You can't expect Bill to drive us into the middle of Arklow when the town is bypassed, Maureen, he has his ferry to catch.'

'They never wanted to be bypassed, Deborah. What town would? They will be only too delighted to have a lorry going through their streets once more. We shall have carte blanche.'

'What is that supposed to mean?'

'What it means, Deborah, is we will have the streets to ourselves. We shall not be delayed or hindered in any way.'

'We can't, Maureen. It's not fair.'

'It's OK, Deborah,' Bill said, 'I've got plenty of time. In any case, I couldn't bear to leave now, now that we are getting close to . . . There's a message coming through. Press that red button, Maureen.'

'Stomping Mary to California Bill. Hi, Bill, your quarry has been sighted. The bus you are looking for has been spotted outside Toughy's garage on the outskirts of Arklow.'

'Thanks, Stump. Thanks a lot. I told you we'd find them, Maureen.'

'No disrespect to your friends in the lorry business, Bill,' Maureen sniffed, 'but we already know they are in Arklow. Oh damn.'

'What is it now, Maureen?'

'I forgot to phone Chief Meyers. With all the excitement it went out of my head entirely.'

'We don't need him now, Maureen. We know where your pensioners are and they are exactly where they were meant to be. It's good to know we're not stranded. We can get a lift back to town with them on their bus. I didn't fancy being stranded in Arklow.'

'Stranded is what my poor residents have been. Stranded with that woman . . .' Bill and Deborah, engrossed in their own conversation, weren't listening. '. . . it won't happen again. I shall make it my business to ensure that . . .'

'"For me and my trew love will never never, laaaaaa", I can't remember the words, "but we'll be in Scotland afore yaaaa."' Nigel had the car window open and was singing his way through the countryside.

'Is that the only bloody song you know?' his partner asked. 'Give one more bar of it and . . . Tell me one thing. Nigel, how in God's name did you ever get picked for undercover work? Hold on. Look. Look down there. It's Avoca. You can see the whole layout of the place.'

'Any sign of anything?'

'Like what, Nigel? We're hardly going to spot a large group of criminals having their afternoon tea out in the open air.'

'I can see a lorry. It's pulling away.'

'Probably a delivery.'

'Sergeant Kelly did say—'

'Shut up, Nigel. Remember what Jones said about Kelly.'

The Escort descended the steep hill into Avoca and

stopped beside car three which had arrived at precisely the same time.

'Anything to report, lads?'

'I wish we had.'

'Right. In for coffee.'

'Christ. I never realized undercover work involved so much coffee. My nerves are rattling. Why don't we forget the coffee? Why don't we just ask if they have seen anything suspicious?'

Annette Connell saw the Escorts from her vantage point in reception. She watched as the men got out of their cars and walked towards her. 'What is it this time?' she asked herself. Buses, ambulances, a mad nurse. To think I changed from the night shift for a bit of peace.

'Can I help you?' She smiled at the rookies.

'We are doing a survey, Miss.'

'Yes?'

'We were wondering . . . have you noticed anything unusual here today?'

'Like what?' Annette looked at the four men lined up in front of her. Creepy, she thought. Are they planning a raid? She put her hand under the desk and felt for the emergency button.

'What my partner means to say is have you noticed a bus? A particular bus, a City Swift. We are with the bus company and we are planning routes and stops we haven't used before which might be favourable to our tourists.'

'Oh.' Annette was relieved. 'A city bus. As a matter of fact there were two of them here today.'

'Which way did they go?'

'The first went to Arklow. I don't know where the second one went. They didn't come in here.'

'Thank you, Miss. That's all we wanted to know.'

'Will you be sending more? We do like to know in advance.'

'Definitely. It's a lovely place to stop. We shall give it ten out of ten. One more thing, Miss. The rest of our survey party will be along shortly. If you could direct them on to Arklow we'd be most obliged.'

Annette stepped out for a breath of fresh air. She was sitting at one of the garden tables chatting to another member of staff when cars one and two drove up. She jumped to her feet, waving her arms above her head and gesturing towards the Arklow Road.

'They've gone to Arklow,' she mimed.

'What's the matter with that woman?' Jones said. 'Could our cover be blown after all?' Annette ran over to the cars. 'They've gone on to Arklow.'

'Who have?'

'The other survey men. They told me to tell you they've gone to Arklow.'

'Right,' Jones replied.

'And may I say how happy we'd be to accommodate as many tourists as you can send up? We like to pride ourselves on our ability to give a warm Irish welcome to all nationalities. Would you hold on a moment and I'll bring you out some of our brochures? They'll give you details of our rates for afternoon tea, lunch and dinner. We do a wonderful after-dinner cabaret for a very reasonable extra. It goes down a treat with the Americans.' Annette ran back into reception.

'Get going, quick,' Jones said. 'The woman is obviously off her rocker.'

Annette emerged from the lobby, brochures in hand, to the screech of cars one and two taking off at high speed.

When he had finished his meal George Perrin had slipped out of the hotel to find a secluded phone box in which to phone the superintendent. He didn't want to use the mobile – it would make it too easy to pinpoint his position. George knew what the reaction was going to be but he didn't care. He wasn't going to play cat and mouse to Lefty Morgan much longer. If the case didn't come up soon he'd pull out of the whole thing. His entire life had been put on hold and he was sick and tired of it. Even as George said these things to himself he knew he wouldn't back out. Morgan deserved everything that was coming to him. He was a big-time gangster who used other people to do his dirty work and he, George, was the only one who could make sure he got what was coming to him. George rang the special number given to him by Headquarters. He wouldn't get a reply – for security reasons he spoke to a recording – but his message would be relayed through channels in some sort of coded form.

'Superintendent. It's Perrin here. Returning to base shortly. No need for alarm. Hope you weren't worried.'

George smiled to himself as he added the last bit. He knew the superintendent would be tearing his hair out. He left the phone box and, following Iris's map, made his way to the pottery shop.

'Vodka and tonic for you and gin and tonic for me. Phew, I don't know about you, Helen, but I really needed this little respite. Imagine, we're halfway through our trip already. I bet now you're glad you came with us.'

'I'm not talking to you, Iris, until you take that stupid hat off.'

'Oh my goodness, I forgot I even had it on. I've been calculating, Helen – even with the delays we've had we're not too far behind schedule. It's three-thirty now, our pensioners will be back at four, which means with our two stops on the way back we should get in at approximately seven-thirty. Do you think I should phone the nursing home, tell them we are running a little late?'

'I wouldn't bother, Iris.'

'You're right. The less I have to do with Sister Carmody the more I like it.'

'She seems to be a bit of a tartar. Her pensioners are afraid to do anything.'

'I expect she is one of those women whose bark is worse than their bite.'

'Even so, Iris.'

'She does have a lot of responsibility. It can't be easy running a big place like that.'

'I'm not saying she doesn't but . . . you know, Iris, you would be very suited to a job like that.'

'Me?'

'Yes, you. You could certainly make their lives cheerier.'

'But I've no nursing experience.'

'I know that but look at it this way. If they were happier they wouldn't need so much nursing. Look at the Fairview crowd. They don't have nurses and they seem to manage pretty well without them. You should think about it.'

'My dad, God be good to him, used to say—'

'Iris. One more word about your sainted Dad . . .'

'I was only going to tell you—'

'Well, don't.'

Chapter Sixteen

'I'm looking for me granddad. He came here on a day trip but he forgot his pills. If he doesn't get them he could drop dead.'

Chalkey led Janice in and out of every hotel and restaurant in Arklow looking for the pensioners but so far he'd drawn a blank. Everywhere he had enquired people had expressed concern about his grandfather's fate but no one had any information as to his whereabouts.

'Poor Chalkey.' Janice was overcome. 'So that's what you meant when you said we might be late. You never mentioned your granddad. Why didn't you tell me?'

'I didn't bleeding know, did I? The ma rang me on the mobile. She knew we were out for a spin and she thought we might be able to find him.'

'When did she ring?'

'What does it matter when she bleeding rang?'

'Oh Chalkey love, you're upset. Keeping all that worry to yourself. You know I'm here for you, love.

You can tell me anything.'

'Sure, doll, sure, it's the worry that made me snap.'

They were nearly at the end of the town. There was only one more hotel to try and Chalkey was praying that would be the one. He knew Morgan's gang were watching his every move and they weren't going to be pleased if he didn't come up with a result.

'Stay here, doll, watch the bike.' Chalkey went into Cassidy's Hotel and up to the front desk.

'I'm looking for me granddad. He came here on a day trip but he forgot his pills and if he doesn't get them he could drop dead.'

'Oh my, how terrible. Actually we did have a group of pensioners for lunch but I think they've left. Hold on a minute, let me check.' The girl popped in to the dining room and came back to Chalkey immediately. 'You're in luck. The manager says they have gone for a walk but they'll be back shortly. The tour organizer is in the lounge. Do you want me to get her?'

'No.'

'But what about your granddad? Shouldn't you let her know?'

'No. Don't say anything to nobody. Me granddad wouldn't like a fuss. I'll catch him when he comes back. He'll be all right till then,' Chalkey added as he went back out to Janice.

'Well?'

'No sign of them. The ma must have been mistaken about Arklow. She gets like that.'

'What are we going to do?'

'Nothing.'

'Nothing? Chalkey, you can't leave your granddad without his pills.'

'What do you want me to do, eh? I told you they're not here. I can't go looking when I don't know where they are.'

'Phone your mam back. Get her to give you—'

'Cut it out, Janice. If he drops dead it's his own fault.'

'Chalkey. You shouldn't say things like that.'

'Yea. And who's going to stop me?' Chalkey started to walk away.

'Where do you think you're going, Chalkey Deveroux?'

'I'm getting crisps.'

'How can you think of crisps when your poor granddad is on the verge? How can you be so heartless, Chalkey?' Janice burst into tears. 'My mother was right all along about you.'

Passers-by stopped and stared as Chalkey and Janice began to shout at each other. Lefty Morgan's man, Smasher, was standing in the doorway opposite the hotel. He got the message. Cassidy's. That's where they were. He was about to go back to the gang when Chalkey strode across the road towards him and sidled past him.

'They've gone for a walk and they're due back.' He went on down the road and turned into a newsagent.

Iris and Helen heard the commotion on the street and went to the door to have a look. They saw Janice slumped over the motorbike, crying her eyes out.

'Poor girl,' Iris said, 'breaking her heart over some worthless idiot I've no doubt. It's the same the world over.'

'Shouldn't we—'

'We can't get involved, Helen. We have enough responsibilities on our plate as it is. Talking about responsibilities, where on earth can Stephen have got to? He should be here by now. Our pensioners are due back soon and I would like to get going straight away. Did he mention which garage he was going to?'

'Not to me.'

The ladies returned to their seats in the lounge.

'Another G and T, Iris?'

'I don't think we have time.'

'Of course we have time. I'm having one, anyway. I need to be fortified in case we have any more emergencies.'

'Don't, Helen. Don't even think it.'

'I won't be a minute.' Helen went up to the counter. 'Same again, please,' she asked, giving a quick look across at Iris to make sure she wasn't watching, 'but could you make it doubles this time?

Smasher reported back to the gang who were lying in wait further down the road. 'Our man is here. They're in Cassidy's Hotel.'

'So what's the plan?'

'There's three main roads out of the town. One goes through a housing estate before it reaches the outskirts, one goes inland to Aughrim, and the main one leads back to the N11. That's the one the fuzz will be on. Here's what we'll do. Kev, you take the bus, drive it to the hotel but keep out of sight of the windows – the tour leader and her mate are in there. You pick up the pensioners, they'll be too doddery to know one bus from another, drive out the Aughrim road and then on to Tinahely where you ditch them. Wear the bus blazer and cap – they'll only see you from the back so they shouldn't cop you until you've driven off. Gus, you get your ambulance lined up beside the bus. When we grab our man, get him into the back of it and head back to the main road. Don't worry about the fuzz, they won't stop you, they're not looking for an ambulance.'

'What about the other bus?'

'There's no sign of it – maybe the driver went for petrol or something. It doesn't matter, he has to come back and when he does, that's where you come in. Marty, you take the driver. The rest of you get on board as quick as possible. Fill the bus out as much as you can . . .'

'Rent a crowd, uh?' A few of the gang chortled.

'Cut it out.'

'Say that again, Smash. We take the—'

'Jesus, Brains, it's simple. Two buses, one ambulance. Their bus, our bus, got it? Their bus goes to Tinahely. Our bus goes back into town and the ambulance heads straight for Lefty's lock-up.'

'What if the fuzz stop our bus?'

'What can they do? You're on an outing. The driver won't talk if he knows what's good for him.'

'I got it now, Smash. It's a good plan.'

The gang moved off to take their position down by the side of the hotel.

The pensioners had settled themselves in the back room of The Lancers. It was a bit of a crush – the publican had obliged with extra tables and stools so that everyone could watch the darts challenge – but they managed to get themselves organized. The ladies grouped together down one side of the darts area and the gents shuffled into positions at the other side. Dessie passed his hat around and collected fifty pence from each of them 'to make the game more interesting.'

'Nearest the bull starts,' Dessie said. 'Who's going to take chalks?'

'What is he talking about?' Mrs Bourke asked. 'What bull? I don't see a bull.'

'It's the little ring in the middle.'

'Why is it called a bull?'

'I don't know. It just is.'

'But it doesn't even look like a bull.'

'This is going to be a cinch,' Dessie winked at the men. 'Candy from a baby.'

'Do we all have to play?'

'We won't have time for everyone to play. Pick your best team. We'll have three on each side and it'll be a knockout. A pint of your best, sir,' Dessie said to the publican. 'I steer better when I'm oiled. As soon as you're ready, ladies.'

'Hold on,' Cissy said, 'give us a chance. We have to pick our team.' The ladies huddled together for a consultation. 'You play first, Olive, then you,

Lillie. We'll keep Miss Poole for our surprise finish. You hold back, Miss Poole,' Cissy whispered. 'I'll give you the nod when it's time. OK, Dessie, we're ready.'

'But I don't know how to play,' Olive said.

'That's the whole point. They won't know what hit them when Miss Poole gets up. Don't worry, Olive. Throw the dart at the board. That's all you do.'

'Nearest the bull so,' Dessie said. 'Off we go.'

'Will you wait a minute till I've had a sip out of me Guinness? And stop hovering over me, you're making me nervous.' Olive threw her dart and the assembled pensioners ducked for cover. The dart hit the board flat on and bounced back into the crowd.

'Hard luck, Olive,' Cissy shouted encouragingly. 'You'll do better next time.'

'Next time? Do I have to do it again?'

'You've got three shots, Olive. Now go on, throw your next one. Aim for the middle.'

'Where is it? I can't see it with all those circles making me dizzy.'

'Will you throw the bloody dart, Olive? The rest of us will never get a shot in with you taking so long.'

Dessie got his team away with a double nineteen. He was followed by Lillie, who was thrilled that her dart, although not scoring, hit the board and stayed in, then Con, then Miss Poole and finally Mr Connor. Miss Poole got her side away with a modest double two, enough to convince the gents that her shot was a mere fluke.

'I do believe I'm getting better.' Olive had managed a shot which landed between the wire and the edge of the board. 'Do I get something for that?'

'You get a medal for not killing anyone, Olive, that's what you get.'

The match became tense. One by one the players were eliminated until it was down to a play-off between Dessie and Miss Poole. The supporters roared on their players. Advice came from every quarter.

'You've fifty-eight left, Dessie. Two nineteens and a double ten.'

'Oh no, Dessie, one nineteen, that leaves you with an uneven number. Go for nineteen double ten. Ouch. Hard luck, Dessie.'

'Now, Miss Poole,' Cissy shouted. 'You're on sixty-three. Go for it. Wipe him off the board. Thirteen, twenty, and two fifteens.' The ladies held their breath as Miss Poole took her shot. 'Thirteen. Hooray, you've got it. Now twenty. Take your time, Miss Poole, take your time. You can do it.'

'Don't worry, men. She'll never do it.'

'Two fifteens. Miss Poole wins. Well done, Miss Poole. I knew you could do it.'

'But I never play for money,' Miss Poole protested as Cissy and Lillie tried to get her to accept her winnings. 'It was against our ethos at Villiars.'

'Ethos, schmeethos, Miss Poole. Our team won fair and square. Don't you think that lot wouldn't take our few bob if it was the other way round. Hand over the money, Dessie.'

'We've been hustled,' Dessie complained. 'You're

supposed to declare if you have a professional on your side.'

'Would you give over, Dessie. Hustled! Listen to yourself. He thinks he's on the waterfront.'

'Was that the one where Paul Newman ate the boiled eggs? I didn't think he played darts.'

'Snooker, Lillie. He played snooker.'

'On the waterfront?'

'Please, please.' Miss Poole was getting agitated. 'Why don't we put the money back in the kitty and we all share it?'

'Do you know, Miss Poole?' Lillie said, 'you're so nice you should become a Catholic.'

'Another round here if you please, sir,' Dessie called over to the barman, 'compliments of our generous winner.'

'Don't you think it's time to go?'

'We've another twenty minutes yet,' Dessie said, 'we can put this money to good use. Didn't the day turn out grand after all?'

The pensioners sipped at the drinks Dessie had ordered with the winnings.

'It's been a wonderful day,' Dessie enthused.

The residents of the Cross and Passion all nodded their agreement. 'It will be very hard to settle back to normal after this.'

'Cheers everyone.' Dessie raised his glass in a toast.

'Look at him,' Cissy said, draining her glass. 'Delighted with himself to be drinking at our expense. I'm going to the powder room, does anyone else want to go?'

'I don't really,' Lillie said, 'but I'll go anyway.'

The ladies all got up and followed Cissy out of the door.

'If I know anything about women,' Dessie said, 'they'll be at least half an hour in there. Anyone for a quick one before they get back?'

'Oh merciful hour.' Lillie blessed herself, 'I hope there's nothing wrong. There's an ambulance beside our bus.'

'It can't be for us. We're all accounted for.' When the pensioners had trooped back to Cassidy's Hotel, the first thing they saw was an ambulance parked beside their bus. As they approached, Kev, wearing the bus company blazer and cap, bent down over the steering wheel as if adjusting something at his feet.

'Is everything all right, Stevie?'

Kev grunted a reply.

'I think we should get on. We don't want to go in to Iris smelling of drink. You know she'll only start off about it. Mrs Clancy, you'd only a mineral. You go in and tell Iris we're on the bus waiting for her. Tell her we're examining our pottery.'

'Me?' Mrs Clancy said. 'I couldn't, not all by myself.'

'Don't be ridiculous, woman.'

'Leave her alone, Dessie Rourke. If she doesn't want to go in she doesn't have to.'

'I could go in with Mrs Clancy,' Mr O'Neill said quietly, 'I have some peppermints in my pocket. I'm sure they would disguise my breath. I did only have one drink.'

The pensioners looked at Mr O'Neill in amazement.

'Good on you, Mr O,' Dessie said. 'A man after my own heart, a volunteer.'

'Well isn't that something else,' Cissy whispered to the ladies beside her, 'there's a man who looked as if he couldn't tie his own shoelaces and look at him now, practically a hero. More power to you Mr O'Neill,' she said aloud. 'It's a pity some of our other gentlemen weren't so restrained. On the bus, everyone. Mr O'Neill, suck two of your peppermints and give me the rest of them.' Cissy stood by the door and handed a lozenge to each of them as they mounted the steps. 'Miss Poole, Mrs Scott, Mr Flood, Mr Carr, Willie, come back for your lozenge, Willie.'

'I don't like them.'

'It's only a lozenge, Willie, it won't kill you.'

'I'm not taking it.'

'You'd think I was trying to give him arsenic. Go on then. Don't blame me if Iris catches you with drink on you. Con, Violet . . . don't give me that look, Dessie Rourke. I know what you're thinking. Mrs Walsh, Mr Mooney, Mr Connor. Mai, I nearly forgot about you you're that quiet on this trip. Now you, Lillie. Is that everyone?'

'Mr Perrin's not here.'

'He's probably inside with Iris. Did you all get a lozenge? Suck it slowly, try to make it last as long as possible.'

'Did anyone notice something different about our bus?'

'It's the drink, Lillie. It has you cross-eyed.'

*

Kev held his position and waited until all the pensioners were aboard. He had seen Mrs Clancy and Mr O'Neill going back into the hotel but there was nothing he could do about it. He couldn't wait for them to come out again, he'd have to get going before the alarm was raised. He turned on the engine and flashed the lights to signal Gus in the ambulance. Gus pulled up alongside him and spoke in through the window.

'Have you got Smith?'

'How do I know? I have them all except the two who went back into the hotel.'

'Shit.' Gus banged on the divider to the rest of the gang in the back. 'Get out and get them, the rest of you get on board.'

The gang members poured out of the back of the ambulance and on to the bus.

'All right, you lot. Which one of you is Alex Smith?'

'Who are these men?' The pensioners were startled by the appearance of the gang on the bus. 'Stevie. Do you know these men? Does anybody know them?'

'What are they doing on our bus?'

'I won't ask you again. Which one of you is Smith?'

'You've made a mistake,' Cissy said, 'there's no one here called Smith. Now get off our bus before . . .'

'Button it, granny, button it if you know what's good for you.'

'Stevie. What's going on?'

Kev turned round to face the pensioners.

'It's not Stevie. Get off everyone. It's not our bus.'

'Stay where you are. Don't move anyone. Hand over Smith and you won't get hurt.'

'We told you. There is no Smith. Come on everybody, get off the bus.' The pensioners got up and moved towards the exit. 'The police will hear of this, young man.'

'Get back to your seats. Kev, what'll we do?'

The bus had begun to sway as the pensioners surged forward.

'We'll have to get the hell outta here. Brains, stick that L-plate in the window. Gus,' Smasher shouted out to the ambulance, 'drive on, we'll follow you. Take the Tinahely road. We'll get it sorted when we get out of town.' As Kev moved the bus forwards the pensioners fell on top of each other in the aisle. 'Keep them down there. Keep them out of sight until we've cleared the town.'

'Wait for us.' The two gang members who had started looking for the missing pensioners came galloping back. 'You're not leaving without us.'

'On the bus already?' Iris said in surprise to Mrs Clancy and Mr O'Neill. 'How very organized of you. Is everybody accounted for?'

'We think so, Iris.'

'Never mind. We'll do a head count. It's odd Stephen never came in for his lunch.'

'He probably went straight in to the dining room, Iris.'

'I certainly hope so, Helen, considering his meal was paid for. Did you have a nice time, Mrs Clancy?'

'Oh yes, Iris, we—'

'I'm not late, am I?' Mr Perrin appeared in the lounge. 'I must congratulate you, Iris, your leaflets were very helpful and very informative. You were right about the historical value of the town, most interesting.'

'Why thank you, Mr Perrin,' Iris gushed with pride.

'You should think about involving yourself in the tourist business, Iris. You have a natural flair for it.'

'Do you really think so? I must admit I spent quite a lot of time on the preparation.'

'That's all we need,' Helen muttered, 'a dancing tour guide.' She raised her voice. 'How many more flairs have you under your belt, Iris, that we don't know about?'

'You know all my secrets now, Helen. As my father, God rest him, used to say, "there's many good goods in small parcels".' Iris giggled as the double gin and tonic began to kick in. 'Well ladies, gentlemen, let's get this show on the road. Tell me Mr Perrin –' she took hold of Mr Perrin's arm as they left the lounge '– which bit did you find particularly informative?' Iris stepped out of Cassidy's arm in arm with Mr Perrin, followed closely by Helen, Mrs Clancy and Mr O'Neill.

Maureen, Deborah and Bill had arrived in Arklow. They drove slowly through the town watching out for any sign of the pensioners.

'We must find Cassidy's Hotel. That's where they were booked in for lunch.'

'It's well past the lunch hour now, Maureen.'

'They were to have a free hour here in Arklow so it

is possible they are still here, although for the life of me I don't know what Miss Fox expected of my pensioners. Hanging around a small country town for an hour is bound to cause difficulties and my residents are very susceptible to chills.'

'It's a beautiful day, Maureen. No one is going to get a chill.'

'There, there's the hotel. Quickly, Bill, drive in. I think I can see Miss Fox at the entrance. Thank goodness we haven't missed them. At last our search is over.'

'Thank you so much, Bill,' Deborah said, 'we are very grateful. I have to admit we would never have made it without you.'

'I'm just glad things have turned out OK for you. Are you going in?'

'I must,' Maureen said. 'I want to see for myself how my residents have fared. I also want to speak to the driver to find out what time he expects to be heading back.'

'We have time for another coffee, Deborah, if you could bear it.'

'I'd love to, Bill.'

Deborah and Bill headed in to Cassidy's as Maureen went to talk to Iris.

'There you all are.' Maureen greeted the travellers as they emerged from the hotel. 'We've been looking for you all over.'

'Sister Carmody. What a surprise! What are you doing here?'

'Miss Fox. Have you been drinking?'

*

All four squad cars had converged on Arklow. After a brief circuit of the town they spotted the City Swift as it was leaving the hotel.

'Car one to Headquarters. Car one to Headquarters. Come in Headquarters.'

'Jones?'

'Our target is in sight, Sergeant Kelly. They have left the hotel and are heading South.'

'Stay on the air, Jones, I have the Chief here. Chief. It's Jones.'

'Jones. Meyers here. Any sign of the rest of Morgan's gang?'

'No, Chief.'

'Good. We may have managed to contain them in Ashford.'

'Chief?'

'The members of Morgan's gang you apprehended in the café.'

'Chief? Sir?'

'Remember, Jones. Do not stop the bus unless you suspect trouble. Let it continue on its course. We have received a communiqué from Smith assuring us all is well so unless there is a threat keep out of sight. Follow and observe, Jones.'

'Copy that, Chief . . . Oh, Chief. I should mention there is an ambulance which seems to be travelling with them.'

'Could be a coincidence or a precaution because of so many elderly persons travelling. Don't worry, Jones, I'll get it checked out. Well, Sergeant Kelly.' Chief Meyers gave a sigh of relief. 'We seem to have nipped that one in the bud.'

'Congratulations, sir. A job well done.'

Stevie had finished his business in the garage. The bus was checked out and to his relief there was no permanent damage. He was in no hurry to get back to the hotel. He was quite happy to forgo the dinner and stay chatting to the lads in the garage. He'd pick up a sandwich on the way back to the hotel – that would do him till he got home. Stevie was enjoying himself, regaling the lads with descriptions of Iris and the pensioners. 'I thought we were done for when we landed in the field. If you could have seen us, half the wall gone. I tell you one thing, it'll be a long time before I put myself forward for an outing again.'

Stevie saw the blue flashing light of an ambulance coming down the street towards him. As he pulled over to allow it more room he was surprised to see another City Swift follow closely behind it. He gave a wave of recognition to the driver but got no response. 'Learner. Probably too nervous to take his hand off the wheel.' Stevie smiled to himself, feeling like an old hand as he turned in to Cassidy's.

'Where is everybody? Stephen, where are our pensioners?' Iris asked as she, Maureen, Helen, Mr Perrin, Mrs Clancy and Mr O'Neill stood looking into the empty bus. 'I thought they were on the bus.'

'I haven't seen them, Iris. Not since I dropped you all off.'

'But Mrs Clancy and Mr O'Neill came to tell us they were getting on the bus.'

'You can see for yourself, Iris. They're not here.'

'Mrs Clancy, Mr O'Neill.' The pensioners turned fearfully to Maureen as she spoke to them. 'Did you or did you not see the rest of your group getting on a bus?'

'Yes, Sister Carmody, they were getting on here right beside the ambulance . . .'

'That's right,' Mr O'Neill said. 'We both saw it and I gave them my peppermints.'

'. . . We came out of The Lancers –' Mrs Clancy waved her hand in the direction of the pub '– and we crossed the road, and then we were sent to tell Iris the message so she wouldn't smell drink. Isn't that right, Mr O'Neill?'

'But why were you in The Lancers?'

'Because nobody wanted any pottery, Sister Carmody.'

'I cannot make any sense out of this, Miss Fox. Kindly explain what is going on. Where are my residents?'

'Stephen, are you sure the pensioners weren't here when you pulled up?'

'There was no one here, Iris. I told you. I was waiting to collect you all when the Sister here got out of her lorry and—'

'Her lorry?' Iris and Helen said together.

'That one.' Stevie pointed to the truck behind him and all eyes followed his finger.

THOMPSONS HAULIERS

REFRIGERATED TRANSPORT

NATIONAL & INTERNATIONAL RO RO SERVICE

EST. 20 YEARS

'There is a perfectly good explanation that I don't have time to go into now,' Maureen said. 'Our priority must be my residents.'

'I've just remembered something,' Stevie said. 'As I was about to pull in I passed another City Swift. Maybe they got on the wrong bus.'

'The wrong bus,' the assembly in the car park chorused.

'The wrong bus, Stephen. How could they get on the wrong bus? Wouldn't the driver know . . .?'

'It was a learner, Iris.'

'Yes?'

'Well sometimes they test learners by getting them to pick people up, unexpectedly like, they don't tell you in advance. If the pensioners got on he might have thought it was for part of his training.'

'That must be it. Why didn't you say something before now?'

'I didn't think of it. I only remembered it seeing that lorry. Don't go blaming me.'

'We must follow that bus. Stephen, which direction did it take?'

'It was going left. Hold on a tick.' Stephen got out a map and traced the road with his finger. 'The trouble is, once you get out of the town there are three roads you can take. They could have gone on any one of them.'

'Quick everyone,' Iris said. 'On the bus. There isn't a moment to lose.'

'Will you be staying with your own transport, Maureen?' Mr Perrin tried to keep an innocent expression on his face as he said it.

'Very droll, Mr Perrin. Miss Fox, we cannot drive willy-nilly in the hopes of seeing them. Young man. Call your employers. Find out who leased the other bus and what is their destination. Mr Perrin, do you have your mobile with you?'

'Yes but . . . I'm afraid it is limited.' Mr Perrin was reluctant to hand over his phone. He knew the call would be monitored.

'Limited. Limited to what? You surely cannot refuse to lend us your mobile. This is an emergency.'

'Now, young man,' Maureen instructed Stevie as Mr Perrin handed the mobile over, 'make that call.'

Stevie turned away and dialled the number of the bus company. He didn't want them all looking at him when he spoke to Mr Maloney. After a series of 'uh-uhs', and 'really, Mr Maloneys', he turned back to the others.

'It's bad news, I'm afraid. Well, sort of bad news. The other City Swift went missing. It was taken out from the garage this morning. It's the strike, you see, no one knows if it's out officially or unofficially.'

'Shouldn't we ring the police?'

'Mr Maloney has already informed the police,' Stevie said, 'and they are keeping an eye out. The trouble is he can't fill up a stolen form in case it's not stolen.'

'I must get Deborah,' Maureen said, 'she's in the hotel with the lorry man. I shall prevail on him to continue to assist with our search.'

'Shouldn't we let the police and the bus company handle it?'

'Not with my residents aboard. No. We cannot

afford to wait for the police. The trail is hot. Young man, check your map. I shan't be a moment.'

'Well, Maureen, are you happy now?' Deborah said. 'After all that drama you finally found your people.'

'I wish that was the case, Deborah. But thanks to that incompetent cheerleader my residents have got on the wrong bus, and what is worse, a bus that was stolen from the city this morning. As we speak they are headed to the outer reaches of Wicklow, for all we know, to be murdered or worse.'

'You are joking. I don't believe you.'

'Come. Come and see for yourself whether I am joking or not.'

Deborah and Bill followed Maureen outside in time.

'. . . I can see your worry, Iris,' Helen was saying, 'but if they were bus thieves, why should they stop to pick up passengers?'

'Hostages,' Maureen announced overhearing Helen's words. 'Hostages.'

Janice had fled to the ladies' room in Cassidy's to repair her face. Tears had dislodged her new Outdoor Girl mascara which had been attached free of charge with every purchase of Outdoor Girl deodorant. She had bought it specially to impress Chalkey, not that he had even noticed. 'Outdoor Girl,' Janice sighed to herself in the mirror, 'Chalkey Deveroux wouldn't know an outdoor girl if she came to him on a horse.' She stifled a sob and continued with her repairs. 'What am I going to do? I'm not going back with him. I never want to see him again. There must be some other way of getting home from here. I'll ask them at the desk, they should know.' Janice finished with her face and left the ladies' room.

'Excuse me, Miss.' Janice went to Reception and spoke to the girl behind the desk. 'Are there any buses going to Dublin from here?'

'I don't think so, love. I think you're too late for the bus. There's a train at seven though, it gets into town at eight-fifteen.'

'Seven. But that's hours away.' Janice felt the tears welling up again. 'Are you sure there's nothing else?'

'Been let down have you?' Janice could only nod. 'I tell you what. There's a tour bus outside in the car park. They'll be going back to the city. Maybe if you asked the driver he'd let you on. It's worth a try.'

'Thanks.' Janice smiled bravely. 'Thanks very much. Where . . . ?'

'Out that way, love, by the lounge.'

As Janice walked through the lounge she saw Maureen talking with Bill and Deborah. 'Funny,' she thought, 'I'm sure I've seen that nurse somewhere before.' When she spotted the City Swift with its decorations and its banners, she gave a quick prayer. 'Please, God, please let them take me.' The bus driver and a few other people were examining a map which was spread out on the bonnet of a car. No one noticed her. They were too busy talking and pointing out various routes. Should she go over to them? Janice made a decision. She reasoned that if she asked they might say no, but if she was on the bus already they were hardly going to throw her off. She crept forward, flattening herself against the back of the bus and waited for her chance. Moments later it came. The nurse, followed by a man and a woman, appeared from Cassidy's and joined the group around the bonnet. Janice ducked, crept further towards the door and jumped on. Keeping low she moved to the long seat at the back and, with her heart pumping for fear of exposure, lay down on the floor.

Chapter Seventeen

The bus, the ambulance and the two back-up cars stopped at one of the many scenic areas on the way to Tinahely. Smasher left two of the gang members on guard at the door of the bus while the rest of them got out and gathered around one of the wooden picnic tables. The pensioners, bemused and bewildered, sat two by two in their rows, afraid to move in case they caught the attention of their captors.

'Is this part of the mystery tour? Is it some kind of test?'

'I'm afraid not, Miss Bourke. I don't know what they're after but they are up to no good, that's for sure. Maybe they kidnapped us to get ransom.'

'Ransom? But we don't have any money. Who would pay ransom for us?'

'It's not us they are after.'

'What are they going to do with us?' Olive cried out, unable to bear the suspense any longer. 'What is going to happen to us?'

'Don't go upsetting yourself, Olive. They can't do anything. They're just trying to intimidate us.'

'They're not having my body,' Lillie said, watching the gang from the window. 'I'll kill myself first.'

'At the risk of hurting your feelings, Lillie,' Dessie said, 'I don't think there's any fear of that.'

'Who is this Alex Smith they're on about, does anybody know?'

'The weird thing is they don't seem to know themselves. One way or the other we'll have to find out what they're up to. It's the only way we'll get out of this mess.'

'But how, Dessie? Muscles there isn't going to let you off the bus.'

'Why don't we just drive off,' Lillie suggested, 'while they're not looking?'

'We can't. They took the keys.'

'We can't sit here like ducks to the slaughter. Hey Mister –' Dessie banged on the window and shifted towards the door '– you'll have to let me off, I need a leak.'

'Stay where you are.'

'Even a condemned man gets a last request.'

'He has a point there, Brains. Let him off but watch him.'

'Atta boy, Dessie,' Cissy whispered, 'get as close as you can.'

Cissy and the others crouched at the windows and looked on anxiously as Dessie got off the bus and walked as near as he dared to the picnic table. He stood half obscured between a rubbish bin and a bush, undid his fly, and strained to overhear the gang's conversation.

'What do we do now, Smasher?'

'Get on to Chalkey. See if he knows which one of them is Smith.'

'An' if he don't know? I don't fancy telling the boss his plan was mucked up because none of you recognize Smith.'

'Maybe we should just torch them all.'

'No. The boss was definite about that, he said do Smith if we have to but no one else. Now get on to Chalkey.'

'Chalkey. It's us. We have everybody here but we don't know which one is Smith. What does he look like?'

'How would I know? I've enough trouble of me own trying to find Janice.'

'Janice? The boss never said nothing about a Janice.'

'She's me mot.'

'For Christ's sake, Chalkey. We're in a bind here. Forget your bleeding mot. Get on to the boss and find out which one of them is Smith.'

'No way. I'm not ringing him. My job was to find them and I found them. It's down to you to talk to the boss.' Chalkey hung up.

'Well?'

'It's no use, Smasher. He doesn't know.'

'Shit.'

'Oi! What's taking you so long?' Brains shouted over to Dessie.

'Give me a minute. I'm nearly finished.' Dessie hung

on as long as he could. He had to find out who the boss was and why they wanted Smith.

'Oi, you're not competing with the bloody Niagaras. Tie a knot in it if you know what's good for you and get back on that bus.'

'Who's ringing Lefty?' Smasher looked from one member of the gang to the other.

'Not me, Smash.'

'Not me either. The last time I rang he said he'd decapitate my dog if I bothered him again.'

'I never knew you had a dog, Kev. What is it?'

'Will you two shut the fuck up about dogs? I can't hear meself think with the pair of you. Gimme the phone.' The gang watched as Smasher dialled Lefty's number. 'Lefty, it's Smasher. Here's the score. We have the coach and we're on our way to Tinahely.'

'So what's the problem?'

'Like I said, Boss, they're all here, but we don't know which one is Smith.'

'Playing cute is he? Hiding behind a skirt-ful of grannies. He's in his early forties, sort of neat, and he's got brown eyes, brown hair, oh, and he wears glasses for reading.'

'Great, Boss. We'll get that sorted.'

'You better get it sorted, Smasher, and quick. I want him back in town pronto.' Smasher grinned at the gang. 'We have him, forties, brown eyes, brown hair and glasses . . . What?' Smasher broke the silence that followed. 'What's the matter with you lot?'

'There's no one on the bus fits that kit, Smash. They're all ancient. Go look for yourself.'

'Naw. This fellow is smart. He's disguised, you numbskulls. Who has a paper?'

'I have. In the car.'

'Get it. I want everyone of them to read it. The one who has to put on glasses is our man.'

Dessie scrambled on board and repeated what he had heard to the pensioners.

'We're none the wiser, Dessie.'

'Oh, but we are. We know it's not one of us.'

'Listen to Sherlock,' Cissy said, 'I could have told you that myself.'

'Once they realize they haven't got Smith they'll let us go.'

'They'll let us go? What makes you so sure, Dessie?'

'Because they were told not to torch us.'

'Oh my God.'

'Get them back in their seats,' Smasher said walking up and down the aisle holding the newspaper up in the air. 'Now you lot. Each one of you is going to read a bit of this newspaper. I want it loud and clear. No funny stuff. You.' He stopped short at Mr Flood. 'You start.'

'Me?'

'Yeah, you. No headlines. I want the small print. Now read.' Smasher gave a menacing laugh down the bus.

'Despite being . . .' Mr Flood's hands began to shake so much he couldn't see the print.

'It's all right, Mr Flood,' Cissy said, 'read it out, you can do it.'

'Despite being down to ten men Wycombe Wanderers pulled off—'

'Where's your glasses?'

'I don't need glasses for reading. Only for the television.'

'Siddown. You.' Smasher went on to Mr Carr.

'Despite being down to ten—'

'Not the same bit. Pick another bit, turn the page.'

Mr Carr fumbled in his pocket and took out his glasses case.

'We got him.' Smasher grabbed Mr Carr by the arm.

'Eh, Smash.'

'What?'

'He's bald as a coot.'

'So he could have shaved.'

'But he don't look forty, Smash, he looks more like a hundred.'

Smasher dropped Mr Carr's arm and moved on to Mr O'Connor. 'Read.'

'Alexander Banquet will miss not only the Tote Cheltenham Gold Cup,' Mr Carr's voice trembled, 'but has been ruled out for the rest of the season . . .'

'Shit,' Marty said. 'I had an ante post on him.'

'Me too,' Gus said. 'I had him at ten to one.'

'. . . The Mullins trained . . .'

'That's enough.' Smasher snatched the paper from Mr O'Connor and passed it from one male pensioner to the other but, glasses or no glasses, no one fitted Smith's description. Smasher began to panic. Time was running out. The bus company would have reported the stolen bus. They were bound to be spotted by a passing patrol. He had a brainwave.

'Wigs,' he shouted. 'Check the women for wigs.'

The ladies screamed as each of them felt their hair being tugged.

'Get off, you blackguards,' Dessie roared as he tried to protect the ladies. 'What do you think you are doing?'

'Pipe down, Pops.' Dessie felt the thump in his ribs and sank to his knees. 'If you don't all shut up there's more where that came from.'

'What do we do now, Smash?'

'Smith must be still in Arklow. Kev. Get this lot outta here. You know where to go. You two, go after him in the car. Gus, head back to Arklow, the rest of us will follow in the other back-up.'

'Gee, Smasher. Do you think that's a good idea?'

'Do you want to face Lefty if we don't have our man?'

'Let's go, boys.'

It hadn't taken much to persuade Bill Thomas to stay with the search party. In spite of Deborah's insistence that it wasn't fair on him he agreed with Maureen – who had temporarily shelved her scruples about him – that two vehicles were better than one for their pursuit.

Tactics were arranged. Stevie would follow the route taken by the other bus, Bill would return to the main road in case they doubled back, and continue on that way. Mr Perrin's mobile was commandeered by Maureen. 'You shall of course be reimbursed, Mr Perrin,' she said as she put it in her pocket.

'There's not much point in you being in the lorry with the mobile, Maureen,' Deborah pointed out. 'Bill has the CB. We can't have all the communications in the one place. Give it to Iris.'

'Certainly not. I shall retain the mobile.'

'I am in charge of this trip, Maureen,' Iris said, 'and I am perfectly capable of co-ordinating the search.'

'Capable!' Maureen snorted. 'We have all seen a sample of your capabilities. I never wanted my residents to go on this trip. I told Doctor Kennedy, as Deborah can witness, that it would end in disaster. I said too much excitement would lead to problems but I never envisaged abduction.'

'It's all my fault,' Iris wailed. 'All I wanted to do was give them a good day out. What have I done? Oh, what have I done?'

'Hold on, Iris,' said Helen. 'Listen Nurse whatever your name is. If you gave even a quarter of the attention to your residents as Iris does—'

'Ladies, ladies. Arguing among ourselves won't help anything. We don't know that anyone was abducted. We don't know that the bus was stolen. There could be a perfectly reasonable explanation for all this. What we must do now is concentrate our efforts and get the pensioners back. Maureen, if you want to stay within reach of the mobile I suggest you stay on the bus. I shall go in the lorry if that's all right with you, Bill.'

'Oh no you don't, Mr Perrin,' Stevie said, 'if this bus breaks down I won't be able to manage without you.'

'Maureen, we're wasting time. Get back in the lorry with myself and Bill.'

'Very well, but I must make a quick call to the Cross and Passion. My staff have been in liaison with the police and they may have some news.'

'How come you were in touch with the police already?' Helen asked. 'The pensioners have only gone missing in the last little while.'

Helen didn't get a reply. Maureen moved out of earshot as she dialled the number of the Cross and Passion.

'The Cross and Passion,' Ann Roberts sang out. 'What can I do for you?'

'Ann. It's Sister Carmody. Have any of our residents called in? Did Chief Meyers contact you? Is Doctor Kennedy there? Have you any news at all?'

'Hello, Sister. Nope, nope, nope and nope. It's really quiet. I'm playing draughts with Garda Cullen and he says I'm cheating because I'm winning all the time but I'm not. I'm very good at draughts. I always win when I play at home.'

'Pull yourself together, girl. I do not want to hear about your draughts prowess. Put me on to Garda Cullen.'

'She wants to talk to you.' Ann was about to hand over the phone when she remembered something. 'And Sister, I hope you're not forgetting I go home at five-thirty.'

'What is your update from Chief Meyers, Garda Cullen?'

'Not much, Sister. Everything is fine now. People have been apprehended in Ashford. The Chief is well pleased.'

'People. What people?'

'The ones after Mr Smith.'

'Has the world gone mad entirely? I have no idea what you are talking about, Garda. Kindly get your Chief Meyers to contact me immediately on this number. Mr Perrin, what is this number? Mr Perrin,' Maureen called into the bus, 'the number please . . . 088 6082761,' Maureen repeated into the phone. 'Do not delay in relaying this message, Garda Cullen, immediate communication is vital. Underlings,' Maureen mused to herself as she hung up, 'even the police it appears cannot get staff.'

Sergeant Kelly put his head round the door of Chief Meyers's office.

'Chief. We have picked up two calls made from Smith's phone. Neither of them were made to the designated number.'

'Can you trace them?'

'The men are working on it, sir. We do know they were made from the Wicklow area.'

'Keep it up, Kelly. I wonder . . . it's not like Smith to use it indiscriminately . . . hold on, let me take this.' Meyers broke off his conversation to answer his phone. 'Meyers.'

'Sir, it's Garda Cullen. I just had a call from Sister Carmody. She wants you to contact her urgently on 088 6082761.'

'088 6082761?'

'That's right, sir.'

'Everything all right, Chief?' Sergeant Kelly asked.

'That –' Chief Meyers looked at his phone in disbelief '– that Sergeant Kelly, was a message for me to phone Sister Carmody on Smith's phone. How in the hell did she get that number unless . . . why didn't I think of it before? . . . She is part of the gang. It's all beginning to fall into place. Think of it, Kelly. If she has his phone, she must have him.' The Chief went up to his wall map. 'The call was made from approximately here –' he ringed the Arklow area '– which means she must be still in the vicinity. Get on to all units, Kelly. Pick her up.'

'Why do you think she called, Chief?'

'She doesn't know the phone is monitored and that, Sergeant Kelly, is our trump card. Keep the trace on. If she makes another call we have her. Anything on the second one yet?'

'It came through, Chief, while you were on to Cullen. It was made to the Dublin Bus Company. A Mr Maloney took the call. He said it was one of his drivers enquiring about a second City Swift.'

'And?'

'He told his driver that there were no other authorized City Swifts out.'

'That's it?'

'That's it, Chief.'

'I'll have to work that one out, Kelly. Never forget Lefty Morgan is clever. He will use any manner of red herrings to throw us off the scent. Get your men into action.'

'All units. Come in, all units. Listen up, men. The nurse from the Cross and Passion is now a suspect. We know she is in the area. She must be picked up immediately for questioning. Break off your surveillance of the pensioners' coach and apprehend the nurse and anyone travelling with her. Do you read? Over.'

'Car one, here. We read you, Sarge and will respond. Over.'

Chapter Eighteen

The sun was blotted out by huge menacing conifers as Kev turned off the road and drove through a dark forestry track. To the pensioners, this track was endless, it seemed to stretch for miles.

'Keep an eye out,' Dessie said, 'try to remember which way he's taking us.'

'What's to remember, Dessie? It all looks the same.'

'I'll never be able to look at my sweet little Christmas tree in the same light again if that's the mothers and the fathers of it.'

'What are you on about, Lillie? Your Christmas tree is artificial.'

They took a sharp right turn and as they cleared the forest the sun reappeared, twinkling over a small lake beside an old stone cottage.

'Thank God,' Cissy said. 'That was scary. I thought we were never coming to the end of it.'

'Isn't that beautiful?' Lillie said. 'It looks like heaven should look like.'

'If only we were with angels, Lillie.'

The track twisted past the old cottage and on up through the open-posted gate.

'Did you see that sign?'

'What sign?'

'On the gate. It said, "Keep Out, Military Area". It's an army-training base.'

'They picked a beautiful spot for their training.'

'They didn't pick it for its beauty. They picked it for the isolation.'

'Look. Over there.' Dessie pointed to a large green hangar-like building with a tarmac stretch in front of it. 'That must be where they are taking us.'

The bus stopped near the hangar. Kev turned off the engine, got out of the driver's seat and faced the pensioners. 'Home sweet home, folks,' he laughed.

'You can't leave us here,' Dessie said.

'What's the matter, old man, afraid the bogeymen will get you?'

'You . . .' Dessie made a run at him.

'Watch it.' Kev raised his arm.

'Don't, Dessie, don't,' Cissy cried, 'you'll only get hurt.'

Kev waved the back-up car over to the bus. 'Let's get outta here, boys. This place is giving me the creeps.'

'At least leave the engine running to give us a bit of heat.'

'No can do, Pops,' Kev jangled the bus keys. 'Got to take them with me.'

'What do we do now, Kev, do we follow the others?'

'Nah. Smasher and the lads won't need us. They

won't have no trouble snatching the Smith geezer once they pinpoint him.'

'You don't think they'll need us then?'

'Are you joking? A tour guide, a bus driver and a yellow-bellied witness? Gimme a break. One splat and they're gone, they'll be smashed like ants.' The pensioners jumped as Kev whacked his hand down on the car bonnet.

'Smasher the smasher, eh Kev?'

'He didn't get his nickname for nothing. In the car, boys, we'll meet up with the others back in town.'

The car drove off, leaving the pensioners stranded.

For a moment no one moved. No one said a word. The pensioners sat in their places trying to understand what had gone on. They listened for the sound of the car coming back to get them. They looked around at the silent, beautiful landscape and slowly, very slowly, the full realization of their situation began to take hold.

'The sun is going down.'

'Give over, you are imagining it. Do you want to put the wind up everyone? It's only after three in the afternoon, it won't be dark for hours yet. Someone is bound to come and find us. I bet Iris has people out looking for us already.'

'What if they don't find us? How will anyone find us in this place?'

'Tracker dogs, Lillie. They'll use tracker dogs.'

'Don't be daft.'

'Do you think we should start to walk back?'

'There's about four miles of forestry before we even

get to the road. We'd never make it. The ladies certainly wouldn't. No, it's better to stay on the bus.'

'Maybe we should send up flares.'

'Flares, Lillie, that's a great idea. I'm sure every City Swift comes equipped with its own life-saving equipment.'

'There's no need for that tone, Cissy. I was only trying to suggest how we could signal someone.'

'That's an excellent idea, Lillie,' Miss Poole said. 'A signal fire. We should get one ready. If we are stuck here till nightfall our rescuers would be able to find us.'

'Well done, Miss Poole.'

'I thought of it first,' Lillie pouted.

'We need wood. Lots and lots of wood to make a pyre. Gather wood everyone.'

The pensioners stood up jostling with each other as they tried to get off the bus. This was something to do. Anything was better than just sitting there waiting.

'Hold on,' Dessie said, 'hold your horses. I think we should make a proper plan in case . . .' he hesitated '. . . first we need wood for the fire and we need food.'

'Food! We're only after our three-course dinner.'

'Cissy, collect up everyone's bags, see what left-overs there are from this morning's sandwiches. Two of you men go down to that old cottage and get some water, there's bound to be a spring or a well there.'

'What'll we get it in?'

'The teapot,' Mrs Scott sprang up. 'I've got a teapot in my handbag.'

'Thank you, Mrs Scott, that'll do for starters anyways, but I'm sure, gentlemen, you'll find an old pail or a bottle or something. Get as much as you can.'

'I don't suppose you have any teabags in that bag of yours, Mrs Scott?'

'Be serious, Cissy.'

'And what are you going to do, Dessie Rourke, while we're breaking our backs getting wood?'

'Con and Willie and myself are going to try and get into the hangar over there. You never know. Maybe the army left supplies in it.'

'I would like to go with you,' Mr O'Connor said. 'I spent some time in the forces in my youth, I may be able to be of some help.'

'Thank you Mr O'Connor. The more brains the better. The rest of you sort yourselves into work parties. If those gangsters think they have left us here to rot we'll teach them a thing or two.'

'Will you look at him. He's enjoying every minute of this. Five minutes in the wilderness and he's gone power crazy. Come on, girls, we might as well, it'll help to pass the time.'

The ladies combed the area for sticks, bits of dry moss, leaves, anything that would burn. They scurried back and forth with their armfuls, dropping them at the spot Miss Poole had cleared for the fire.

'Give me a hand with this will you?' Lillie was staggering across the field dragging a big branch behind her. 'I've got a great one. This will last for ages,' she said proudly.

'Well done, Lillie,' Miss Poole said as she took the end of Lillie's branch and helped her carry it over to the pile. 'This reminds me of when I was a young girl.'

'Picking up sticks, Miss Poole?'

'In a way. I was in England during the war, I worked as a land girl.'

'Really, Miss Poole?'

'Oh yes. I was stationed in Kent. Goodness, when I think of it now. A group of us girls were sent down from London to help out on a farm. I have to tell you we knew absolutely nothing about farms, but, by golly, we learned fast. We had to. There were no young men left you see, they were all conscripted.'

'They were hard times, Miss Poole.'

'Very hard, Cissy, hard on everyone.' Miss Poole gave a little sigh. 'But we did have some fun times as well. There were dances and fêtes and all manner of fund-raisers.'

'Did you get paid, Miss Poole, all you land girls?'

'We got our board and a little pocket money. Not enough to keep one in stockings, of course, but then they weren't to be got.'

'Do you know what this reminds me of, Miss Poole? It reminds me of the invasion of the Danes in 1014. That was when our very own poor Brian Boru breathed his last on a beach in Clontarf, we did it in school. He was very short and . . .'

Miss Poole looked at Lillie in some confusion.

'Would you give over, Lillie,' Cissy said, 'How could this remind you of Brian Boru? You weren't even there. Don't mind her, Miss Poole, it's the wood gathering, it brings it out in her.'

'I was only going to explain to her that it reminded me that our Brian Boru was at his own camp fire when it happened.'

'Lillie!'
'What?'

The ladies spread out raincoats and set out what food there was. Miss Poole got the fire going aided by several pages of Olive's large-print novel, *Love is no Stranger*. The men duly returned from the cottage with two buckets of water plus the teapot full to the brim, as well as several rather dubious-looking tin mugs.

'Pick some nettle leaves, ladies.' Miss Poole stoked at her fire. 'Nettle tea can be quite delicious. I shall scald these mugs and they will be perfectly all right for use.'

'Look at us, we're like Tarzan and Jane,' Cissy said to Lillie as they scoured the field for nettles.

'Speak for yourself if you don't mind.'

'Watch your hands. There's an awful sting off those nettles if you touch them.'

'How are we going to drink the tea then?'

'I think the sting goes out of them when you boil them.'

'Well, bags I'm not the first to try it in case it doesn't.'

Dessie, Con, Willie and Mr O'Connor had circled the hangar looking for a way to get in. They tried the door, giving a few shoulder heaves, but there was no budge out of it. They stood back and looked up at the windows but they were too high. There was no way they could reach them.

'Maybe we could dig underneath.'

'With what, Con, our bare hands?'

'A human pyramid,' Mr O'Connor said. 'We form a human pyramid and get in through one of the windows. I've seen it done before. Mr Rourke, you and I are the heaviest, we shall kneel. Con can get on our backs and Willie can use the pyramid to climb up to the window.'

'Willie, get in through the window?'

'It's the only way. None of the rest of us would fit through.'

'Willie,' Dessie said, 'if we got you up there, do you think you could get in that window and open the door for us? Willie?' Willie stood looking blankly at Dessie as he tried to explain. 'We're going to get you up to the window, you get in and open the door for us.' Dessie repeated very slowly and deliberately: 'Do you understand, Willie? Jesus. He'll probably get in and forget what he's supposed to do. Well I suppose there's no harm in trying, we can only give it a go. Which one is the best to try, Mr O'Connor?'

'I don't think it matters, they're all the same.'

Dessie and Mr O'Connor knelt down under one of the windows.

'Now, Con,' Dessie said, 'you get up on our backs. That's it, easy does it. Ouch, bloody hell, Con, what have you got on the bottom of your shoes, running spikes? Not both feet on me, Con, get one leg over on to Mr O'Connor.' Con jiggled perilously on the two backs. 'Kneel down, Con, kneel down. Christ, he's choking me.' Con had put his arm around Dessie's neck to try and steady himself as his knees began to slide off. 'It's no use, Mr O'Connor.' Con had slipped off sideways, dragging Dessie down on to the grass on top of him, 'this will never work.'

'It will. I'm sure it will. Dessie, you keep your knees and arms as wide apart as you can. Con, you kneel on our backs keeping your hands flat, like so.' Mr O'Connor put his hands flat down on the ground to demonstrate what he wanted. 'It will help to keep you steady. Willie, use us as you would a ladder. One step, two steps and up. Now let's try again.'

'What if he can't get the window open when he gets up?'

'We'll soon sort that out.' Mr O'Connor walked around until he found a large stone. 'Stand back, everyone.' He threw the stone at the window, breaking the glass into smithereens. 'Put these on.' He took a pair of gloves out of his coat pocket. 'We don't want you cutting your hands. It's simple, Willie, when you get up put your hand through and open the window. If you are ready, gentlemen?'

The human pyramid was formed.

'Are you at the window yet, Willie?'

'No.'

'No?'

'I'm kneeling on Con but I still can't reach the window.'

'Stand up, man. You've got to stand up.'

'I can't. I'll break me neck.'

'I'll break your neck if you don't. You're killing us down here.'

Willie made a move to stand but as he tried to take his hands off Con's back to reach for the window the pyramid wobbled dangerously.

'I can't, I can't,' Willie cried out. 'Help me, I'm going to fall.' He dropped back down on to Con.

'Get down, Willie. We'll try another way.'

'I can't. I'm stuck. I can't move. Help! Help!'

'What'll we do now, Mr O'Connor?'

Willie's cries reached the group. Everyone stopped what they were doing and rushed in the direction of his voice. When they got to the hangar they gazed in amazement at the four men kneeling on each other's backs beside the wall.

'In the name of the Good Lord what are you lot at?' Cissy said. 'Do you want to have heart attacks playing circus at your age?'

'Get me down,' Willie cried.

The pensioners swarmed around the pyramid helping Willie and then Con to the ground leaving Dessie and Mr O'Connor kneeling side by side in the grass.

'What's the matter, Dessie, can you not get up?'

'Of course I can get up. I'm just having a rest.'

'I couldn't reach,' Willie said. 'They wanted me to get in the window but I couldn't stand up.'

'It's all right, Willie. Sure even if you did get in you wouldn't have been able to get down the other side, or did those two geniuses forget to think of that?'

'I think my spine is bent,' Dessie said as he and Mr O'Connor were hauled to their feet.

'There's more than your spine bent if you ask me. Putting poor Willie in through a window. Did you ever hear the like?'

'Never mind,' Miss Poole said, 'it was a very brave effort.'

'Oh I agree,' Mrs Walsh added, 'so brave.'

'Come back to the fire and have some hot tea.' The gentlemen were escorted like heroes back to the camp fire.

As they sipped at the nettle tea and ate the bits of leftover food, Mr Mooney cleared his throat a few times and then spoke up.

'If you still want to get into that building –' Mr Mooney hesitated when he got a glare from Dessie '– I was only going to say . . .'

'Go on, Mr Mooney, spit it out, don't mind that fella.'

'There's an old wooden ladder in the cottage.'

'Now he tells us. Why didn't you tell us that before?'

'You were halfway up your pyramid before we came back with the water. I didn't want to interrupt.'

Maureen, Deborah and Bill drove through the crossroads heading back to the main road.

'Keep alert, Deborah. Watch every side road.'

'I am, Maureen.'

'Bill, can you call up your friends on the CB and tell them to look out for the coach?' Maureen was fretting and fussing, she couldn't sit still; she kept jumping around in her seat afraid of missing some sign that the other bus had passed that way.

'We'll find them, Maureen. Between all of us, we'll find them.'

'You know I knew this trip would prove a disaster. Would anyone believe me? Why, only last night I said it to Deborah in the cocktail lounge . . .'

'Cocktail lounge, no less.' Bill raised an eyebrow at Deborah.

'. . . when we return I shall speak to the board. I shall insist that Doctor Kennedy gets his walking papers. The last thing the Cross and Passion needs is a doctor with liberal notions.'

'Surely it's not Doctor Kennedy's fault.'

'It was his responsibility to veto this trip.'

'Come, Maureen. You can't mean that.'

'I most certainly do, Deborah. They should never have been allowed to leave the nursing home.'

'It's not a prison, Maureen. You can't lock the old people in and turn a key.'

'I know what is best for them.'

'Do you, Maureen?'

'Routine. Routine is the key that holds things together. A well-regulated day is the secret of running a harmonious ship. My residents appreciate a well-run home and so do their relatives. If you could see the thank-you cards I receive from . . . what on earth is that?' Squad car four, with its siren blasting, had come racing up behind the lorry. As the car came alongside, Nigel waved at Bill indicating for him to pull over.

'Don't stop, Bill. We don't have time.'

'For goodness' sake, Maureen, we have to, look.'

Car four had stopped, sideways on, a little way ahead of them, blocking the road. Nigel grabbed a megaphone from the back seat and jumped out of the car.

'Get out of the lorry and put your hands above your heads.'

'Is he mad?'

'I repeat. Get out of the lorry and put your hands above your heads.'

'They're not proper policemen, they've no uniforms. Who are they? What do they want?'

'I'll find out what this is all about.' Maureen and Deborah watched from the lorry as Bill got out and started to walk towards the squad car.

'Stay where you are,' Nigel boomed at him through the megaphone. 'Stand up against the truck and place your hands behind your head.'

'Maybe they are customs men checking the truck. Deborah, what has Bill got in his truck?'

'I don't know, Maureen.'

'Drugs, it has to be drugs. You've taken up with a drug pusher.'

'I've taken up. That's a good one, you're the one who kept asking him to drive us around.'

'We are sitting on a cargo of contraband.'

'Stop being ridiculous. I'm sure Bill has nothing to do with drugs or anything else. It's probably nothing more than a routine check.'

'The rest of you,' Nigel boomed again, 'get down from that cab.'

'Let me do the talking, Deborah. We must get this over with as quickly as possible and continue with our search. As it happens I do have police connections. Once these men hear I am on terms with a chief inspector they will co-operate. I may even manage to commandeer their car.' Maureen and Deborah got down from the truck. 'What is this all about, officer? We are on a very important mission – every moment is crucial.'

'Up against the truck, ma'am.'

'I am not your ma'am, young man. I am Sister Maureen Carmody of the Cross and Passion and I demand to know what is going on.'

'Hands above your head.'

'This is absurd. Let me assure you we have nothing to do with this man. He merely picked us up.'

'Maureen!' Deborah was horrified. 'How could you? Why won't you tell us what this is all about, officer?'

'We have our orders, ma'am.'

'What orders? Is this some sort of prank?'

Nigel walked back to his partner in the car. 'What's taking the rest of them so long? We have this lot here but I don't know what we are supposed to do with them.'

'Should I get on to their Chief?'

'No, better not. We'll wait for the others. I just wish they'd hurry up.'

'Maybe we should frisk them.'

'Frisk them?'

'Well, it would look good. Better than leaving them standing there.' Cars one and two swung out suddenly from the crossroads and car three appeared driving from the opposite side. They screeched to a halt beside Bill's lorry and their occupants scrambled out.

'Let's have your names, then.' Jones took out his notebook. 'We'll start with you.'

'I have already told this person I am Sister Maureen Carmody, but who are you? Where is your identification? I demand to see identification.'

The eight rookies rooted in their inside pockets and produced their police wallets.

'We've got to play this by the book, lads,' Jones whispered. 'No mistakes or she might get off with a technicality.' Jones collected the wallets and read from each one of them. 'Special agents Jones, Byrne, McHale, Nolan, McGovern, Walsh, Duffy and Sinclair. We are placing you under arrest, Sister Carmody, on suspicion of being a member of a gang led by Lefty Morgan, who is attempting to interfere with a major witness, namely, Alex Smith. You have the right to remain silent, but anything you do say will be taken down and may be used in evidence . . .'

Maureen, Deborah and Bill stood flabbergasted as Jones finished his speech.

'Enough is enough,' Maureen recovered herself. 'This is definitely some sort of prank. I don't know what university you are from gentlemen, but let me tell you I do not hold with rag weeks or any of your other nonsensical games. Your superiors shall hear of this.'

'Book her, Sinclair. Get her back to Headquarters.'

'Take your hands off me. Deborah, do something, talk to them, tell them I don't know anything about Alex Smith.'

Deborah heard no more. Nigel led Maureen off and bundled her into the back of the squad car.

'Officer, you are making a terrible mistake. I give you my word Maureen is not who you think she is.'

'That's enough, unless you want to accompany her to the station.'

'I promise you, she doesn't know anything about a gang or a Lefty Morgan.'

'Give her a chance,' Bill said. 'What have you got to lose? You'll look pretty silly when you discover you have the wrong person, not to mention the publicity it will attract. Police harassment, nurse picked up on trumped-up charge, people won't like it.'

'Car one, come in car one.' Sergeant Kelly's voice came through the radio in all four cars.

'Car one here, Sarge.'

'Have you picked up the suspect?'

'Yes, Sarge, we have her in custody.'

'Have you questioned her?'

'Not yet, Sarge, we've only just got her.'

'Find out if and when the gang plan to snatch Smith from the bus.'

'Roger.'

'Smith,' Maureen said, 'we don't have a Smith.' She rolled down the window of the car. 'Deborah, tell them we don't have a Smith. Get the itinerary and the list of names and show it to them.'

Deborah raced to the lorry and grabbed up Maureen's papers. 'Look, officer, here's the list of everyone on the bus. There is no Smith.'

Jones took the papers and examined them carefully.

'There he is.' Jones pointed out the name on the list. 'Perrin. George Perrin alias Alex Smith.'

'Perrin!' Maureen cried out. 'I should have known! Let me out, let me out, officer, I must speak with the person in charge. I know now what this is all about.' Agent Duffy, who had been guarding Maureen in the squad car, opened the door and led Maureen across to Agent Jones.

'She has something she wants to tell you, Jones.'

'Officer. You must listen to me. I can explain how this has all come about.'

'I'll give you one minute,' said Jones. 'One minute to convince me or I'm taking you all in.'

Maureen spoke rapidly to Agent Jones. She told him of her role in the Cross and Passion, of Doctor Kennedy, of the outing, and of how she had been against it all along, and finally she told him about George Perrin – how he had been landed on them and how she, Sister Carmody, had known from the beginning there was something not right about his being there but had been outvoted by the Board. 'So you see, officer, I knew nothing about his dual role, none of us did, and while we are standing here talking, my poor residents are in danger, terrible danger. Iris Fox is the woman you want to question. She is the instigator of all this. I wouldn't be surprised if she were not the right-hand woman of your criminal, Lefty Morgan.'

'Car one to Headquarters. Come in, Headquarters.'

'Kelly here.'

'Let me talk to the Chief, Sergeant . . . Chief. I have questioned the suspect, sir, as you requested, and I have to tell you that I think she is innocent. In fact I would stake my reputation on it.'

'What reputation? You don't have a reputation.'

'Trust me, sir, I know what I am doing. Don't worry, we won't let her go. She'll stay in the squad car with us, they'll all stay.'

'Could you stand back, Iris? You're making me

nervous. I can't drive with all of you up here.' Stevie was feeling the pressure. Iris, crouched down behind his seat, kept a running commentary going in his ear. Helen and Mr Perrin, holding on to the rails at the disembarkation white line, blocked his view from the side mirror. The two pensioners, Mrs Clancy and Mr O'Neill, standing side by side in the luggage area underneath the ticket clicker, called out encouragement every time they imagined they saw something.

'You'll all have to sit down. There's no standing allowed in the aisle.'

They drove on, skirting a housing estate where a gauntlet of small children, on seeing the decorated bus, ran after it cheering and shouting.

'Will you sit down,' Stevie roared, 'all of you.' He was terrified in case any of the children darted out in front of him. 'That's better,' he said as his passengers meekly took their seats. 'At least now I can see out.' He checked his rear-view mirror, grateful that the children were receding into the background, when he saw a face peeping up from the back row. 'Christ. What now?'

'What is it, Stephen? What's the matter? Why are we stopping?'

'Look behind you, Iris. We have a stowaway.'

All eyes turned to the back of the bus as Janice emerged from her hiding place.

'Howya.' Janice smiled, 'I'm Janice.'

'It's the girl from the hotel,' Helen said. 'The one who was crying outside the door. How did you get here?'

'What are you doing on our bus?' Iris asked.

'I didn't mean any harm. I was only trying to get a lift back to town. My boyfriend ditched me and I'd no way of getting home so when the girl in the reception said you'd be going back I crept on when no one was looking.'

'You poor girl,' Mrs Clancy said. 'What a thing to happen.'

'You *are* going back to town?' Janice looked pleadingly from one face to the other. 'I won't be any trouble, I'll just sit here quietly in the back, I mean, you've loads of room so I won't be in your way or anything.' Janice started to cry. 'Don't leave me here – I have to get home.'

'It's OK, it's OK, Janice. We're not going to throw you off. It's only that . . . Iris, you explain.'

'What Helen is trying to say Janice is yes, we are going back to Dublin, but unfortunately not directly so it might be better for you if we let you off at the next village. I'm sure you'll find transport back from there, there's bound to be a bus or something.'

'There isn't. The girl in the hotel told me everything was gone. I don't mind if you're not going directly. It doesn't matter to me how long it takes once I know I'm getting home. Please. I'll pay my fare.'

'It's not a question of fare, Janice.'

'For God's sake, Iris. Janice. Here's the situation. We have to find a group of pensioners who somehow managed to get on the wrong bus back in Arklow. We're out here looking for them, we can't go back without them.'

'A group of pensioners?' Janice repeated slowly. Janice started to think about Chalkey, and about

Chalkey's granddad, and about Chalkey's granddad's pills and a funny feeling she couldn't explain came over her.

'Yes, Janice. Have you seen them? Did you see them in Arklow?'

'No.' Janice thought it would be better not to mention anything, not yet, anyway.

'Iris, we're wasting time,' Stevie said. 'The longer we delay the less chance we have of finding the other bus.'

'Yes, Iris. Let's get going.'

'Come and sit with me, dear.' Mrs Clancy patted the seat beside her. 'We can have a little chat.' Janice slid into the seat beside Mrs Clancy, glad that the focus had been taken off her. 'I have a granddaughter about your age. She's at college – perhaps you know her?'

'I never went to college, I'm training to be a hair-dresser.'

'How nice, dear. I used to love going to the hairdresser's but it's a long time now since I've been to one. Sister Carmody doesn't like us to leave the building. She did promise once she'd get a hairdresser to come in . . .' Mrs Clancy stopped mid-sentence.

'And did she?' Janice asked.

'Did she what, dear?'

'Never mind, it doesn't matter. I want to ask you, Mrs, Mrs . . .'

'Clancy, dear, I'm Mrs Clancy.'

'I wanted to ask you, Mrs Clancy, did you have a Mr Deveroux on your bus?'

'I don't think so, dear. There's no Mr Deveroux in

our home, but there were other ladies and gentlemen on the tour, perhaps he is one of them. Iris would know, she knows all the names.'

'Which way now, Iris?' The bus had reached a Y-junction and Stevie was unsure which road to take.

'Give me your map. If we take this left fork and continue on that road we should eventually link back up with the main road. What do you think, Mr Perrin, does that seem the best plan?'

'I don't see any alternative, Iris. That way goes to Aughrim via Tinahely, the other road seems to peter out.'

'If we don't see them by the time we get to Tinahely I don't know what we'll do.'

'Don't forget, Iris, the lorry is looking as well – we have all the main routes covered.'

'Let's contact the lorry. They might have some news. Mr Perrin, will you ring the number they gave us?'

Mr Perrin tried his phone. He'd given up worrying about the line being traceable. He had already decided that if things went on much longer, and there was still no sign of the pensioners, he would call Meyers himself and elicit his help. It meant blowing his cover, he knew that, but there was nothing else for it.

'I got Bill Thomas's office, Iris, but they say there is no reply from the truck. They're not responding at all.'

'That's all we need, Mr Perrin. Ask them to keep trying.'

'Maybe it's a good sign, Iris. Maybe they've left the

lorry because they're with the others.' Helen tried her best to sound convincing.

'Nice try, Helen. I wish I could believe it.'

Janice slipped up to the front and sat beside Helen. She had turned over in her mind her day out with Chalkey again and again and the more she thought about it, about Chalkey's behaviour and his phone calls and his story about his granddad, the more she felt there was a connection between him and the missing people. She would have to find out first if there really was a Mr Deveroux on the bus. If there wasn't then she'd know, she'd know for sure.

'Was one of your old people called Mr Deveroux?' she asked Helen.

'I don't know, Janice. I don't think so. Why do you ask?'

'Oh no reason, I think I know one of the old fellas on the trip, that's all.'

'I'll ask Iris for you.'

'No, don't ask her,' Janice said quickly. 'I mean, don't bother her, she's enough on her plate. Could you find out for me on the quiet like?'

'You're being very mysterious, Janice. Is he a relation?'

'You could say that he might have been.'

Helen got the seating plan from Iris's clipboard.

'No, Janice, there's no Deveroux here.'

'I had a feeling there wouldn't be. Listen. I have to talk to you.'

Janice poured out all the details of her outing with Chalkey. How they stopped first at the roundabout where they saw the police cars, then Chalkey's funny behaviour in Ashford – going in and out of the toilet all the time and watching what they thought were Jehovah's Witnesses, and doing a runner out of the place. She told her about Avoca and Arklow . . .

'We were in all those places, Janice,' Helen said in surprise.

. . . and about going looking for his granddad and how he picked a row with her. Janice stopped to get her breath. 'And I don't know how.' Janice finished her story. 'But I think it's all connected up with your missing old people.'

'My goodness, Janice. I don't know what to think. We'll have to tell the others. There are too many coincidences for it not to be connected. Maybe they can make some sense out of it. Stephen, pull up.'

'Why, Helen?' Iris said. 'We can't waste any more time.'

'Pull up, Stephen. Iris, Mr Perrin, all of you. You have to hear what Janice has to say.'

Janice repeated her story exactly as she'd told Helen. When she'd finished, Mr Perrin asked a question.

'Janice. Was your boyfriend, Chalkey, ever involved in a gang?'

'He was. Well, he used to be, but he gave all that up for me. He swore he was going straight and he was getting a proper job so we could save up and get married.'

'Think hard, Janice. Did he ever mention the name of the leader of this gang?'

'Everybody knows that gangster's name – it's Lefty Morgan.'

Mr Perrin slumped in his seat.

'Mr Perrin! What's the matter? Are you all right? Do you know this man?'

'I know him, Iris. I know him very well indeed. I'm afraid I have some explaining of my own to do.'

Chapter Nineteen

'My name, my real name, is Alex Smith. George Perrin is the name I adopted when I went into hiding. Poor old George, if he only knew . . . I work for a shipping company based on the North Quay docks called Transo Shipping. About seven months ago, November to be exact, I was working late, catching up with some paperwork. I was alone, the rest of the staff had gone. When I finished, I switched off the light in my office and took a last look out of the window. It was a clear night and I stood there admiring the view – the harbour lights shining on the berthed ships, the cranes, the ropes, all the paraphernalia of a busy quayside. It was so still, it looked like a beautiful painting. I was about to leave when I saw some activity below me. A car drove up to one of the ships' gangways and a group of men got out. The ship had arrived that day from Amsterdam. Its cargo had been unloaded so I knew there was only a skeleton crew left on board. A member of the crew came down the gangway carrying a bag. He placed this on the bonnet of the car and opened it. After a few minutes one of the other men opened the boot of the car and took out a suitcase. I couldn't hear what they were saying but it was obvious some deal was going down. They switched the bag for the suitcase and the crew member returned to the ship. It was then that I saw a man, a man whom I discovered later was the criminal, Lefty Morgan, as clear as daylight, picked out by the headlights. A second car appeared, a type of jeep; the bag was put into that and driven off. I was in a panic at that point, torn between watching what was going on and phoning the police, terrified they might look up at the window and see me. As soon as the coast was clear, when both cars were out of sight, I phoned the police and told them what I had seen. They picked up the jeep as it was leaving the port area and recovered about five-hundred thousand pounds' worth of drugs. They stopped the other car, but there was nothing to connect them with the deal, so they had to let it go. That's where I come in. I can identify Lefty Morgan. I can place him at the scene. I recognized him immediately from the photographs the police showed me. I was persuaded by the Chief Inspector to give evidence – he told me they had been after Lefty Morgan for a very long time and this was the first real chance they had to nail him. I have to tell you there have been many many times since then when I wished I had said no, but when the Chief pointed out to me the terrible destruction these drugs cause, I felt I had no choice. I was placed in the Cross and Passion Nursing Home under my alias and was supposed to stay underground until the trial. Now you know the whole story. You know I am responsible for all this trouble. I should never have come on the outing. I am so sorry.'

'Why weren't the police watching you? I thought you would be kept under strict security.'

'That was where we got too clever. Safe houses can become known to the gangs. There's always someone who can be bribed. We thought it was the perfect solution. And it was, until today. I have no idea how the gang found out about our little outing and, because they found out, I've involved all of you in it. The only thing I can possibly do now is refuse to testify.'

'He's right,' Janice said. 'Lefty Morgan is evil, he'll stop at nothing to prevent you testifying.'

'What can I say? How can I make this up to you? Not only have I spoiled your outing, but I've put everyone in danger. I must try to contact the gang and persuade them to take me and release the pensioners. It's the only way.'

'We can't let you do that, Mr Perrin, Alex, they might kill you.'

'They will kill us all if I don't.'

'There must be something we can do,' Helen said, glancing round the bus for inspiration. 'Think, everyone, think.'

'I'll get on to Chief Meyers, see what help he can give us.'

'It'll have to be quick, Mr Perrin,' Stevie said. 'The gang can't be very far behind us. Once they discover none of the pensioners fit the bill they'll come after you again.'

'My poor pensioners,' Iris cried. 'What will they do to them?'

'Don't worry, Iris. We'll get them back safe and sound.'

'We can't stay here,' Helen said, 'we're sitting targets. Stevie, we passed a farm a few minutes ago. Why don't we go back and try and hide the bus in there? It would give us a bit of time while we wait for Mr Perrin's chief to get here.'

'I don't see how you can hide a bus, Helen.'

'We have to try, Iris, unless you have a better suggestion.'

'It's a good idea,' Stevie said. 'It's the only idea we have so we might as well try it.' Stevie reversed into a laneway, swung his bus around, and then headed back the way they had come.

'Well, everybody,' Mr Perrin had finished his phone call. 'I've spoken to a Chief Meyers who has taken over the case. He assured me he already has four cars on the road looking for us, and the good thing is, they are already in the area. If we can stall the gang, keep ourselves out of sight until the police get here, we might stand a chance.'

'We might stand a chance but what about my pensioners?'

'They won't harm them, Iris, I am sure of that. It would cause too much of a furore, bring too much attention on themselves.'

'Let's get the decorations down. We won't stand out so much if we take them down. Come on everyone.' Helen started tearing down the bunting. 'Give me a hand with this, Janice, we'll try to yank it through the window.'

'Try to be careful, Helen,' Iris said. 'I was hoping to be able to use that banner again next year.'

'Smasher, have we got any idea what we're gonna do? Have we got a plan?'

'Yea, we have a plan. Get Smith and get the hell away, that's what we do.'

'Do you think we might look a bit conspicuous going back into the town?'

'What do you mean "conspicuous"?'

'Look at us.' The gang were back on the road to Arklow. 'We are going at hearse pace. If we keep on like this we could be pulled for kerb crawling.'

'That's a good one, Kev,' Brains said, 'I wish I'd thought of it, only thing is there ain't no kerb, we haven't seen a kerb for ages.'

'Will you two shut the bleeding hell up? I'm trying to think. Get Chalkey back on the blower. He found Smith once – he can find him again. Tell him it came directly from Lefty. That'll fix him in case he tries to wriggle out of it.'

Moments later Chalkey was on the other end of the line.

'Chalkey, old flower, guess who?'

'What do you want?'

'Smith is what we want.'

'Oh no, no you don't. I already found him. If you lost him that's your problem.'

'How's your mot, Chalkey? Found her yet?'

'Leave Janice out of this.'

'But she's not out of it, is she Chalkey? Lefty wants

Smith. You know what he's like if he don't get what he wants. You still there, Chalkey?'

'Yeah. I'm still here.'

'Attaboy. We're coming back in to town. Have him fingered.'

'Shit,' Chalkey said, banging the handlebars on the bike. He knew he was in a fix. That was no idle threat. He would have to find that bleeding Smith again or they'd do Janice. He cursed himself for getting involved. 'Shit, shit and more shit.' Chalkey looked behind him to the pillion seat. He could almost hear Janice say, 'language, Chalkey,' in that voice of hers. Chalkey started thinking about Janice. She wasn't so bad a mot to have, he could get used to her. 'Cop yourself on, Chalkey, don't go getting soft, or before you know it you'll find yourself in a Corpo flat with three squalling brats.' Chalkey swore again. He'd have to find Smith for Lefty. Lefty was the man, the numero uno. The gang would do anything for Lefty, no questions asked. He knew he couldn't let them hurt Janice.

Chalkey had been sitting on his bike trying to figure out where Janice had got to when he got the call. He had tried the bus and train stations, scooted up and down a few of the streets, but there was no sign of her. There was no sign of the group on the tour either. Where was he going to start this time? 'Stupid bleeders, letting Smith fall through their fingers,' he muttered to himself as he went back in to Cassidy's.

'Hello. Aren't you the young man who was looking for his granddad?'

'Yeah, that's me,' Chalkey said, relieved. He had been standing at the reception desk wondering what the hell he was going to say this time, but the girl spoke to him first.

'You would not believe the comings and goings we've had with that group. The manager was only saying these tours were hardly worth the trouble considering the discount we give.'

'Yeah, right miss.'

'It doesn't look good for our business when an ambulance pulls up outside your premises. Did it come for your granddad?'

'No, he's fine. I'm still looking for him though.'

The receptionist took a minute for this to sink in. 'How do you know he wasn't in it?'

'I rang through to the hospital. It wasn't him.' Chalkey had to think fast. 'It was some other geezer.'

'That's good.'

'So where did they go?'

'Who go?'

'The blee . . . the rest of them.'

'That's the funny thing – they came in one bus and it took two buses to take them home. That's our manager's point. I mean to say, if they can afford two buses you wouldn't think their tour operator would haggle so much about the price of our Saturday special, would you?'

'The buses, miss, where did they go?'

'Out the Aughrim road. Probably soft-soaped another establishment to give them a cheap evening tea. I hope you find him,' the receptionist called out after Chalkey as he made a beeline for the exit.

*

'Smasher. It's Chalkey. They took the Aughrim road out of town. I'm going to head out that way and see if I can spot anything.'

'OK, we're on it. You better be sure, Chalkey.'

'That's what they told me in the hotel. Where are you?'

'We're heading right their way. Good work, Chalkey. Lefty will be proud of you. Right lads, lady luck is with us. The stupid bus is coming right to us. All we have to do is wait.'

'Cissy, don't you know the wardrobe in my house?'

'Intimately, Lillie.'

'There is no need for that, Cissy.'

'Well, ask yourself. How would I know the wardrobe in your house?'

'There's a wardrobe in my bedroom and on the top of it is a brown valise suitcase.'

'Why are you telling me this?'

'It's got my papers in it, that's why. If we don't get out of this I want someone to know.'

'Know what, Lillie? What are you talking about?'

'The funeral arrangements. I have everything written down, the hymns and all. There's a policy in the case in a brown envelope, you'll see it as soon as you open it, it's a Credit Union policy I've been paying into for years that'll cover all the expenses and after me beneficiaries get what's coming to them, there's a few bob put aside separately for a party.'

'Who'd be at the party? Everyone you know is here.'

'Look around you. There's nothing for miles. Hypochondria is going to set in and we'll all die of exposure.'

'Will you stop that, Lillie? You're only upsetting yourself with that kind of talk.'

The pensioners were sitting round the fire. They were sipping the nettle tea and swopping stories. Dessie had tried the hangar – the ladder had been carried up from the old cottage and he had managed to get a look in – but there was nothing in there that could help them. All he could see was a few tables and chairs, a pile of green camouflage nets and some rusting machine parts, nothing that was worth risking life and limb getting in for. They'd laughed about it, teasing Dessie and making jokes about what he could do with his camouflage nets. They started a sing-song which was abruptly halted when Lillie said she could feel a drop of rain.

'We better get back on the bus,' Cissy said. 'Come on, everyone, let's get back on the bus in case the ground gets damp.'

'It'll be colder on the bus.'

'That may be so, Olive, but at least you won't get piles,' Cissy said, making an effort to raise a smile. 'Collect up all your stuff everyone.'

The pensioners picked up their belongings and got back on the bus and Cissy had a quiet word with Dessie. 'We have to try and do something, Dessie, we can't just sit here. Is there no way we can start the engine?'

'I don't know anything about buses.'

'You've had a car. How different can it be? At least

try, Dessie. It'll make us all feel better if something is being tried.'

Dessie got out and opened the bonnet of the bus.

'What do you think, Dessie?'

'I'm freezing me balls off for nothing in this bit of drizzle, Cissy, that's what I think.'

'Fiddle with something, can't you? See if anything moves.'

'I know what I'll fiddle with in a minute,' Dessie muttered under his breath. 'Oh, Miss Poole, I didn't see you there. I'm having a look . . .'

'May I?'

'Be my guest.' Dessie stood back to let Miss Poole in beside him. 'Do you know anything about buses, Miss Poole?'

'I'm afraid not, Mr Rourke. Tractors were more my field.' Miss Poole and Dessie stood side by side peering in at the engine. 'I wonder . . . Mr Rourke, can you trace this wire, see if it goes in towards the dashboard?'

'No. She goes the other way.'

'Try this one.' Miss Poole handed him another wire.

'Do you know where you're taking them wires out of?'

'Don't worry, Mr Rourke, I think I know what I am doing.'

'By jeepers, this one does, it goes right up.'

'Good. Keep your hand on it.' Miss Poole took the other end of the wire and stretched it across to the battery. 'I'm going to see if we can connect this up, Mr Rourke. The trouble is I don't know if it's the positive one or the negative.'

'We'll soon find out.'

'What's happening, Dessie?' Cissy cried from the bus.

'I don't know. Miss Poole has half the wiring out, I only hope she doesn't fry herself.'

Miss Poole touched some wires together and sparks began to fly.

'Christ.' Dessie jumped. 'Have you got it, Miss Poole?'

'I may have. Mr Rourke, would you get on the bus and put your foot on the accelerator? When you get my signal, press down on it and keep it pressed until you hear the engine begin to fire.' Miss Poole bent over the engine again as Dessie got into the driver's seat. 'On my signal,' she called. 'Now, Mr Rourke, now.'

The engine spluttered a bit, as if doing its best, but then it died. Dessie pressed the accelerator as hard as he could and then began pumping at the pedal.

'Don't pump, Mr Rourke. Don't pump, you might flood her.'

'What is she saying, Cissy? I can't hear her.'

'Get your foot off, Dessie.' Cissy relayed the message, having stationed herself at the door to watch the proceedings. 'She says you'll flood her.'

'Don't worry, Mr Rourke, I think I know what I was doing wrong. We'll have another go. This time, if we get a fire, ease the pedal, just barely tip it. If it catches then pump like mad and whatever you do don't let it cut out.'

The pensioners craned to watch as Miss Poole disappeared under the bonnet again. Dessie sat rigid in his seat, his foot poised above the accelerator, terrified of making a mistake.

'Cross your fingers.'

'I've everything crossed already,' Lillie said.

They heard the same spluttering as before but this time the splutter seemed to get stronger.

'Now Mr Rourke, press gently. Gently does it, that's it. Now, pump!' Miss Poole roared her command. '*Pump*!'

Dessie walloped his foot up and down as the engine roared into action.

'Hooray, she's done it. She's hot-wired the bus.'

Flushed and blackened, Miss Poole stepped on the bus to an outburst of clapping and cheering.

'You've done it, Miss Poole, you're a marvel.'

'What about me?' said Dessie. 'The sweat's pouring off me, I'm losing stones here.'

'What about you, Dessie? Don't worry, I'm only joking, you were great. Three cheers for Miss Poole and Dessie. Hip, hip, hooray.'

'We must keep the engine idling, I don't know if I could do it again.'

'Don't worry, Miss Poole, I'm not taking my foot off this pedal for all the tea in China.'

'Can we go home now?' Willie asked.

'We don't have anyone to drive the bus, Willie.'

'Why can't she do it?' Willie pointed to Miss Poole. 'She's done everything else.'

'I am afraid I couldn't. I've never driven a bus. I could get you all killed.'

'Dessie, what about you? Could you do it?'

'Through that forest road? I don't think so. I mean

I'd be willing to give it a try but if we went off the road we'd be worse off than ever. I don't think any of us can do it.'

'In my army days I drove the supply truck,' Mr O'Connor said. 'I am sure the principle is the same. I could perhaps give you some guidance.'

'That would take too long, Mr O'Connor. We'd be out of petrol before I learned the ropes. Why can't you do it?'

'I would, Mr Rourke, but the problem is I don't see very well any more. My eyesight is not what it used to be.'

'We could guide *you*, Mr O'Connor. There's enough of us here to steer you, and once we get out on to the main road we can get help. Could you do it, Mr O'Connor? If we were your eyes, could you do it?'

'You don't think it would be too risky?'

'What have we got to lose? Even if we end up stuck on the forest road we won't be any worse off than we are now. I say we should give it a shot.'

'I don't know if this is such a—'

'Let the man in there, Dessie,' Cissy said, leading a reluctant Mr O'Connor to Stevie's seat. 'Let him get the feel of the wheel. Now. Who has the best eyesight?' Handbags and pockets were raided as everyone dived for their glasses. 'Maybe I'd better rephrase that. Who can see further than their hand in front of them? Right, that's that then. Miss Poole, you come up here. Stand behind Mr O'Connor and watch for his right. Dessie, you stand on his left. The rest of you, station yourselves at the windows and stick your heads out. If anyone spots an obstacle, call out. I'll take Iris's place here with the intercom. Are you ready, Mr O'Connor?'

'I don't think I will ever be ready.'

'Nonsense, you'll be fine. Hold on, everyone, hold on to the rails in case we have any jolting.'

'Drive over to the tarmac, Mr O'Connor, it will make it easier to turn.'

'Where is it, Miss Poole?'

'Drive straight ahead, Mr O'Connor, I'll tell you when you can turn.' The bus jerked forward. 'Slightly to your left, Mr O'Connor, that's it, a bit more, a bit more. Now, swing right, swing, swing, a big circle, all the way round.'

'I can't see a thing.'

'Don't worry, just keep swinging, we're nearly there. Start to straighten out, easy easy, straighten, straighten. Mr O'Rourke?'

'All clear this side.'

'Forward, Mr O'Connor, forward. Once we get through those gateposts we'll be on the forest road. Steady now, the gateposts are directly in front of you. That's it. Steady, steady, we're through.'

'Thank God for that.'

'Bravo, well held, Mr O'Connor. It's plain sailing after this.'

'I wish I had your confidence, Miss Poole.'

'We're going past the cottage,' Dessie said. 'It's on your right, Mr O'C.'

'Goodbye, lonely old cottage,' Olive cried. 'We won't ever see you again, we're going home.'

The bus inched on as Dessie and Miss Poole steered Mr O'Connor through the dark forest road. The tension was broken by a scream coming from halfway down the bus.'

'Ohhh,' Lillie shouted, 'damn it.'

'What's the matter, Lillie?'

'A big branch is after smacking back and taking the eye out of me.'

'Well, don't stick your head out so far.'

Detective Chief Superintendent Meyers strode into the operations room and addressed his sergeant.

'Kelly, get yourself a replacement on the desk, we are going out.'

'But, chief—'

'No buts, Kelly. Get on to your team in the field, tell them to stand by until we arrive.'

'But, Chief—'

'Get on to them, I want them standing by. We are taking over personally. What those rookies need is leadership – leadership and co-ordination. We shall take the reins and steer this operation through ourselves.'

'Don't you think sir, that by the time we get there . . .?'

'When I was a rookie, Kelly, there were leaders and there were learners. You looked up to your leaders, were guided by them, your commanding officer was your king and you were the foot soldiers. Instinct and intuition doesn't grow on trees, it has to be nurtured, and we, Kelly, are the nurturers. We need to instil in our men the need for discipline and co-operation, and above all—'

'Chief?'

'What is it now, Kelly?'

'I have Jones on the line, what do I tell them?'

'I just told you what to tell them. They are to stand by.'

'Are you there, car one?'

'We're here, Sarge.'

'I have been instructed to tell you to stand by.'

'But Sarge, what about Alex Smith? He's still on the bus. We can't—'

'Those are Chief Meyers's specific orders. He is leaving immediately and will join you ASAP.'

'That's crazy, sarge. It'll take him ages to reach us.'

'What's the problem, Kelly?'

'Officer Jones is afraid the delay could have consequences, sir.'

'Give that to me.' Meyer snatched the phone from Sergeant Kelly. 'Jones, this is your Chief. Your orders are to stand by. Do nothing until we arrive. Do I make myself clear?'

'Yes, Chief, but—'

'Are you questioning my orders, Jones?'

'No, sir.'

'Find yourselves a strategic position in which to stand by. Sergeant Kelly and I shall communicate with you when we arrive in the area. Maintain radio silence until then, none of Morgan's gang must know the direction of my approach. We have heard from Smith. He is still at liberty and I intend to keep him that way.'

'Did you all hear that?'

'Roger, car one.'

'Switch off your radios and get out of the cars. We

need to have a confab.' The cars pulled over to the side of the road and lined up behind Jones.

'Golly,' Nigel said. 'The Chief is coming himself? Isn't that a bit unusual?'

'It's a bummer, it means we have to sit here twiddling our fingers while the target gets further and further away.'

'Why, Jones, why is the Chief coming himself?'

'How do I know?'

'If the gang are not supposed to see us, where are we going to find a strategic place to wait?'

'The whole thing is stupid. We were supposed to escort Smith back to town.'

'What about our prisoners?' The eight rookies turned to look at Maureen, Deborah and Bill who were in the back seat of car four. 'What do we do with them?'

'We can't let them go. They'll have to stand by with us.'

'This is intolerable,' Maureen said. 'Why are they staring at us like that? I can't make out a word they are saying. Deborah, can you hear them? Open the window a bit.'

'We better not, Maureen.'

'What did that radio message mean? What's stand by?'

'I think, Maureen, they have to wait for reinforcements.'

'Reinforcements? There are eight of them. How many more can they want? This is wasting valuable time.' Maureen stretched over to the front of the car and reached for the horn. 'I won't have this.' *Beep, beep, beeeep, beep, beep, beeeeep*. Maureen kept up the racket as the rookies ran to the car to stop her.

'Stop that. Get your hand off the horn.'

'I demand to know what is going on. Why are we sitting here? Why aren't we following my residents?'

'Madam, if you don't take your hand off that horn I shall be forced to have you cuffed.'

'Tell me what is going on.'

'Back in your seat, madam.' Jones grabbed hold of Maureen's arm as she stretched forward again and tried to reach the wheel. 'Oh no you don't! Nigel, cuff her. Make sure she doesn't reach that horn again.'

Nigel opened the passenger door, took hold of Maureen's wrists and slapped handcuffs on her.

'Unhand me. Don't you dare! Deborah, do something.'

'Now, madam, back in your seat.' Nigel took Maureen's shoulder and pushed her back beside Deborah.

'You can't do this to me.'

'We just did. Now sit down and shut up.' He slammed the car door.

'That damn horn has probably attracted attention,' Jones said. 'We better get out of here.'

'Where to?'

'We'll go back to Arklow. We can sit somewhere and wait for the Chief.'

'What about our cover?

'Same as before.'

'But the prisoners . . . how do we . . ..?'

'Converts. To your cars, men. Leave two-minute

intervals and then each of you make your way back to Arklow. Stop at the first hotel or coffee shop you come to. We will liaise there and wait for instructions from Chief Meyers.'

'What did I say to you?' Nigel whispered to his partner. 'I knew we'd be in for more coffee somewhere along the line. Did you see me with those cuffs? Honestly, I never thought I'd be able to do it. My very first bust – I wish someone had had a camera.'

'Keep that woman cuffed, Nigel. When we get into town you can disguise them, throw a scarf or something over them, but don't take them off.'

'What about the other two? Will I cuff them as well?'

'No. I don't think they'll be any trouble. Tell them if they don't co-operate they'll be looking at ten years for obstruction, that'll keep them quiet.'

'Has it come to this?' Maureen said, lifting her arms out and rattling her cuffs. 'Handcuffed in a police car. I will never be able to hold my head up in public again.'

'It's all a ghastly mistake, Maureen. I am sure as soon as the head man comes along it will be straightened out, won't it, Bill?'

'I don't know what to say. This whole thing is a farce. I mean they are supposed to be chasing a dangerous criminal gang and what do they do? Arrest us.'

'Can't you do something? Anything?'

'Like what? If we try anything we'll end up handcuffed like Maureen.'

'Handcuffed like Maureen,' Maureen wailed, sinking

her head into her cuffed hands. 'The humiliation of it.'

'It's all right, Maureen. It won't be for long.'

'That is no consolation, Deborah. Any time is too long to be . . . I can hardly bring myself to say it . . . to be chained like this.'

'They're coming back. Don't say anything. We'll wait for the first chance we get and contact the police.'

'They are the police.'

'I mean the local uniform police, not these Keystone Cops trainees. It's obvious that they don't know what they are doing. What I don't understand is if this witness is so important how could they send such idiots to track him down?'

'Maybe, Bill, they're decoys for the real police.'

'Decoys. Some decoys. They're about as subtle as a ton of bricks. The gangsters must be laughing their heads off.'

'Where are you taking us now?' Maureen asked Nigel as he and his partner got into the car.

'We are going to Arklow.'

'But that's going backwards – we've already been in Arklow. My residents are up ahead somewhere. We must go on. I insist that we go on.'

'Lady, you are not in a position to insist anything. I suggest you keep quiet or you'll find yourself having your holidays in the Joy.' Nigel nudged his partner and spoke to him out of the side of his mouth. 'I'm getting really good at this tough stuff, aren't I?'

Sergeant Kelly and Chief Meyers left Headquarters and headed south. The sergeant drove in silence, trying to figure out why Meyers had taken this course of action. It wasn't like him. He knew from sources that Meyers never went into the field, yet this was the second time he had left Headquarters to intervene personally. Unprecedented for Meyers. Other Detective Inspectors were more actively involved, but not him. He preferred to sit at his desk and then bask in the limelight and get the glory when culprits were brought in. He has something up his sleeve, Sergeant Kelly thought to himself, something to play for. Meyers was well up when it came to the inner workings of the police hierarchy.

'Nothing to say, Kelly?'

'Concentrating on the road, sir.'

'It feels good to think that Morgan is within our grasp.'

'Morgan is fly, sir. He's cute as a fox. I don't think we should count our chickens, as they say.'

'We'll have him, Kelly, don't you worry. When we get Smith back we'll have him right where we want him. And this time, Kelly, Smith stays under lock and key. I want twenty-four hour security.'

'He's not going to like that, sir.

'He can like it or lump it, Kelly. I want him where I can see him. It won't be long before the trial. He can have his freedom after that.'

'I doubt that, sir.'

'What do you mean?'

'I doubt he'll have his freedom. Morgan's gang will be out to get him. If Morgan gets sent down for years, they'll want revenge.'

'Are you forgetting, Kelly, that we have gang

members being held by the local force slap bang in the middle of Ashford? There won't be any of them left on the outside when I get finished with them.'

'As you say, sir.'

'Absolutely as I say, Kelly.' Both men lapsed into silence. 'Kelly, get Commander Reinhart on the line. I want to brief him.'

'Do you think that's wise, sir? There are no charges preferred yet, no paperwork done.'

'Of course I think it's wise. I wouldn't call him up on a Saturday unless I was utterly confident of success. He is probably out playing golf. Have him paged.'

'Commander. Meyers here . . . and a good day to you too, sir . . . yes, Commander, and it's going to be an even better day in a very short time. We are on the brink of success with Morgan's gang. Yes, Commander . . . absolutely sure, sir . . . yes, Commander . . .'

'Three bags full, Commander,' Sergeant Kelly hissed to himself. 'So that's his game. That's what he's playing for. Full credit and more promotion. I should have known.'

Chapter Twenty

The City Swift, carrying Iris, Stevie, Helen, Mr Perrin, Mr O'Neill, Mrs Clancy and Janice, hurtled into the hay barn sending up clouds of straw and dust in its wake. Stevie stopped dead in front of a 20-foot-high wall of baled hay.

'We're in. Thank God for that. They'll never find us here.'

'They may not,' Helen said, glancing out the back window of the bus, 'but someone else has. Don't look now but there's a very angry farmer, with a shotgun in his hand heading this way.'

'Leave this to me,' Iris said. 'I'll go and talk to him. I have a way with country folk. Hello,' she sang out as she stepped off the bus. 'How nice to meet you and what a lovely day.'

Bang. Bang. The air was shattered as Henry Pilkinton, the owner of the barn, raced across his yard and fired two shots over Iris's head.

'Help! Help! I'm being shot,' Iris screamed. 'He's trying to kill me.' She fell backwards into the bus.

'Oh my God, Iris. Are you all right?' Helen knelt over Iris who had fainted to the ground at her feet. 'Iris, speak to me. Speak to me, Iris.'

'What happened?' The others crowded forwards. 'What was that?'

'Someone shot Iris.'

'Is she all right?'

'Stand back, give her some air.'

'Oh dear, is he part of the gang?' Mrs Clancy asked. 'Is he going to shoot all of us?'

'No he is not, Mrs Clancy,' Janice said, patting her hand. 'I've seen the likes of him before. Don't you worry, he's just a big bully with a gun. I'll handle him, I'm not having him firing at us like that. Let me off. Don't you fire that thing at me,' she shouted out to Henry, 'or you'll be sorry.'

'Janice, don't. Come back.'

'Mrs,' Janice called out to the farmer's wife who had run from her kitchen when she heard the noise. 'Mrs, I'm coming out. Get that gun off your man before he kills someone.' Janice sidled past Iris's inert body and got off the bus.

'Iris. Can you hear me?' Helen knelt over Iris's prostrate body. 'Speak to me, Iris.'

'Pour some water on her.'

'I haven't got any water. Look, she's coming round.'

'Am I hurt? Am I alive? Where am I?' Iris opened her eyes. 'Would you stop slapping my face like that, Helen?'

'We thought you were dead. Here, let me help you up.'

'No, don't move me. Let me lie here a minute, I feel all dizzy.'

'You've had a nasty shock, Iris, we all have.'

'Henry. It's a girl.'

'I'm not blind, woman, I can see it's a girl. Don't come any closer, Miss. What do you want? Why are you in my hay barn?'

'Why are you shooting at us? Stop pointing that thing at me, we just want to talk to you.'

'Henry. Give me the gun. The gun, Henry.'

'Get off. Get off all of you and stand where I can see you.' The passengers got off the bus and lined up in front of Henry Pilkinton. 'You're not all off.' He waved his shotgun towards the bus.

'Iris,' Mr Perrin called back to her, 'Iris, you must get off, this gentleman wants us all off.'

'No way, Mr Perrin. I am staying exactly where I am.'

'Musha, the poor girl is frightened out of her wits,' Mary Pilkinton said. 'Would you put that thing down like I told you, Henry?'

'I know this must seem very strange to you,' Mr Perrin said, 'but I can explain. We are in a very difficult situation. We need your help. If we could go somewhere and talk . . .?'

'Of course you can. Come in to the kitchen, I'll make us all a nice cup of tea and—'

'Mary.'

'You've done enough damage for one day, Henry Pilkinton, can't you see these nice people are in trouble?'

'This is very kind of you, Mrs, Mrs . . .?'

'I'm Mary Pilkinton and this is my husband, Henry. Come on now, I'll put the kettle on. Don't mind about him.' The passengers were looking warily at Henry Pilkinton and his gun. 'He takes a bit of time to get to know people.'

'I'm not surprised,' Helen whispered to George Perrin, 'if he shoots first and gets to know them afterwards.'

'Will you get your friend off the bus? Henry will apologize to her, won't you Henry? He didn't mean any harm. We are plagued here with young lads coming out messing about, and not just the village lads. We're so near the city we get hordes of them out on their bikes looking for mischief. They have Henry's heart scalded with the trouble they cause.'

'Don't tell me about lads on bikes,' Janice said, 'I know all about it.'

'Iris.' Helen went back to the bus for her. 'Iris. Get up off the floor, we're going in for tea.'

'Going in for tea!' Iris snorted. 'Going in for tea! No one seems to care that I've been shot. I could be dead, and now I'm expected to jump up, as if nothing had happened and go in for tea.'

'Stop being so dramatic.'

'Dramatic? Is that what you call it?'

'Think of your dad, Iris. He'd be so proud you were in the front line, that you took the flak for all of us.'

'He would, wouldn't he,' Iris said, somewhat mollified. 'I expect he's up there watching me, waiting for me to resume control.'

'He's sure to be. Come on now, take my arm and I'll help you up.'

'My legs feel like jelly.'

'You'll be fine, Iris.'

'We must get our pensioners back, Helen, no matter what it takes.'

Mary Pilkinton set the table in the kitchen. She laid out pots of tea, brown bread and butter, scones and raspberry jam.

'Henry, bring in two more chairs from the front room for our guests.'

'Guests, Mary? Since when does a bus full of strangers become guests?'

'Pay no heed to him, we don't get many visitors around these parts. Get the chairs, Henry. Sit down everyone, and help yourselves. It's all home-made, my Henry loves his bit of home-made.'

'I thought so. You'd never get bread like this in the shops.'

'I must give you some to take home, and I've a nice batch of eggs, laid only this morning. You'll have some of them as well.'

'Is there anything better than a really fresh egg to start the day? My dad, God keep him, used to swear by it . . .'

'She has definitely recovered, Mr Perrin,' Helen said. 'Wait for the next bit: "He was a soldier, you know." '

'. . . He was a soldier, you know. He always used to say, "You can march all day if you have a good breakfast inside you." I can almost hear him.'

'Is he still with us?' Mary Pilkinton asked kindly.

'No. Sadly he passed away a few years ago.'

'And your mother?'

'I am an orphan.'

'Eh, excuse me,' Stevie said. 'I don't want to spoil the party, I mean, this is lovely and all, but I have a bus in a hay shed, there's a gang out to get us, Mr Perrin here is on the run and no one but me seems to be worrying about any of it, and that's not even mentioning the fact that we have no idea where the other old ones are. I can tell you one thing for sure, Mr Maloney is not going to like it.'

'Mr Maloney?'

'My super at the depot. That is if he is still my super which, after the day that's in it, I very much doubt.'

'Stevie's right,' Mr Perrin said. 'We must prepare ourselves. If that gang discover our whereabouts there's no knowing what will happen. Mrs Pilkinton, Mr Pilkinton, let me try to explain what is going on.'

'It's about time somebody did,' Henry Pilkinton said.

'It was a perfectly ordinary senior citizens' outing.' Iris jumped in, determined to be the one to tell the story. 'This is my second year running the trip and I must reassure you that nothing like this ever happened before. We started out from Fairview—'

'Oh no, Iris. It was Drumcondra,' Mrs Clancy said. 'I know it was Drumcondra because that's where we live, isn't it, Mr O'Neill?'

'. . . Thank you Mrs Clancy. The bus started out from Fairview. It's a terrible pity you didn't get to see it before we took down the decorations. Anyway . . .'

'Iris. Will you shut up and let Mr Perrin explain?'

'But it's my outing, Helen.'

'Iris, we don't have time for a bloody blow-by-blow account. Mr Perrin, tell the Pilkintons your story, tell them what you told us.'

'I can tell it just as well.'

'Iris, shut up and let Mr Perrin get on with it.'

The Pilkintons nodded and shook their heads at the right moments as Mr Perrin, assisted by interjections from Iris, recounted the details of his plight. He told them what he had witnessed on the dock and how he had been placed in the Cross and Passion for his own safety; how he had spent the last few months in hiding trying to keep up a front while all the time afraid of being discovered. He told them that when the outing was first mooted he saw it as a much-needed escape from worrying about Morgan, about Chief Meyers and above all about the ordeal of the forthcoming trial, and how it had turned into a nightmare for all concerned. He told them how everyone he met he had brought danger to and, even now, here in the safety of their kitchen . . . Mr Perrin broke off; he couldn't continue.

'Don't, Mr Perrin. It's not your fault. You were only trying to do the right thing.'

'That's right, Mr Perrin, and don't forget, the police are on their way.'

'What about your family, Mr Perrin?' Mrs Pilkinton asked. 'Didn't they know where you were?'

'I am a widower, Mrs Pilkinton. My dear wife passed on some years ago.'

'I am sorry. I hope you don't think I was prying.'

'Oh, Mr Perrin, we never even asked you. We were so het up with ourselves.'

'Understandably too, Iris, considering the circumstances.'

'Have you family, Mr Perrin?'

'We had no children. The doctors didn't advise it. My wife wasn't a strong woman and we thought it best . . .'

'Alone and hunted,' Mrs Pilkinton said. 'Does anyone ever know what's in store?'

'How did the gang find out about you, Mr Perrin?'

'I have been racking my brains trying to figure that out, Stevie. No one in the nursing home knew my true identity. Not the doctors, not the nursing staff and, although Sister Carmody wasn't too happy about my presence there, it wasn't because she knew about me. No, the only one in on the plan was the governor of the board.'

'I couldn't take to that Sister Carmody,' Iris said. 'I had dealings with her when I was organizing the trip. She didn't want it to happen. She didn't approve of her residents leaving the premises.'

'That's why I ruled her out,' Mr Perrin continued. 'If she had been an associate of Morgan's she wouldn't have kicked up such a fuss about it.'

'I hope you don't think it was one of us,' Mrs Clancy said. 'We didn't know, Mr Perrin, honestly we didn't. Tell him, Mr O'Neill, tell him we didn't know.'

'We didn't know,' Mr O'Neill repeated.

'We only found out about the outing when we saw

the notice.' Mrs Clancy started to weep. 'And we put our names down . . .'

'I was waiting for my son, I didn't want to come at all.'

'Of course you were, Mr O'Neill,' Iris murmured, putting her arm around Mr O'Neill's shoulder while Helen tried to comfort Mrs Clancy.

'This is terrible,' Mr Perrin said, 'and it's all my fault.'

'The important thing now is not how they found out but what we are going to do.'

'I know,' Janice said quietly. Then she raised her voice. 'I know how they found out. At least I think I have a fairly good idea. It was Chalkey.'

'Chalkey?'

'My boyfriend, the one I was telling you about. The one who ditched me.' Janice's voice quivered.

'What do you mean, Janice? How is your boyfriend involved in this? Is he part of the gang?'

'Chalkey part of the gang? That's a laugh, they wouldn't have him. Oh, he wants to be, he's always trying to be a big shot, hanging out with them, trying to get in with them. They'd use him when they'd need a runner or a messenger boy, but he'd never really be in.'

'But if he's not part of the gang . . .?'

'Let the girl speak.'

'We were out for a spin, me and Chalkey. We were stopped, trying to decide where to go, when a load of cars pulled up beside us. We thought at first they were police cars, though they weren't in uniform or anything. Anyway, Chalkey heard them say something and after that he got all funny. I think now that they were talking about you, Mr Perrin. Anyway, Chalkey gets on the mobile to someone and then all of a sudden he makes up his mind where we're going. When we get to a café the same fellas are there, only now they're Jehovahs.'

'You are losing me, Janice,' Helen said.

'The girl said they were Jehovahs and I thought that was funny because, like I told you, we thought they were police, but they really were police and after a while when Chalkey came back from the toilet and he was mortified because he thought I thought he'd had an accident and we had a big row and then everybody started arguing and that's when they started arresting everybody and we slipped out.' Janice stopped to draw her breath.

'Go on, Janice.'

'We went to the next place and Chalkey wouldn't say anything to me and then we went to Arklow 'cause he wanted to look for his granddad. He said his granddad was on a trip and needed his pills and that's when we had our next row and he walked away from me and his granddad wasn't on the trip anyway because I asked Mrs Clancy and she said there was no Mr Deveroux so I think he was making all that up, I think all the time he was looking for you, Mr Perrin, for Lefty Morgan because he wanted to get in with them.'

'What you are saying, Janice, is that Chalkey followed our bus and kept the gang informed?'

'That's exactly it, Mr Perrin. When you were talking and all, all the bits came back to me. How could he do it? I loved him, I thought we were going to get married. How could he use me like that?'

'There there, my dear.' Mrs Pilkinton put down her teapot and held Janice. 'Don't cry. Why, if I had a pound for every time Mr Pilkinton made me cry I would be a rich woman.'

'Hold on there!' Mr Pilkinton started to protest but stopped when he got a sharp look from his wife.

'They're all the same,' Iris said, 'with a few exceptions of course, Mr Perrin. Even my dad, God be good to him, could try my patience.'

'It's not quite the same thing, Iris.'

'Oh, but it is, Helen. You don't know, you don't know anything.'

'Iris?'

'I never told you this, Helen.' Iris, who was still holding Mr O'Neill, squeezed him tight and rocked him back and forth before she went on. 'I was engaged once, I know what Janice is going through. Oh yes, Helen, hard to believe isn't it? Me, plain old Iris. My father didn't approve. "Wrong side of the tracks," he used to say, "he's not right for you, girl. You can do better for yourself." I can still hear his voice. I was in a situation where it was either my dad or my fiancé. Dad was ill at the time, I couldn't leave him, I couldn't walk away and leave him . . .'

'He doesn't sound much of a fiancé, Iris if he put you in that position.'

'Dad could be difficult, he didn't make it easy for Seamus.'

'Even so, Iris.'

'I thought he'd wait. I knew given time things

would have settled down, sorted themselves out, I hoped—'

'Oh, Iris,' Janice cried, 'he didn't wait.'

'Wait? No, he didn't wait. He hooked up with Mary Cummins from down the road. I had to watch them every day, hand in hand, coming and going,' Iris struggled to blink back her tears and rocked poor Mr O'Neill even harder. 'Every time I looked out the window I seemed to see them.'

'Oh Iris, how awful for you. What a horrible thing to happen. Maybe, maybe if he was that fickle you are better off without him.'

'Am I, Helen? Look at me, I'm nearly middle aged, I'm on the shelf . . .'

'Don't be ridiculous, Iris, you're not near middle age, you're only thirty-seven.'

'Thirty-six if you don't mind. Thirty-six and nothing to show for it.'

'Here you are, ladies.' Mrs Pilkinton placed a box of tissues on the table and all hands made a dive for it. 'I'm that choked myself listening to your stories. Is any man worth the sacrifices we women make?'

'You shouldn't upset yourself, Iris. Any man would be lucky to have you.'

'Thank you, Mr Perrin.'

'They do say there's someone in this world for everyone.'

'With my luck, Mrs Pilkinton,' Iris sniffed, 'my someone is probably the undertaker.'

'We'll all be near the undertaker if we don't make a plan,' Stevie muttered under his breath.

Henry Pilkinton, Mr Perrin and Stevie stood

helplessly at one side of the kitchen as the ladies, all of them in tears, consoled each other. They felt sorry for Mr O'Neill, who was still trapped in Iris's bosom, but hadn't the courage to rescue him.

'This could go on all day,' Mr Pilkinton said morosely. 'I've seen it before.'

'What do we do?' Stevie asked. 'We haven't got all day.'

'Nothing you can do, lad. Ride it out is all.'

'Mr Pilkinton, could I use your telephone? I'm afraid my mobile may be tapped. I want to contact the police and let them know where we are.'

'We don't have a phone.'

'That's just great,' Stevie said. 'We're cannon fodder here.'

'The first thing to do is disguise the bus, with your permission, Mr Pilkinton. We must make sure it can't be seen from the road. I shall leave the farm and make my way back to town. If I am on my own, with a bit of luck I might—'

'No,' Iris suddenly rallied, 'you can't do that, Mr Perrin. You are not going to offer yourself up to those criminals, I won't allow it. I have a plan. Stephen and I will take the bus and steer the gang away from here. When they see we don't have you they won't harm us.'

'I can't let you do that, Iris. It's too risky.'

'Nonsense, Mr Perrin. I'm still in charge of this outing, you know. Anyway, Stephen and I will be well able to cope with a few ruffians. Won't we, Stephen?'

'I don't fancy taking the bus, Iris. They might destroy it.'

'Well we have got to get help somehow. Do you have transport, Mr Pilkinton?'

'I've the tractor.'

'You have the moped, Henry. You could go down to Arklow and get Sergeant Keogh up from the station.'

'No. I shall go, I insist. It would be better if your husband stayed here, Mrs Pilkinton. He could help defend Mr Perrin and the others from an assault. If the gang does spot me, what could be more innocent than a woman out for a jaunt on a moped?'

'Do you know how to drive one, Iris?'

'What's to know? You sit on and steer. I'm sure I am perfectly capable of driving a moped. Don't everybody look at me like that. I promise you, there is nothing to worry about, I shall be back with help before you can say "Jack Robinson". Mrs Pilkinton, lead me to the moped. Stay here, everyone, and stay out of sight.'

'It's not that way, dear,' Mrs Pilkinton said as Iris headed for the barn. 'It's in the back shed.'

'I'm getting my tracksuit bottoms from the bus, Mrs Pilkinton. It will be easier to ride the moped in my bottoms.'

'There she goes,' Helen said as they heard the moped roar into action. 'She doesn't look too steady.' They all watched from the Pilkintons' kitchen window as Iris wobbled her way down the driveway.

'You need to change gear,' Mrs Pilkinton shouted after her.

'Where is it?' Iris shouted back.

'On the handlebars. Twist the handlebars. Oh dear.' Iris had vanished out of sight.

'Do you think she'll make it?' Stevie asked.

'I don't know, Stevie, I don't know.'

Chapter Twenty-one

While Maureen remained in the back seat of car four, agent Nigel Sinclair, his partner James Duffy, and Bill Thomas and Deborah stood arguing on the pavement directly outside Cassidy's Hotel. Bill was demanding his right to make a phone call and the rookies were trying to stall. They didn't want him making any calls until Jones got there.

'Get them inside, Duffy. Bring them in to the hotel before the whole town is looking at us. I'll get the nurse. Out of the car, lady.'

'Do what you will to me,' Maureen said, 'but I shall not step out of this car in handcuffs. It is an affront to any woman, let alone an SRN in charge of an exclusive retirement home.'

'She is absolutely right, you know,' Bill said, 'this is harassment. We have not been charged with anything. You can't go round handcuffing people if they're not charged. I insist on calling my lawyer.'

'Get back in the car. Not you, Duffy – them, get them

back in the car.' Bill and Deborah were bundled in beside Maureen. 'What do you think, Duffy, is he right? What if he rings his lawyer and we are not supposed to have her in handcuffs? We could be done for.'

'I only know Jones said to keep her cuffed.'

'Yes, but it's not his head on the line with lawyers, is it?'

'Maybe we should call Sergeant Kelly.'

'We can't call Kelly, Chief Meyers is with him. You heard the Chief say radio silence.'

'What if we take the cuffs off, just until we get inside, and then put them on again? Better still, we cuff just one of her hands to something solid, that way she'd have the use of the other one and she wouldn't have so much to complain about.'

'Good thinking, Duffy, we'll do it. Get them out.' Nigel opened the car door. 'Get out of the car.'

'Again?'

'Yes, again, and no funny stuff.' Nigel bent in to Maureen. 'Come on out, lady.'

'I already told you, agent whatever your name is, I am not getting out.'

'Listen, lady. We're going to uncuff you. You walk beside my partner here into the hotel and sit exactly where we tell you to sit.'

'Would you kindly desist from addressing me as "lady"? I am Sister Maureen Carmody.'

'Have it your way, Sister. Now out.' Nigel undid the cuffs. 'Duffy, take hold of her arm.' Maureen, Deborah and Bill were escorted into the hotel.

'Grab a table in the lobby, Duffy, so we can keep an eye out for the others. Over here, you lot. Watch them carefully,' he whispered to his partner, 'we don't want anyone taking off.'

'Good evening, sir. What can I get you? Oh.' The receptionist looked at Maureen. 'Are you with the ambulance?'

'She is with us,' Nigel replied before Maureen could speak.

'Oh good, I mean, sorry, I thought, as she is in uniform, she must be with the ambulance although it did leave some time ago, and I was hoping, for our guests' sake you understand, that it hadn't returned.'

'We'll have coffee,' Duffy said. 'Coffee all round, Nigel?'

'I suppose there's nothing else for it. We can't sit here with nothing in our hands, but I'm telling you, Duffy, I'm sure I'm going to be sick.'

'I'll have a pint of Guinness, please,' Bill said. 'Ladies, what is your pleasure?'

'You can't have drinks.'

'And why not? We're not in official custody or you would have taken us to the station. I order a drink, right now, or I call my lawyer. What's it to be, gentlemen?'

'Stay where you are. Duffy.' The two agents moved out of earshot. 'What do you think?'

'We better let him, Nigel.'

'This doesn't feel right.'

'I know it doesn't but we don't want him calling his lawyer before the Chief gets here, do we?'

'I mean, look at it, Duffy – the suspects having drinks, us having more bloody coffee. I don't think this is by the book.'

'It's not a by-the-book situation, is it, Nigel?'

'We'll let them have one drink, let's hope they finish it before the others arrive.'

'We'll make sure they do.'

Nigel turned to Bill. 'One drink. We're going to allow you to have one drink each and that's it.'

'Deborah, Maureen, what can I get you?'

'Gin and tonic, Bill, please. Make that two. I'm sure, Maureen, you need one as much as I do.'

'That's one pint, two gin and tonics and two coffees.'

'Duffy.' Nigel leaned behind Maureen's back. 'The cuffs.'

'Do we have to? I mean she's in between us. Let's leave it for a little while, at least until we've had our coffee.'

'Where do you think you are going, Sister?' Maureen had stood up and was trying to slide herself past the rookies.

'The ladies' room.'

'You can't.'

'What do you mean, I can't? You surely don't expect me to urinate on the floor?'

'Duffy, you'll have to go with her.'

'Me? I'm not going. Why can't you go?'

'I have the others to mind.'

'No way, Nigel. You're not getting out of it with that.'

'You accompany her,' Nigel said to Deborah.

'I don't need to.'

'If I let you go, I want your word of honour you'll come straight back.'

'You have my word, young man,' Maureen said as she made her way across the lobby to the ladies' room. 'You have my word that this day will return to haunt you.'

'Stand by the door, Duffy.'

'But, Nigel, she gave you her word.'

'I don't trust her. Wait outside the door till she comes out.'

'That's a bit much,' Deborah said, 'loitering outside a ladies' loo. Hardly in keeping with . . .'

'Quiet!' Nigel snapped. 'I have more handcuffs.' He jiggled the cuffs in his pocket. 'And I am not afraid to use them.'

'Your drinks, sir.' The receptionist had returned with the drinks and was placing them on the table as Nigel referred to the handcuffs. Normally, this being a hotel, she would present the bill when the customers were leaving, but handcuffs . . . she thought she'd better get the money up front. 'That'll be eleven pounds seventy, please.'

'This gentleman here is paying,' Bill explained.

'What?' Nigel said.

'You brought us here, you can pay for the drinks.'

'Eleven pounds seventy? That's a bit steep, isn't it?'

'Those are our prices, sir. It is all written up on our tariff list. Guinness, two pounds fifty, two G and Ts, six pounds twenty, and two coffees, two pounds fifty. That makes eleven pounds seventy in all.'

'I need a receipt,' Nigel said, handing over the cash.

'Certainly, sir, no problem.'

'I don't want to see Sergeant Kelly's face when you put in for this, Nigel.'

'Well, it's not my fault, is it?'

'Mr Lewis.' The receptionist had gone back to her desk and was ringing through to the manager's office. 'This is Marianne here at reception. I don't want to worry you, Mr Lewis, but we have some customers in the lobby that I'm not too happy about . . . No, I don't think they are but they are acting very strangely, and Mr Lewis, one of them has handcuffs . . . No, Mr Lewis, they haven't asked for a room yet, they're having drinks . . . Three men and two women. One of the women is wearing a nurse's outfit and, I have to tell you, judging by the state of it, it's not bandaging she's wearing it for . . . yes, Mr Lewis, I know we don't make a habit of prying into our guests' affairs but . . . I agree with you, Mr Lewis, and I have no problem with that type of carry-on in the privacy of their own homes, but when they come to a respectable hotel bringing equipment, I shudder to imagine what they get up to . . . I know, Mr Lewis, but I'm thinking of our reputation as a family hotel. I mean, if we let that sort up into our bedrooms there's no knowing . . . We do have empty rooms, Mr Lewis, there was a cancellation this morning . . . I am aware bookings are down, but . . . whatever you say, Mr Lewis, you're the boss.' Marianne hung up. It was all very well for Mr Lewis, upstairs, in his ivory tower. He didn't have to deal with things on the floor. He didn't have to cope when things got difficult. Marianne took a little swig of the brandy she kept under her desk for medicinal purposes. 'Of course, it could all be totally innocent,' she told herself, 'the remains of a fancy dress party or something like that.' She began to ease up when the main door opened and six more men entered the hotel and joined the first group.

'Jones. Am I glad to see you?' Nigel greeted his fellow agents enthusiastically. 'We've been having a terrible time with that nurse.'

'Where is she? Is she handcuffed?'

'She was creating merry hell about the cuffs, Jones. We had to leave them off while she went to the ladies. Don't worry, she's not going anywhere. Duffy is standing guard. Any more news from the Chief?'

'Not yet. I don't expect them to be much longer. Why are those prisoners drinking, Nigel? What's going on here?'

'Prisoners?' Deborah exclaimed 'Bill, did you hear that?'

'I had to let them, he threatened to call his lawyer.'

'That's right,' Bill said, 'and I intend doing so if I don't get some answers pretty quick. Are you in charge of this charade?' He addressed Jones.

'I ask the questions here.'

'Why are we being detained, officer?' Deborah asked. 'Do you have something to charge us with? Maureen has already explained her connection with your Alex Smith so I don't see any reason for our being held here against our will . . .'

'I have been forced to abandon my truck,' Bill joined in, 'bullied into a police car and driven here, and no explanation has been given.'

'I told you, Jones,' Nigel said. 'It's been like this the whole time.'

'The case we are dealing with is of the utmost

sensitivity. You are being held for – no, you are being asked to assist the police with their enquiries. Chief Meyers will answer your questions as he deems fit as soon as he arrives. Miss,' Jones called the receptionist to the table. 'Remove these drinks and bring more coffee, please. Duffy, stop standing around with your hands in your pockets. Get in there and cuff that woman. I want her under submission when Meyers gets here. I want him to know we have the whip hand.'

Duffy cautiously pushed open the door of the ladies' room and was greeted by a slight breeze. The cubicles were ajar, the window was open. Maureen was gone.

'Mr Lewis, it's Marianne again. I don't want to be too alarmist but there's more of them, Mr Lewis, and – I can hardly bring myself to tell you – the one with the handcuffs is gone into the powder room and one of the new ones is talking about his whip hand.'

Maureen had no intention of returning to the lobby to be chained to a coffee table like some common criminal. She checked out the window in the ladies' room: it was high and narrow but if she manoeuvred herself around she should be able to squeeze through. She placed her right leg in the sink and, bouncing up and down a couple of times on her left leg to gather momentum, she propelled herself upwards. There was a creaking noise as the sink threatened to come away from the wall but she quickly placed her bottom on the sill to take the weight off it. She peered out the other side. Not too big a drop, but she would need to lower herself carefully – it would be all too easy to turn an ankle on her descent.

Leaning forward as much as she could, she thrust one leg out over the sill and down. For a moment she was balanced precariously with a leg dangling down each side of the window, but she managed to shift her position and get the other leg through. She was out. She lowered herself and dropped lightly to the ground, crouched for a moment to check she hadn't been spotted, then, keeping low, she crept behind some beer kegs to get her bearings. Maureen's brain was racing. Her plan was to get out of the town as fast as she could and follow her residents. If she could get to Bill's truck she could contact his CB friends again; she could even take the truck and continue her search. The keys. How would she get in? She'd have to break a window, there was nothing else for it. There was bound to be another set of keys in the dashboard or somewhere handy like that. Anyway, the CB was the main thing. She must get to the outskirts of the town and hitch a lift back to the lorry.

'McHale, radio the Chief, tell him where we are. The rest of you, follow that nurse, she can't have got very far. Spread out and find her. You two.' Jones addressed Deborah and Bill Thomas. 'Stay where you are. If you move I will have you picked up and arrested.'

'I thought we were already arrested,' Deborah said.

Marianne threw her eyes up in despair as the seven rookies disappeared into the ladies' room. 'I don't care what Mr Lewis has to say,' she muttered aloud. 'I'm not having this.' She strode from her desk and entered the toilets in time to see the last of the rookies climbing out through the window. She opened her mouth as if to scream then snapped it shut again. Without a word Marianne turned on her heel and walked straight across the lobby to the bar area, poured herself a stiff brandy and took it down in one swallow. It was too much for Mr Lewis to expect her to cope with this sort of carry-on. Three years of Tourism and Business Studies plus one year's work experience under her belt . . . Marianne refilled her drink and downed that one as well. And for what?

'Excuse me, Miss,' Bill called over to her, 'when you get a chance, could we have the same again please?'

'The same again is it? Well I am sorry to disappoint you but I'm all out of whips and cuffs at the moment . . .'

'What is she talking about, Bill?'

'. . . You do your best. You smile and smile. Tourists, foreigners, weddings, funerals, smile and smile, backpackers, pensioners, ambulances, men waving bondage weapons, "all in a day's work, Marianne", according to Mr Lewis, "ours is not to reason why, Marianne". What does he care . . .'

'Eh, Miss. A pint of Guinness and a gin and tonic, please.'

'Get it yourself.' Marianne's glass went up to the optic again.

*

Chief Meyers and Sergeant Kelly curled off the motorway and, following agent McHale's directions, drove directly to Cassidy's Hotel.

'Our quest is almost over, Kelly.' Chief Meyers allowed himself to smile. 'As soon as we pick up Smith and return him to Harcourt Street we can relax. I'm not worried about the gang. Once Morgan's trial is over they'll fall apart. In fact, in my experience, they'll fall over each other giving evidence in return for amnesty. I've seen it happen before. Take away the leader and the rats turn tail. Here we are. Pull over, Kelly. Good, there's no sign of our squad cars. Remind me to congratulate the lads on their discretion. I must admit, Sergeant, I half expected them to be parked out front.'

Chief Meyers and Sergeant Kelly walked into the lobby of the hotel. They looked around for their agents. There was no sign of them. There was no sign of anyone except a couple sitting over drinks and another lady, sitting alone on a bar stool, talking incoherently to herself.

'Check around, Kelly. You try the other rooms and I'll try to get someone at reception.' Meyers stood by the desk waiting for attention when he noticed a bell with a sign over it: IF RECEPTION IS UNATTENDED PLEASE PRESS. He gave three short rings and waited but there was no response. Impatiently he pressed the bell again, this time keeping his finger on it, and the lady at the bar jerked to attention. She reeled across the lobby and to his surprise went in behind the desk.

'Yess?' she slurred. 'Whatcha want?'

'Hello. I'm looking for some gentlemen I was to meet here. Quite a large group; there were eight of them actually. They may have been in the company of a nurse. Have you seen them?'

'Oh I've sheen them, I've sheen them coming and going with their whipsh 'n' handcuffsh.'

'Miss, this is extremely important. Where did they go?'

Marianne pointed to the ladies' room.

'I repeat, Miss. Where did they go?'

'Tsat way.'

'May I inform you that I am Chief Detective Inspector Meyers?'

'Whipsh 'n' handcuffsh.'

'I think she means handcuffs.' Bill Thomas had joined Chief Meyers at the desk. 'She may have seen your men with them.'

'Who are you, sir?'

'My name is Bill Thomas. I, and my friend there –' Bill indicated Deborah '– were brought here by some of your agents. I take it they were your agents?'

'Do you know where they are?'

'The girl is right. They did disappear into the ladies' room.'

'That is preposterous.'

'I agree, but that's what happened. Why don't you join us, Chief Meyers? Why don't we sit down and try to the bottom of this?'

'Whipsh 'n' handcuffsh,' Marianne repeated.

'Enough, Miss, or I shall call my sergeant and have *you* handcuffed.'

Marianne fainted to the floor.

'The poor girl,' Deborah rushed up to the desk. 'You've frightened the wits out of her.'

'Leave her. If there's one thing I can't abide it's people drinking on the job. Kelly.' The sergeant had returned to the lobby. 'What news?'

'Nothing, sir. No sign of them at all.'

'Like I said, Chief Meyers, I think we should sit down and talk this through from the beginning. Your agents are after the wrong person.'

'That nurse . . .'

'Maureen has nothing to do with your Alex Smith,' Deborah said. 'Her only concern is for her missing pensioners.'

'I think she's right, Chief,' Sergeant Kelly said.

'There's coffee on the table. Why don't we sit down? Deborah and I will tell you all we know. If we put our heads together we can try and find a way to get the pensioners back.'

'I have eight agents in the field,' Chief Meyers spluttered. 'What makes you think that you . . .'

'If you don't mind my saying it, Chief Meyers, your agents seem a little ham-fisted. Like I said, they've gone after the wrong person.'

Chapter Twenty-two

Guided by his passengers, Mr O'Connor drove the bus slowly and tortuously along the forestry road. Miss Poole and Dessie held their positions behind him, the other pensioners manned the side windows, while Con and Willie, who were kneeling on the back seat, kept up a running commentary on all the obstacles and dangers they might have run into but didn't.

'There's no point looking out the back window, Willie. It's the front and sides we need to watch.'

'There's no room for us anywhere else. You have all the windows taken up.'

'You can come over here beside me, Willie, if you want,' Lillie said.

'You'd want to watch yourself, Willie, she's out to get a lodger. She wants to double up on her fuel allowance. Jesus.' Cissy lost her balance and fell over as the bus gave a lurch.

'Serves you right for telling lies,' Lillie said.

'Steady, Mr O'Connor. Keep her steady.'

'Oh dear. I think I'm losing my hold. I can't go on like this much longer.'

'Nonsense Mr O'C, you're doing great.'

'It's all clear on the port side,' Lillie called out.

'You're not on the port side, Lillie, you're on the starboard. You're supposed to be watching your own side, not minding anyone else's.'

'I am minding my own side. I'm blurry-eyed looking at it. How far have we gone now?'

'About two miles.'

'Two miles? Is that all? My neck feels as if it's been sticking out this window for longer than that.'

'I can see daylight ahead.'

'Thank God.'

'You can pull your head in now, Lillie, if you want,' Miss Poole. 'We're coming to the end of the forest. It won't be so difficult to steer on the road.'

'I'm glad you think so, Miss Poole,' Mr O'Connor said.

The bus finally cleared the forest and came out at a T-junction on a secondary road.

'Which way should I turn?'

'Right,' said Cissy.

'No, left.'

'We can't go left, it will bring us back to Arklow. We might meet up with those men again. Go right, Mr O'Connor, right.'

'Stop, please. It's hard enough driving this bus without conflicting instructions. I'm going to pull over until you make up your minds.'

'No!' everyone chorused together.

'For God's sake, Mr O'Connor, don't stop the

bus. We might not get her going again. We'll go right.'

The bus jerked several times as Mr O'Connor turned the big wheel and swung out round the corner. They swayed dangerously but he managed to steady the bus and straighten it up.

'Whew,' Lillie said when the danger was over. 'I'm nearly dizzy. That reminded me of being in a chairoplane – I used to hate them things when I was a kid.'

'We're in the middle of the road, Mr O'Connor. Do you not think we should move over a bit?'

'If I move in any closer we'll end up in the ditch.'

'You drive whatever way you are most comfortable, Mr O'Connor.'

'Thank you, Miss Poole.'

'If we're stopped by the police for dangerous driving,' Miss Poole whispered to Dessie, 'so much the better.'

'Giddyup, Mr O'C, I reckon if we keep going at this rate we should reach the city in time to collect six months' pension.'

'Leave him alone, Lillie. He's doing his best.'

'Stop. Stop the bus. We have to go back.'

'Are you mad, Cissy? What are you thinking of?'

'She's flipped,' Lillie said. 'She's gone off her rocker. I seen it once before.'

'We have to go back. You all heard what those men said.'

'Too right we heard them, that's why we're getting as far away as we can.'

'Are we going to leave Iris and Helen and Mr Perrin and poor Stevie to those men? They don't know what's in store for them. They'll be taken completely unawares.'

'But they're dangerous criminals, Cissy. What can we do?'

'I don't know what we can do but we have to think of something. Don't forget, they think they left us stranded so we have the element of surprise on our side.'

'Oh that's great, Cissy,' Lillie said, 'the element of surprise. Well, let me tell you the only element I want to know about is the one in the bottom of my electric kettle.'

'Suppose it was you, Lillie? Suppose it was you the gang was after. You'd expect us to do something, wouldn't you?'

'I would not. I'd sign over the pension straight away.'

'They are not after Mr Perrin's pension, Lillie. You heard them. He's a witness. He's a witness to something and it must be really big or they wouldn't be after him like that.'

'Mr Perrin is a very nice man,' Miss Bourke said. 'He always brings us back treats when he goes to town.'

'So what are you saying, Cissy? What do you want us to do?'

'We've got to go back to Arklow. We've got to warn Iris and the others, tell them what's going on. Turn around Mr O'Connor, we're going back.'

'I can't.'

'What do you mean, you can't?'

'I can't turn this bus around, it's too big.'

'We'll go in reverse then.'

'What?'

'It won't make any difference to Mr O'Connor. All he has to do is hold the wheel and follow our instructions.'

'This is madness, Cissy, we'll all get killed.'

'Tell me, what's the difference? He can't see either way. Into reverse, Mr O'Connor. Now, start backing.'

'Wheeee,' Willie and Con shouted, 'we're leading.'

'Shit. To the back everyone. Take up positions at the back.'

The countryside reverberated with noise as Iris moved the moped up into full throttle and belted along the road. Luckily, since she'd left the Pilkintons' farm she'd had the road to herself so she'd had a chance to get the knack of the bike without having to contend with any other vehicles. 'Full steam ahead, Iris,' she told herself. She discovered that the faster she went the easier it was to stay upright. 'Dear God, and St Anthony, and anyone else up there listening, help me get my old folks back and I promise . . .' There was something up ahead. Iris slowed a little, trying to make it out. It looked as if some cars were parked sideways across the road and they were definitely not police cars. The gang. It had to be them, and she was heading straight for them. Yes. There was an ambulance half hidden behind some low-lying branches. Iris stopped the moped. What could she do? She turned off the engine and glided towards the ditch, pulling on the almost non-existent brakes and scooting frantically as she tried to come to a halt. She got off the bike and wheeled it on a bit further, keeping as close to the ditch as she could. They obviously hadn't seen her yet but she'd have to get off the road.

She opened a big metal gate – no easy task, trying to hold on to the bike with one hand while undoing the big bolt with the other – and pushed the bike into a field. So far, so good. She remounted and started her engine. 'With any luck they'll think it's a tractor,' she thought as once again the moped shattered the silence. Hanging on for all she was worth, Iris bumped her way down along the ruts inside the hedge, terrifying a herd of Friesians who up to then had been grazing peacefully in their field. The cattle started to run from the noise. They ran until they got to the open gate where they stampeded to freedom. 'Damn,' Iris said, 'the gate. I forgot to close it. I can't go back now. I must remember to send a note of apology to the owner as soon as I get back to town.'

Lefty's gang, sitting in ambush in their back-up cars, became aware of a thundering noise.

'Did you hear that?'

'Yeah. Where's it coming from?'

The noise got louder and louder and Smasher stepped out of the car to investigate.

'Holy shite! Get out! Get out of the cars! Whoa, whoa,' he shouted. He jumped up and down and waved his arms in a feeble attempt to divert the stampede, but the cattle were too freaked to heed him. 'Stop them. Stop them for God's sake. They're heading our way. They'll wreck the cars.'

It was too late. The gang could only jump out of the way as the cattle, big eyed and frothing, burst through the cars, banging and clanging off them and sending them crashing into each other, before they began to slow down.

'What the fuck are we going to do now?' Smasher stood in the middle of the road staring at the cars. 'Look at them, they're bleeding wrecked.'

'It could be worse, Smash. There's still the ambulance, they didn't get the ambulance,' pointed out Brains.

'Shut up, you stupid get.'

'I was only trying to . . .'

'What's Lefty going to say when he hears we were run over by a bunch of stupid bleeding cattle?'

'What'll we do, Smash? We better get out of here.'

'Yeah, Smash. Someone's bound to come along.'

'Will you for Christ's sake shut up and let me think? OK, everybody, in the bleeding ambulance.'

'And then what, Smash? It's going to look pretty funny if we're sitting here and—'

'Just get in, dammit, and close the doors.' The gang piled into the back of the ambulance. 'I have it. Nobody tells him, right? No one says a word to Lefty about cows.' Smasher waited for a reply. 'Right?'

'Sure, Smash, sure. Whatever you say.'

'Mum's the word. Now keep quiet; shut your traps till I formulate another plan.'

'Jesus. What was that?' The gang leaped in their seats as they heard someone knocking on the side of the ambulance.

'It's probably the farmer. If we don't answer he might get on to the cops. Quick, Brains, get under that blanket. You too, Kev. Not the same stretcher, dope, take one each, make as if you are hurt. The rest of you, when I opened the door, look worried. We're here because we got injured in the stampede. I'll get rid of him. If he kicks up a stink I tell him we're going to sue for the cars.'

'Are we, Smash? Are we going to sue?'

'"Are we going to sue?" How the hell do you think we sue for two hot cars and a hot ambulance?' The knocking started again. 'Is everyone ready? I'm going to open the door.' Smasher opened the back door and leaned out.

'Hi, Smasher.'

'Chalkey. You bleeding idiot. What are you doing here?'

'I was looking for . . . What's going on, Smasher? What's with the cars, they're all banged up?'

'It's Chalkey. Hi Chalkey.'

'What happened to you, Brains?'

'Nothing.'

'Why are you all wrapped up in the blanket?'

'It's on account of the cows.'

'Enough. Knock it off. You're doing my head in. Listen, Chalkey, you ain't seen those cars, right? You don't know nothing.'

'Sure, Smash. So where's Smith? How come you haven't got him?'

'We'll get him, don't you worry. Now get lost, Chalkey. I have everything sorted. That bus will be along shortly and I don't want you messing things up.'

'Me?'

'Yeah, you. Go on, skeddadle.'

'If you're sure you don't need me any longer I'll . . .'

'Beat it.'

'Get off that stupid stretcher,' Smasher said as soon as Chalkey had headed away. 'Pete, go up to the front and start driving.'

'Which way, Smasher?'

'I don't bleeding know yet, do I?'

Iris rode the bike through a gap in the hedge at the other side of the road. She shook from head to toe, every bone in her body had been jolted, and when she got off the bike to test her legs they nearly went from under her. 'Damn.' She swore silently as she looked down and saw the snags in her new tracksuit bottoms. They were ruined. Briars sticking out from the hedge had picked out threads all down the right leg. She wanted to dump the bike there and then but she knew she couldn't. She had no idea how far away from Arklow she was or, for that matter, which way to go. Left or right, there was nothing on the road to help her get her bearings. Her instinct was to go left, and to continue in that direction until she came to a signpost. For all she knew she could be going the wrong way but there was nothing else for it. When she felt sufficiently recovered she gave the bike a push start and remounted. She putt-putted on, slowly and carefully, wary of coming across any more gang members.

THOMPSONS HAULIERS. Iris spotted the truck parked at the side of the road. Funny, she thought, she could have sworn she had seen that truck earlier but she couldn't be sure, so much had been going on. If the driver was in it she could ask him for directions or, better still, he might have a mobile phone he'd let her use. Iris drove up to the truck and circled it but it was empty. Then, out of the corner of her eye, she thought she saw a flash of something white.

'Hello,' she called out. 'Anyone there?'

Maureen stepped out from the back of the truck.

'You,' Maureen said. 'Stay where you are, Miss Fox. I am making a citizen's arrest.'

'You, Sister Carmody. What are you doing here? Why are you lurking behind this truck?'

'I am here because you lost my residents.'

'I lost your residents?' Iris retorted. 'That's a good one. You are the one who should be arrested, subjecting my poor pensioners to the clutches of criminals. And as for poor Mr Perrin, words fail me.'

'Poor Mr Perrin,' Maureen snorted. 'Poor Mr Perrin. I'll have you know that your poor Mr Perrin is wanted by the police. In fact, your Mr Perrin is not Mr Perrin at all.'

'Of course he's not, he's Alex Smith.'

'Ah-ha. I was right – you do know him. Shame on you, Miss Fox.'

'Shame on you, Sister Carmody. Subjecting Alex Smith to such persecution, the same Alex Smith who is prepared to put his life on the line for others.'

'What are you talking about?'

'Don't play the innocent with me.'

The ladies argued bitterly. Harsh words flew back and forth and voices were raised until Iris, suddenly remembering their proximity to the gang, called a halt.

'Listen, Sister Carmody. It is becoming clear that you don't know about the gang and, obviously, I didn't know about the gang. We are wasting valuable time with this fruitless talk. However, help is at hand. Even as we speak there's a bevy of policemen on their way to apprehend the gangsters. Mr Perrin made contact with the department dealing with his case and we have been assured assistance is close at hand. I was on my way to find a telephone to let them know where Mr Perrin is hiding when I encountered the gang. It was only by dint of diving into a field that I managed to avoid them, but they are out there looking for him and if they catch him the Lord only knows what they will do. It's not just Mr Perrin that's in danger now, it's all of our pensioners.'

'If you are waiting for the police to help, Miss Fox, you are wasting your time. Your bevy of plainclothes men are at this very moment sitting in a hotel in Arklow drinking coffee. They arrested me and my companions; I was held against my will and only managed to escape by climbing out a toilet window.'

'I don't understand.'

'I was forced into a car. Held in chains.' Maureen held out her wrists dramatically. 'Handcuffed, Miss Fox, like a rogue animal.'

'Oh, Sister Carmody. But why?'

'Because, Miss Fox, they're making a hames of the whole situation. Arresting the wrong people, refusing to listen, and now, instead of chasing those dreadful men, they are sitting in the hotel waiting for their chief to arrive and tell them what to do and, in the meantime, my residents are out there somewhere . . .'

'Alone and frightened,' Iris said.

'. . . alone and frightened, Miss Fox.'

Both ladies stood silently reflecting on the situation.

'Sister Carmody, this won't do at all. If we can't rely on the police we must pool our resources and rescue the pensioners ourselves. Are you with me, Sister?'

'I'm with you, Miss Fox.'

'We need a plan. My dad, God be good to him, always said, "Half the battle is won, Iris, if you plan well." Do you have a pen or pencil and a piece of paper on you, Sister Carmody?'

'I have nothing, Miss Fox. My bag is in an abandoned car somewhere in the mountain forest.'

'Sister?'

'Don't ask, Miss Fox, the explanation is too painful.'

'And my bag is on the bus, so we'll have to make notes mentally. Note one . . . can you memorize, Sister Carmody?'

'Perfectly, Miss Fox.'

'. . . Note one. Original bus now in farmyard. Helen, Mr Perrin, Stephen, Mr O'Neill, Mrs Clancy and Janice . . .'

'Janice, Miss Fox? I did not see the name Janice on your list.'

'She wasn't on the list. We picked her up in Arklow. Well, we didn't pick her up in so far as she stowed away.'

'Stowed away, Miss Fox?'

'She, Janice that is, had had a row with her fiancé

and needed a lift back to town.'

'Don't you think it a trifle irresponsible to have unauthorized persons aboard your bus, Miss Fox?'

'Coincidentally it happens that she was the lead we needed to link our outing with the gang. Janice discovered that Chalkey, her fiancé, was in on the plan. He was the one who reported Mr Perrin's whereabouts.'

'And you let her on board?'

'Janice is totally innocent, Sister Carmody, you have my word on that. She was used, used most cruelly. You as a woman will know that bitter taste.'

'Does it show that much, Miss Fox?'

'What, Sister Carmody?'

'It takes so little to bring it all back. A chance word, a gesture . . .' Maureen paused for a moment in memory while Iris, unsure where this was going, waited uneasily for her to continue. '. . . yes, Miss Fox. I know that bitter taste . . .'

'Sister?'

'. . . and although it was some twenty years or so ago now, I can still get the taste.'

'Dear me.' Iris did a quick subtraction in her head and concluded that Sister Carmody was a little older than she had thought. 'Go on, Sister.'

'It was early summer when he proposed. A foolish heady afternoon when the world seemed fresh and exciting. I had taken a half day, not easily done in those days, Miss Fox, as I'm sure you know . . .'

Iris opened her mouth to protest but closed it again. It wouldn't be an appropriate time to point out age differences.

'. . . I was in my final year. A few months to go before sitting the SRN Examinations.'

'SRN?'

'State Registered Nurse, Miss Fox. Where was I? I seem to have lost my thread.'

'You didn't say where you were, Sister Carmody. You said it was early summer and you had taken the half day.'

'Ah yes, thank you, Miss Fox. I was on St Theresa's ward at the time. Naturally we weren't allowed personal calls but Marcus had phoned the nurses' station, pretending to be a relation of one of the patients, and got through to me. He begged me to meet him that afternoon and when Marcus begged, no one, least of all me, could refuse. I invented some story or other for Matron so I could get off duty after the patients' dinners and fled, as soon as I was relieved, to the Nurses' Home to change. Marcus had hinted that there was something special he was going to ask me and I wanted to look my best. I was to get the one-thirty train to Dalkey and Marcus would meet me at the station.'

'Oh, Sister Carmody,' Iris sighed, then she added for no particular reason, 'Did you know him long?'

'Three weeks, Miss Fox. Three glorious weeks of wining and dining, the cinema, parties, I can't begin to tell you how wonderful it was.'

'When you met him at the station, did he . . .'

'No, Miss Fox. I missed the train. Can you imagine my dilemma when I saw it pulling out of the station as I ran down the platform? I panicked. What could I do? I raced back up to the main road and jumped on a number eight bus praying that it would reach Dalkey as quickly as the train. I pictured Marcus standing alone on a deserted platform as all the passengers disembarked and I wasn't among them. It was a terrible journey, Miss Fox.'

'Was it long, Sister Carmody?'

'About three miles.'

'Was he there? Was he waiting for you?'

'No, Miss Fox, he was not. I raced from the bus terminus to the station but there was no sign of him. I questioned the porter, describing Marcus in every detail. He had seen him. He remembered the handsome young man, cursing and swearing, and enquiring what time the next train would arrive, and was able to point out to me where Marcus had gone to wait. I could have kissed him for his news. I could imagine Marcus, cursing and swearing with disappointment because I wasn't on the train and I forgave him because in the whole time since I had known him Marcus had never uttered as much as the mildest of swear words. I popped into the ladies' waiting room to tidy my hair and freshen up my lipstick and then followed him to the public house beside the station, the Loreto Arms.'

'Was he there, Sister Carmody? Please tell me he was there this time.'

'When I saw him, sitting in the lounge of the Loreto Arms, a ray of sunshine beamed through the window and seemed to shine directly on him. My heart soared, Miss Fox, the vision was almost biblical.'

'When did he ask . . . ?'

'I didn't care about anything. I knew from that moment I would do anything for him. We went for a walk. We walked along the Vico Road, on up to Killiney Head, and returned to Dalkey a few hours later. It was then he asked me. He wanted to elope – "he couldn't wait any longer for me to be his" were his exact words. I told him I had only a few more months to go and I would be finished but he insisted he couldn't wait. If I didn't leave with him immediately he would do something terrible. I agreed to elope. I couldn't bear to see him so upset, and over me, it was exciting and thrilling. We spent the next few hours planning everything. We would go to London to a registry office. "Who needs the trappings of convention?" Marcus said. "We're young and in love. We can let everyone know afterwards." There would be no engagement ring, another convention according to Marcus; instead we would put that money to good use. We agreed that I should lend him another two hundred pounds so he could handle the tickets, the accommodation, book the registry office and so on, and he would repay me everything he owed as soon as he got his first job. He was most insistent that he would be the breadwinner of the family. The following Friday I withdrew the money from the bank and gave it to Marcus. The money had been put aside for the remaining tuition fees, exam fees and papers but I wouldn't need that now. I was going to London to be married. I told no one. It was my secret, mine and Marcus's.'

'Please don't tell me that—'

'I stood at the ticket barrier at Dún Laoghaire

Harbour until the boat disappeared beyond the horizon.'

'Oh, Sister Carmody.'

'So you see, Miss Fox. I do know the bitter taste.'

'What did you do?'

'Nothing. I did nothing.'

'And your exams?'

Maureen didn't reply.

Iris couldn't contain herself. She threw her arms around Maureen, hugging and squeezing her until Maureen begged her to stop.

'My uniform, Miss Fox. I am trying to keep some semblance of appearance together. If you persist like this it will be damp as well as crumpled.'

'I'm sorry, Sister. I couldn't help it. Your story is so sad.'

'You will, of course, keep this to yourself.'

'Scout's honour, Sister Carmody.'

'I believe we were on note one. Miss Fox, pull yourself together.'

'Sorry.' Iris sniffed, wiping her nose with a tissue. 'Note one. Original bus hidden in farmyard and persons already referred to hidden there also.' Iris didn't want to mention Janice's name again. 'They will remain there until the arrival of rescue troops. Note two. The whereabouts of the main body of our pensioners remains unknown. This must be our priority. We know they have to be somewhere in the area and we must find them. Note three. The gang are also in the area and have at their disposal cars, an ambulance, and a duplicate bus, and my gut feeling is if we find the bus we find our pensioners.'

'Is that part of your notes, Miss Fox?'

'It's just a feeling, Sister, there is no need to memorize it. That seems to be about it. Whatever happens we must avoid the gang at all costs. The good thing is we have the element of surprise. They won't be expecting us. Sister? Sister Carmody? What are you doing?' Maureen had picked up a large rock and was aiming it at the truck window.

'Stand back, Miss Fox.' She hurled the rock through the window, sending slivers of glass in all directions.

'Have you gone mad, Sister Carmody?'

'Trust me, Miss Fox.' Maureen climbed up on the step of the lorry, put her hand through the window and opened the door. Once inside she turned on the CB radio and spoke urgently into it. 'Mayday. Mayday. Come in anyone.' The CB crackled for a while and then cleared and Maureen repeated her message.

'Howdedoody. What's the SOS, ma'am? Where's the fire?'

'Is that Mr Stomping Mary?'

'Sure is, ma'am.'

'I am Sister Maureen Carmody, I am a friend of California Bill. We, that is, Bill spoke to you about some pensioners who were missing. The situation is much more serious now and I need your help.'

'Where is old Billy boy?'

'He has been arrested. He is in police custody in Arklow. That's why I need your help. It is imperative that we find the pensioners. They are being pursued by a gang of ruthless drug dealers operating a bus, an ambulance and some cars. Bill is implicated and cannot prove his innocence until the pensioners have been found. Will you help us?'

'You can bet your bottom dollar I will.'

'Please, Mr Stomp. Get all your people on it. I and my companion, Miss Iris Fox, will continue our search. Alert your office, we will phone in regularly for updates.'

'We're on it, Moe. Keep in touch.'

'Moe.' Maureen winced at the nickname but decided to ignore it. She got down from the lorry to where Iris was standing in awed amazement.

'You are extraordinary, Sister Carmody. How did you do that? How did you know about that radio?'

'To the bike, Miss Fox. We must be on our way.' Maureen hitched up her uniform and straddled the bike behind Iris.

Chapter Twenty-three

Lefty Morgan paced his cell. He was waiting for his boys to call. He wasn't worried. Nothing to worry about, he told himself, the boys were more than likely in a black spot and couldn't reach him. He'd give it another twenty minutes and then he'd try them again. By rights they should have Smith in the lock-up by now. What's to go wrong? The job was a cinch – all they had to do was get rid of a few auld ones and nab Smith. Too bloody busy enjoying themselves giving Smith the once over. He'd give them a bollocking when they did get in touch – no one kept Lefty Morgan waiting, least of all his own men. Lefty did a few more turns in the cell and phoned Smasher.

'It's the phone,' Smasher said to the gang. 'Move over, I can't get at me pocket.'

'Ouch, watch it, your bleeding elbow is like a razor.'

The gang were squashed together in the back of the ambulance. They hadn't moved very far from the site of their damaged back-ups. They'd reversed up a small lane and were lying in wait. Smasher had reckoned that if Chalkey's information was correct the bus would soon appear along the road. It would have to slow almost to a crawl to get past the cars, and that would be their chance; they would be ready to pounce.

'Boss. How's it going? Shut up you lot, it's Lefty . . . Yeah, Boss, I had it switched off, we were lying in ambush and I didn't want to give the game away by the bloody thing ringing at the wrong time . . . Eh, not yet, Boss, we ran into a few snags, nothing we can't handle but . . . Yeah, Boss, it's swarming with fuzz, they even had some undercovers on the bus but we out-foxed them, the dumb cruts . . . Yep, we're all in place, the bus is purring towards us, right into our laps, it'll be a piece of cake . . . Sure, Boss, we'll call you the minute the job is done . . . There's nothing to worry about, Boss, you'll be out on bail by tomorrow and with us taking care of Smith you won't be going back in . . . Yeah, Boss I am sure, you can go ahead, break out the champers, we'll all be celebrating.' Smasher pressed the off button and stared into the mobile. 'Shit,' he said, 'Lefty's getting rattled, I can tell by his voice. We gotta do something, and fast.'

'I didn't know there were undercovers on the bus,' Brains said.

'Well you do now, right? And if Lefty asks you, the place was swarming with them, right? Here's how it's going to go. We get Smith in the ambulance, shift whoever is on the bus off, and Bob's your uncle, the job is done. I'll keep two of you with me to guard

Smith, the rest of you boys can travel back to town in the bus.'

Smasher and his boys waited and waited but nothing passed down the road.

'Nothing yet, Smasher,' Pete repeated for the umpteenth time from his vantage point in the driver's seat.

'Bloody hell. How much longer are they going to be?'

'Don't worry, Smasher, they'll be along. It's a tour bus, they're touring, looking at the sights and stuff.'

'Knock it off, Brains.'

'The heat in the back of the ambulance had become almost unbearable. The boys removed jackets and jumpers and were down to their shirtsleeves. Smasher knocked on the ambulance partition window.

'Anything?'

'No, Smash. Like I told you seconds ago, nothing. Nada.'

'That bleeding Chalkey. I'll wring his bloody neck. I'll be dug out of him when I get my hands on him. Get him on the blower. He's going to answer to Lefty for this cock-up.'

'I don't think Lefty is going to care whose cock-up it is, Smash. He's going to blame us anyway.'

'Shut the fuck up. I can't hear myself think with you lot muzzling in on me.'

'We can't help it, Smasher. We ain't got room to breathe.'

'He, ha, ha.' Gus started to laugh. 'Ha ha ha ha ha.'

'What's the matter with him? He says nothing the whole bleeding day and then he starts to laugh.'

'I just thought of something funny, Smash.'

'What? What's so funny?'

'It's to do with breathing.'

'Yeah, so?'

'There was this fella, an' he had a problem with his nose . . .'

'Is this a joke, Gus? 'Cause if this is a joke I'll . . .'

'No, Smash, honest to God, it's the truth.'

'Go on, Gus, tell us your story.'

'Well there was this fella, and he had a problem with . . .'

'Yeah, yeah, we know, with his nose.'

'Anyway, he goes to the doctor and he says, Doc, I've a problem with me nose . . .'

'Jesus Christ, Gus. I'm warning you. This had better be good.'

'. . . An' the doc says . . .'

'Smasher.'

'The doc says "Smasher"?'

'Smasher.' The voice came from the front of the ambulance. 'It's the bus.'

'The bus. Where is it?'

'Look to your left. I don't know how it happened but it's coming from the wrong direction and Smasher, it's coming backwards.'

'Who gives a shite what way it's coming? Get ready, everyone. Brains, you stand in the middle of the road. Make out you need help so they stop. The rest of you, file out and stay behind the ambulance till you get my signal, then come forward. Pete, keep your engine ticking and edge out, face the ambulance the way we want to go, we want a smooth getaway. Brains, where are you going?'

'I thought you said stand out and—'

'Not yet, you bloody idiot. We wait until the bus gets past the cars and then we go.'

Mr O'Connor yanked the gearshift and the bus chugged along in reverse. 'I don't like this. I'm getting a very weird sensation in my body. It's not natural to be driving like this when I can't see where I'm going.'

'*Now* he's worried,' Lillie whispered.

'What does it matter, Mr O'Connor?' Cissy said. 'You couldn't see when we were going forward.'

'Places, everyone. To the rear windows,' Miss Poole called out. 'We must be Mr O'Connor's eyes.'

'I think I can see something,' Willie said.

'You've been seeing things all day, Willie.'

'Willie's right. There's something big up ahead.'

'I can't make it out. Miss Poole, can you see? What is it?'

'It looks like a road block.'

'A road block?' Everyone crowded to the back. 'That's good, isn't it? It means that the police are there.'

'Hooray!' The pensioners shouted out loud. 'Hooray, we're saved!' The pensioners were still cheering and clapping as they approached the barricade.

'That's odd,' Miss Poole said, 'I don't see anyone.'

'Shove over, Miss Poole, and give us a look. She's right. There is no one there. What do you make of it?'

'I know one thing,' Dessie said. 'The police would never go off and leave cars like that in the middle of the road.'

'Maybe it's a booby trap,' Cissy suggested. 'There could be a bomb.'

'Oh my God, a bomb!'

'Steady on, girls, let's not panic, I don't think . . .'

'I've seen it before, you know,' Miss Poole said, 'during the war. Cars hijacked and filled with explosives.'

'With all due respect, Miss Poole, that was years ago. We're not at war now.'

'Says who?' Cissy said. 'When you think of all we've been through we might as well be at war. Stop the bus, Mr O'Connor.'

'Cissy's right, we should stop the bus.'

'Don't, Mr O'Connor. It will be worse if we get stuck here. Look, somebody's coming.' Brains appeared out of the hedgerow and was walking towards them. 'He's waving us down.'

'Yoo-hoo,' Lillie called out. 'Are you looking for us?'

'Be careful, Lillie,' Dessie said. 'I don't like this. I don't like this one bit. I think that's one of the criminals. It's an ambush.'

'Stop the bus, Mr O'Connor, but don't let the engine stall.'

'Are you mad, Dessie?'

'Yes I'm mad. I'm mad and I'm sick of being bullied around by those mobsters. We're going to get him. Look, he's on his own and like you said, Cissy, there's a coach-load of us. Now, Mr O'Connor, when he gets alongside of us open the door, let him get on, and as soon as he's on the bus we rush him. Get ready. The door, Mr O'Connor.' Brains had stepped up on to the bus. 'Now, everyone. Get him.'

The pensioners charged at Brains. Bony fingers grabbed at his arms and legs while Dessie landed a headbutt to his chest.

'Drag him in.'

They hauled the unfortunate gangster into the bus and threw him down the centre aisle.

'Sit on him, girls. Don't let him up.'

'The door, Mr O'Connor. Close the door.'

'Help! Let me up!' Brains tried to move but the combined weight of Violet, Mrs Scott and Miss Bourke – the heavier ladies of the party – sitting on his back and legs was too much for him and he couldn't move.

'What now, Dessie?'

'Forward, Mr O'Connor, forward, as fast as you can. All eyes to the front. Miss Poole, Cissy, Lillie, man your windows please. Hold on tight, everyone. Now, Mr O'Connor, go!'

Mr O'Connor put his foot on the accelerator and the bus lunged forward.

'Where am I heading, Miss Poole?'

'Don't worry about that for now, just keep going.'

Smasher watched his man getting on the bus. 'Like I told you, boys,' he said, 'a piece of cake. One look at Brains and they'll cave. Pete, get down there with the ambulance and pick up Smith. We'll deal with the rest of them. We get them off the bus and then we . . . What the . . .?' Smasher saw the bus taking off. 'What the hell is Brains up to, the thick bloody stupid git? I'm goin' to . . . Get back in the ambulance, all of you. Pete, get after them. Tell that eejit to stop fooling around. Wait for us. Pete, come back.' Smasher was left jumping up and down in frustration as Pete shot forward and took off after the bus at top speed.

'We are being chased. It's that ambulance.'

'Mr O'Connor,' Miss Poole said, 'wait until he's nearly upon us then pull out to the middle of the road and stop dead.'

'What are you saying, Miss Poole?'

'We can't possibly outrun the ambulance. We must wait until he's nearly upon us and then force him off the road. The bus is much heavier, he'll have to give way, it's our only chance.'

'Oh my God.'

The ambulance was heading straight for them.

'Brace yourself. Sit down and brace yourselves for impact.'

'Hail Mary, full of grace, the Lord is with you.' Lillie dropped to her knees between the seats and started to pray. 'Forgive me for all my sins and intercede for me with Him on high.'

Pete raced the ambulance towards the bus. He planned to get ahead of it and get it to stop. 'Christ!' The bus screeched to a halt directly in front of him forcing him to swerve sharply to avoid running into the back of it. 'Shiiite . . .' Pete roared as he tried to swerve out of the way, but he was going too fast; he lost control and the ambulance plunged into a deep ditch at the side of the road.

'Hooray, bravo, Mr O'C, you've done it! Three cheers for Miss Poole and Mr O'Connor!'

The pensioners got to their feet and looked out the window at the stranded ambulance.

'Is it over?' Lillie poked her head up over the seat. 'Can I get up now?'

'It's over, Lillie. He's not going anywhere.'

'Do you know, me whole life flashed before me? I never believed that stuff before but it's true.'

'It didn't take long, Lillie,' Cissy said, 'you were only down there for a minute.'

'What do we do now, Miss Poole?'

'I don't think we will have any more trouble, look.'

They all looked to where Miss Poole was pointing and saw the gang who had chased after the ambulance stop dead when they saw it hit the ditch. Smasher wasn't minding them, he was occupied boxing the heads of his fellow criminals.

'I can't go on, Miss Poole. I'm done for. My hands are shaking so much I can hardly hold the steering wheel.'

'Try to keep going a bit longer, Mr O'Connor. If we can put a few more miles between us and those ruffians we'll be out of danger and we can stop the bus.'

'I can't drive that bus again.' Mr O'Connor began trembling. 'Please, don't try to make me.'

'The poor man has done enough. If it wasn't for him . . . don't worry, Mr O'Connor, it's OK. We'll think of something.'

'Ohhh.' Brains groaned from the floor as Mrs Scott, who had taken off one of her shoes to use as a weapon, hit him on the head once more. 'Knock it off, granny, that hurts.'

'I nearly forgot about him in all the excitement,' Cissy said. 'What are we going to do with him?'

'We'll take him with us to the police station. Hand him over to the authorities.'

'And how do you propose we get there? Poor Mr O'Connor's done in. We can't expect him to keep driving this bus.'

'I have an idea,' Lillie said. 'Hey, mister. Yes you, you big galoot,' she said to Brains. 'Can you drive?'

'Huh?'

'I said, can you drive?'

'Yeah. I can drive, but I ain't driving this.'

'You ain't aren't you? We'll soon see about that. Girls, you know what to do. Strip him.'

'Get off. Leave me alone,' Brains cried out, clutching at his clothes as the ladies advanced towards him. 'Help!'

'I wouldn't want to be in your shoes,' Dessie said. 'I think we should get off the bus, men, this could get ugly.'

'Don't leave me. Don't leave me with them,' Brains appealed to the gentlemen.

'You have two choices. Drive the bus or we leave you to the ladies.'

'I'll drive, I'll drive,' Brains cried. 'Just get them off me.'

'That's settled then. Back off, girls but watch him. You know what to do if he tries any funny stuff.'

'Can't you go any faster, Miss Fox?' Maureen was clinging on to Iris on the back of the moped and they roared along the road.

'I can't hear you, Sister Carmody. What did you say?'

'I said can we not go any faster? Can you pick up more speed?'

'What direction do you think we are headed in, Sister?'

'I have no idea, Miss Fox. I can't see.'

'Can you see now?' Iris bent down over the handlebars and Maureen got the full blast of the wind in her face.

'Sit up, Miss Fox. I can't hold on with you bent over like that. Stop! Stop! My cap's blown off. I've lost my cap.'

'We can't stop now, Sister.'

'We must.'

'Can't you get another one?'

'No. That cap has great sentimental value. It is irreplaceable.'

'For goodness sake, Sister Carmody, we don't have time to waste on a cap.'

'Slow down. Stop this bike or I will throw myself off.'

Iris slowed the bike, turned around and went back the way they had come while Maureen kept a lookout for the missing cap.

'It could have blown anywhere, Sister Carmody.'

'Stop here. This is the spot where it blew off.'

'I never heard such rubbish,' Iris said to herself as she watched Maureen searching at the side of the road. 'We're in the middle of a crisis and we're looking for a cap.'

'There it is, in that hedgerow. I need your

assistance, Miss Fox. It's landed too high up for me to reach.'

'Get a stick,' Iris said, getting off the bike.

'I need you to give me a lift up.'

Humour her, Iris, Iris told herself. Help her get the damn cap and then we can get on with rescuing people. Iris put her arms around Maureen's legs and struggled to lift her. 'I can't budge you, Sister Carmody. You're too heavy for me.'

'Nonsense, Miss Fox. I'm not heavy at all. Try harder.'

Iris gave another heave and managed to shift Maureen enough to get her feet off the ground. They were in that position when the bus containing the pensioners drew up alongside them.

'It's Iris.'

'And Sister Carmody. What on earth are they doing?'

'Yoo-hoo, Iris. It's us.'

'Sister. It's our pensioners. Oh, thank God, they're safe.'

'Miss Fox. Kindly put me down.' Iris had forgotten for a moment she was still holding Maureen. She opened her arms and let her slip to the ground.

'Fiend, abductor!' Maureen rushed on to the bus and before anyone could stop her she had rained several blows on to the back of Brains's head. 'You won't get away with this. I will have you imprisoned for life.'

'Stop, Sister Carmody, stop. Don't damage him or we won't have anyone to drive the bus.'

'We captured him, Iris. All by ourselves.'

'Where are the others, Iris? We thought they were with you.'

'Are they not still in Arklow?'

'The only ones in Arklow,' Maureen said, 'are my friend Deborah and a truck driver called Bill.'

'Your friend Deborah?' Iris enquired. 'Are you here with a friend? I must admit, Sister, I am a bit confused. I think we all are.'

'Yes. My friend, Deborah and Bill are being held by a group of deviant, misinformed, plainclothes policemen in a hotel in Arklow.'

'In Arklow?'

'Miss Fox, would you please stop repeating everything I say? I am trying to explain the situation. Deborah and Bill are being held in Arklow under the misconception that they are involved with a Lefty Morgan and his fellow conspirators.'

'They weren't on the outing,' Mrs Scott said. 'We never had a Bill or a Deborah on the outing, did we?'

'No, Mrs Scott,' Iris said. 'They are friends of Sister Carmody's.'

'What's she doing here anyway?'

'I don't really know.'

'We should get out of here,' Dessie said. 'Remember the gang aren't far behind. I bet you a grand as soon as they get more transport they'll be after us again.'

'They weren't after us in the first place. They're after Mr Perrin and he's not with us.'

'I know that, Lillie, but they don't know that.'

'We were heading for Arklow, Sister,' Miss Poole said. 'We were going to go to Arklow and hand this man over to the police.'

'I don't think that's a very good idea, Miss Poole. After the way those policemen treated myself and Deborah I don't trust them to handle this situation at all.'

'Maybe we should drive straight back to the city.'

'No,' Iris said, 'we can't. We have to go to the farm and get the others.'

'Farm, Iris? What farm?'

'The farm Mr Perrin and the others are hiding in. Don't worry, Sister Carmody, they are quite safe there, no one is going to find them.'

'No one would have found us in the aerodrome,' Willie said from the back of the bus. 'We could have died there and no one would have found us . . .'

'The aerodrome?' Iris and Maureen said together.

'. . . They would have found our bones, bleached by the sun, no identifying marks, nothing at all except our teeth to tell anyone who we were.'

'They'd have had a hard time at that considering we're all wearing dentures, Willie,' said Cissy.

'I'll have you know, at least three of the teeth in my mouth are my own.'

'We know, Lillie. You're always telling us.'

'Oh, Willie.' Iris went down to him. 'Of course we would have found you. We would have searched the countryside till we did.'

'I want to go home, Iris. I'm tired.'

'We are going home, Willie. As soon as we pick up the others we'll go straight home, I promise you.'

'Drive on, fiend,' Sister Carmody instructed Brains.

'Where to? I can't drive on if I don't know where I'm going, an' don't call me "fiend", I ain't no fiend, I'm Brains.'

'You must have a proper name, young man,' Maureen said. 'I cannot allow my residents to be driven hither and thither by someone called Brains.'

'Sister Carmody, he's a gangster. What does the name matter?'

'It matters, Miss Fox. There is a certain etiquette which . . .'

'I'll guide you to the Pilkintons' farm,' Iris said. 'We can collect everyone there and head for town.'

'To the farm,' Maureen said. 'Miss Fox, directions please.'

'The moped. I can't leave the Pilkintons' moped behind. Could we get it on the bus?'

'For heaven's sake, Miss Fox, we haven't room for a motorcycle.'

'We'll have to make room. It will fit down the aisle.' Iris struggled to get the moped aboard and put it down the centre of the bus. 'There. That's fine. I couldn't very well leave it when the Pilkintons were so kind as to lend it to me. Willie, what are you doing, Willie?' Willie had left his seat and was heading for the moped.

'I've always wanted a go on one of these,' he said.

'Up you get so.'

Willie was hoisted on to the moped.

'Vroom, vroom.' Willie, all smiles now, sat astride the moped. 'Vroom, vroom.'

'Way to go, Willie.'

'Isn't that great?' Iris said. 'It's really cheered him up.'

Maureen threw her eyes to heaven but kept her mouth closed tight.

Chapter Twenty-four

'Ah yes indeed, the hurly-burly of a busy Detective Inspector's office can take its toll but it has its rewards as well.' Chief Meyers sat back contentedly in the hotel armchair and smiled at his audience – the fact that this was a captive audience didn't seem to deter him in the slightest. 'Wouldn't you agree, Sergeant Kelly, that the satisfaction of a job well done has its own reward?'

'As you say, sir.'

Bill and Deborah sat opposite Chief Meyers as he went on discussing not only his career but also the changes he would make in the force if and when he was appointed Commissioner. Nailing Lefty Morgan would be a big feather in his cap. 'The icing, so to speak.' The Chief had had it from the horse's mouth.

'That's all very interesting, Chief Meyers,' Deborah said, 'but we've been here for ages now and there's still no sign of your men returning. They obviously haven't found Maureen and, in the meantime, we haven't a clue where the pensioners are, let alone

Morgan's gang, and I don't see how you are going to get anything done about it sitting around here drinking coffee.'

'Easy, Deborah,' Bill said. 'We don't want to upset the Chief now, do we?'

'Sergeant Kelly, can we have an update on our men's position if only to satisfy our friend here? I have every confidence in my team's ability, Miss. Sergeant?'

'Like I told you before, Chief, there is no news.'

'What are you doing here then, sergeant? Get out there and get after them.'

'I would have been after them already but you started talking and . . .'

'If I could get back to my truck, Chief,' Bill said, 'I'm sure I could find them.'

'Stay where you are. I want you where I can see you. Kelly, make sure they don't move.'

'This is madness,' Deborah said. 'We are not the ones you want.'

'Chief, give me a minute to check the car radio. Something might have come in.'

'Very well, Kelly, but don't be long. I want these people watched.'

'Did you hear that, Bill?' Deborah said. 'We're to be watched. You are going to be very sorry, Chief Meyers, when the full story comes out.'

'Save your breath, Miss. I've heard it all before.'

'What is it, Kelly? What have you got?'

'There's been some developments, sir.'

'Get on with it, man.'

'It appears that Headquarters got a call in from Ashford. The local police are still holding a number of customers in a café. They've been there all afternoon.'

'Go on.'

'It's causing quite a stir, Chief. A number of television crews are at the scene. Headquarters want to know what we're going to do about it.'

'Do about it?'

'Yes, sir.'

'They are all suspects, Kelly. Plants. Part of Morgan's clever plan to divert our attention. They will continue to be held until we have Alex Smith back in protective custody. Do I make myself clear, Kelly?'

'Perfectly clear, sir.'

'How can they be involved, Chief? The bus didn't even stop there.'

'I decide who is involved and who isn't, Miss. It's called expertise. I don't expect you lay-people to understand. We policemen work on hunches and ninety-nine per cent of the time those hunches are spot on. Right, Kelly?'

'If you say so, sir.'

'Tell the local men to hold everyone until I get there. How many television crews did you say there were?'

'I don't know exactly, sir.'

'Never mind. I shall leave directly. An impromptu press call can do wonders for police morale.'

'What about us?' Deborah said. 'We can't stay—'

'Sergeant Kelly, I will take the car. You will continue to control operations from here.'

'But, Chief—'

'Those are your orders, Kelly. Public relations cannot be left to local men to handle. The keys, sergeant.'

Chief Meyers departed, leaving Sergeant Kelly, Bill Thomas and Deborah looking in disbelief at each other.

'Sergeant Kelly, I appeal to you. You know this situation is out of hand. Come with us to my truck. We have more chance of finding the pensioners, and your Alex Smith, on the road than sitting here in the hotel. I have CB on board, we can tune it in to your police frequency. What do you say, sergeant?' Sergeant Kelly took a moment and then nodded his assent. 'Great. Let's get going then.'

Deborah walked over to reception to settle the bill but found Marianne passed out behind her desk. She left the money on the counter and followed the others.

Chalkey cruised aimlessly around Arklow. He didn't have any idea where he was going but he was so glad to be off the hook with Smasher and the boys he didn't care. He was trying to figure out where Janice could have got to. He'd checked the station; there wasn't a train due for a while so he reckoned she must be still around somewhere. Would she have hitched? No, Janice wasn't a hitching sort of girl. No use looking in pubs for her either, she wouldn't go into a pub on her own. There were a few coffee shops in the town but he had looked in and she wasn't in any of them. That only left the hotel and there was no way he was going back there, that'd be asking for trouble. He knew if he went back to the city without Janice her ma would kill him. Janice's da was bad enough but he was shit-scared of her ma. It would be all right if she had got home but how was he to know when he couldn't find her? This day was turning out to be a bloody nightmare.

'Holy smoke . . .'

Chalkey spotted Sergeant Kelly leaving the hotel with two other people. He watched as the sergeant stepped into the road and waved down a passing car. Kelly spoke to the driver and then beckoned to the other two. They all got in the car and took off.

'Weird,' Chalkey said aloud, 'bleeding weird, I never saw the likes of that happening before.' Janice was momentarily forgotten as his curiosity got the better of him and he turned the bike to follow after them.

Jones stopped his car and waved down the others. He realized they were not going to find the fugitive nurse this way, they'd have to fan out. He was beginning to feel the pressure. What if they didn't find her? How could he explain to Meyers that eight plain-clothes had failed to recapture one woman in a nurse's outfit? Meyers would have a fit. If he could only contact Sergeant Kelly without the Chief finding out, he could ask his advice. There was nothing else for it. Meyers or no Meyers, he would have to break radio silence.

'Car one to Sergeant Kelly. Come in Sergeant Kelly.'

'Is that you, Jones?'

'Yes, sir, Chief Meyers, sir.'

'I trust everything is under control, Jones.'

'Yes, sir.'

'I mean *everything*, Jones.'

'Absolutely, sir.'

'And Smith?'

'Under our fingertips, sir.'

'I'm very glad to hear that, Jones, because I am on my way to Ashford for a news conference. I want to be able to announce on television that we have retrieved our witness, that the gang involved are in custody and that once again the guardians of the law have served the public as it deserves to be served. Am I free to say that, Jones?'

'Yes, sir, very free, sir.'

'Good. Now, Jones, I want you to link up with Sergeant Kelly and return to Headquarters in convoy. I might suggest to the media that if they happen to be outside Headquarters at a certain time they could perhaps witness the triumphant return of a well-planned, well-co-ordinated, mission. What do you say to that, Jones?'

'It would go down very well, Chief.'

'I think so. It's not often we get a chance to bask, as it were, in the media spotlight.'

'No, sir. We don't often get to bask.'

'We shall have a debriefing back in the office as soon as I can get away from the television people.'

'Right, sir.'

'Over, Jones, and well done.'

'Thank you, sir.'

'Jones? What is it, Jones?' Nigel got out of his car and ran up to Jones. He found him and his partner rigid in their seats staring straight ahead of them. 'What's the matter with you? Hey guys,' he called to the others, 'there's something wrong in car one. Speak to us, Jones, say something.'

'Chief Meyers,' Jones spluttered, 'Chief Meyers is going on national television to announce that Alex Smith has been rescued and that the gang are in custody.'

'That's brilliant, Jones. No wonder you are surprised. When did they get him?'

Jones could only whimper and shrink into his seat.

'You fool, Nigel,' agent Sinclair said. 'Don't you see? Jones is trying to tell us that Smith is still at large but the Chief is under the impression that we have him.'

'Oh dear. I wonder how he thought that one up.'

'We've got to contact Sergeant Kelly.' Jones sat up suddenly. 'He's our only chance.'

'Why don't we call him?'

'Because, Nigel, we don't know where he is. I tried to get him on the radio but Chief Meyers is driving his car.'

'I see. Well, actually, to be truthful, I don't see. I don't see at all unless, Jones, you told the Chief we had Smith.'

'I didn't.'

'Then how did he think we did?'

'All I said was he was under our fingertips. Is it my fault he drew the wrong conclusion from that?'

'Of course not. Anyone with even half a brain wouldn't rush to the conclusion that under one's fingertips doesn't mean one has. It is close, though.'

'There is only one way to save the situation.'

'Yes, Jones.'

'We must get Smith, get the nurse, get the gang and get them all back to Headquarters before Chief Meyers arrives with the television crew.'

'Good for you, Jones,' agent Sinclair said. 'Think positive. We must all think positive. It's the only way.'

'To your cars, gentlemen.'

'I don't know about Jones,' Nigel said as he and his partner went back to car four. 'I mean, you heard him say – "only one way to save the situation" – then he lists three, no, four things. Do you think he's OK?'

'He's probably still in some sort of shock. We'll play along with him for the moment but if you want my opinion I think we're fighting a losing battle.'

'You and me both,' Nigel agreed.

'Thank you, sir,' Sergeant Kelly said. 'The police force is indebted to you.'

The car that had picked up Sergeant Kelly, Bill and Deborah and deposited them at Bill's truck drove away.

'He'll have a story for his grandchildren,' Bill said, 'about the day he assisted in a police chase. Did you see him respond when you told him to ignore the speed limit?'

'It made his day,' Deborah said. 'Look, Bill, your window's broken.'

'Bloody hell. Damn hooligans. Well, we've no time to worry about that now. What's our best plan, Sergeant?'

'Get your CB going. Get me on to Police Headquarters.'

'I can't put you through directly, sergeant, all our calls go through the office switchboard. I can tune in to your airwaves but I can't get you a direct line out. Let me talk to my depot first. If there were any messages for me they will have them.'

'What good is that?'

'Bill has all his friends on the lookout for your bus, sergeant. Somebody might have spotted something.'

'Nothing,' Bill said after a few moments, hanging up the CB. 'No luck so far.'

'What now?' Deborah asked.

'We search, we ask.' The sergeant said. 'Two Dublin buses on small country roads, somebody has to see them.'

'What about your local force, sergeant? Can we contact them?'

'No. Best they keep out of it. We already have four cars in the area. Any chance of surprising Morgan's gang is probably lost already. And there's no way of knowing if Chief Meyers hasn't already briefed them and if so—'

'They're on to the wrong people, right sergeant?'

'That could be the case.'

'You don't have to be tactful with us, Sergeant Kelly. We saw your chief in action.'

Chalkey's bike purred quietly as he watched the truck from a vantage point further down the road. For the life of him he couldn't figure what was going on. He saw, but couldn't hear, the CB calls. He watched as the Sergeant consulted a map and then directed the driver on to a small road that would lead back to Arklow. 'Barmy,' he said to himself, 'they're all barmy.' Chalkey knew that Morgan's gang were only a few minutes away, lying in ambush for that bus. Two, three turns at most and they'd all meet up with each other. That would be a gas, Chalkey thought. Serves them all bleeding right, serves Smasher right if he got picked up. What would Lefty Morgan have to say about that then, his right-hand man picked up? Smasher shouldn't have threatened Janice. That wasn't right. Jesus. Janice, he forgot. Where the bleeding hell could she have got to? Why didn't she phone him? Chalkey checked his mobile; it was OK, plenty of credit on it still. He turned the bike but thought the better of it. 'Let's see what happens if that lot meet,' he chuckled to himself.

Smasher and the boys spotted the truck in the distance. They had climbed a small hill to get the lay of the land and saw it coming in their direction.

'We're saved, boys,' Smasher said. 'A piece of cake and it's falling right into our laps. We grab the truck and . . . move those cars, make enough room so they can get through without slowing. The driver is bound to get curious about that ambulance. He'll probably get out. No, better still, one of you lie down beside it. That'll make sure he stops and when he does, grab him and get him out of the way. Pete, you drive – I'll come in the cab with you. The rest of you, when we get past the cars, move them back to the middle and then get in the truck. Dug, get down to the ambulance and lie down.'

'Sure, Smash.' Dug scampered down the hill.

'Get going, boys.'

'The extraordinary thing about it, sergeant, is that neither myself nor Bill are involved with these people at all. I'm here because Maureen, Sister Carmody that is, got me out of bed to help her look for her lost residents, and Bill is here because we broke down on the way and needed a lift and he was kind enough to stop for us. Now, even though I don't know her people, I feel worried about them. I mean, to think that an outing, sergeant, an innocent outing for a group of elderly people, could end up like this. The Lord only knows how they are coping with it all.'

'In my experience,' Sergeant Kelly said, 'older people have a remarkable ability to cope with most things. Look at the changes they have been through in their lifetime. We don't even come up to scratch when it comes to their resources. They have seen it all.'

'Sergeant,' Bill said. 'Look ahead. There's been an accident. It must have just happened, there's a man lying in the road.'

'Oh my God,' Deborah screamed. 'He could be dead. Stop, Bill. Stop.'

'Stop here, Bill. It's better not to drive too near, they could be leaking petrol.' Bill and Sergeant Kelly prepared to jump out of the truck.

Dug was lying on the road near the ambulance. He had just lifted his head to gauge how far away the truck was when he found himself looking at the face of Sergeant Kelly. He dropped his head back down and closed his eyes.

'I should have known,' Sergeant Kelly said. 'It's a set-up, Bill. Get back in the truck, quick.'

'But, sergeant?'

'I know that lowlife. He's one of Morgan's men. If he's here the others can't be far away.'

'But he's hurt, sergeant,' Deborah said.

'Oh no he's not. Bill, drive on up towards him. Make as if you are going to drive over him.'

'You can't do that.'

'It's all right, Deborah. The sergeant knows what he is doing.'

Deborah couldn't look as Bill moved the truck forward. He got closer and closer and was almost beside Dug when he honked his horn. Dug opened his eyes and saw the front wheels of the truck practically on top of him. He leaped up and ran for all he was worth, calling out to the rest of the gang.

'Smash,' he shouted, 'we've been rumbled. Run, Smash, run!'

'Bloody hell.' Smasher had watched the proceedings from the hill. He saw it all going wrong. 'Where the hell did Kelly come from?' he roared at his boys. 'Get lost, scarper, Kelly will have the whole force down on top of us.'

'Where'll we go, Smasher?'

'I don't bleeding know, do I? Just get outta here.'

'Wait for me, Smash.' Dug struggled up the hill. 'Don't leave me.'

Smasher and the boys had already gone.

'Will we give chase, sergeant?'

'No. Our priority is Smith. This episode confirms that they haven't got him. They wouldn't be hanging around in those bushes if they did. They won't be driving anywhere – by the look of those cars their transport is kaput. It'll be easy enough to pick them up between here and town. Morgan's boys are not used to Shank's mare, Bill, it'll take them a long time even to get to Arklow.'

'I hope they don't run into Maureen,' Deborah said. 'I wonder where she got to. Mind you, if she managed to elude eight plain-clothes policemen . . .'

'They are new in the field,' Sergeant Kelly explained.

'What field, sergeant? They don't seem to have a clue.'

'I agree they don't have much know-how but in the normal course of events each one of them would be assigned to an older, more experienced man. It was unfortunate the way the rota was worked out for the weekend.'

'Meyers?'

'No. To be honest it was me. Our men had been working round the clock on the Morgan case. We thought it was sewn up. I gave the order for the investigating team to be relieved so they could spend some time with their families. It was a bad call but I take full responsibility for it.'

'Where to now, sergeant?'

'Get on your CB, Bill, and give this number to your office to phone. I couldn't use it before. I couldn't take the risk it might be intercepted. Ask them to leave this message. "Perrin. Contact the station immediately and leave information of your position for Sergeant Kelly. We are in the area and can pick you up."'

'That's it?'

'That's it. The call will go through to Perrin's mobile. If he gets it he will reply.'

'And in the meantime?'

'We continue to search. They are hiding somewhere in the area. It's only a matter of time before we find out where.'

Chapter Twenty-five

'Vroom, vroom, vroom.'

'Where are you headed for, Willie?'

'Texas. I'm heading for Texas.' Willie was still astride the moped in the centre of the bus.

'On you go, cowboy.'

'Vroom, vroom, vroom, vroom.' Willie continued to enjoy himself.

'Must you do that?' Maureen asked. 'It is impossible to hear oneself think with that racket going on.'

'Lighten up, Sister. He's only having a bit of fun,' Iris said.

'Well it certainly wouldn't be tolerated at the Cross and Passion. I am happy to say that none of my residents would behave in that manner. Horseplay down the centre of a bus – it isn't dignified at his age.'

'And at what age would you consider that people should stop having fun?' Cissy asked. 'Or do you not believe in fun in that mausoleum of yours? I wouldn't go into that place if you paid me. I wouldn't be seen dead in it.'

'I don't think there is any fear of that. Our residency is quite restricted. We pride ourselves on our selection.'

'Restricted is right. A boa wouldn't be so restricted. I bet you people pay through the nose for your restrictions. I think it's a disgrace. You've all that space and Miss Poole tells us she's not even allowed to put in a few plants in the garden and she's an expert.'

'Yes,' Lillie said, 'and you won't even let her have a donkey.'

'This is preposterous,' Maureen said. 'I refuse to listen to this ridiculous criticism.'

'A donkey, Lillie?' Iris asked. 'What makes you think Miss Poole wants a donkey?'

'I don't know. Something that happened earlier on, or maybe it was an ostrich. Miss Poole, which was it you wanted, a donkey or an ostrich?'

'The part I don't understand, Sister, is if your nursing home is so restricted, how come you had Mr Perrin? Surely he wouldn't be on your selected list?'

'Mr Perrin was placed in the Cross and Passion without any consultation with staff members. Naturally, had I been consulted, there is no way I would have allowed it. Endangering my residents by exposing them to criminal elements would be unthinkable. Rest assured, on our return to the city this matter will be taken up at the highest level.'

'That's a great comfort,' Cissy said, 'when we've all nearly had our throats cut. We've been exposed, Sister Carmody, whether you were consulted or not. We've been hijacked, abandoned and left for dead in an airfield and if not for Miss Poole and Dessie and Mr O'Connor we'd be still there.'

'That's right,' Lillie agreed, 'and I've got a twitch in me eye from looking out that window that'll probably never go. Do you see it?' Lillie blinked around the bus and her eyes came to rest on the back of Brains's head. She stared at it for a minute. 'Oi, you, gangster man,' she called up to Brains. 'What's your name? Your real name?'

'Don't talk to him, Lillie. Don't encourage him.'

'I can't be sure, Cissy, but there's something very familiar about the back of that fella's head.'

'Give over.'

'I'm telling you. Wait here a minute.' Lillie reeled up to the front of the bus and stood behind Brains. 'What's your name?'

'What's it to you?'

'I'll give you what's it to you if you don't keep a civilized tongue in your head. Do you want me to call up the girls?'

'Me name's Brendan. Brendan Barlow.'

'I thought so.' Lillie lowered her voice. 'And your mammy's name is Theresa Barlow, isn't it?'

'So what?'

'"So what," he says. Listen to me, I know your granny, she only lives down the road from me. How do you think she's going to feel when I tell her that her grandson kidnapped us, threatened to murder us and hijacked us? She'll never get over it. She'll never have another night's peace when she hears.'

'You're not going to tell her?'

'And why wouldn't I tell her that her little Brendan,

the little chap she used to knit jumpers for, is a low-down, good for nothing . . .'

'No don't tell her. It'll break her heart, she'll kill me.'

'Well, you better start co-operating. You drive this bus the way you are told, no funny stuff, no messing, or else.'

'Don't worry, missus, I'll co-operate. I'll do whatever you say, just don't tell my granny.'

'That's better, that's more like it. Where do you want to go, Iris? Brendan here wants to co-operate. Just come up here and give him your directions.'

'How did you do it, Lillie? What did you say to him?'

'I let him know what's what. I told him he'd have to answer to me if we didn't get where we are going, and pronto.'

'Well done, Lillie,' Helen said.

'Where to, Miss?' Brains asked Iris. 'Just tell me where you want to go.'

'We keep straight on this road, then there's a sharp turn to the left for the Pilkintons' farm. I'll show you when we reach it.'

'Lillie Fogerty,' Cissy said, 'get down here to me and tell me what that was all about.'

'Do you remember Mary Kavanagh that was?'

'No. Is she dead?'

'No she's not dead, she married Jack Donevan.'

'Oh, Mary Donevan. I know Mary Donevan.'

'Well hers and Jack's young one, Theresa, married a Barlow from Percy Place.'

'So?'

'That's their young fella, Brendan.'

'Go on, it's never.'

'It is. Would you believe it?'

'You could knock me down with a feather. That nice family. They can't know what he's up to, it'll break their hearts when they find out.'

'That's what I told him. He begged me not to tell his granny, said he'd co-operate if I didn't.'

'But sure they're going to find out anyway. He's going to be handed over to the police.'

'I know that, Cissy, and you know that, but he doesn't seem to know it. I don't think he's the full shilling, if you know what I mean.' Lillie and Cissy both looked up at Brendan.

'Easily led.' Cissy said.

'I'm afraid so, Cissy.'

'Vroom, vroom, vroom.'

'Would you please stop that racket,' Maureen said.

'Leave him alone, he's not doing anyone any harm.'

'Willie.' Miss Poole stood up in the aisle. 'When you are finished, could I have a go please?'

'Miss Poole!'

'Yes, Sister Carmody?'

'Miss Poole, I am surprised at you. I hope you're happy now, Miss Fox. Just look at the damage you have caused – you've turned my residents into a bunch of hooligans.'

'You have a beautiful place here, Mrs Pilkinton. It's so peaceful it's hard to realize how close it is to the city.' Mr Perrin, Helen, and the pensioners who'd been left behind were sitting round the big kitchen table in the Pilkintons' kitchen while Janice and Stevie huddled in a corner listening to pop music on the radio.

'I love this one, it's great for dancing.'

'In your dreams, Janice. They're crap. The lead guitar is useless.'

'Shows how much you know. They were in the top twenty last week.'

'Yeah. That's only because people like you buy the tape. If you really want sound you should listen to—'

'What do you mean, people like me . . .'

'So much for your peace and tranquillity, Mr Perrin.' Helen laughed. 'How much longer do you think we'll be here?'

'With any luck Iris should have been in contact with Chief Meyers by now.'

'That's providing she hasn't got lost or fallen off the bike.'

'We'll have to hope for the best. In the meantime, this is as good a place as any to hide.'

'More tea, anyone?' Mrs Pilkinton asked.

'You're an angel, Mrs Pilkinton. I never thought I'd be so grateful to see tea.'

'We were just saying, Mrs Pilkinton, that Iris has been gone a long time.'

'Devil a bit, dear.'

'It shouldn't have taken all that time for her to get to Arklow. Do you think something has happened to her?'

'Maybe she ran into the gang,' Stevie said.

'Ran over them, more like,' Helen said. 'Did you see the way she handled the moped?'

'I'll give it another thirty minutes,' Mr Perrin said. 'If there is nothing after that I'm going to Arklow myself. No, Helen, don't try to talk me out of it, there is no other way.'

'You'll walk right into the gang, Mr Perrin. It will be like giving yourself up to them on a plate. All we've been through will have been for nothing.'

'My mind is made up.'

'And the gang will have won. Is that what you want?'

'Of course it's not.'

'Well then, you are not budging. If nothing happens in thirty minutes Stevie and I will take the bus and make a run for it, right, Stevie?'

'Sure thing, Helen, I'm game. I'd rather meet the gang any day than listen to this crap.'

'Listen to him, he hasn't got a clue,' Janice said.

'What's that noise? Did anyone hear a noise? It sounds like a bus.'

They looked up anxiously in time to see the second bus drive into the farmyard.

'Well, I'll be blowed,' Mr Pilkinton said, scratching his head.

'Look, dear,' Mrs Pilkinton said, 'more visitors.'

'Yahoo,' Stevie shouted. 'It's our lot. Come on.' Everybody rushed out of the kitchen.

Iris was the first to alight, followed by Maureen and then the pensioners.

'It's Sister Carmody,' Mrs Clancy said. 'Hello, Sister Carmody, have you come to collect us?'

'Well done, Iris, you made it,' Helen said, 'and you have the pensioners. Where did you find them?'

'I didn't actually find them, Helen, they found us. I met the gang and they crashed because of a stampede and then we – Sister Carmody and I – met the others and . . .'

'I don't follow you, Iris. Didn't you get to Arklow? How did you meet Sister Carmody?'

'The gang, Iris,' Mr Perrin asked. 'Did you say they crashed? Are they immobilized?'

'Don't talk to us about immobilized. That same gang left us completely stranded, they took the keys, didn't they Cissy, and left us for dead . . .'

'Tea, anyone?' Mrs Pilkinton called out through the clamour as everyone began talking at the same time. 'Would anyone like to come in for tea?'

'Mrs Clancy, Mr O'Neill,' Maureen called out. 'Do keep off the grass, it's bound to be damp and you will catch a chill. Go back inside.'

'I don't want to go back to the kitchen, I am sure my son will be waiting for me.'

'. . . that's only the half of it,' Dessie said. 'There I was, Mr Perrin, halfway up a ladder trying to get into the aeroplane hangar when I felt the rung going from under me. I tell you, I thought I was done for.'

'We had a lovely tea here, Miss Bourke, with scones and home-made jam and everything.'

'How nice, Mrs Clancy. We didn't – ours was rather weak and weedy, and it was very green. We lit a campfire, you know.'

'Hello dear,' Mr O'Connor said to Janice, 'are you with the farm? I wonder, could I have a cup of tea? I'm quite parched.'

'How wonderful, a farm,' Miss Poole said. 'There is

nothing more satisfying than a good field of potatoes.'

'Hold it. Hold it,' Lillie shouted. 'All of you. This is worse than the blooming Mad Hatter's tea party. Brendan,' she called out to Brains who was still sitting behind the wheel of the bus, 'belt the horn or there'll be no stopping them.'

Brains obliged and kept his hand on the horn until everyone had stopped talking.

'Don't, don't,' Helen cried. 'You'll give the game away. You'll attract the gang.'

'No fear of that, Miss. We left them miles back.'

'It's OK, Helen. We don't have to worry about them. They've lost their transport and they're walking around out there like headless chickens.'

'We ran the ambulance off the road,' Dessie said proudly. 'Mr O'Connor drove backwards and forwards . . .'

'Mr O'Connor drove the bus?' Maureen sank to her knees. 'But he can't see, Mr O'Connor cannot see his hand in front of him. Hooligans in aisles, blind men driving, what next? Lord, what more can you throw at me?'

'Get up off the grass, Sister,' Cissy cackled. 'You'll get piles.'

'Who are you?' Helen asked as Brains got out of the bus.

'Don't take any notice of him, Helen,' Lillie said, 'that's Theresa Barlow's lad.'

'I don't understand. How . . .?'

'Stop. Let me on the bus.'

'What is it, Willie? What's the matter?'

'I left my mac on the bus.'

'It's all right, it's not our bus, Willie.'

'Whose bus is it? It looks like our bus. Where is our bus?'

'It's hidden in the barn.'

'I hope my mac's in it. My daughter bought it for me. She'd get very cross if I lost it.'

'Don't worry,' Iris reassured him. 'Everybody's belongings are on our bus. Now, say hello to the Pilkintons, Maureen. They hid us from the gang.'

'How do you do. I am sure this is all very confusing for you but I assure you I had no part in any of this.'

'It is so good that we're together again. You've no idea how worried I was about all of you.'

'If the gang are immobilized, Iris,' Mr Perrin said, 'I think we should leave as quickly as possible. We don't want to give them time to regroup.'

'Mr Perrin,' Maureen said, 'or should I call you Alex Smith?'

'You can call me whatever way you want, Maureen.'

'Have you any idea what you have put us through?'

'I know exactly what I have put these good people through, Maureen, though I'm not sure where you come into it, considering you refused to come along in the first place.'

'I am here because I knew from the start that this trip would be a disaster. Deborah and I set out the moment I realized that Miss Fox had managed to get lost with my residents.'

'I did not,' Iris protested.

'There is no point in denying it, Miss Fox. A Mr Scully of Ashford was waiting for you and you didn't show up. If you had, this whole sorry episode could have been avoided. I spoke with Chief Meyers personally and he assured me . . .'

'Meyers,' Mr Perrin said, suddenly dashing off to the barn. 'I'm going to get the mobile, there could be a message.'

Chalkey turned off his engine as he neared the farm. Not that he needed to – the noise from the crowd gathered in the yard would have blotted it out anyway. He had decided to follow the bus. When he had seen the fiasco with the ambulance and had watched the lads as they scattered in all directions, he knew to make himself scarce, he knew what the consequences would be if he hung around long enough for Smasher to see him. Not that any of it was his fault. He gave them the information and they blew it. What happened after that had nothing to do with him, not that Smasher would see it that way. He'd follow the bus and see where it went.

So one of them down there was Smith. For a moment he was tempted to call Lefty but he thought better of it. Lefty would want to know where Smasher was and why he hadn't got the squeal already and Chalkey wasn't going to be the one to tell him. He was about to turn tail and head for home when he spotted Janice. What the hell was she doing there? How had she got mixed up with that lot? Now what was he going to do? He watched one of them run into the barn and come out again. He had a mobile in his hand. That must be him – Alex Smith in the flesh.

*

'Mr Perrin,' Maureen said, 'did you get anyone?'

'Yes. I had a message from Sergeant Kelly. I gave him our position and he's on his way. As a matter of fact, he's only minutes away.'

'Does he have reinforcements?'

'I don't think so, Maureen. He's travelling in a truck.'

'Heavens to Betsy, Mr Pilkinton,' Mrs Pilkinton said to her husband, 'there seems to be an army coming. A truck, sir?'

'I don't understand it myself, Mrs Pilkinton. I am afraid we have rather upset your day.'

'I'll say,' Mr Pilkinton said. 'I don't know what you city folks are about. You're being chased by a gang, I have not one but two buses in my yard, and now there's a truck on the way?'

'You go back to your drills, dear,' Mrs Pilkinton said. 'I'll put the kettle on again.'

The truck drove into the yard at full speed and screeched to a halt. Sergeant Kelly jumped out, followed quickly by Bill Thomas and Deborah.

'Alex. You're all right?'

'I'm fine, sergeant.'

'Don't worry about the rest of us, whatever you do, sergeant,' Cissy said.

'I'm sorry, Mrs, I didn't mean any offence.'

'Sitting decoys,' Lillie said, 'that's what we've been, and he doesn't even ask about us. I'm writing to my GP.'

'I think you mean TD, Lillie.'

'Whatever.'

'More company,' Mrs Pilkinton said to Deborah and Maureen, 'and who are you?'

'Deborah is a friend of mine,' Maureen explained. 'She drove me out to look for my residents, and this gentleman is Mr Bill Thomas who picked us up.'

'This is getting so confusing I'm almost dizzy,' Cissy said.

'May I suggest that we leave all the explanations until we are back at the station?'

'The station, sergeant?' Iris said.

'Police Headquarters, Miss. I shall have to ask you all to give statements.'

'We can't, sergeant. Not now. My old folks have been through enough. I must get them home. We're way behind as it is. Their families will be worried.'

'Humph,' Maureen snorted. 'It's a pity, Miss Fox, you didn't think of the families before you careered all over the countryside with my people.'

'It is procedure, Miss.'

'I don't care, sergeant. I'm taking my people home. I'll give you all the names and addresses and you can talk to them tomorrow.'

'Iris is right, sergeant. You have no idea what's been going on.'

'I believe I do, Alex.'

'Sergeant,' Maureen said. 'I wish to lodge a strong complaint about your men. I have been abused in the most vile manner by a team of incompetents.'

'I am aware of the situation, Sister. Like I said, we'll get everything sorted down at Headquarters.'

'Where are your men now?'

'Out looking for you, Sister.' The sergeant turned to

Mr Pilkinton. 'Mr Pilkinton, would you allow us to leave one of the buses here on your farm? We shall alert the bus company and have someone come and collect it as soon as possible.'

'I don't know about that.'

'Of course he will, sergeant,' Mrs Pilkinton said. 'It would be no trouble, no trouble at all. Tell him, Henry.'

Mr Pilkinton muttered something which the sergeant interpreted as a yes.

'Thank you, sir. We are grateful. Right, on the bus if you please, and don't worry, I shall be accompanying you the whole way.'

'I'm not driving that one, sergeant,' Stevie said. 'I want my own one.'

'Yes, sergeant,' Iris said. 'We must travel on our own bus. All our belongings are on it, and a lot of expensive decorations.'

'Very well. Go get your bus but be as quick as you can.'

'Goodbye, Mrs Pilkinton.' Iris hugged the farmer's wife. 'You have been so good, thank you, thank you so much for everything.'

'Don't be a stranger, dear. Anytime you're out this way, call in and see us. Henry and I would be delighted, wouldn't we, Henry. Henry?'

Mr Pilkinton had ducked into the pantry. He saw Iris bearing down on him, her arms open, ready to embrace him.

'Goodbye, everyone. Drive carefully now.'

'Goodbye, Mrs Pilkinton, goodbye.'

'Come along, folks. We must get a move on.' The

sergeant bustled everyone aboard the bus. 'Keep it moving, now.'

'Dear me, sergeant,' Maureen said. 'This is not traffic control. Deborah, why aren't you getting on?'

'I'm travelling back with Bill.'

'With Bill?'

'Yes, Maureen. He's missed his ferry, his whole day's been ruined, and I don't think it would be very nice to abandon him now after all he's done for us.'

'Well really, Deborah, I do think that's over and above what is necessary.'

'It may not be necessary, Maureen, but I am doing it.'

'Hold on,' Janice had jumped off the bus and was running back towards the kitchen. 'I forgot something.'

'Janice, what are you doing?'

'I'm getting potatoes. Mrs Pilkinton said I could take some home for me mam.'

'What a nice thought,' Miss Poole said. 'Sister Carmody, couldn't we—'

'Most definitely not, Miss Poole.'

'Bloody hell,' Chalkey exclaimed. 'It's like a bleeding convention down there. I'll never get to Janice. There's so much babbling going on I can't make out a word.'

Chalkey watched as Sergeant Kelly herded the pensioners on to the bus. First there was a lot of hugging and kissing with the farmer's wife. Then he saw Janice run back and get a big bag of something that was so heavy she could hardly carry it. Finally, the man and the woman got back into the truck and the Sergeant got on the bus. They took off in convoy. The bus and then the truck pulled out of the farm with all their occupants waving out of the windows to the farmer and his wife. Maybe he should call Smasher. Let him know there was fuzz on board in case they made another attempt to grab Smith. No. To hell with it, he wasn't getting involved no more.

'I'll tuck in behind them,' Chalkey thought, 'and pick up Janice when she gets off.'

Chapter Twenty-six

'It feels good, doesn't it, Iris – Stephen back in the driving seat, the pensioners safe and sound, and with the sergeant on board we shouldn't have any more trouble. Straight home, eh Iris? Back to dear old Dirty Dublin.'

'You know, Helen,' Iris said, 'we do have comfort stops booked for the return journey.'

'I think you can forget about that. Look at the time; they're hardly expecting us now.'

'It is paid for, Helen. I hate to think of that money going to waste.'

'So get a refund. Ring them, ask them to send you your money back. Not that I think you have much chance in succeeding.'

'That's an excellent idea, Helen. We can put it by and it will help to start the fund off for next year.'

Helen groaned silently. She and Iris were sitting together at the front of the bus with Mr Perrin and Dessie in the row behind them. Sergeant Kelly, with Brains Barlow safely on his inside, sat in the opposite aisle and the pensioners, keeping a few rows' distance between them and the gangster, spread themselves over the rest of the bus. Maureen had stationed herself on the long seat at the back. 'I shall stay where I am,' she said when invited to sit beside Cissy. 'I want to be able to keep my eye on everyone.'

Iris stood up and faced the passengers. 'Hello. Attention everyone. Here we are on the homeward trail . . .' Iris got no response, no one was paying any attention to her. The passengers were slumped in their seats in a state of exhaustion.

'Leave it, Iris. They're all too tired.'

'I'm not having my pensioners returned home in a state of torpor, Helen. I don't want their last memories of our outing to be downbeat. They just need something to lift their spirits.' She stood up on her seat and clapped her hands. 'Attention, everyone. Now, I know you are all a little tired, but what about a little singsong to keep us going, keep our spirits up? What about, "It's a Long Way to Tipperary"? I know everyone knows that one.'

'Is she joking?'

'I don't think so, Cissy.'

'Come on, everybody, it'll help to shorten the journey home and cheer us all up at the same time. On the count of three. And a one, and a two, and a . . . "It's a long way to Tipperary, it's a long way to go, it's a . . .'

'. . . "Long way to Tipperary, to the sweetest girl I know . . ."' To the astonishment of the assembled passengers Brains Barlow took up the song and began to sing it with gusto.

'Of all the nerve,' Lillie said. 'You keep your singing voice for the police, Brendan Barlow, remember what I told you.'

'A singing criminal,' Cissy said. 'Where would you get it? All we need is for the sergeant to join in.'

'Perhaps we should let him sing,' Miss Poole said. 'I seem to remember reading somewhere that singing is recommended for rehabilitation.'

'I know a few on this bus need rehabilitation, Miss Poole, naming no names of course, but I don't think singing is going to help.'

'Are you looking at me, Lillie Fogerty?' Dessie asked. 'Because if you are . . .'

'Ladies, gentlemen, please.' Iris flapped her arms about. 'We mustn't argue among ourselves. We don't have to sing that one. There are plenty of other songs we can sing. Would anyone like to start one off?'

'No.' The entire bus, with the exception of Brains Barlow, was unanimous.

'Well, Iris, if nothing else, you certainly woke them up,' Helen laughed.

Stevie concentrated on the road. He reckoned it would take about an hour to get back to town. He wondered if there would be anyone at the depot to take in the bus. Not that he was worried about it – if there wasn't anyone there he'd leave it outside and drop the key into the letterbox. It will be a great relief to be shut of it, he thought to himself. He'd had enough for one day. They had flashed through Avoca without any delay and hit the main road heading back the way they had come. He gave a little shudder when he passed a sign: WELCOME TO ASHFORD, THE GARDEN OF IRELAND.

'What is it, Stephen? Why are we slowing down?'

'There's a pile of traffic up ahead, Iris. Look.'

'Oh no, not a road block,' Helen said. 'I hope they're only checking for tax or something. I don't think I could bear it if it was anything else.'

'Can't you detour, Stephen?'

'No way, you must be joking. I'm not going up one more side road, not even for you, Iris. We are sticking to the main drag all the way home. It won't take long to get through.' Sergeant Kelly walked up to Stevie. 'What is it, lad?'

'A road block, sergeant.'

The Sergeant peered out through the window. He could be mistaken but no, there was car one, parked on the hard shoulder, and standing by the side of the road was Agent Jones.

'Leave this to me, lad,' he instructed Stevie as he pulled up alongside the squad car. 'I'll speak to them.'

'Young man, Stephen,' Maureen called out from her seat, 'why have we stopped?'

'Road block, Sister.'

'Of all the . . . let me off. I won't have this delay when my residents are exhausted.'

'The Sergeant is dealing with it, Sister.'

Maureen didn't listen. She bustled up the aisle and got off the bus.

'You,' she said, recognizing Jones. 'Sergeant, arrest that man. He's the one who ordered me handcuffed.'

'Let me handle this, Sister. Get back on the bus.'

'I will not.'

'Back on the bus now or I'll have you handcuffed myself.'

Maureen leaped back on board.

'Jones, do you want to tell me what the blazes you think you are doing?'

'Hi, sarge. Look what we've got.' Jones led Sergeant Kelly to the back seat of his car. In it Smasher and Dug sat handcuffed and subdued. 'We caught them red-handed, sarge. They were trying to hot-wire a car when we pounced.'

'Well I'll be . . .'

'Nigel has three more. The rest of them got away, sarge, and we thought they might try to hitch a lift so we decided to stop all vehicles and search them.'

'I'll be . . .'

'I know, sarge. It's wonderful, isn't it? Sergeant, wasn't that the nurse that . . .?'

'Yes, Jones. Never mind that now. Go on ahead and book this lot. We'll ask the local boys to pick up the others. And, Jones, well done. Well done all of you. I'll see you all later.'

'Thank you, sarge.'

'Oh, and Jones, do something for me on your way back . . .' The sergeant whispered into Jones's ear.

'Car one to cars two, three and four. We're going in, men. Fall in behind the bus.'

'We roger that car one.'

'And I roger back to all of you.'

The road block was lifted and the convoy moved forward.

*

'Look, Helen, look at Scully's. I wonder what's going on?'

The area around Scully's was floodlit and, in spite of a small cordon of policemen attempting to hold them back, television crewmen and interviewers were all over the place. They had set up arc lights, camera and sound equipment, and were trying to film the customers inside who were alleged to be part of a ruthless criminal gang. Mr Scully was dancing up and down on the pavement. He ran from the café to the street, appeasing his customers on the one hand and appealing to the crew members to respect the laws of privacy and private property on the other.

Chief Meyers paced the floor inside the café. He was awaiting the arrival of the Commander who had been summoned by the local police. The Commander wasn't happy. He'd had words with Chief Meyers on the telephone about an unauthorized news conference, sanctioned by the Chief, which went out live to the nation on the early evening news. On it Chief Meyers had implied that all was well. That the witness who was under police protection had been returned safe and sound. The Commander had had no confirmation of this and he had set out to do some damage relief.

'I tell you something for nothing, Iris,' Stevie said, 'it looks like right bedlam in there. I'm glad we're not involved in that.'

The convoy drove past Scully's and on to the dual carriageway, unnoticed by anyone.

*

Lefty Morgan had watched the evening news in the recreation room. Although he didn't usually mix with the prison riff-raff, preferring to watch his own set in his cell, tonight was an exception and he felt the need for a bit of company. When Lefty appeared in the recreation room a silence descended among the men. Lefty's presence usually meant trouble. It usually meant he was looking to single out someone for something. Even the screws got nervous when Lefty joined in the normal prison activities. The men nearest the telly shifted over to give Lefty the best seat.

'Boys,' Lefty acknowledged the move.

'Hiya, Lefty.'

'How's it going, Lefty?'

Lefty watched the programme without moving a muscle. There was no reaction from him when Chief Meyers, speaking from a village in County Wicklow, spoke of the safe return of a witness for the state in the case of The State versus Mr Lawrence 'Lefty' Morgan. When the news was over he stood up and, without a word to anyone, returned to his cell.

'That's twenty years for him,' one of the prisoners said.

'I wonder why he didn't get his boys to bump your man off?'

Quietly and calmly Lefty closed the cell door before giving vent to his anger. He ranted and raged with frustration. That shower of no good . . . when he got hold of Smasher even his own mother wouldn't recognise him. He had no fallback plan. He had been so sure of getting Smith. Smith – who was he anyway?

A nobody, that's who. An easy target for the likes of Smasher and the boys. Lefty's phone rang and he grabbed it. Newsmen often got things wrong. Could be the fuzz put out that message because they didn't have Smith and they thought it might rattle the boys into doing something stupid.

'Morgan.'

'Hello, lovey, it's Imelda. I can't talk long because I'm in a call box. I didn't use our own phone to ring you like you told me not to and I don't have much change, you know the way the mobiles eat up money from a public box.'

'Get on with it, Imelda.'

'Don't take that tone with me, Lefty Morgan. I'm not one of your boys.'

'I'm sorry, love, I'm sorry. Just tell me what you phoned about.'

'It's not as if it's easy for me with you banged up.'

'Imelda, I said I was sorry. Now will you get on with it.'

'I just thought I better tell you that it doesn't look like you are going to get out because one of your boys phoned me to say that Smasher and some of the rest were picked up and . . .'

'Imelda. What's your bleeding number . . . ? Imelda . . .' Imelda Morgan's bowl of artificial flowers hit the cell floor.

'Oh look, Iris, we're back at the Meetings of Moore's Waters again. Are we stopping?' Lillie had had a nap and was alive and alert again. She proceeded to wake everyone else. 'Wakey, wakey, you lot. We don't want to miss the end of the outing now, do we?'

'I think that's where I left me mac, Iris, at old Moore's.'

'He's at it again,' Lillie said. 'Willie. Old Moore's an almanac, he's a weather reporter, he hasn't got your overcoat, love.'

'Don't forget, Iris, you promised we could stop at the ostriches. I want to bring home some feathers.'

'That's not the Meeting of the Waters, Lillie, we passed that ages ago, that's the sea. And no, I'm afraid we can't stop, we are behind as it is.'

Iris stepped up beside Stevie and picked up the megaphone, tapping the head of it.

'Testing, one, two, three, testing.'

'What's she doing?'

'She's testing.'

'Sure didn't she do that before and it was working fine?'

'Listen to me, all of you. We are not making any stops. The Sister is anxious for us to get back to town and so am I. I don't want your families or your loved ones to be worried about you.'

Sobs from Janice filled the bus.

'Who was that?' Iris asked.

'It's Janice,' Helen said. 'I better see what's the matter with her. Janice, what's the matter? What's wrong?'

'Your loved ones,' Janice sobbed. 'I thought I had a loved one. Chalkey hinted that he and I, he and I . . .' Janice buried her face in her hands.

'Don't cry, Janice. I'm sure everything is going to work out.'

'How can it? I couldn't marry him now, could I? If he can dump me like that when we're not even married what'll he be like when we are? Out every night enjoying himself, leaving me alone with the kids . . .'

'You have children?' Maureen asked.

'Of course I don't. What sort of girl do you think I am?'

'You could talk to him, Janice. These sort of misunderstandings often happen between couples.'

'Do you think so?'

'I'm sure about it.'

'I'm not so sure,' Iris said. 'If he's part of that gang, Janice, you might be better off without him.'

'I don't think he is really. He's just easily led.'

'Aren't they all?' Cissy said. 'Me and Lillie were only talking about that earlier, weren't we Lillie?'

'Speak for yourself, woman,' Dessie Rourke said quickly.

'Listen, Janice, when we get back to town phone him. Everyone has tiffs and they blow over. For all you know he could be sick with worry, he could be searching for you right now.'

'Searching for me? Do you really think so?'

'Of course I do.'

'Stevie, will you stop at the next phone box? I want to ring Chalkey.'

'Can't you wait until we get to town?'

'No, I can't. Please, Stevie, please.'

'Love,' Lillie sighed. 'Could you beat it?'

'Easily,' Cissy replied.

'You could use my mobile, Janice,' Mr Perrin said.

'I warn you, your call may be monitored, but if you don't mind that . . .'

'I don't care. I won't be saying anything private. I only want to know where he is and why he dumped me in that town and if he still loves me or what. And I want to find out if he really is mixed up with that gang and to tell him that if he is it's all over between us, especially after what they tried to do to all of you.'

'I hope your battery is fully charged, Mr Perrin. It sounds as if she could be on it for quite a while.'

Chalkey heard the mobile going off in his pocket and tried to work out who it could be. It couldn't be Smasher. He'd seen Smasher and some of the boys in the squad cars. Lefty – could it be Lefty? No. Lefty couldn't know they had been picked up yet so why would he be ringing? It must be Brains or Kev. Shit. He should have turned it off. He'd have to answer it now. If he didn't, Lefty might get to hear of it. He slowed and took out the phone.

'Chalkey here.'

'Chalkey?'

'I just said so, didn't I?'

'It's Janice.'

'Janice! I've been looking all over for you.'

'You have?'

'Of course I bleeding have.'

'Oh, Chalkey.' Janice cupped the phone and repeated Chalkey's words down the bus. 'He's been looking for me.'

'Ahh,' Lillie sighed again, 'isn't that nice? He's been

looking for her.'

'If you are going to slobber all the way home, Lillie, you can sit on your own.'

'Are you there, Janice?'

'Of course I'm here, Chalkey, you're talking to me.'

'So what do you think?'

'What do *you* think, Chalkey?'

'I don't know what sort of conversation that is supposed to be,' Maureen said. 'Stop shilly-shallying and articulate, girl. Tell that boyfriend of yours exactly what's on your mind.'

'Leave her alone. It's not your phone call.'

'She already told us she wants answers, so why doesn't she tell him? She won't get answers if she doesn't ask questions.'

'I hate questions and I hate telephones,' Con said, 'they make me nervous.'

'I know what you mean, Con. I like to be able to see who I'm talking to.'

'To think you can make a telephone call from a bus. My goodness, in my courting days, and that's not so long ago, one had to go through the village operator. One was always sure the postmistress was listening in.'

'They do say though that soon you'll be able to phone from your television, then you can see who you are talking to.'

'I'd hate that. You could be caught wearing any old thing.'

'How will that work? There's nothing to lift.'

'Mr Perrin, is it true that mobile phones can damage your eardrums?'

'I don't know, Dessie.'

'It's probably the sonar. I heard it's supposed to be very bad for you.'

'I'd never get a mobile.' Brains spoke up. 'Not if it's bad for me.' The conversation stopped dead as they all looked incredulously at Brains. 'It'd do my head in.'

'Who asked you?' Lillie said. 'There's no one on this bus interested in your opinion, so kindly keep your trap shut and don't be interrupting decent people's conversation.'

'I didn't mean any harm.'

'Well you just keep it that way.'

'Janice. Are you still there, Janice? Speak to me.' Chalkey was screaming into his phone. 'Oh for Christ's sake.' He revved the bike and picked up enough speed to overtake the truck. Staying on the outside lane he moved up alongside the bus and tried to catch a glimpse of Janice through the windows.

Beep, beep, beep, beep. Chalkey banged on the horn as he kept abreast of the bus and Stevie caught sight of him in his side-view mirror.

'Sergeant. There's a biker trying to get our attention. What do you think? Could it be a trap?'

'No,' Iris said. 'Not more trouble. Where is he, Stevie?'

'Right-hand side.'

'It's Chalkey,' Janice cried. 'Chalkey, I'm here.'

'Isn't that beautiful? He's come to get her.'

'How on earth did he appear like that?' Iris wondered. 'Pull over, pull over, Stephen, before he gets himself killed.'

'Sergeant. What do you make of it?'

'Highly suspicious, Mr Perrin. I don't like it one bit.'

Stevie pulled in at the side of the road and stopped.

'Mr Perrin. Move down to the back of the bus. Stevie, don't open those doors until I tell you.' The Sergeant lowered the window.

'I'm looking for my girlfriend,' Chalkey said. 'I want to talk to Janice.'

'How do you know she's on this bus?'

'I followed you. I saw her getting on back in Arklow but then I lost you. I've been sitting here for ages waiting for the bus to pass. I knew it would have to come this way.'

'How come I know your face? What's your name, lad?'

'I'm Chalkey Deveroux, sergeant.'

'Deveroux. That's it. I knew I knew you. I've had you in before.'

'I was in a bit of bother when I was a nipper, sergeant, but I'm straight now. You can check me out. Honest, sergeant, I'm only looking for Janice.'

The Sergeant hesitated. He looked round the bus at the anxious faces of the pensioners, then he weighed up the story Chalkey had just told him. He must be telling the truth. No one would be stupid enough to stop a bus full of people and mount an attack on his own.

'Open the door, Stevie.'

Stephen opened the door and Chalkey stepped on to the bus.

'Chalkey.'

'Janice.'

The two looked awkwardly at each other.

'Well, don't just stand there, give her a hug,' Cissy said.

'Hiya, Chalkey,' Brains gave a big grin.

'Brains! What are you doing here?'

'It's on account of my granny.'

'Are you going to spend all day talking to your mate, Chalkey Deveroux? I'm waiting. I'll be getting off now, Iris. I'll go back to town with Chalkey. Thanks for everything. It's been lovely meeting all of you and don't forget what I told you, Mrs Clancy – any time you want a hairdo you've only to call me. Goodbye everyone, goodbye.'

'Remember, Deveroux, I'll be keeping my eye on you.'

'Sure, sergeant. Any time.'

'We all will,' Iris said. 'You make sure you treat Janice right.'

'Don't forget your parcel, Janice,' Stevie said.

'My potatoes.' Janice reached for the bag.

'You can't take them on the bike.'

'Says who? The farmer gave them to me and I'm taking them home for me mam.'

'But, Janice . . .'

'Don't "but Janice" me, Chalkey Deveroux. I'm taking them.' Janice lugged the bag off the bus.

'I can see who is going to wear the trousers in that relationship,' Dessie said.

'It's only a few potatoes.'

'I know that, Cissy, but there's where it starts.'

*

Ann Roberts and Garda Cullen were sitting in the day room of the Cross and Passion. It had been a long day and Ann was bored. She wanted to go home and meet up with her friends and it was all the Garda could do to stop her slipping off when he wasn't looking.

'Why can't I go home?'

'I'm sorry, Ann, I can't let you go. You have to wait until Chief Meyers gives the all clear.'

'The all clear for what? I haven't done anything.'

'I know, Ann, but orders are orders. I'm stuck here too, you know. I could be out catching robbers and joyriders.'

'Oh yeah.'

'Have you ever thought of becoming a policewoman when you grow up?'

'No I haven't. And I am grown up.'

'And what do you want to do, Ann, or do you not know yet?'

'I'll either be a model or a singer.'

'Very nice.'

'Anybody mind if I put on the television?' Doctor Kennedy had come into the day room to join them. 'I want to get the test results.'

'Go ahead, doctor.'

When the television came on the news was halfway through. Doctor Kennedy and Garda Cullen weren't paying attention to it – they were discussing the possibilities of the next day's hurling match – when Ann let out a scream.

'There's that man. What's he doing on the telly?'

They turned to the television to see Chief Meyers

being interviewed outside a café. He was saying that a witness had been rescued and that the police had everything under control.

'Great news, Garda.'

'It's odd, doctor, that no one has called me. I better get on to the station.'

'Does that mean I can go home?'

'Not yet, Ann, but I'm sure it won't be long.'

'We are approaching Kilmacanogue everyone, and then it's on to Bray.' Iris had picked up the microphone again.

'Iris, Iris, can we see the ostriches now, Iris?'

'Lillie, one more word about those ostriches and . . .'

'There's no point in stopping, Lillie, you wouldn't be able to see them anyway, they'd be asleep.'

'What do you mean "asleep"?'

'Ostriches are Australian – it's the middle of the night over there.'

'What's she talking about? That's daft, Cissy. If I was transported to Australia I wouldn't keep Irish hours now, would I?'

'You wouldn't, Lillie, because you would know where you were, but the ostriches don't know they're in Ireland, do they?'

'She's making a point. I don't know what it is yet but she's making one.'

'Mr Perrin,' said Maureen, 'could I possibly use your phone? I would like to call my staff and let them know where we are.'

'Certainly, Maureen.'

'How long do you estimate it will take us to get in?'

'Within the hour, I'd say, Maureen.'

'Hello. Cross and Passion, who do you want?'

'Ann, is that you?'

'Yep.'

'It's Sister Carmody, Ann.'

'My mother wants to talk to you, Sister Carmody.'

'Is your mother there?'

'No. She says you are to phone her. She wants to talk to you about my exploitation.'

'Such nonsense, Ann. Pull yourself together, girl, we have had an extremely difficult day and I am altogether too tired to listen to anything frivolous.'

'Well, don't say I didn't warn you.'

'Get Doctor Kennedy for me.'

'I can't, he's gone out for a minute.'

'Gone out?'

'Yep.'

'Who is there, Ann? Who is handling things?'

'The policeman is still here. He won't let me go home even though we saw that man on the telly telling everyone that they had their witness person.'

'They have their witness, Ann?'

'That's what they said on the telly.'

'Put me on to the policeman . . . Sergeant Kelly, a member of my staff has just informed me that a news bulletin announced that the witness is in custody. How could that be, sergeant? Mr Perrin is with us.'

'Give that phone to me, Sister . . . Cullen, it's Sergeant Kelly here. What's going on, Cullen?'

'I don't know, sergeant. I saw Chief Meyers on the

television myself but when I rang Headquarters they knew nothing about it.'

'I don't know what Meyers is playing at. Stay at your post, Cullen. We will be with you shortly.'

As they approached the suburbs and joined the heavy throng of traffic heading back to the city, the convoy got separated. Bill did his best to remain directly behind the bus but the weaving cars and lane hoppers made it impossible.

'I feel terrible about this, Bill,' Deborah said. 'I could have got on the bus. You have been arrested, missed your ferry, you might even lose your job because of us, and now you are heading into town in all of this.'

'Don't worry about it, Deborah. I want to do it and anyway I couldn't bear to go off and not see this to the finish.'

'But what about your delivery? Shouldn't you . . .?'

'Nothing that can't wait until tomorrow.'

'I don't know what to say.'

'Say you will have dinner with me tonight.'

'Of course I will. It's the least I can do after all we've put you through.'

'Not as a duty, Deborah. Don't come as a thank-you.'

'I'm not, Bill.'

'Back to the fumes and the traffic. Makes you wonder why we don't all move out and live in the country.'

'A day like today would really enforce that, Iris.'

'Today was an exception, Helen. You wouldn't

normally be running into that sort of thing.' Iris picked up the microphone. 'We won't be too long now, folks. If you would start to think about gathering your belongings . . . Stop, stop, wait a minute . . .'

The pensioners had got up and started rummaging under seats and in the aisle.

'Would you get up, Con? You're sitting on me handbag.'

'Did anyone see a green cardigan? I can't find it, I hope I didn't leave it in the aerodrome.'

'It'll have to stay there, we're not going back for it.'

'Oh dear, I can't seem to remember where I started. Was I sitting beside you, Miss Bourke?'

'I don't think so, Mrs Clancy. I think I was beside Mrs Scott.'

'Our cuttings,' Miss Poole said. 'We mustn't forget our cuttings from the booth.'

'. . . Stop. Stop,' Iris continued ineffectively. 'Please everyone, stay in your seats. Wait until the bus has stopped. Sit down, please.'

'Cross and Passioners,' Maureen bellowed above the uproar. 'Keep to your seats. Remain seated until the bus stops.'

'Thank you, Maureen,' Iris said as all the pensioners sat down again.

'That reminds me of *Aeroplane*.'

'What does, Lillie?'

'Remember I was telling you on the way out? Yer man tells them to stay in their seats and then he jumps out with his parachute and they can't move because they're fastened and he breaks both his legs but he gets to fly again.'

'I think you are mixing up your films, Lillie,' Miss Poole said. 'I seem to remember the one with the broken legs. It was about an RAF pilot during the war, wasn't it?'

Chapter Twenty-seven

Fairview Park, the Marino end, was to have been the first drop-off point on the return journey but Iris decided they would do the Cross and Passioners first and then deliver the other pensioners to their homes.

'You don't mind do you, Stephen? It won't take us too long.'

'Of course not, Iris. They've been through enough without having to find their own way home from Fairview.'

They drove on through the city without further mishap and, when they reached Drumcondra, Stevie turned into the Avenue of the Cross and Passion Nursing Home. He pulled up at the front steps and gave a toot on the horn.

'Don't, Stephen,' Helen laughed, 'this is not the sort of place you toot in.' Helen looked across at Iris who pretended she hadn't heard.

'Well, well, well,' Doctor Kennedy said as he, Garda Cullen, and Ann came out on to the front steps to greet the travellers. 'Welcome back, everyone. All present and correct, I hope?'

'Sister Carmody. Look at the state of you.' Ann giggled behind her hand as the dishevelled figure of Maureen got off the bus. 'You look as if you've been —'

'That's enough, Ann,' Maureen said.

'It's good to see you back in one piece, Sister.'

'Thank you, Doctor.'

'Can I have a go on the bus, Sister?'

'You certainly cannot, Ann.'

'Why not? You've been on it all day.'

'How does it feel to be back, Mr Perrin?' Helen said, leaning over her seat to talk to him. 'I hope you are going to look after him from now on, sergeant. We can't let him get captured after all this.'

'Don't you worry, Miss, I will make his safety my personal responsibility.'

'Will you be staying here, Mr Perrin? Will he, sergeant?'

'No, Miss.'

'I don't see why not, sergeant,' Mr Perrin protested. 'You have the people who were out to get me. There's nothing Lefty Morgan can do now. You also have a bus full of witnesses who have been kidnapped, threatened, and harassed, not to mention the stolen bus and the ambulance and the cars. What more could you want? Surely that's enough to deter any further assaults, and don't forget our extra passenger who has sworn to give evidence against the gang. Isn't that right, Lillie?'

Before the sergeant could answer, Iris had picked

up the microphone. 'Home sweet home,' she said. 'I am sure you are all delighted to be back. Now, before you Cross and Passioners get off I know you would like to give a big thank-you to our driver, Stephen, who has done such a terrific job. Stand up and take a bow, Stephen.' Iris started a handclap and everyone joined in. 'Three cheers for Stephen, hip, hip . . .'

'Hooray.' The pensioners chorused.

'Don't be modest, Stephen. Up you get and acknowledge your applause.'

'Doctor Kennedy, help me get our residents off the bus. Ann, go in and ask cook to prepare tea. Our people are quite traumatized, Doctor Kennedy. It's going to be difficult to settle them.' Maureen stepped back on to the bus. 'Miss Poole, Miss Bourke, Mrs Clancy, Mr Walsh, Mr O'Connor, Mr Flood, Mr O'Neill . . .'

'I would like to tick people off my own list, Sister,' Iris said. 'I am responsible for everyone's safe return, you know.'

'Nonsense, Miss Fox. I do know my people. Mr Connolly and Mr Carr, this way if you please.' The pensioners didn't budge as Maureen stood at the door of the bus and addressed them. 'Come along, get your things together. I'm sure Miss Fox wants to get on.'

'Hello, everyone.' Doctor Kennedy had stepped up on to the bus behind Maureen. 'Well, you certainly all seem to have had quite an adventure.'

'Adventure, Doctor Kennedy? Is that what you call it?'

'Now, Sister.'

'We have had a spiffing time, Doctor Kennedy,' Miss Poole said. 'I wouldn't have missed it for the world.'

'Neither would I.'

'Nor me.'

'Not for anything.' The voices came from all over the bus.

'I'm looking forward to hearing all about it.'

'Oh yes, Doctor, we've been all over the place.'

'And we rammed some convicts.'

'And Mr O'Connor drove the bus.'

'Don't forget, Miss Poole got it started.'

'And when Mr O'Neill and Mrs Clancy got off and went to look for the others we were abducted and . . .'

'We had a lovely dinner in Arklow.'

'Whoa, whoa,' Doctor Kennedy said. 'Slow down. I can't keep up with all of you. And who have we here?' The doctor smiled around the bus at the other pensioners. 'More adventurers?'

'That's Cissy and Lillie and Dessie and Willie and Con and Iris and . . .'

'So you are Iris?'

'Yes, Doctor.'

'You are the woman who organized the outing?'

'Yes, Doctor.'

'I see.'

'And this is Helen. I couldn't have done it without Helen.'

That's it, Iris, Helen said to herself, land me in it. 'Hello, doctor, nice to meet you,' she said out loud.

'Ah, and here is Mr Perrin. The dark horse of our establishment.'

'Ladies and gentlemen,' Sergeant Kelly said, 'may I suggest we all go inside?'

'Why, Sergeant?' Maureen asked. 'I'm sure there is no need to detain these people any longer.'

'Sister Carmody, I took the liberty of asking agent Jones to call ahead. I asked him to have your people organize tea and sandwiches all round. I know, Iris, you didn't want this but I would like to get some statements while things are fresh in everyone's mind.'

'Really, sergeant, this is too much.'

'I think it's a great idea, sergeant,' Doctor Kennedy said. 'I'm sure our friends would like a chance for a last chat before everyone decamps to their homes. What do you say to tea, folks?'

'I could murder a cup of tea,' Cissy said.

'It's not nettle tea, is it? I don't think I could drink it if it was nettle tea.'

'Don't worry, Mrs B, it's not nettle tea, it's our finest green label.'

'We'll come in for tea, sergeant,' Iris said, 'but I don't want anyone put through a third degree.'

'Nothing like that, Iris. No one will be questioned. Garda Cullen and I will simply pick up any of the bits and pieces of conversation we think might be relevant. After that you are all free to go home.'

'What about Mr Perrin, sergeant?' Maureen asked.

'Mr Perrin will be coming with us.'

As the sergeant spoke, Bill Thomas's truck turned into the drive.

'Deborah,' Maureen said. 'I almost forgot about her.'

'Some friend,' Helen whispered.

'Well, really. Did she have to bring her lorry driver right up to the steps? It doesn't look good to have a lorry so near the front porch.'

'Hooray!' The pensioners cheered and clustered round the truck as Deborah and Bill got out. 'We're all here now.'

'Not quite.' Helen had turned her head towards the entrance and saw the four squad cars enter the Avenue.

'What are they doing here?' Maureen screeched. 'Sergeant, is this your doing?'

Sergeant Kelly stood out from the crowd and waved his arms at the advancing cars. 'Not here, Jones,' he shouted above the noise. 'You weren't meant to come here.'

'Hi, sergeant. Sorry we're late. We got a bit lost.'

'Tea's ready.' Ann came out the front door in time to see the squad cars arriving in the front garden. 'Wow,' she said, 'are there crooks in there? I want to have a look.' Before anyone could stop her she raced down the steps to the cars and looked in the back to where Smasher and Dug sat handcuffed. 'Double wow. Wait till my friends hear about this.'

'Ann! Get back from there! Those men are dangerous.'

'They don't look dangerous to me.'

'Stand back, Ann.' Garda Cullen pulled her away. 'You don't want to get too close to them.'

'Real crooks.' Ann stuck her tongue out and Smasher and Dug retaliated by rattling their handcuffs at her. 'Wow. Wait till I tell my mother.'

'That's enough of that, Ann. Sergeant, what are you going to do about this?'

'Are those nice policemen coming in for tea?' Mrs Walsh asked.

'They certainly are not,' Maureen answered.

'Take your people inside, Sister Carmody. I'll get this sorted out,' Sergeant Kelly said as he went across to his team.

'Inside. Everyone inside for tea.'

'Leave your things on the bus,' Iris said to her Fairview contingent. 'We'll have a quick cuppa and then we'll head for home.'

'Jones. What are you doing here? You were supposed to bring that lot to Headquarters and book them.'

'Sorry, sarge, we thought . . .'

'Back to Headquarters, men, and bring our friend here –' the sergeant nodded over to the bus '– Brains with you. I'll be along as soon as I get some statements.'

'Great bunch of boys you have working for you, Kelly,' Smasher grinned up at the Sergeant. 'Me and Dug fancy a spot of luxury in a retirement home.'

'You'll get to retire all right, Smasher, and for a long time.'

'I want to talk to Meyers.'

'You don't talk to anyone, Smasher.'

'Oh yeah. Tell Meyers I want to see him. Tell him I might have something to say that might interest him.'

'Like what?'

'Let's just say you might not need your witness after all.'

'Take them in, Jones.'

'Morgan's going down, come what may. We don't feel like joining him, do we Dug?'

'Are you telling me you are prepared to turn state's evidence, you are prepared to do a deal?'

'Let's just say we want to talk to Meyers.'

'Bingo nights,' Iris was talking to Doctor Kennedy as they sat around the day room over the tea and sandwiches. 'That sounds fun, Doctor, and you certainly have the room for it.'

'And that's not all, Iris. I hope to organize all sorts of different activities.'

'What does Sister Carmody think about it?'

'Don't worry about Sister Carmody, she'll come round. Her bark is worse than her bite. You might not think it but she does genuinely care for her residents. I've seen her put in any amount of extra hours making sure everything is shipshape and running smoothly.'

'She should have been in the army. My dad, God rest his soul, he was in the army. He liked everything to run like clockwork.'

'So you can understand Maureen's – Sister Carmody's – way of doing things.'

'It can't be easy running a big place like this.'

'It's not, Iris. That's why I think you would be such a great help to her, taking care of the social side of things, leaving her free to do her stuff. Will you think about it?'

'I don't know, Doctor. We didn't exactly hit it off.'

'Nonsense, Iris. I know once you are working together you'll get on like a house on fire. Think about it, please. You are just what this place needs.' The doctor moved on.

'Think about what?' Helen asked. 'I saw you in cahoots with the doctor. What was he asking you to think about?'

'I'll tell you later.'

'Lovely sandwiches,' Lillie said. 'Is there anything to beat a good sandwich?'

'A pint,' Dessie said.

'Trust you, Dessie Rourke. Can you not behave yourself?'

'It's some time since I went out for a pint of beer,' Mr O'Connor said. 'I used to enjoy going out to the pub.'

'No reason you can't meet us for one any time you want, Mr O'Connor. We always go in to Grogans on pension day. That's not far from here at all, it would only take you a few minutes down the road.'

'And if you don't want to meet that reprobate, Mr O'Connor,' Cissy said, 'we ladies go into the lounge.'

'You can get your dinner there as well,' Lillie said. 'They do a nice stew on a Thursday.'

'Pubs are not for having your dinner in, woman, they're for drinking in.'

'Don't mind him, Mr O'Connor. That fellow has no class at all.'

'There's someone on the phone for you, sergeant,' Ann said. 'It's that man who won't let me go home.'

'Never mind, Ann. As soon as I'm finished here I'll run you home.'

'In a squad car?'

'In a squad car.'

'Can we put on the siren?'

'You can have one turn with the siren on.'

'And do I get to say when we put it on?'

'You do, but remember, only once.'

'Wow. I know exactly where I want to put it on . . . That Amanda Kelly is going to die when she sees me.'

'Kelly here.'

'Sergeant Kelly, I have had words with the commander and he is in full agreement with me that we need more men on the Smith case.'

'Why, Chief?'

'Why, Kelly? Surely that's obvious.'

'I heard you were on the television, Chief.'

'A routine press conference, nothing more.'

'Nothing more, sir. The Commander didn't wonder why you announced Smith's return even though you didn't know we had him?'

'A technicality, sergeant. It's only a matter of time . . . What did you say?'

'I said, Chief, you didn't know we had him.'

'You have him?'

'Yes, sir, we have him and most of the members of the gang.'

'Why the hell didn't you say so?'

'I was about to, sir.'

'Where is he? I want him brought in immediately.'

'You have it, sir. But by the way, Chief, don't you think you should have those people at the café in Ashford released? The Commander won't be pleased if they sue for false arrest.' Sergeant Kelly smiled to himself as he pictured Chief Meyers's expression.

'They have been held all afternoon.' Let's see him wriggle out of that one. The Sergeant hung up and then dialled another number. 'Hello. This is Sergeant Kelly. Put me through to the Commander.'

'A word, Mr Perrin.'

'Sergeant?'

'I don't want to be too optimistic, Mr Perrin, but I thought I should tell you, you may be off the hook.'

'What do you mean?'

'I mean we may have other witnesses willing to testify against Morgan.'

'You may or you do, sergeant?'

'I'd say it's pretty definite. The people who want to testify are out to save their own skins.'

'You mean Morgan's own people?'

'It could be, Mr Perrin, it could be.'

'Helen, I think I have good news.'

'That's a funny way of putting it, Mr Perrin. People usually have good news or they don't.'

'It's possible I won't need my alias much longer.'

'I don't understand.'

'It's hush-hush for the moment but it seems Morgan's gang are going to testify in return for certain favours from the police.'

'That's wonderful, Mr Perrin.'

'Smith. Could you get used to me as an ordinary Mr Smith?'

'It sounds very suspicious. I suppose as long as your first name isn't John.'

'As you know already, it's Alex.'

'I think I prefer George Perrin.'

'So you wouldn't venture to go out with an Alex Smith?'

'I hadn't thought about it before, especially as Alex Smith is a fugitive.'

'But from the criminals, Helen, not from the law.'

'Goodbye, goodbye everyone, we'll meet again soon.' Iris was hugging and kissing the residents of the Cross and Passion before shepherding her other pensioners back on to the bus.

'We have all had a wonderful time, Iris,' Miss Poole said, 'haven't we, everyone?'

'Oh yes, Iris. We'll never forget it.'

'Goodbye, Iris,' Doctor Kennedy said, 'and don't forget what I said.'

'I won't, doctor. Helen, a hand here please. Helen?' Helen was embracing George Perrin, it wasn't the sort of embrace that Iris had been dishing out. Iris couldn't believe it. What had got into her? 'Helen.'

'Coming, Iris.'

'You can wipe that smirk off your face for a start.'

'What smirk?'

'You know what smirk. It's time to board our passengers. Have you got the list?'

'For God's sake, Iris.'

'Stephen, your copy of the itinerary please. Lillie, Cissy . . . Ladies first please, Dessie, that's the way they are on the list. Olive, Mai . . . Move them down the back please, Helen. Now Dessie, up you come. Reggie, Willie, Con . . . No Con, that belongs to the Cross and Passion, we must put that back. Helen, could you bring this plate of sandwiches back to the room we were in? Now Stephen, prepare yourself. We are almost ready and we can take off.'

'If we don't see you beforehand, although I'm sure we will,' Lillie called out to the Cross and Passion pensioners, 'we'll see you on the next outing.'

'Oh yes, Lillie.'

'Definitely.'

'Get your head in, Lillie,' Cissy said. 'You're getting far too fond of sticking it out windows.'

'Very funny.'

'Goodbye, everyone.'

'Goodbye, goodbye.'

The bus turned down the Avenue and drove off.

'That was some day, eh?'

'You said it, Dessie. Though I'm not sorry to be going home.'

'Three cheers for Iris.'

'Hip-hip, hip-hip, hip-hip, hooray!'

*

'Deborah. When I have our residents settled perhaps you'd care to join me in a sherry?' Maureen asked.

'I'd love to, Maureen, but I've already arranged to have dinner with Bill.'

'Dinner with Bill?'

'Yes, Maureen.'

'Well really, Deborah. It's none of my business, but he *is* a lorry driver.'

'I know that, Maureen.'

'I wouldn't have thought he was your sort of person.'

'What do you mean, my sort of person?'

'For goodness sake, Deborah, think about it.'

'There's nothing to think about, Maureen. I'll give you a call tomorrow.' Deborah walked over to the lorry where Bill was waiting for her.

'All dispatched, Sister,' Doctor Kennedy said. 'I'd say you are ready to retire yourself. Care for a night-cap, or should I say early-evening-cap, before I go?'

'Thank you, no, Doctor.' Maureen was still watching the lorry as it drove down the Avenue.

'Nice chap, that Bill Thomas. Offered his services any time we need a hand.'

'Services, Doctor?'

'Seems he owns a whole fleet of lorries, inherited them from his father, a very handy chap to know if we ever want things shifted. I'll push off myself so, my wife will think I am lost. Goodnight, Maureen.'

'Good night, Doctor.'

Sister Maureen Carmody and Iris Fox sat together in the cocktail bar of the Russell Hotel. It was their first tête-à-tête. Maureen, keen to show her familiarity with the cocktail bar, smiled all round as if to a huge circle of friends while Iris, dolled up up to the nines – she had spent about two hours deciding what she should wear – tried not to appear ill at ease.

'What would you like, Sister Carmody?'

'Let me, Miss Fox.'

'No, Sister Carmody. I insist. I did ask first.'

'I usually have a gin and tonic when I'm here.'

'Won't be a mo.' Iris hopped up to the counter and soon returned with two large, brightly coloured drinks.

'What is that?'

'Tequila Sunrise. I thought as we are in a cocktail bar we might as well have cocktails. We'll start with these and I asked the young barman to send over two Brandy Alexanders as soon as we are ready.'

'Miss Fox.'

'Down the hatch, Sister.'